THE
FAILURE
OF
FEMINISM

THE
FAILURE
OF
FEMINISM

NICHOLAS DAVIDSON

PROMETHEUS BOOKS
Buffalo, New York

90 89 88 87   4 3 2 1

Library of Congress Cataloging-in-Publication Data

Davidson, Nicholas, 1955-
    The failure of feminism.

    1. Feminism—United States. 2. Sex roles—United
States. 3. Sex differences (Psychology) I. Title.
HQ 1421.D38   1987   305.4′2′0973   87-7190
ISBN 0-87975-408-4

Contents

Introduction

This is not a book about women. It is a book for and about women and men. Its message is simple—so simple that in a few years it may be a puzzle why anyone should have bothered to make a case for it: Men and women are different. In their difference they need each other. The human race needs them both.

This view, which more and more Americans are coming to share, conflicts with powerful cultural ideologies epitomized by feminism, the "Women's Liberation Movement" which wielded such influence on American life from the late sixties to the mid-eighties that those years can be called "the Feminist Era."

Feminism has been a force for progress and a force for alienation. It has given positive direction to women's lives and created personal anguish. It has given some women greater pride in themselves and created unspeakable difficulties in their relations with men. It is time to evaluate its merits.

Women's rights are too important to be left to feminists. Indeed, gender issues are too important to be left to women. Many men assume "all that emotional stuff" isn't really as important as the next upturn in the stock market or America's ability to face down the Soviet Union. This is a serious oversight. Gender issues involve some of the most important questions the human race will ever encounter. They affect how our businesses, government, military, schools, colleges, churches, families, dinner dates, sex acts, and, in short, all aspects of our lives are to be run. The answers we choose over the coming years will determine the future course of civilization. If we do not choose, others will do so for us.

This book looks beyond the Feminist Era to the future of gender in American life. But to accomplish this task, we must plunge into the cultural archeology of the recent past. The experience of the baby boom generation, even in its worst excesses, has been a valuable proving ground and must not be wasted through a failure to come to terms with it. Amid the flotsam and jetsam of experience and the appalling circuitousness of historical evolution, some permanent lessons have been learned. These lessons are of value to future generations of Americans, and to people everywhere who seek to build better societies. Along with a warning against the devastating human cost of feminism, this book thus offers a fundamental message of hope: that we can learn from past experience in order to build a better future—indeed, a future good beyond our parents' or grandparents' fondest imaginings.

To this end we must now come to terms with the period through which America has just passed, the Feminist Era.

PART I

The Sixties: A Legacy of Protest

Chapter 1

A Short History of American Feminism

America has known two waves of feminism, separated by a fifty-year period in which almost nobody wanted to be known as a feminist. The first wave ran from the second half of the nineteenth century to the end of World War I and the incorporation of female suffrage into the Constitution in 1920. The second wave began in 1969 as one of the many social brush fires of the 1960s and has continued to the present. In each case, the intellectual genesis of the movement preceded the dissemination of its ideas and the formation of effective political pressure groups by a number of years.

Nineteenth-century feminism was a by-product of abolitionism. The white, middle class, predominantly Northern women who were participating in the campaign against the enslavement of Southern blacks found that their ability to participate in public events was limited because of the restrictions placed on their sex. Together with some of the male abolitionist leaders, two of these abolitionist women drew up a "Declaration of Sentiments" modeled after the Declaration of Independence. It is convenient to date the birth of American feminism from the publication of this manifesto in the eventful year 1848.

The early movement was concerned with such wide issues as property rights for women and, among its more radical members, the establishment of sexual equality. By the 1890s, the movement had come to focus more narrowly on obtaining the vote for American women. It broadened its appeal by limiting its scope with such success that by 1917 it may have numbered over two million enrolled members,[1] and in 1920 it helped to secure the passage of the Nineteenth Amendment, which granted the vote to women.

Throughout this period there was a large overlap between the suffrage movement and the temperance movement. Some of the same principles were involved. Drinking by men created a social blight whose effects were felt primarily by women, who were often poorly supported, beaten, or abandoned by alcoholic husbands. It was thus no accident that the Eighteenth Amendment, prohibiting the manufacture, sale, and importation of alcoholic beverages, was passed just a few months before the Nineteenth Amendment.

But while the American fundamentalist tradition gave a lasting though inadequate base to the temperance movement, the nineteenth-century feminist movement failed to find a permanent constituency. Once the vote was obtained, American women ceased to function as a pressure group. They voted according to class, region, race, and individual views, just like men. To the despair of their feminist elders, American women in the 1920s lost interest in the larger cause of sexual equality. A wave of social conservatism swept the country. And a relentlessly conformist peer culture inundated American youth: to be a feminist was hopelessly passé.[2] Unresolved, the issues raised by the feminists remained as it were hanging in the air, fading gradually from inattention and lack of interest. But never disappearing entirely, they awaited the opportunity to assume new substance.

Over the next five decades, from 1920 to 1969, it was routine for any woman in a publicly visible position to declare "I am not a feminist." Eleanor Roosevelt and Margaret Mead were only two of the thousands of American women who made such declarations in those years.

And then toward the end of the 1960s something happened, the impact of which we are still absorbing almost a generation later. Feminism reappeared as part of the revolt of the sixties and early seventies. In a time when all the bases of society were being challenged, it was perhaps inevitable that women's traditional roles should also be called into question.

Any discussion of the sixties must deal with the "generation gap." Just as every child must separate from its parents to achieve autonomy, so every generation revolts against the preceding one. But exceptional demographic circumstances made the separation between the sixties generation and that of its parents unusually complete.

America had experienced a low birth rate during World War II, when millions of young men were away in the military and society at large was holding its breath awaiting the outcome of the conflict. Victory, mass demobilization, and America's newly dominant position in the world led to an explosion of optimism and energy beginning in the late forties. Carried away with enthusiasm—for the opposite sex after years of separation, for material joys after years of enforced austerity, and for private life after years of direct and indirect service to the struggle against totalitarianism—couples married and had children in unprecedented numbers. The low birth rates of the Great Depression of the thirties and World War II in the forties gave way in the fifties to a "baby boom." The coming generation was thus both exceptionally numerous and demographically isolated from that of its parents.

The generation of its parents had itself achieved an unusually strong cohesiveness, based on powerful shared experiences. Many of them were old enough to have been touched by the rebellion of the twenties, which pitted jazz, dance halls, lipstick, romance, cigarettes, and cocktails against Prohibition and the remnant puritanism of the Victorian era. All remembered the Great Depression of the thirties as a time of desperation and struggle, when workers lost their jobs, families lost their savings, and life became a bitter and uncertain struggle, a matter of high seriousness.

By contrast, the generation born in the baby boom of the fifties grew up amidst the affluence, rising expectations, and low unemployment of the sixties. Where its parents were indelibly marked by an awareness of the constraints in life, the sixties generation was as thoroughly imbued by a sense of possibility. Unlimited ambition was to be its hallmark.

This basic difference fueled the generation gap and made communication across it difficult. Rarely had two such radically opposed generational mentalities coincided.

Additional factors widened the gap. The new generation was affluent, or felt itself to be. Its parents were overwhelmingly blue collar: factory workers, laborers, and farm hands. The baby boom generation's defining experiences were different. Its members aspired to white collar jobs, or to artistic and creative roles. Their parents had worked hard to achieve financial security and considered themselves unusually fortunate if they had had a chance to earn a college degree. The baby boomers, on the other hand, grew up surrounded by the fruits of the preceding generation's success, and viewed college less as an opportunity than as a right. If they worked at all in their youth, it was usually for pocket money or "to build character," not as a necessity for literal survival.

This contrast in education had begun early on. The baby boomers were the first "Spock generation." Disturbed by Freud's accounts of adult neuroses caused by parental harshness, Dr. Benjamin Spock wrote books that provided America with an immensely popular new approach to child rearing. The older generation had been brought up by parents who viewed their main role as character formation, with an emphasis on cooperation, respect, and discipline. Corporal punishment was a staple of this regime. The baby boomers, by contrast, were brought up by lenient parents who viewed their main role as the providing of love and security; they hoped each child would "actualize itself" and "live up to its full potential." Corporal punishment fell into disfavor. Millions of parents came to view the idea of striking a child with horror. In this regard too, there was a fundamental difference between the generations: the principal felt responsibility of preceding generations was toward others, but that of the baby boomers was toward themselves. By "actualizing themselves," they were making the greatest possible contribution to the progress of humanity. A profound selfishness and a profound idealism were thus mixed together inextricably in the consciousness of the baby boomers. We cannot truly appreciate them without giving due weight to both these elements.

Of course not all the baby boomers were Spock babies. Indeed, it is probable that Spock's ideas reached only a minority of parents even in the upper middle class, which was most thoroughly imbued with them. But they affected enough of the baby boomers to give their generation a very different tone from the one preceding it.

This new psychology combined with mass college education to create a political gap as part of the generation gap. At the universities that had been newly expanded to accommodate them, the baby boomers encountered disciplines like sociology and cultural anthropology which had begun as adjuncts to the social movements of the Age of Reform of the late nineteenth century. (We shall return to this topic in due course.) The universities were peopled with professors who stood for the most part well to the left of the American political center of gravity, nourishing warm memories of Franklin D. Roosevelt's New Deal of the thirties and bitter recollections of Joe McCarthy's persecution of Communists and suspected Communists in the fifties. The baby boomers, sons and daughters for the most part of working class parents who had never known the ins and outs of intellectual life, were charmed by these tweedy, sophisticated, self-assured creatures, and responded eagerly to their repeated praise of youthful idealism. Why not, indeed, build a better vorld today? They came to believe that they had touched the Tree of Knowledge in a way their parents had not: that they had become conscious of themselves and their place in social process, through the perspective granted by intellectual knowledge. They were in this not wholly wrong; but, as we shall see, they were not wholly right either.

The most charismatic of the left professors, like Richard Hofstadter, subtly mocked the values of the uneducated, sneering at the "laissez-faire" economic notions and quaint belief in "human nature" of "the businessman on Main Street." Many baby boomers came to feel ashamed of their parents, people, it seemed, of narrow views and limited life experience—hick farmers, money-grubbing small businessmen, and right-off-the-boat immigrants whose imperfect grasp of American language and culture had sometimes embarrassed their children.

Indeed, this new generation was possessed of a new refinement, and felt itself to be profoundly out of place in the mainstream America in which it grew up—a world of garish neon signs and crassly sculpted roadside diners, of openly manipulative television ads and aggressively oversized automobiles—of, in essence, an apparently all-powerful commercial conformity that reigned in the absence of any trace of the high culture they had come to know and prize through their education. In reaction to a perceived cultural consensus against which they felt initially almost powerless, they were driven to almost any other source of identity, and searched for it everywhere from the concert halls of Europe to the juke joints of the Chicago ghetto. As they grew up, they would introduce mainstream America to an almost limitless variety of strange artifacts discovered in the course of their travels, from quiche to karate.

The new generation was truly superior to that of its parents in some ways; but it knew no way to assess the worth of its discoveries except through trial and error—the grim, costly process of experiment through which progress so often proceeds. Along with much of value, more disturbing new imports surfaced, including the drug culture of Negro hustlers and bebop musicians, and a politics of violent revolution. The winnowing process would be far from complete by the late eighties.

Family life was seen as a dishonorable compromise and a trap by this generation as, filled with the dreams and frustrations of adolescence—frustrations honed to a brittle knife edge by the agonized battles across the generation gap—it stepped forward to claim its place on the national scene. As is often the case, more as the result of discretion than of the facts, the love life of its parents seemed hopelessly tame, perhaps nonexistent, to the next generation. Largely isolated through historical circumstances from the countervailing example of older peers, many of the baby boomers came to believe their generation had invented sex. In love, sex, marriage, family life, and child rearing, the example of the older generation did not seem so much irrelevant as nonexistent. The puritanism that had prevailed in the West since the early nineteenth century made it difficult to penetrate the veil of silence beneath which previous generations concealed their experience of the facts of life. Yet here was a generation suddenly cut off by its peculiar demographics from the older peers who could have made up for the lack of printed wisdom with the handed-down culture of word of mouth.

The civil rights movement of the late fifties and early sixties, which sought to end the legally enforced segregation of blacks in the South, worked further to convince the younger generation that "the system" was the source of error, and opposition to it the only viable course. Words like "dissent," "change," and "struggle," always in favor among left activists, in or out of power, thus acquired a special charge for millions of members of the new generation.

Finally, there was the immense contrast in the two generations' experience of war—a basic difference that has in many cases proved unbridgeable and immune to the subsequent efforts of reason. The parental generation had fought a harsh and bloody war on the side of right. Anyone could see that Hitler and his allies had to be stopped at whatever price. The soldiers came home as heroes to a happy nation proud of their accomplishment. The crippled, the shell-shocked, and the bereaved could take comfort in the knowledge that their sacrifice had not been in vain.

The young men who straggled back to the country towns and working class neighborhoods after their tours in Vietnam, on the other hand, had no such experience. They had fought a defensive war with no clear goals, in the midst of an uncomprehending people who looked just the same as the Communist guerrillas they were supposed to be repulsing. To many of their peers, they came home as villains—traitors to humanity at worst, dupes of a system gone wild at best. During World War II, girls would not look at a man out of uniform; during the Vietnam War, they would not look at a man in one.

Nor were combat troops the only casualties of the Vietnam War. Tens of thousands of young men fled across the border to Canada to avoid conscription in a war they had concluded was immoral. Millions more were driven into varying degrees of opposition to their government, ranging from time- and energy-consuming political activism to an artificial prolongment of education in order to take advantage of the draft deferment granted college students. Some went to jail.

Alienated from the past represented by their parents and from the present represented by "the system," millions of the new generation devoted themselves to creating a different future. The word "different" itself was often used as a high compliment. "You can't trust anyone over thirty" became a popular saying. The nihilist chic of European youth crossed the Atlantic with the anthem "My Generation" by the British pop group the Who, who snarled "Hope I die before I get old" before smashing their instruments onstage. At the Monterey Pop Festival in 1967, Jimi Hendrix went them one better and burned his guitar. It may have been utterly mindless, but it sure was exciting. The way seemed opened to endless change, endless self-exploration, endless excitement— and at the end of the deep hurt of the generation gap and the bitter anger over the Vietnam War loomed, perhaps, happiness, or a better world.

It was in this atmosphere that the new feminist movement began.

The female political activists who were responsible for the reemergence of an American feminism in the late sixties had received an education substantially identical to that of the male activists with whom they made common cause in the civil rights movement. Implicitly, they believed their contribution to the movement to be equal to the men's. Furthermore, as the generational revolt gathered steam, there developed a rejection of the values of the older generation, particularly the norm of marriage and the ideal of the nuclear suburban family, with its sharply defined gender roles.

Expecting to be accepted by the men as equal collaborators, these activist women instead often found themselves relegated to tasks like doing the paperwork and fixing the coffee while the men attended to the more prestigious questions of ideology and strategy. Moreover, sixties radicalism often exhibited a vigorous misogyny. As the black radical Stokely Carmichael declared, "The correct position for women in the movement is prone." This clash between the expectations and the experience of radical young women led at first to puzzlement and then to revolt, fueled by the discovery of Betty Friedan's *The Feminine Mystique* (1963). The consequence of this revolt was the emergence of the feminist movement as we know it. This movement proposed to generate a comprehensive analysis of society, complete with prescriptions for the remedy of its ills.

The feminism that resurfaced in the American press around 1969 shared the general characteristics of the larger countercultural revolt from which it developed. It was idealistic, believing in the possibility of a better world, even of the best of all possible worlds, if only people could get rid of their hang-ups and act together. It was American, at a time when America dominated the world as few nations have in the course of history, and badly informed about other times and places, despite a systemic fascination with the exotic. It was generational, suspicious of the motives and values of the generation of its parents, convinced that only the new youth culture was capable of defining the right questions or supplying the right answers. It emphasized the importance of the individual and the group at the expense of personal relationships—an emphasis that seemed to be justified by the high divorce rate of the parental generation and the transitory character of adolescent life in dormitories, crash pads, and campgrounds. And it was angry, believing that women were being cheated of things which were rightfully theirs, which could only be won back through organized confrontation and the maintenance of a high level of rage against the "system."

It was a revolutionary period, or aspired to be: as in all such periods, everything seemed possible. The continuance of any perceived injustice was interpreted as nothing short of a crime, either of commission or omission. Much of the sixties generation succumbed to a muckraking mentality. Its favorite form of literature was the critique: *Unsafe at Any Speed* debunked the auto industry, *Subliminal Seduction* did the same for advertising, *The Myth of the Britannica* attacked America's favorite reference work. No activity, sector, or set of concepts was exempt from assault as authors, breathless with outrage, crossed and re-crossed the shaky line between reform and revolution, flattering the generation's opinion of itself and its mission as adroitly as any demagogue.

The new feminists thus believed they had the right, the duty, and the ability to remake "traditional" female roles, or even to radically redefine the female. Such self-confidence is essential to conceptualize change, and the new feminists undoubtedly promoted change. Whether they had the necessary wisdom is another question altogether. Almost a generation later, it is time for us to reevaluate the philosophy of gender that they developed.

Chapter 2

The Feminist Devaluation of the Feminine

The new feminism spread through a variety of means: word of mouth, parallel personal experiences, and, above all, the mass media of magazines, newspapers, and television—through all the ways that a modern mass society uses to stay informed about itself. But to a remarkable degree it spread through books. The most influential feminist publications were runaway best-sellers which presented often rather sophisticated anthropology, psychology, and sociology to a mass audience. Although many readers probably never bothered to read them from cover to cover, the feminist best-sellers were effective vehicles for ideas. Even their more opaque passages served to increase the aura of intellectual legitimacy of the notions they presented. The most influential of these feminist best-sellers were Betty Friedan's *The Feminine Mystique* (1963), Kate Millett's *Sexual Politics* (1970), and Germaine Greer's *The Female Eunuch* (also 1970). These books are important both as influences on subsequent thought and as examples of the thought of their time; they are both causes and results of the emergence of contemporary American feminism.

Having examined the seminal arguments of contemporary feminism in these books, there is no need to refute their various retreads in the seventies and eighties. If you can penetrate the argument of *The Feminine Mystique* or *The Female Eunuch,* you will not be very impressed by Colette Dowling's *The Cinderella Complex* or Susan Brownmiller's *Femininity.*

The seminal work of contemporary American feminism is Betty Friedan's *The Feminine Mystique.* First published in 1963, *The Feminine Mystique* attacked the 1950s cult of femininity and family life to the exclusion of other life possibilities for women.

The background to understanding *The Feminine Mystique* is that, after World War II, Americans came to idealize family life as never before. The reasons for this development are a subject of dispute, but they certainly include the prolonged separation of millions of men and women from the other sex during the war years and the economic expansion of the fifties which made it possible for the majority of American women to stay out of the job market.

According to Friedan, women fared badly by trading jobs for careers as wives and mothers. The result was a pervasive alienation, which she claimed was practically universal at the time she wrote *The Feminine Mystique*. Women everywhere suffered from "the problem that has no name," a sense of directionlessness which manifested itself in depression, insomnia, and other neuroses. These difficulties, Friedan said, could not be successfully treated in terms of the psychological categories that were then current, like those inherited from Sigmund Freud. Indeed, they could not be understood at all as individual problems. What was needed instead was a fundamental change in women's lives. If women lacked a sense of purpose, it was because they needed to redirect their energies away from the inadequate satisfactions of the suburban domesticity that had become the fifties ideal, in order to find a more significant and enduring outlet for their abilities in careers. The solution to "the problem that has no name" was for women to change their primary allegiance from the world of the family to the world of paid work. Instead of defining themselves as wives and mothers, women were to define themselves first and foremost as professionals.

According to Friedan, part-time or volunteer work could not fill the yawning gap of meaning in the lives of American women. "The amateur or dilettante whose own work is not good enough for anyone to want to pay to hear or see or read does not gain real status by it in society, or real personal identity." Only professional careers, she claimed, remunerated by money, could give American women the self-esteem she believed they lacked.

Friedan pointed out that "A great many suburban housewives today step back from, or give up, volunteer activity, art, or job at the very point when all that is needed is a more serious commitment. The PTA leader won't run for the school board. The League of Women Voters' leader is afraid to move on into the rough mainstream of her political party." She argued that, if women were afraid of commitment to careers and leadership positions, "the false dilemmas and guilts of the feminine mystique" were to blame.[1]

The possibility that women avoided consuming career commitments because they placed a higher value on their home and family lives was precisely the problem, according to Friedan. The imposition of universal domesticity by the cultural climate of the fifties was suffocating American women's self-esteem, strangling their talents, and threatening their very sanity. Family life was a trap from which all women needed to escape.

It was a stark vision. Women had no real choice. Good lay on the side of higher education and careers as the sources of women's identity; bad on the side of traditional female values and modes of coping. Friedan made frequent use of an analogy between Nazism and American culture. "We are committing," she wrote, "quite simply genocide, starting with the mass burial of American women and ending with the progressive dehumanization of their sons and daughters."[2] The home, in Friedan's view, was a "comfortable concentration camp" whose prisoners, housewives, had been brainwashed by "femininity." Such women were not "fully human."[3]

The first objection feminists had to American women was thus that they were "feminine." Femininity was not just irrelevant to women's humanity; it was what prevented them from achieving it. Progress required that women give up "an immaturity that has been called femininity." Women had to reject "the old feminine image" in order to become "a different kind of woman." Only then could they hope to become "complete human beings."[4]

Femininity was epitomized by the role of the housewife. Too many American women, Friedan wrote, "have been deceived, or have deceived themselves, into clinging to the outgrown, childlike femininity of 'Occupation: housewife.' "

> Women, as well as men, can only find their identity in work that uses their full capacities. A woman cannot find her identity through others— her husband, her children.[5]

Only by learning to compete directly with men could a woman "break out of the housewife trap." "She must learn to compete then, not as a woman, but as a human being."[6] Femininity and humanity were incompatible.

Dire consequences awaited the woman who failed to heed this message: "She will fritter away her energy in neurotic symptoms, or unproductive exercise, or destructive 'love.'"[7]

Women who were content with their lot had the longest road to travel, for happy housewives were sickest of all—virtually beyond redemption as human beings. Their brainwashing had been so effective they had lost the ability even to resent having been "denied the right to become fully human."[8] The future lay with the aggrieved.

> The adjusted, or cured ones who live without conflict or anxiety in the confined world of home have forfeited their own being; the others, the miserable, frustrated ones, still have some hope.[9]

American women had no alternative to the "progressive dehumanization" of the housewife role but to seek fulfillment elsewhere, namely, in the masculine world of work and careers. It was an uncompromising message, and it was widely believed. But was it true?

There is no doubt the alienation Friedan saw was common among upper middle class American women in the 1950s. But alongside this situation was another whose existence Friedan was reluctant to admit. That was the reality of millions of American women who were more or less content with their lot in life, who did not want to switch their primary identity from family to job, and who were not prepared to view their gleaming new houses as "comfortable concentration camps." In a new ending added to her book in 1974, Friedan wrote "[T]hat strange hostility my book—and later the movement—seemed to elicit from some women amazed and puzzled me. Even in the beginning, there wasn't the hostility I had expected from men." Friedan explained this hostility as a sign of psychopathology: "If you were afraid to face your real feelings about the husband and children you were presumably living for, then someone like me opening up the can of worms was a menace."[10] In the course of this book, we will see that the ready acceptance of Friedan's ideas by many men and their vehement rejection by many women may have a different explanation.

The Feminine Mystique established two cardinal points that were to orient American feminism for the next generation. The first point was that femininity, as embodied in the role of the housewife, was no longer, indeed had never been, a viable life strategy for women. The second point was that the only way to escape the housewife role, with its soul-destroying limitations, was to reject feminine characteristics, or at any rate to relegate them to a secondary place in one's scheme of existence, and to seek a new emotional center of gravity in a professional career. Women were to abandon their traditional life strategies and adopt those of men.

The architects of the role revolution never envisioned giving women a choice between being housewives and being career women. Even "moderate" feminists like Betty Friedan never described the occupation of housewife as a valid life choice, but rather as an oppressive role from which women had to be weaned. The belief that "feminists just want to give women a choice" was and is mistaken. Among feminists, it is always assumed that a better future requires the complete elimination of the housewife role. As Simone de Beauvoir, author of the *The Second Sex,* pointed out in a talk with Betty Friedan, "No woman should be authorized to stay home and raise her children. . . . Women should not have that choice, precisely because *if there is such a choice, too many women will make that one.*"[11] Similarly, in *The Second Stage* (1981), Friedan continues to criticize "that obsolete, traditional family in which mothers, by necessity or choice, stayed home and were supported as housewives by breadwinning fathers."[12]

The feminist goal has been to change the cultural climate of the fifties, which tended to force all women into marriage and motherhood, into a climate which channels women into careers, which will if necessary force them onto the job market. Girls who were being told they had no choice but marriage and motherhood were to be told they had no choice but professional careers. As Friedan said,

> A massive attempt must be made by educators and parents—and ministers, magazine editors, manipulators [i.e., advertisers], guidance counselors—to stop the early-marriage movement, stop girls from growing up wanting to be "just a housewife," stop it by insisting, with the same attention from childhood on that parents and educators give to boys, that girls develop the resources of self, goals that will permit them to find their own identity.[13]

And "identity," of course, had been defined as a professional career. *The Feminine Mystique* aimed to replace one prescriptive set of values with another that was equally unbending. "Educators," Friedan wrote, "at every women's college, at every university, junior college, and community college, must see to it that women make a lifetime commitment (call it a 'life plan,' a 'vocation,' a 'life purpose' if that dirty word 'career' has too many celibate connotations)."[14] The success of this effort may be gauged by the precipitous decline in the marriage and birth rates in the seventies and the simultaneous influx of millions of young middle class women onto the job market.

As an advocate for American women, Friedan selected the wrong targets: femininity, the roles of wife and mother, and the home. Family was portrayed as incidental to a woman's life, a manifestation of her lower, "merely biological" side, which required little attention or fore-thought. To replace the devalued family in Friedan's "new life plan for American women" came new notions. One was careerism, the belief that the central focus of a woman's life should, and for her mental stability had to be, a career of full-time paid work. The message of *The Feminine Mystique,* which millions of women were to heed, was that "careers can't wait, men can."[15] With careerism went a new mystique of pro-fessionalism: the belief that participation in the professions represents the acme of fulfillment for all women. These fundamental mistakes were to mark the new feminist movement from its inception.

Friedan's attack on femininity, as epitomized in the housewife role, had by the late sixties exploded in the emerging mass "women's move-ment" into a virulent hatred directed against the institution of the family itself.

Kate Millett's *Sexual Politics* was published to effusive and nearly universal acclaim in 1970. Her book was saluted in the *New York Times* as "Supremely entertaining to read, brilliantly conceived, overwhelming in its arguments, breathtaking in its command of history and literature." Its author, an aggressively dowdy individual, her face obscured behind heavy black eyeglass frames, overweight, and given to wearing nondescript pantsuits, was praised in ethereal, almost mystical terms by *Cosmopolitan:* "The Movement has found the ideal spokeswoman! . . . Silver-tongued . . . velvet-gloved . . . her history of the political aspects of sex and sexual repression was a revelation, a swift kick."[16]

Kate Millett, a self-described radical lesbian feminist, believes that a relationship of coercion exists between the sexes. The object of *Sexual Politics* is to expose the workings of "patriarchy," to show that it is destructive, to demonstrate that it is not inevitable, and to further a "revolution" to replace it with a just sexual order.

> The situation between the sexes now, and throughout history, is . . . a relationship of dominance and subordinance. . . . [S]exual dominion obtains . . . as perhaps the most fundamental ideology of our culture.
>
> This is so because our society, like all other historical civilizations, is a patriarchy. The fact is evident at once if one recalls that the military, industry, technology, universities, science, political office, and finance—in short, every avenue of power within the society . . . is entirely in male hands. . . . What lingers of supernatural authority, . . . together with the ethics and values, the philosophy and art of our culture . . . is of male manufacture.[17]

The universality of "patriarchy," Kate Millett argues, cannot be explained by any known biological characteristics; it is a cultural phenomenon. "Endocrinology and genetics afford no definite evidence of determining mental-emotional differences [between men and women]." Men and women differ only in "[t]he heavier musculature of the male" and in their reproductive organs. It is doubtful that there are "any significant inherent differences between male and female beyond the bio-genital ones we already know." These genital differences are of little importance:

> For the sexes are inherently in everything alike, save reproductive systems, secondary sexual characteristics, orgasmic capacity, and genetic and morphological structure. Perhaps the only things they can uniquely exchange are semen and transudate.[18]

With such assertions, Millett pushes the doctrine of environmental determinism to its logical extreme. According to environmental determinists, socialization, not biology, can best explain human behavior. Humans, in this view, have few—extreme environmental determinists would say no—inherent traits. Taking her cue from this idea, Millett argues that people have no instincts or drives which are relevant to an analysis of the human condition. "Patriarchy" takes the blank slate of the infant and writes its program on it, endlessly perpetuating itself.

> Conditioning runs in a circle of self-perpetuation and self-fulfilling prophecy. To take a simple example: expectations the culture cherishes about his gender identity encourage the young male to develop aggressive impulses, and the female to thwart her own or to turn them inward.

There is thus no "natural" basis for sexual differentiation in role, temperament, or status. Whatever gender differences do exist are the product of "patriarchal society."

The main purpose of the institutions of society is to maintain patriarchal oppression. Chief among these instruments of oppression is the family.

> Patriarchy's chief institution is the family. It is . . . a patriarchal unit within a patriarchal whole. Mediating between the individual and the social structure, the family effects control and conformity where political and other authorities are insufficient. As the fundamental instrument and the foundation unit of patriarchal society the family and its roles are prototypical.

The family is a "feudal" institution that reduces women to "chattel status." Its role toward children is simply to force them into subservience to the oppressive values of the larger society:

> The chief contribution of the family in patriarchy is the socialization of the young (largely through the example and admonition of their parents) into patriarchal ideology's prescribed attitudes.

Millett cautions her readers that since the family is extremely ingrained as an institution, its elimination will demand an exceptional effort:

> Although there is no biological reason why the two central functions of the family (socialization and reproduction) need be inseparable or even take place within it, revolutionary or utopian efforts to remove these functions from the family have been so frustrated, so beset by difficulties, that most experiments so far have involved a gradual return to tradition. This is strong evidence of how basic a form patriarchy is within all societies, and of how pervasive its effects upon family members.

The family is equated with patriarchy; the one arises from the other. Fortunately, there is hope:

> Radical social change cannot take place without having an effect upon patriarchy. And not simply because it is the political form which subordinates such a large percentage of the population (women and youth) but because it serves as a citadel of property and traditional interests.

To the presumed shock of her readers, Millett has discovered that the family is an economic institution: "Marriages are financial alliances, and each household operates as an economic entity much like a corporation."

One might have thought that the family is of necessity an economic institution, and that as such it has made human life possible through the ages, but Millett is supremely uninterested in such mundane matters. According to her, "traditional sexual alliances" are "corrupted" by their "crass and exploitative economic bases."[19] Is she then perhaps a romantic who yearns for a pure form of relation based solely on love? Not at all. "The concept of romantic love affords a means of emotional manipulation which the male is free to exploit." However the deck is stacked, in Millett's view, women come out on the bottom. Heterosexual love always works against women. This is nowhere more apparent than in the institution of marriage.

According to Millett, marriage is essentially an exploitative rather than a cooperative institution. It is a one-sided pact that works to the benefit of the husband and the detriment of the wife. Although the exchange of goods and services, the pooling of resources, and the sharing of responsibility have usually been seen as the basis for marriage, Millett can see nothing in marriage except the exploitation and degradation of women: she describes wives as "domestic servants" and "slaves." Women's "chattel status" is degradingly apparent in "the general legal assumption that marriage involves an exchange of the female's domestic service and (sexual) consortium in return for financial support."

The problem with these claims is not that women and men have historically had identical rights under the law in marriage; certainly they have not. It is that Millett systematically exaggerates the negatives of this difference in order to make the situation of women in marriage appear as unpleasant as possible. Recklessly sacrificing facts to rhetoric, she asserts that

The principle of "coverture" or *femme couverte,* general throughout Western jurisprudence, placed the married woman in the position both of minor and chattel throughout her life. Her husband became something like a legal keeper, as by marrying she succumbed to a mortifying process which placed her in the same class with lunatics or idiots. . . . The husband was the sole "owner" of wife and children . . . her offspring were his legal possessions. . . . A father, like a slaver, could order the law to reclaim his chattel-property relatives when he liked. . . . Lest a woman entertain any doubts over her serf status, the wedding ceremony . . . was perfectly clear upon this point.[20]

If Millett was arguing that morally, or even in practice, Western law ever made women into "chattels" her case might have some limited validity. But her repeated assertion that women were legally men's chattels is an outright falsehood. Wives have never been their husbands' chattels under Anglo-American law—no more so in the time of Alfred the Great than at present. Her flaky legal history is not designed to inform but to shock.

Such outrageously false passages cannot be explained as technical disagreements in areas like legal history, where no reputable scholar would agree with Millett's inventions. Similarly, Millett asserts that "The closest analogue to marriage was feudalism." Neither legal scholars nor medievalists, who have studied feudalism, nor anthropologists or sociologists, who have studied marriage, could be found to support this baseless declaration. But people lacking specialized knowledge of these fields are apt to be snowed under by the blizzard of specious evidence.

Unquestionably the radical rage of the sixties and seventies was fueled by this sort of rhetoric, which portrayed women as the penultimate victims of history. However meretricious Millett's scholarship may be, it must be admitted that her misrepresentation of technical evidence was successful as a rhetorical tactic. The dozens of passages in which Millett misrepresents technical evidence are not careless mistakes but effective political rhetoric, designed to shock, persuade, and motivate.

There can be, then, no question here of an honest disagreement over a historical interpretation. These passages are better explained by the facts that Millett is a lesbian advocate in a society that favors heterosexual marriage, and above all that she hates and fears men.

The evidence of Millett's hatred of men seethes just beneath the surface of *Sexual Politics*. If we were to treat her argument as a pure intellectual proposition without considering this obvious source of her motivation, we would fail to grasp what she has set out to accomplish.

Regardless of one's views on Freud's theory of penis envy, it is evident that some such desire inflicts itself on Millett. There is a curious gingerish quality in her references to the male genitals which seems to reflect not some remnant of prudery but rather an odd mixture of admiration, disgust, and fear, of fascination and repulsion. She is infinitely more concerned with the male genitals than any man I have ever known.

Rather than using the many available matter-of-fact terms to refer to the male genitals, Millett gives them elaborate, sneering characterizations like "the male indicator" and "the penis, badge of the male's superior status." It is impossible to avoid the conclusion that her hatred of men is bound up with this hatred of what she perceives as the primary symbol of masculinity.

One might expect Millett, as a lesbian, to show some identification, if only in principle, with homosexual men, but her hatred of men overcomes any feelings of gay solidarity she might have had. This is made clear in passages like the following, in which Millett generalizes from her assessment of a primitive culture to "patriarchies" in general:

> [The atmosphere of the men's houses in Melanesia] is not very remote from that of military institutions in the modern world: they reek of physical exertion, violence, the aura of the kill, and the throb of homosexual sentiment. . . . The tone and ethos of men's house culture is sadistic, power-oriented, and latently homosexual, frequently narcissistic in its energy and motives. . . . Considerable sexual activity does take place in the men's house, all of it, needless to say, homosexual. But the taboo against homosexual behavior . . . tends to effect a rechanneling of the libido into violence. This association of sexuality and violence is a particularly militaristic habit of mind.[21]

Although the defense of female homosexuality is the pervasive theme that runs unacknowledged through Millett's book, male homosexuality is entitled to no such legitimation. The implicit message of the above passage is nothing more subtle than that "soldiers are faggots." Homosexuality is good in Millett's eyes—unless it is practiced by men.

The task of invalidating male sexuality is thus complete. Not only is men's sexual activity with women corrupt, so is their sexual activity with each other. In the new feminist ethos, men are fundamentally suspect as sexual beings. Only women can engage in sex without destructive consequences. Therefore, sex between women becomes the highest, indeed the only acceptable form of sexual activity. The allure of this ideology to lesbians scarcely requires comment.

Millett claims that men distance themselves from women by depersonalizing them, by objectifying them, by making them into members of a category rather than seeing them as individual human beings. It therefore comes as something of a shock to realize that such dehumanizing objectification is precisely what Millett does to men. This pervasive tendency is most strikingly seen in the habitual use of the generalized term "male" when a specific term like "husband" would be more appropriate, as in "All that the wife acquired by her labor, service or act during 'coverture' became the legal property of the male."[22] The effect of this repetitive misuse of the word "male" is, first, to remove the immediacy of the reader's perception of the human actor in question by depicting him primarily as a member of the impersonal category of "males," second, by a process of guilt through association, to make the category of maleness suspect, and so finally to make the word "male" into a term of abuse. This usage of the word "male" occurs again and again in feminist writing.

To Friedan's assault on femininity, Millett thus adds an assault on masculinity. Maleness is defined as pathological; it is a perversion of humanity, "the deformation of the 'masculine' personality, e.g., a certain predatory or aggressive character."

Millett's hatred of men is bound up with her belief that men hate women. By choosing the most extreme cases of the always ambiguous relationship between the sexes, she is able to make a case that patriarchy causes men to hate women and that as a result women are systematically degraded in their contacts with men. The following example sets the tone:

> Patriarchal myth typically posits a golden age before the arrival of women, while its social practices permit males to be relieved of female company.

Men, Millett thinks, really don't like women. It is therefore best that women avoid them.

To take another example: Millett states—and here one must emphatically agree with her—that "women entertain, please, gratify, satisfy and flatter men with their sexuality." It is a symptom of the web of negativity into which she is trying to draw her reader that by the end of her second chapter Millett expects this statement—which only describes what is natural, normal, and good—to be met with shock. How outrageous, the reader is supposed to think, that women entertain, please, gratify, and so forth, men! What an unjust culture it is that would make them want to do such a thing! Rationality recedes; rage builds.

Rage is highly valued, for it is a key ingredient in "revolution." The revolution is social and economic, but it is above all cultural.

We are speaking, then, of a cultural revolution, which, while, it must necessarily involve the political and economic reorganization traditionally implied by the term revolution, must go far beyond this as well.[23]

In this Marxist-feminist nirvana, the institutions of society are to be completely transformed. The family is to be abolished. Its function of providing care for children will be taken over by the state. Millett believes this will benefit all concerned, as most parents are unfit to raise their offspring.

The care of children . . . is infinitely better left to the best trained practitioners of both sexes who have chosen it as a vocation, rather than to harried and all too frequently unhappy persons with little time nor taste for the work of educating young minds.[24]

Universal day care will help free women by hastening the imminent dissolution of the family:

The collective professionalization (and consequent improvement) of the care of the young . . . would further undermine family structure while contributing to the freedom of women.[25]

But as "patriarchy's chief institution," the family deserves no better: "The family, as that term is presently understood, must go. In view of the institution's history, that is a kind fate."[26]

If men and women persist in wanting to form relationships, the revolution is willing to show tolerance: "Marriage might be replaced by voluntary association, if such is desired."[27] But marriage, like the family, is irredeemably corrupt and must be permanently destroyed as an institution. Millett expects these actions will result in the creation of "a world we can bear out of the desert we inhabit."[28]

Such was the "scholarly" end of the new feminism as it emerged from the late 1960s.

Readers put off by the man-hatred and the aridity of Millett's book (it was originally written as her doctoral thesis) were relieved to discover Germaine Greer's zippy, zany *The Female Eunuch.* Published within a few months of *Sexual Politics,* it promptly overtook the more academic work on the best-seller lists.

The Female Eunuch helped to invest women with a truly world-historical role in contemporary times. Invoking the role of Lysistrata, the heroine of Aristophanes' comedy who persuades the women of Athens and Sparta to forswear sex until their men end the Peloponnesian War, Greer defined women's mission as nothing less than to coerce men into saving humanity.[29] This message was taken seriously by millions of women influenced by feminism around the time Greer wrote. With the horrors of war invading television screens every day in the Vietnam era, men and Western civilization seemed corrupt to many. Redemption would have to come from women and non-Western civilization.

The terrain for the idealization of the non-established and the non-Western had been in preparation for perhaps a century as the viewpoints of the homosexual, the insane, the alcoholic, and the sexually obsessed were explored in art and literature. The cult of the powerless had by the 1960s exploded into a veritable celebration of marginality, fueled by the alienation of the baby boomers from the commercial culture around them, and also by the experience of marginality of white civil rights workers early in the decade.

Blackness became excruciatingly hip. Many blacks reacted with embarrassment to overenthusiastic young whites smitten by a projected fantasy of black culture. The great blues singer Albert King protested to a deferential white interviewer in 1969: "I ain't no star, I'm just a guy trying to make a decent living. I don't want to get big."[30] But the unscrupulous cashed in. Popular books like Eldridge Cleaver's *Soul On Ice* were read by millions of college students who considered the world through the eyes of an avowed rapist. Books like *Manchild In the Promised Land* gratified the newfound cultural insecurity of the white upper classes, while political radicals like the Black Panthers made outright fools of them, as mercilessly documented by Tom Wolfe in *Radical Chic*. The popular novels of the sixties generation, like *One Flew Over the Cuckoo's Nest, Catch 22,* and *Slaughterhouse Five,* idealized the perspective of the outsider. When the members of that generation reached college, they were assigned texts like Camus's *The Rebel,* which reinforced the notion that the farther a person was from society's center, the closer he was to the truth.

Even legitimate literature in this period like Anthony Burgess's *A Clockwork Orange* and V. S. Naipaul's *A House for Mr. Biswas* used the outsider's perspective as a point of departure, though the corrosive skepticism of such superior works toward the era's politico-literary clichés was undoubtedly missed by their trendier readers. The inside perspective on society was universally rejected in favor of the outside one.

A corollary of this xenocentrism was that the greater the degree of victimization one could lay claim to, the more authority attached to one's pronouncements.[31] The description of abuse received at the hands of authority figures like parents, policemen, judges, bosses, or simply men, became part of a sort of collective rite, and was eagerly listened to by one's contemporaries with a heady mixture of breathless voyeurism and sympathetic rage.

Drawing on this confessional mode, Germaine Greer directly based many of her arguments in *The Female Eunuch* on her own experiences. She describes her home as an example of

> the unbroken home which ought to have been broken. . . . My father had decided fairly early on that life at home was pretty unbearable; and he lived more and more of it at his club, only coming home to sleep. My mother did not protest about this, as it gave her an opportunity to tyrannize the children and enlist their aid to disenfranchise my father completely. . . . She used to mutter to me that my father was a "senile old goat." Once my mother knelt on my small brother's chest and beat his face with her fists in front of my father and was threatened with violent retaliation, the only instance of my father's rising to her bait that I can recall. My brother was three years old at the time. . . . I can recall being beaten for giving away all my toys when I was about four. I really didn't want them anymore.[32]

Greer, the product of an unhappy home whose mother made life a torment for her father and herself, externalized the loathing she felt for her family of origin onto the institutions of marriage and the family in general. Her mother's inadequacies left her with an antipathy toward femininity and a deep fear of having children, as shown by the impossibly complicated conditions she sets for having children.[33]

Greer's book came as a relief to many men who wanted to remain up-to-date but were repelled by Millett's man-hating brand of lesbian feminism, as well as to feminist women who wanted to continue to love men. Greer became known as "the feminist men like." Many men find women to be collectively irritating at times, as many women do men. Greer's book seemed to justify men in this feeling: There really was something wrong with women. Rather than obliging men to accept women as they are, difficulties and all, Greer's book held out the promise women would change. If Millett's emphasis is on her opposition to men and

masculinity, Greer's—like Friedan's—is on her opposition to women and
femininity. Greer's critique of the feminine begins with her title, which
implies that women are incomplete, damaged beings, "female eunuchs,"
and continues relentlessly throughout her book.

> The female's fate is to become deformed and debilitated. . . . Every girl
> whose upbringing is "normal" . . . is a female faggot. . . . Woman is never
> genuine at any period of her life. . . . Women cannot love. . . . Women
> must be frigid. . . . The ignorance and isolation of most women mean that
> they are incapable of making conversation. . . . Women are always precipi-
> tating scenes of violence in pubs and dancehalls. . . .[34]

Greer identifies "femininity" as the source of "the miserable destructiveness of womankind."[35]

> Any . . . aim is likely to be followed in a "feminine" way, that is, servilely,
> dishonestly, inefficiently, inconsistently. . . . We can, indeed we must, reject
> femininity as meaning *without libido,* and therefore incomplete, sub-
> human. . . .[36]

By the end of all this, Greer's reader is apt to be convinced that
women as they exist are pretty awful, and had better change. But like
Millett and other feminists, Greer cannot decide if women are inferior
to men, the same as men, or superior to men. Part of the reason for
this quandary is that she is almost as hostile to men (as they presently
exist) as she is to women.

> Male energy is contoured and deformed too . . . so that it becomes aggression
> and competitiveness. . . . How sad it is for men to have feeling and thought
> in opposition! . . . The male perversion of violence is an essential con-
> dition for the degradation of women.[37]

Men, who in Millett are violent and brutal, are in Greer violent and
vulnerable. The male is wounded as surely as the female. The conditioning
to masculinity, although it does not reduce its recipient to "impotence"
like femininity, creates a tragic split between thought and feeling, leaving
men with a propensity for violence that is responsible for the world's
worst problems, including the threat of nuclear annihilation.[38]

Like Millett, Greer believes the sexes can and must radically change.
The artificiality of sex differences is apparent, she says, even in the bones
of the body.

> We tend to think of the skeleton as rigid. . . . In fact it is itself subject to deformation by many influences. The first of these is muscular stress. Because men are more vigorous than women their bones have more clearly marked muscular grooves.[39]

The impression Greer gives is that if women exercised as much as men they would develop equally large muscles. This is simply not true, which is why there is perennial concern at the Olympics over women athletes taking male hormones: in most sports contests, and in all those involving physical strength, maleness is a decisive advantage.

What is true for physique, Greer says, is equally true for behavior: "the 'normal' sex roles that we learn to play from infancy are no more natural than the antics of the transvestite."[40] Greer maintains that researchers have been unable to find any differences at all between male and female minds. "No such differences have ever been established."

Greer's source on this subject is Eleanor Maccoby's widely respected *The Development of Sexual Differences*. Greer carefully lists the behavioral sex differences Maccoby documents, such as girls' greater verbal abilities and boys' better performance in "situations requiring enterprise and lack of shyness." Then—in one of her trademark *non sequiturs*—Greer asserts that "we must refrain from assuming anything about the female psyche from such evidence, except that the sex of mind is still to be demonstrated."[41] In other words, Greer presents evidence of sex differences—and then claims to have done just the opposite. The unwary reader, bemused by all the scientific-sounding jargon, is presented with the seemingly authoritative conclusion that "the sex of mind is still to be demonstrated." What the scope and implications of these differences are would have been a valid topic for discussion, but a very different one from claiming that there are no such differences at all.

Greer does concede elsewhere that male and female temperaments differ at present, but argues that the difference is purely the result of "conditioning." "The masculine-feminine polarity is actual enough, but not necessary."[42]

To refer to this polarity as if it were real is wrong, Greer argues.[43] Women must "refuse to accept the polarity of masculine-feminine."[44] (Note that the emphasis here is on women's actions, not on men's: women are the potential saviors of humanity; they have become the active principle.) The innocuous and useful phrase "the opposite sex" becomes a perverse euphemism in the new feminist frame of reference. So does the wonderful French exclamation of delight in the two sexes, *Vive la différence!*[45] To become whole, men and women must assume each other's better characteristics, so that human temperament will no longer be divided by sex into a "polarity" but unified along a "continuum." Men and women will no longer be masculine and feminine, but instead male and female.

What will men and women be like, once freed from the crushing burdens of masculinity and femininity? What is maleness without masculinity and femaleness without femininity? These questions cannot be answered at present, according to Greer. Like Millett, she argues that the natures of maleness and femaleness cannot be known until masculinity and femininity are destroyed. As Millett writes, "Whatever the 'real' differences between the sexes may be, we are not likely to know them until the sexes are treated differently, that is alike."[46] Greer expresses the same idea with added rhetorical verve: "the sex of the uncastrated female is unknown."[47] Because she thinks the true nature of women is unknowable until after "the revolution," she dodges considerable evidence to the contrary that was already available at the time she wrote her book.

Her readers are thus sent forth to do battle, believing they have been informed about the nature of their mission and their enemy, when in fact they have been systematically misled about the nature and degree of differences between the sexes. They have been deprived of more knowledge than they have been granted, through the delegitimation of traditional wisdom, with its component of genuine insight into the natures of men and women, and through the misrepresentation of scientific data. That women are passive and despicable, that men are brutal and pitiable, so that both sexes must change not just their behavior but their very "souls";[48] that masculinity and femininity have no relation to maleness and femaleness, whose nature, if any, cannot be ascertained until after "the revolution"; that even the physical differences between the sexes are caused by differing lifestyles: these were among the key ideas with which a generation of activist women went out into the world, ideas which they then tried to apply to their relationships with men, their scholarly research, their jobs, and the raising of their children—if they had any.

For it was a uniquely barren generation in the annals of American history, and the higher you climbed the social ladder, the fewer children women had. Graduates of Radcliffe College were having almost none, it was discovered in the seventies. Where their mothers in the fifties had been swept up in a generational enthusiasm for marriage and child rearing, college women in the seventies were moved by a different set of imperatives. The "feminine mystique" gave way after 1969 to a "feminist mystique" that was just as prescriptive, life-denying, and divorced from the real needs of women. In both cases, individual American women—and indirectly men—were the losers, swept up in two successive floodtides of ideology which even the strongest personalities found it impossible to resist.

According to the new mystique, men and women, perverted by masculinity and femininity, find it impossible to live with each other. Their relations are "A battle which is fought through inauthenticity and hypocrisy by concealed blows and mutual treachery."[49]

Married life is presented as a condition of misery and unremitting conflict. To Friedan's characterization of the wife as a brainwashing victim and Millett's description of her as a "domestic servant," "chattel," and "slave," Greer adds even more vivid color. She portrays the wife as a drudge without hope of betterment, a shrew who destroys the man in her life, a desexed, trapped, miserable creature who is almost too contemptible to pity and whose example must be avoided at any cost by the woman lucky enough to find herself still single.

Not only is a woman who marries doomed to the gradual destruction of what is best in herself and in her mate: she is also working against progress in history. The refusal to marry is one of the most important steps women must take to fulfill their mission to redeem the human race. When young upper middle class American women began to marry again in significant numbers in the early 1980s, this view of marriage as the betrayal of a collective cause was to bring them no end of conflict and guilt, as documented by Megan Marshall in *The Cost of Loving: Women and the New Fear of Intimacy* (1984). Millions of young women had internalized the message against marriage of works like *The Female Eunuch*:

If women are to effect a significant amelioration in their condition it seems obvious that they must refuse to marry. . . . If independence is a necessary concomitant of freedom, women must not marry . . . a woman who seeks liberation ought not to marry.[50]

This hostility to marriage is oddly reminiscent of views expressed by the feminist character Olive Chancellor in Henry James's great novel *The Bostonians* (1886).* *The Bostonians* is of course not an official feminist document, but it has the advantage of being the product of a uniquely gifted observer who was personally acquainted with the types of people about whom he wrote.

In a moment of high drama, Olive asks Verena Tarrant, the playful, feminine girl whose future is up for grabs between Olive and the masculine man Basil Ransom, for the supreme sacrifice: "Promise me not to marry." But when they meet next, Olive has decided that Verena must give her even more, for a promise might fail to bind her actions forever. Instead of making a promise she might later break, Verena must internalize Olive's ideas so that they will have a lasting effect. With this goal in mind, Olive expounds the message against marriage to her protégé:

> I hope with all my soul that you won't marry; but if you don't it must not be because you have promised me. . . . No man that I have ever seen cares a straw in his heart for what we are trying to accomplish. . . . Oh yes, I know there are men who pretend to care for it; but they are not really men, and I wouldn't be sure even of them! Any man that one would look at—with him, as a matter of course, it is war upon us to the knife. . . . Any man who pretends to accept our programme *in toto,* as you and I understand it, of his own free will before he is forced to—such a person simply schemes to betray us. There are gentlemen in plenty who would be glad to stop your mouth by kissing you! . . . Then you will see what he will do with you, and how far his love will take him! It would be a sad day for you and for me and for all of us.

Olive's monologue is so similar to the message against marriage of recent feminists that the question arises, has society progressed so little in the century since *The Bostonians* was written, or have feminists learned so little? There is yet another possibility worth considering: Does the triad of Olive Chancellor, Verena Tarrant, and Basil Ransom, circled in the novel by the immature man Burrage and the unmasculine man

---

*A remarkably faithful film version of *The Bostonians* was released in 1984 and is widely available on videotape.

Pardon, represent some permanent aspect of the human situation, a perennial source of personal and ideological conflict rooted in conflicting sexual personalities?

The message against marriage was accompanied by warnings against the destructive effects of motherhood. Motherhood destroys whatever shreds are left of a woman's well-being; it holds no true rewards. As Greer writes:

> The plight of mothers is more desperate than that of other women, and the more numerous the children the more hopeless the situation seems to be. Most women, because of the assumptions that they have formed about the importance of their role as bearers and socializers of children, would shrink at the notion of leaving husband and children, but this is precisely the case in which brutally clear thinking must be undertaken.

Recent studies have shown that children fare better psychologically with their own parents except in the most severe cases of abuse and neglect. But Greer argues that even a low level of unhappiness justifies the breaking of homes: "It is much worse for children to grow up in the atmosphere of suffering, however repressed, than it is for them to adapt to a change of regime." According to Greer, children are likely to benefit from their mothers' departure: "It is probably better for the children in the long run to find out they do not have undisputed hold on mother."[51]

Not only is motherhood bad for women and not needed by children: it is actually bad for children. Like Millett, Greer believes that most parents are incompetent to raise their own children. She is sure that professional authorities could do a far better job. "Schoolteachers," she maintains, are able to clearly perceive "the anti-social nature of this mother-child relationship."

Thus, "the unfortunate wife-mother finds herself antisocial."[52] Nobody wants or needs her: not her husband, to whom she is a shrew and a sexual bore; not her children, who would be better off in a motherless, communal setting; not her society, which must struggle with her resistance to the greater wisdom of professional educators. But there is one source of hope, for the family is disappearing as an institution. The housewife can thus—if she has the courage—abandon her family with no regrets.

According to Greer, "The family is already broken down: technology has outstripped conservatism."[53] The interesting question, then, is not how to save the family—it must without question be destroyed—but rather with what to replace it. The reader who considers Greer's proposals for an alternative institution must be touched by her naiveté, but may well wonder why such notions have so recently been taken seriously.

> For some time now I have pondered the problem of having a child which would not suffer from my neuroses and the difficulties I would have in adjusting to a husband and domesticity. A plan, by no means a blueprint, evolved which has become a sort of dream. . . . I . . . hit upon the plan to buy, with the help of some friends with similar problems, a farmhouse in Italy where we could stay when circumstances permitted, and where our children would be born. . . . Perhaps some of us might live there for quite long periods, as long as we wanted to. The house and garden would be worked by a local family who lived in the house.

Greer maintains this would be a stable arrangement:

> The rambling organic structure of my ersatz household would have the advantage of being an unbreakable home in that it did not rest on the frail shoulders of two bewildered individuals trying to apply a contradictory blueprint. This little society would confer its own normality . . . , but it may well be that such children would find it impossible to integrate with society and become dropouts or schizophrenics. As such they would not be very different from other children I have known. . . .
>
> If we are to recover serenity and joy in living, we will have to listen to what our children tell us in their own way, and not impose our own distorted image upon them in our crazy families.[54]

It is certain that the first thing Greer's hypothetical child would tell her if placed in such a situation would be "Mama, please don't go." Greer's fantasy commune would be as fragile as the other ill-conceived "experiments in communal living" of the late sixties. The days of her "unbreakable home" would be numbered in months—more likely in days. The nuclear family, even in Greer's hostile depiction of it, appears as a bedrock of stability by contrast. This is so because it rests on the mutual commitments and interdependencies of individuals, whereas Greer's "a sort of dream" is clearly an attempt to formulate a plan for living that would require *no* commitment, in which the individual is unfettered by any responsibilities whatever. And never mind the kids: she is as unconcerned about their welfare as can be, cheerfully speculating they might "become dropouts or schizophrenics." This attitude toward children's well-being, however, is fully consistent with Greer's general attitude; she goes on to call for "the undermining of our civilization," proclaiming that "it is time for the demolition to begin."[55] Such was *The Female Eunuch*—far and away the most widely read feminist book of the seventies.

Radical leftism's hostility to the family, dating back to Marx and Engels, is one of its most dishonorable traits. America was fortunate indeed that the revolution of the sixties failed; China less so, as Mao's hostility to the family helped precipitate the chaos and famine of the Cultural Revolution; while Cambodia, under Pol Pot's policy of the separation of family members, showed the true fruits of which this view is capable if only it acquires power and freedom of action. Quoting Lenin, Greer writes that "Revolution is the festival of the oppressed."[56] This may seem to be just an amusing conceit if the festival leaves behind it the beer can mountains of America's privileged youth at Woodstock, rather than the bound skeletons of Cambodia's innocent men, women, and children in the killing fields. Those who fail to respect the conditions necessary to maintain human life exhibit a fundamental disrespect for life itself. Because we are never as wise as we would like to think, tradition is an irreplaceable *sine qua non* of human existence. Irresponsibility is far too weak a word for the radical readiness to jettison all the institutions of society in the vague belief that progress will somehow thereby result.

In their rhetoric, Millett and Greer share a predeliction for sensationalism. They are both lavish users of the appalling anecdote that is intended to reveal something horrible and hidden about the relations of men and women. Millett starts *Sexual Politics* with a description of intercourse taken from one of Henry Miller's sordid but arousing novels which is, she claims, revealing of the way men think of women and sex. Greer reproduces a long account of a gang rape in Brooklyn as a characteristic example of the way men feel about women.[57] The effect is to shock the female reader with the violence done to what ought to be beautiful, the sex act, and to both arouse and disgust the male reader. By simultaneously evoking these conflicting emotions, the writer evokes a sense of horror in the female reader, and of uneasiness and guilt in the male reader, creating in each an opening of vulnerability in which they are temporarily rendered more suggestible. "*This* is how men think of women?" thinks the appalled female reader—and chances are there is no man at hand who can answer her question. "*This* is what the way I feel about women leads to?" thinks the similarly shocked male reader—and he is not about to be treated to any reassurances by our two feminist authors. The readers will then, if all goes well, eagerly grasp at the explanation put forward by the author to explain the confusion created by the initial shock tactic. The goal is to weaken the readers' critical faculties so as to make them more receptive to the author's point of view. This tactic is repeated literally *ad nauseam* by both writers. We will see that these were not to be the last uses of sensationalism by feminist tacticians.

Between them, Friedan, Millett, and Greer represent the three main strands of the feminist movement. Friedan exemplifies the so-called moderate feminists, who emphasized legal and orthodox political methods like lobbying and get-out-the-vote campaigns. Millett accurately represents the radical feminism that was so prominent in the early seventies and now serves as the basis for "Women's Studies." In her dogmatic Marxism, her lesbian advocacy, and her aggressive self-righteousness, she is representative of the radical feminist *esprit*. Greer, an incorrigible iconoclast with few organizational ties, represents a more popular strain of radical feminism than Millett. Greer presents the most detailed script for a revolution in consciousness of the three, which typifies the comprehensive, interpersonal feminism that colored the lives of an entire generation.

But it must be remembered that feminism, for all its amorphous lack of organization and its bitter internecine quarrels, retained the allegiance of millions of women throughout the 1970s. However great their disagreements, the belief persisted that they belonged to a single grand movement to liberate humanity, "the women's movement." Although the feminists held views that ranged from the extreme left of the American political spectrum, like Friedan, to beyond the pale of American electoral politics, like Millett, and included idiosyncratic thinkers like Greer, the differences between their theoretical positions should not obscure the extent to which they were simply working on different aspects of the same problem. One can say that Friedan represents the political, Millett the intellectual, and Greer the personal aspects of modern feminism. The same feminist may sound like Friedan when she speaks before the university administration in the morning, Millett when she teaches a Women's Studies class in the afternoon, and Greer when she goes out to dinner with a male colleague in the evening. What united feminists was greater than what divided them, especially as the "radicals" succeeded in their effort to push the "moderates" yet farther to the left and as attitudes of the sort recommended by Greer were disseminated and became common points of reference through which feminist insiders could recognize each other—and get the upper hand in contacts with those outside the movement, in particular with men.[58]

It is striking that in the works of these three authors, purportedly advocates for women, there is scarcely any praise for women, who are consistently described as weak, inferior beings. Friedan characterized women (as they presently exist) as "inferior to men, dependent, passive, incapable of thought or decision."[59] Only by escaping from marriage, home, and children can women become "strong." The habits of mind, the emotional styles, and the life strategies associated with femininity must all be discarded, condemned as "soulless and degrading."

Femininity was commonly described as a lower stage of evolution, to be left behind by the march of progress. The feminine woman was "merely biological"; the feminist woman was a creature of a higher order. Feminist writings often display a curious contempt for biology. "The biological" was an inferior plane of existence to be overcome or avoided; it held no useful or interesting lessons. Biology could not inform but only hinder the progress of women.

Friedan repeatedly castigated "biological function" as a trap in which the feminine woman was caught and reduced to the level of a dumb brute. In the same spirit, Millett speaks of biology with unconcealed distaste: "The limited role allotted the female tends to arrest her at the level of biological experience. Therefore, nearly all that can be described as distinctly human rather than animal activity (in their own way animals also give birth and care for their young) is largely reserved for the male."[60] Millett thus neatly begs such questions as whether there might be any difference in the ways that animals and humans care for their young. Another prominent feminist, Shulamith Firestone, argued that humanity was in transition "between simple animal existence and full control of nature."[61] The obsolescence of biology was eagerly awaited.

Feminists were thus able to comfort themselves in their tribulations with the thought that they represented the future of humanity. They were better or at least, well, more *advanced* than those other, lesser women, such as their mothers.

And whatever their trials might be, they would be slight compared to the horrors that awaited women who obstinately clung to "the outgrown, childlike femininity of 'Occupation: housewife.' "[62] Feminist writers were full of dire warnings for those who failed to heed their message. The consequences of femininity, as presented to the young women of the baby boom, were severe. Friedan warned that a woman who failed to build her life primarily around a professional career, "remunerated by money," would "fritter away her energy in neurotic symptoms, or unproductive exercise, or destructive 'love.'. . . By choosing femininity . . . these girls are doomed to suffer ultimately that bored, diffuse feeling of purposelessness, non-existence, non-involvement with the world that can be called *anomie,* or lack of identity."[63]

The one virtue the new feminist ethic was willing to concede women was their greater innate pacifism: they had escaped the "enculturation" which made men more violent, aggressive, competitive, and divorced from their emotions. On the other hand, the opposite virtues, which had been traditionally imputed to women, were seen as condemning them to continued inferiority. At the same time she was urged to cherish the noncompetitiveness that made her superior to men—as men were, of course, not as they might become if only they could be separated from their masculinity—the new feminist was also being given the contradictory message that everything worth doing was being done by men, so that in order to retain any sense of self-worth, she would have to acquire the male virtues. For having rejected the female virtues, there was nowhere else to turn. The resulting conflict between the concepts of woman as pacifistic and woman as identical to man was smoothed over by the widespread acceptance of environmental determinism, which could always be invoked to argue that temperament and gender were not linked. The feminists' arguments shifted according to context, as was necessitated by the conflicting assumptions about gender on which the feminist perspective had been built.

In any case, men's objections were easy to dispose of. Men who pointed out inconsistencies in the feminist line could be accused of limitations like "linear male thinking." The devaluation of men and maleness ensured that the male viewpoint could always be discounted. Mad, androcidal Valerie Solanis captured the spirit of the feminist perspective in the manifesto she wrote for SCUM (The Society for Cutting Up Men) in 1968:

Men who are rational . . . won't kick or struggle or raise a distressing fuss, but will just sit back, relax, enjoy the show, and ride the waves to their demise.[64]

Men have no place in feminist discourse except as the objects of scrutiny and attack. The feminist dialogue consists exclusively of women talking to women. Feminists in search of wider public support often emphasize that the lesbian separatists who advocate the legal separation of the sexes, or even the genocide of all men, were always a minority of "the sisterhood." The feminist movement's ideological basis, though, involved a separatism of a different sort: the rejection of the validity of the male perspective. The feminist regeneration of humanity would proceed without benefit of the counsel of half the population.

But for all their vilification of men and masculinity, the feminists doomed themselves and the millions of women they influenced to male imitation. For regardless of whether their emphasis was on the rejection of the housewife role like Friedan, the rejection of female sexual passivity like Greer, or the rejection of heterosexual relations altogether like Millett, traditional female forms of behavior, thought, and association were invariably condemned. All these writers, and the whole massive effort to write and publish "women's books" that they spearheaded, were united in the feminist devaluation of the feminine.

PART II

The Feminist Era, 1969–1984

Chapter 3

The Feminist
Perspective

By the mid-seventies, the talk of radical versus moderate feminism had largely subsided. A unified point of view had emerged from the various strains of radical and moderate feminism. The internal disputes of feminism would henceforth focus on priorities and tactics rather than underlying principles, on which there was broad agreement. This unified point of view can be described as "the feminist perspective."

Something curious was going on among feminist writers in the seventies. As feminist books proliferated, so did feminist issues. To equality under the law was soon added a host of other causes. Some of these causes were understandable as aspects of the feminist focus on sex, the family, and work: contraception, abortion, rape, pornography, day care, divorce law, sexual harassment, and the Equal Rights Amendment. In addition to these expectable issues, though, a veritable plethora of other complaints began to crop up. To me the most striking of these was the book whose title proclaimed that "Fat Is a Feminist Issue."[1] It began to seem that *anything* could be a feminist issue. Clearly, something was wrong. The problem lay in the feminist perspective.

Upon its public reappearance in 1969, American feminism seemed to many to embody a single grand goal: equality in principle and in practice between men and women in all aspects of life. Because this goal seemed to fit in with the larger sixties push for social justice and with the egalitarianism that is such a central and enduring feature of the American personality,[2] it was easy for Americans to support "Women's Liberation" and to write off its follies as the inevitable excesses of a new movement.

But the quest for justice was not the only force driving feminism. The feminism that appeared at the end of the sixties was a reaction against the anomie of some undetermined number of housewives, the misogyny of male members of the New Left, and the exclusion of women from many levels of society. This reaction was to some extent justified. Modern life *had* presented women with unsolved problems, unthinking misogyny *was* often culturally acceptable, and women *were* excluded from many activities for reasons that were usually obscure and often indefensible. But the form that feminists' reaction to these facts took was heavily colored by the habits of the larger countercultural revolt. It was a period that glorified the act of protest and accepted the Marxist notion (without, on the whole, recking for its origin) of rage as a healthy, cleansing force in societal matters, and that constantly informed its youth that they were inventing new and better ways of living. Feminism succumbed to all these blandishments.

So, although some of the conditions that motivated the feminist revolt were well founded, the form the revolt took was at best a mixed bag. That form soon spewed up a whole demonology of new forces to fight against. Its sixties legacy left feminism with a hypercritical, dogmatic tendency that severely hampered the feminist effort to remake the nation's intellectual, individual, and political lives.

This self-defeating tendency is dramatically illustrated by the targets chosen by Friedan, Millett, and Greer. They vented their rage against men, women, masculinity, femininity, the sex act, marriage, the family, the home, medicine, social science, and capitalism. It became routine for feminists to attack some of the most powerful supports of women's welfare and to assault potential allies of the feminist cause—starting with men as a class.

Before the current feminist wave, it was common to deride feminists (who were not around to defend themselves) as man-haters. Contemporary feminists made short work of these sneers, which soon ceased. But we have overlooked the extent to which feminism *is* an anti-male movement, not in the sense that feminism is an agglomeration of man-haters, but in the sense that the assumptions which underlie feminism posit men and maleness to be the enemy.

These underlying assumptions were established by the sixties legacy, which emphasized the revolt of the oppressed against the oppressor as a cause of social progress. It was assumed that the condition of woman was unjust. Ever since some unspecified point in the past, the whole weight of society had been used to oppress her. Marriage reduced woman to "serf status," under which she and her children became the "chattel-property" of her husband, who was seen as having all power—power that he was inclined to use in a self-interested way. Woman thus existed in a condition of "enslavement to the family."[3]

The principal intellectual task of the new feminism was to reveal the nature of this oppression across time and space. Millett had argued that every known society is a "patriarchy." If all societies are patriarchal, then to analyze women's oppression by men or their oppression by society comes down to the same thing; patriarchy and society become synonyms. The equation of human society with male oppression threw open the whole sphere of human experience to feminist analysis. Feminists set out to document the oppression and exclusion of women in psychology, medicine, literature, history, and across the diverse cultures of the globe. The struggle to escape the influence of patriarchy is the grand theme of contemporary feminism.

The feminist perspective is thus the idea that *men are collectively responsible for all the evils of history and for their perpetuation in the present.* Both the form and the facileness of feminist analysis follow from this concept. Find something that bothers you, explore how it is caused, directly or indirectly, by tradition and by men, and you will have reproduced the structure common to all feminist analyses. If the cause is indirect, so much the better: you will win points for subtlety and thrill your readers with horror as you reveal to them the perversity of concealed influence.

The corollary to the exploration of women's oppression was to discover how they had resisted it. Had any women escaped the stultifying effects of male oppression and, if so, what could be learned from them? A search was instituted for female heroes, women who could provide "positive examples" by virtue of their successful defiance of society's norms of femininity.

The feminist perspective imposes a new schema on human history. Since "patriarchal" society is a distortion of the natural human condition, it must have had a point of origin somewhere in the past. Millett (whose views on this matter are paradigmatic) argues that an original state of "pre-patriarchy,"[4] in which societies were ruled by women, but which "might have been fairly equalitarian," preceded the introduction of "male supremacy."

> Since what we are dealing with is an institution, patriarchy must, like other human institutions, have had an origin and arisen out of circumstances

which can be inferred or reconstructed, and . . . if this is so, some other social condition must have obtained previous to patriarchy.[5]

The rise of patriarchy is the feminist version of the Fall from the Garden. It caused all the subsequent ills of human society.

Patriarchy was accompanied by . . . the ownership of persons, beginning with women and progressing to other forms of slavery, the institutions of class, caste, rank, ruling and propertied classes, the steady development of an unequally distributed wealth—and finally the state.[6]

"Pre-patriarchy" is the feminist equivalent of the Enlightenment myth of "the state of nature," the feminist Eden. History, viewed from the feminist perspective, is the story of the fall of woman and her subsequent slow rise. The biblical tale is reversed. Man is the cause of the Fall; the suffering of humanity, the punishment; woman the redeemer. The feminist movement has been pervaded by this messianic belief. And beside the moral imperative to end humanity's misery loomed the most terrible of threats: only by recovering female values could the human race avert nuclear Armageddon.

As we shall see when we examine issues of science and gender, pre-patriarchy, though a widely disseminated notion, makes very little sense from a scientific standpoint and is universally rejected by professional social scientists. There is no matriarchal Eden to which we can return. The human race will have to find other solutions to its problems.

The feminist perspective rearranges the peaks and valleys of history in accordance with the status of women (which is often extremely difficult to determine). Classical Greece becomes highly suspect because of its androcentric culture. It is barely redeemed by the presence of the poet Sappho, the original Lesbian. The Renaissance is labeled a period of "regression" because of the belief that women then lost some rights that they had possessed in the Middle Ages. This notion made the front page of the *New York Times* in 1981. The idea itself, though, goes back to Simone de Beauvoir, who had written much earlier that "Woman still retained a few privileges in the Middle Ages, but in the sixteenth century were codified the laws that lasted all though the Old Regime."[7]

Simone de Beauvoir's *The Second Sex*, written in the fifties, is often viewed as a mysteriously prescient work by modern feminists. But in fact there is no mystery. Beauvoir's application of Sartre's Stalinist dialectic to the sexes, in which Woman was defined as the Eternal Other, simply parallels the feminist perspective.

The one-dimensionality of the feminist perspective is just as evident in literature as in history. Of course art can be made of anything; there is no formula for great art. Precisely. The plot of a feminist fiction goes like this: An event shows a woman that her life is being dominated by men. Wishing to escape this fate, which she thinks was her mother's, she decides to strike out on her own and embarks on a course of action that lets her "assert" herself and "take control of her own life." Men are always the enemy in this petty but ubiquitous brand of fiction. Weak, abusive, manipulative, or simply unfathomable, they are rarely to be trusted and never to be relied on. The mature interdependence expressed in the country song "In My Eyes" or the movie *On Golden Pond* is alien to the feminist mindset. A feminist fiction depicts a woman's escape from a relationship.

The feminist perspective seemed novel to the point of exoticism when it was first widely introduced in the early seventies. But by the following decade it had come to permeate American popular culture—had itself become a new norm. Hollywood marched to a feminist drum.

In *Out of Africa,* the relationship between the characters played by Meryl Streep and Robert Redford cannot be allowed to work out permanently, for that would violate the Myth of Independence by suggesting it is possible for a woman to survive by means other than professional success. Streep's crowning achievement in the movie is not lasting love, but acceptance by the local men's club. The disturbing aspect of this vision is not its validation of female responsibility for self but its one-dimensionality. Like Friedan's warning against the lobotomizing effects of femininity, there is no either-or. The message is that women must choose between love and survival. Personal validation requires the rejection of serious relationships with men and the single-minded pursuit of career success. This dogma, which had played the foreign-film circuit in *My Brilliant Career,* was thus carried to mainstream America.

These tendencies, which in *Out of Africa* are dusted on to a competently produced, entertaining Hollywood epic, dominate *The Color Purple,* which is in all essential respects a faithful screen rendition of Alice Walker's Pulitzer Prize-winning novel of the same name. *The Color Purple* drew cries of outrage from many blacks, who argued that its relentlessly negative portrayal of black men perpetuates racist stereotypes. The men of *The Color Purple* make up a veritable rogues' gallery of sadists and weaklings. The story begins as a father wrenches a newborn from its mother's arms to give away or kill—she, the victim of his incest—and continues in the same vein, as the various women in the story experience life as an endless round of male abuse, with women's rejection of men the only hope for either sex, and lesbianism the one way to sustain life and love.

Men are Walker's villains: In *The Color Purple,* they represent Evil. Women, the victims, heroes, and eventually the redeemers, represent Good. Neither the sometimes inspired acting, the superlative cinematography, nor the excitement of glimpsing a Deep South honky-tonk in the thirties can redress the utter perversity of this message.

Dare we tolerate unquestioned in our midst works that rationalize the hatred of a whole biological category of human beings, whether defined by race, ethnicity, or, as in *The Color Purple,* by sex? Forty years after Allied troops smashed the genocidal machine of Hitler's Third Reich, some twenty years after Martin Luther King, Jr., was awarded the most deserved of Nobel Prizes, it had once more become fashionable to hate an entire category of people on the basis of a biological characteristic—only this time, instead of a race or an ethnicity, it was a sex that was associated with all that is bad and threatening.

In literature, feminism offered an escape from the soul-shredding alienation and complexity of the twentieth century into a simpler, more predictable world. Thus the childlike ending of *The Color Purple*: the men give up their masculinity and discover that what they really like is to sew and be bossed around by their aggressive wives; the women benevolently oversee the new order; and all the desperate conflicts that marked the early pages of the novel are resolved, with nary a loose end or a doubt in sight. "The color purple," indeed!

Despite the mediocrity of this vision, Walker's conformity to feminist ideology has given her a secure and prestigious place among her peers. Alice Walker is one of the brightest lights on the feminist literary scene, a writer whose brilliance no one questions, the very voice of wisdom. In contrast a writer who, like Joyce Carol Oates, dared to ignore or contradict the feminist perspective could count on being criticized for her defection. The collectivist movement could not afford the breaking of ranks.

Popular literature is of course at least as responsive to macrosocial developments as is other fiction, and it did not fail to reflect the new norms. A fantasy of a warrior woman, free, bold, and brave, as fierce and deadly as any man, made its appearance in the seventies and spawned a whole new genre of science fantasy novels. Revealingly, these sword-wielding, swashbuckling women typically exist as a superior race or class and are constantly threatened with reduction to the status of ordinary women at the hands of their male foes.

Let us apply the feminist perspective ourselves. Why not? Consider anything . . . a movie . . . a flower arrangement . . . the way you make love . . . your relationship with a pet . . . the arrangement of the rooms in your house . . . the psychology of Alexander the Great. All these are susceptible to a feminist analysis. The most banal thing can "prove" female subordination.

Consider my apartment. It is in a brick building in Chicago, built in the 1930s. From the street, you push open a gate, chest-high with a spiked top. You walk down a path lined with shrubs and grass, into an entrance hall with mailboxes, and up three flights of stairs. Inside, there is a foyer. Off to the right is a living room with a brick fireplace. On the left is a largish dining room. Straight ahead is a corridor that opens onto a small bedroom (where I am writing these words), which I use as a study. A bathroom also lies off the corridor. The kitchen, which is rather small and has a tiny pantry, lies beyond the dining room, and is entered through a swinging door. The walls of the entire apartment, except the kitchen and the bathroom, are plaster, painted white, and set off by dark wood doors and moldings. The floors are oak.

You begin to get the picture, so to speak. Clearly, this apartment reflects an oppressive culture that subordinates women. Perhaps I should move out of it.

Consider the moldings. Their dark wood is intended to suggest the men-only atmosphere of turn-of-the-century clubs: formal and soaked in cigar smoke. The small kitchen reflects the low value our society places on women's work. The swinging door that sets it apart from the rest of the house "shields" men from the baser, and possibly dangerous, feminine world. Too, this door will not lock: Women must be constantly vulnerable to masculine penetration. The contrast between the large dining room and the small bedroom reflects the pressure bourgeois society places on men to succeed financially. The spacious dining room gives a false impression of affluence, which enables the couple who inhabit the apartment to pretend they are fitting better into the corporate world than is actually the case; such pretensions and games-playing are endemic to patriarchy. In the meantime, real comfort is sacrificed to the pursuit of business success, or its image: the cramped bedroom signifies, and indeed actively reinforces, the devaluation of the personal in their lives. We can read the arrangement as, "There is only a very small place for love in the rat race." We have not even begun to consider the bathroom. . . .

The way the feminist perspective works is readily seen through such examples. The reader can easily continue this investigation for himself, given time to spare and perhaps a few drinks. Those who don't believe that ideas influence people will be astonished at the regularity with which the feminist perspective asserts itself.

Hundreds of articles, books, dissertations, and other cultural productions of the past fifteen years have been based on this method. Like other reductionisms, the feminist perspective can achieve a certain power in its single-mindedness. The problem is that when the reductionism of a principle goes unrecognized, the level of distortion it introduces readily undermines whatever insights it produces.

Because of the numbing one-sidedness of the feminist perspective, feminist intellectual productions tend to have a repetitive, stultified quality. And yet in one respect feminist scholars are constantly surprised. Every time they examine a new culture, a new period, or a new group of women, they have the pleasant shock of finding women who have escaped the soul-crushing oppression of the presumably male-dominated culture, who are interesting, lively, and even brilliant. This would be expected, and would be no cause for comment, if feminists did not make the mistake of believing their own rhetoric. For a secondary result of the feminist devaluation of the feminine is the belief that women who do not enjoy the fruits of "women's liberation" must be beaten-down, dull-eyed drudges, dehumanized by a lack of opportunities for self-expression and personal fulfillment. Fatal arrogance, to so overrate the virtues of one's own time!

For history has been no kinder to men than to women. If toil and suffering have been women's lot, they have also been men's. It is no accident that women live longer than men, even in cultures that are said to oppress women (and may actually do so in some cases). Men have faced agony on blood-soaked battlefields, been worked to death in mines and on galley ships, and in all cultures die younger than women. Proof that patriarchy is bad for the oppressors as well as the victims, say the feminists. Perhaps, though, we may be allowed to step aside from the feminist perspective just far enough to view it too with a little distance. It then becomes clear that the lot of the human race has been both worse and better than feminists admit. Worse, because the toil and pain of life were not caused by men exploiting women, and could not have been remitted through any role revolution. They are in our own time only reduced through the increase of wealth and of political and scientific knowledge. Better, because life for most people in most times has included satisfactions such as marriage and children.

The feminist perspective is unable to cope with a woman such as Pauline de Meulan. Meulan supported herself as a journalist in France in the early nineteenth century and was by all accounts both strong-minded and highly intelligent. Yet when she married Francois Guizot in 1812, her letters to him were filled with passion of a level that eludes feminists (unless they are writing to women): "As I have often told you, you have killed all my faculties; but there's no harm done, since it is you whom you have put in place of me."[8] The feminist perspective is equally bemused by both aspects of Meulan. On the one hand, since it expects to find weak, mindless women in the past, it can only explain Meulan's intellectualism as an aberration in her society; on the other, it cannot account for the selflessness of her love for her husband except as a reaction to men's oppression of women—which stretches a point to the limit of credulity, and beyond.

In the end, the most destructive impact of the feminist perspective was on individuals. The ideology of feminism—so fervently believed in that to disagree with it clear into the eighties was to invite condescending scorn or withering hostility—led to a distancing of women from their emotions and from men that inhibited and destroyed relationships without count. It placed men in a position of tutelage to women that must count as one of the supremely ridiculous deviations of our century. For women, this newfound hegemony turned out to be a hollow victory.

Chapter 4

New Woman, New Man

From Friedan's initial call for a new life plan for American women, a whole new mindset emerged among American women in the early seventies, colored partly by the necessity for changes in attitudes in order for women to compete with men, partly by the cultural baggage of the counterculture, and partly by the contradictions of trying to live in equality with men. A "new woman" emerged, who in important respects truly did differ from her predecessors. At the same time, as a result of the meeting of countercultural philosophies with the aggressive new women's movement, there also appeared a "new man." The New Woman and the New Man may have failed to live up to the feminist ideal, but they were very much the product of that ideal, which led to actual and widespread changes in beliefs and behavior among millions of Americans in the 1970s.

The New Woman

As Greer said in *The Female Eunuch,* women's messianic mission was to begin with each individual woman examining and changing her own self. The goal of this self-examination was to "raise consciousness." A woman's consciousness was raised once she had internalized the feminist perspective as the guiding principle of her life. The first revolutionary act was "understanding"; that is, to do a feminist analysis of one's own life and goals. A feminist analysis means the application of the feminist perspective: how one's life and goals have been determined by the oppression of the patriarchal society and of men. The remedy was "to take control of one's own life." To do this, a feminist would reject her former values and "define" new ones. She would, for instance, "redefine her sexuality." This analysis was supposed to change her life for the better, but it was also an act of high social responsibility.

"Consciousness-raising groups" were formed on an *ad hoc* basis by women throughout America, often taking Friedan, Millett, or Greer's work as a guide. The consciousness-raising groups aimed to help women analyze what had gone wrong with their lives, and what was wrong with the world, from the feminist point of view. Relations with members of the group were intended to counterbalance the women's relations with men, so as to maximize their ability to think and act independently of them.[1] By their very nature, these groups helped define the feminist perspective by its opposition to men.

The first step in raising consciousness was to convince the individual that the present situation of the sexes is intolerable to women. This is the reason for the sensationalism of Millett, Greer, and of the later Women Against Pornography campaign: an appeal to the emotions is made to convey the alleged injustice of the existing situation. Once this is done, it must be shown that change is possible: this is the function of environmental determinism in feminist theory. By acquiring a common set of beliefs, in opposition to those of the broader society, and a common vocabulary, feminists come to recognize each other as members of an in-group and to reject outsiders as non-members.

When the movement emerged around 1970, women became feminists through participation in "consciousness-raising groups" and political causes. Today, the feminist perspective is more often acquired in high school or college through the influence of peers, teachers, and the general cultural climate as conveyed by the media. In the sixties era, becoming a feminist often resembled a conversion experience, as reflected in book titles like *It Changed My Life*.[2] In the late seventies and early eighties, by contrast, feminism was the established church. Young upper middle class women picked up feminism through habit and docility, the way many people get their religion. Being a feminist was simply an accepted and expectable property of an intelligent and forward-looking young woman in many parts of the country, including most leading colleges and universities.

Regardless of how she acquired her feminism, it became the task of the new feminist to uphold the torch of the women's movement in daily life, by showing that she was the equal of men in all ways and by constraining the people in her life to act in accordance with the movement's values. For, as the most famous feminist slogan declared, "the personal is political."

"History has been the holocaust of women," wrote the feminist writer Rosemary Ruether in *New Heaven New Earth*. Believing this, feminists rejected the past as a source of lessons. The humane revolution would proceed, not just without the advice of men, but also without benefit of past experience. Gloria Steinem wrote in the early seventies: "I have met brave women who are exploring the outer edge of human possibility, with no history to guide them."[3]

The feminists believed their generation had a special mission in history. Their mothers were "transitional women" who were tragically stranded between traditional femininity and liberated womanhood. The feminists, by contrast, embodied a new type of woman who would be the equal of men—the first generation of women not to be sacrificed on the altar of history.

Where her mother—or her older sister in the fifties and early sixties— had been soft and plump, the new feminist aspired to be hard, lithe, and muscular. Feminine fat was to go. Greer defined the traditional female physique as that of the eunuch:

> The characteristics that are praised and rewarded are those of the castrate— timidity, plumpness, languor, delicacy and preciosity. . . .
> Eunuchs tend to fatten like bullocks, and so we need not be surprised to find that the male preference for cuddlesome women persists.[4]

Women struggled in gyms and on jogging trails across America to overcome the hips and thighs their genes had given them. Strength, both psychic and physical, had become the highest female virtue. There was widespread agreement that men were not physically stronger than women, except through the habit of exercise.

In the early seventies, before the need to appear neat on the job changed the image of the feminist woman, there was a general rejection of pretty clothes, cosmetics, and all forms of self-adornment. To adorn oneself was seen as a dishonest artifice.

The bra was temporarily rejected by many feminists on ideological grounds, as a form of oppression that forced women to conform to an ideal stereotype. The rejection of the bra didn't last because large-busted women were often physically uncomfortable without its support, and because feminists in general found this particular attempt to feel liberated was inhibited by men's constant stares.

Anything that emphasized the physical dichotomy between the sexes was frowned upon: high heels, which emphasize the swaying gait caused by the female pelvis; smooth-shaven legs, which emphasize the difference in hair distribution between men and women; and any garment that seems to emphasize the relative helplessness and vulnerability of the female before the male. Many women who continued to shave their legs, use cosmetics, and wear pretty dresses felt they somehow weren't quite up to snuff. They acknowledged that their behavior was wrong in principle, even though they persisted in it.

Recent works by feminist writers like Lois Banner and Susan Brownmiller have continued to call for a "natural" approach to dress. The fashion historian Valerie Steele has supplied an interesting critique of the feminist hostility to fashion.[5]

> According to the neo-feminist critique, fashion is bad because it is sexually exploitive and artificial. It is also conducive to self-absorption, and it is a waste of time. . . . Although women no longer wear "tight" corsets and long skirts, nevertheless trousers are still superior to modern skirts, on both practical and ideological grounds. . . . Far better . . . to adhere to the "feminist" ideal of the "natural" woman, and the beauty of "spiritual qualities, healthy bodies, and useful lives."

Valerie Steele goes on to argue that the feminist conception of "naturalness" in dress is itself highly artificial.

> Certainly fashion is erotic and artificial, but are those necessarily negative features? It is apparently a difficult concept for most people to accept that there is no "natural" way to look. . . .
>
> The contemporary belief that athleticism equals feminism and is "based on sound medical knowledge" is as culture-bound as an Edwardian doctor's approval of "healthy" fatness for both men and women. . . . To minimize gender distinctions and to emphasize a mesomorphic body type is no more "natural" than fashion's various exaggerations or stylizations of the sexual body.

Steele challenges us to look beyond the beliefs of our own time by comparing them with similar beliefs of earlier times. She locates the feminist hostility to feminine attire in a long tradition of anti-sexual moralizing.

> Historically, attacks on the artificiality of fashion have been almost as common as attacks on its immorality. Yet why should the ideal of artificiality arouse such deep hostility? . . . [T]he artificial creation of the self is human, even superhuman, whereas the natural and unmodified is equivalent to remaining in an uncivilized, animal state.

The feminist hostility to fashion is thus particularly contradictory in view of the environmental determinism on which feminist ideology heavily depends. If human beings do things through culture that other animals do through biology, then it makes sense that we should express our temperament and status through dress. It is no less natural for us to use clothes to differentiate the sexes or to send sexual signals than it is for us to use clothes to keep warm in cold weather.

As one might expect, feminists are at least as self-conscious about clothing as are other people. In *Femininity* (1984), Susan Brownmiller spends page after page explaining why women should wear trousers, not skirts; why they should not shave their legs, wear fancy shoes, or in general make themselves attractive to men. But this does not mean that clothes are less important to Brownmiller; rather the contrary.

> Who said that clothes make a statement? What an understatement that was. Clothes never shut up. They gabble on endlessly, making their intentional and unintentional points.[6]

It is thus particularly important to many feminists that their clothes send the right "message," and particularly irritating to them that most women continue to dress in a "feminine" manner. Justice Sandra Day O'Connor, for instance, is ridiculed by Brownmiller for wearing nylon stockings on the Supreme Court bench.[7]

Susan Brownmiller herself appears in an approved uniform on the jacket of *Femininity*—and femininity is just what no one would accuse her of displaying in the photograph. It might be the start of a new genre: the author as ideological fashion plate. Perhaps I shall ask my editor if future editions of *The Failure of Feminism* can show me as a bare-chested caveman, a sort of Conan the Barbarian type. For Brownmiller is making a fashion statement in this picture, despite her disparagement of fashion.

She is wearing a dress, not the trousers of which she approves,[8] but what a dress! Formless, sacklike, it gives no clue to what lies beneath. One cannot tell if she has a bust, where her waist is, whether she has hips, or even whether her arms are plump or thin, slack or muscular. It is the body desexualized. Even the fabric, a dull linen, is without pattern or color. No patterns for the woman freed from the patterns of conditioning; no color for the woman who fears to excite men's attention. This nondescript smock is belted with a man's belt: not too wide, with the plainest of buckles. Brownmiller's assumption of the belt, an archetypal symbol of masculinity, shows her determination to assume the masculine qualities it represents: in her case, presumably intellectualism and the search for identity through extrafamilial activities. The rejection of accentuation and ornamentation extends beyond clothing to the body itself. No item of jewelry is visible, for jewelry might suggest feminine frivolity or narcissism. Brownmiller's bushy, unplucked eyebrows remind the male viewer not to expect concessions to his flawed notions of female sexual attractiveness. Is she wearing penny loafers, nondescript sandals, or perhaps, in an ambivalent concession to femininity, espadrilles? We may never know, as the photograph is cropped at mid-thigh; but it can safely be predicted that her footwear is as ideologically correct and as bland as the rest of her attire.

This photograph is a portrait of the woman as Graham cracker. In the nineteenth century, Dr. Sylvester Graham invented his famous cracker as the main food in a diet that, by providing no stimulation to the senses, was supposed to reduce sexuality, which he saw as a dangerous force to be suppressed. It is a sign of the tendency of human plans to go awry that many people now consider Graham crackers a treat. That is not at all what Dr. Graham had in mind. If this is liberation, who wants it? Would a world as bland as the Susan Brownmillers and Dr. Grahams of this world want to see be worth living in?

Although the Brownmillers are still very much with us, the majority of women influenced by feminism adopted a different standard in the seventies, at least during the working day. The watchword of the seventies was "dress for success," a theme which gave rise to dozens of books and hundreds of magazine articles. The dressed for success woman selects her wardrobe to impress her bosses and coworkers with her competence on the job. She does not dress for men; she pleases herself through her own career and does not need a man to validate herself; and on the job she wishes to get ahead through her professionalism, not through her sex (although a little bit of affirmative action would be acceptable). And she certainly doesn't dress to please herself. Thus, under the closely related pressures of feminism and careerism, a new image of the flower of middle class American womanhood appeared—one of the most pathetically conformist norms ever seen in a culture as diverse as our own. Fighting back as they could, women spent a part of their new job dollars on sexier underwear. Beneath her drab business suit, complete with collar bow to echo the male necktie, the professional woman often swathed her skin in luxurious whiffs of silk and lace. The scuffy running shoes with which the urban legions of women replace their heels at 5 o'clock for the ride home are partly a rejection of the corporate ethos to which the quest for independence has consigned so many American women, and partly a rejection of the femininity implied by more attractive footwear: a fittingly ambiguous symbol of our era.

For many women no longer know where they stand, or if they do, they hesitate to articulate themselves in the face of perceived cultural norms. Massive conflict prevails over what it means to be a woman. The change in the image of woman has created conflicts that cannot be resolved until the premises of feminism are reexamined. Only then will we be able to think once more about the role of gender with a sense of perspective.

As Megan Marshall expressed the difficulty of the Me Generation woman,

> The vision of a mother inseparable from her family was replaced by a working woman attached to no one; a dream of giving was replaced by a dream of doing; a life defined by connections to others was replaced by a life of solitary self-exploration. Inevitably, I learned, the second vision eclipsed the first, the self-motivated woman in tweeds—or in a painter's smock or doctor's coat— promising release from a life of selflessness in the home. A good many of the women I interviewed had lived up to that second vision, learning to wear the tweeds and carry the briefcases of success as if they'd been born to them.
>
> But they hadn't been, and that was the whole problem. Whether because the earlier dream could not be forgotten, or because it represented something basic to female nature, by the time I interviewed these women in their late twenties and thirties, parts of the mother image were beginning to haunt the woman in tweeds. "Some days I look in my closet full of carefully tailored suits, simple blouses and blue jeans for the weekend," admitted a thirty-two-year-old lawyer, "and it makes me very sad. I don't think I'd ever feel comfortable in frilly clothes again—but it's as if there's some part of me that I've had to hide even from myself."[9]

Regardless of whether she listened to the Brownmillers or to the dress-for-successers, the one piece of advice the feminist woman was never likely to hear was: Wear what makes you feel good personally, not what someone else thinks you should wear. The New Woman might be a brave explorer of uncharted paths, as Steinem had hoped. But she was likely to explore them along relentlessly stereotyped lines. The personal searches of feminist women in the seventies were as conformist in inspiration as their mothers' rush into domesticity in the fifties.

By the early eighties, the futility of the independent quest as a means to fulfillment for most women was becoming apparent. One by one, women who had rejected marriage as a way of life began to marry, sending the marriage rate up for the first time in decades. Women in their late twenties and early thirties, faced with the prospect of having children soon or never, led the new trend. Women who had publicly denounced the housewife role as impractical and destructive often became housewives themselves. Many who kept their careers reduced their professional ambitions for the sake of stabilizing their family lives, which had come to seem more important. At the same time women began to show more of the stress-linked illnesses that had long bedeviled men, a movement away from the focus on careers began, at first outside the media limelight. The New Woman had discovered the limits of the value of independence. And so some New Women became Traditional Women, often discovering a belated respect for the values of their parents' generation. Older couples with successful marriages of long standing were bemused to suddenly find themselves objects of admiration and scrutiny to many younger Americans. The question of how to have an orgasm on a one-night stand had come to seem crass and irrelevant; the newly interesting question was, how do you make a marriage work? Another often asked question, especially among professionally successful women, was, where are all the men?

The New Man

The New Woman sought a new kind of male creature, the New Man. The primary task of the New Man was to catch up with the newly liberated woman. It was believed that women had made advances in consciousness but that men remained backward by comparison. Throughout the seventies and early eighties, they were routinely urged in the media to move beyond the "constraints" of traditional masculinity; by doing so, there was a chance they might become as liberated and insightful as their women already were.

The characteristic flavor of the feminist attitude toward men's prospects for progress is found in *The Female Eunuch*. Greer argued that men are damaged by masculinity, though apparently not as severely as women are by femininity. Thus, although she did not reject men as Millett had, she remained anti-male in the sense that her acceptance of men was predicated on the change in their nature that the women's movement was expected to bring about. Although men as they existed were pretty awful, liberated women would be able to remake men and so make them good. The condition for men's reacceptance into the human race was to give up their masculinity.

If men refused to go along, it was legitimate to force them to do so. To this end, Greer advocated a primitive form of emotional blackmail:

> Many men are almost as afraid of abandonment, of failing as husbands as their wives are [*sic*], and a woman who is not terrified of managing on her own can manipulate this situation. It is largely a question of nerve.[10]

By assuming they had this right to pressure and emotionally manipulate men to advance the feminist cause, the cause of humanity, feminists laid the ground for a great deal of inauthentic male behavior in the seventies. Many men were forced to proclaim their respect for feminism by insistent wives or girlfriends, who, by the very act of insisting on such deference, guaranteed that male participation in the humane revolution would be limited and inauthentic, that is to say, not grounded in any genuinely felt personal experience. Feminism was thus obliged to prescribe for humanity without benefit of either the feminine or the male point of view.

One of the most effective feminist tactics was to get control over the terms of discussion. New words were invented, with highly specific meanings; certain old words were given new meanings, and others were tabooed. By insisting that arguments be conducted in their vocabulary, feminists gained a tremendous tactical advantage: they were able to fight on their own ground, that of such loaded terms as "sexism," "male chauvinism," and so forth. Even more important, they were able to befuddle their targets through surprising and—to the uninitiated—unpredictable valuations of perfectly ordinary terms. The struggle was waged from the board room to the bedroom, and feminists dearly wished it could be carried to the locker room. The phrase "the opposite sex" was shunned because it implies that the sexes form a dichotomy instead of affirming that men and women are the same in all ways. The word "girl" was virtually abolished, because women were no longer to be defined by their marital status—a rationale that also underlay the invention of the term "Ms." It was an insult to draw any distinction between married and unmarried women. Too, the term "girl" was felt to imply immaturity; ignoring the fact that men often refer to themselves as "boys" in certain contexts, and that the use of the word "girls" for women can be equally innocuous, feminists rejected the word so completely that it became suspect to use it even for females hovering on the brink of puberty.

Body language was called into service. Men who held doors for women, helped them with their coats in restaurants, or performed other culturally standard acts of intersexual courtesy were apt to find themselves reviled as "chauvinist pigs" who wanted to keep women down, or as simply not "with it." Considerable confusion came to prevail in the stylized body language of the sexes.

Any action that seems to suggest greater male competence tended to be perceived as a threat. Even offers to walk a woman home through a dangerous neighborhood could lead to bristling reactions. The idea that men could ever protect women was treated as an insult—even when true.

"Men's groups" were recommended by the feminists to emulate the consciousness-raising groups that had had such an impact on women. In these groups, men were supposed to reveal to each other deep insecurities that masculinity had produced in them—fear hiding behind a facade of toughness, uncertainty concealed beneath a veneer of decisiveness, unresolved hate disguised under a mask of aggressiveness. Masculine characteristics like toughness, decisiveness, and aggressiveness were to be analyzed according to environmental determinism as products of early conditioning. Men were to proceed to overcome these limitations, through the help of their liberated women and by learning to "open up," to be weak and vulnerable, and to cry freely together.

It didn't work. Although a spate of men's consciousness-raising groups was founded around 1970, practically all fell apart in a matter of months— often after just one or two meetings. If men had truly expressed themselves to each other in these groups, a new human manifesto might have appeared; but, since feminism was the only available philosophy of gender in the radical-liberal consensus to which any man who joined such a group was likely to subscribe, and since feminism was the property of women, the men's groups were pervaded by inauthenticity. To truly evaluate masculinity from a male point of view would have shattered the feminist perspective, whose inadequacies are somewhat easier to gloss over from a female point of view. As attempts to foist off an anti-male ideology onto men, the men's groups brought out the contradictions in the feminist perspective too glaringly; and so they fizzled.

The failure of the men's consciousness-raising groups did not stop other pressures to create the New Man. The hippie ideal had already provided a base on which to build. Hippies were to be tolerant, unconcerned, dreamy, impractical, androgynous if they wished; above all, they were not to impose their wills on others. "Hey man, don't lay that head trip on me" was the characteristic hippie response to a disagreeable idea. The hippie ideal was to "do your own thing" without interference from anyone else. The highly directive feminist ideology, with its manifold prescriptions and prohibitions, was diametrically opposed to this countercultural spirit; but the men who grew up under the countercultural regimen were ideal candidates for the New Man: tractable and easygoing, they provided suitably malleable material to receive the imprint of feminist ideology.

The hippie also provided an invaluable counterbalance to older, unreconstructed men who worked as, say, airline pilots or newspaper editors or were otherwise attached to a macho point of view. By reminding such men that they were not quite up-to-date, that they were engaged in a losing battle with the spirit of the times, the hippie ideal helped to discount traditional male perspectives, creating a lingering insecurity among many men who were far from countercultural themselves.

So under the pressure of feminism the New Man began to emerge, from young men who had grown up in a time of widespread cultural insecurity and had as yet no direct experience of adulthood, from sensitive and artistic men who had never felt comfortable with masculine bluster, from homosexual men to whom relations with women were of slight concern anyway, and to a lesser extent from older men who struggled to escape their "conditioning."

A book called *Ah, Men!* published in 1980 accurately voiced the reaction of many men to feminism.

> Profound and rapid changes in women have left men lagging far behind, reeling in quiet confusion as to what their roles should be. . . .
> Suddenly, the old familiar male pattern seems to be changing before our eyes. We find ourselves in a different arena, where the very meaning of words

like *masculine* and *feminine* are [*sic*] rapidly changing. It's new and exciting—and frightening.

Of course, some men are much more fortunate than others in their ability to adjust. Their fluidity, sensitivity, and sense of themselves are strong; but they also speak of a nagging feeling that many of their new attitudes are hedged with contradictions. These men tend to be younger, in their twenties and thirties, and have grown up in a countercultural environment. They generally have been more receptive to the feminist influence than any other segment of the male population. They are quick to respond to new currents in our culture, recognizing the positive, potentially liberating possibilities of new male values.

Such tractable men, ready to jump on the bandwagon of social change, represent the wave of the future, according to this view. There is no alternative to cooperation with the feminists in their search for new values.

Others resist the winds of change with steadfast determination. And, in the long run, they will be unsuccessful at stemming the tide of history.[11]

There is no hope, according to the men who are trying to catch up with the feminists, of men finding themselves without respectful attention to the feminist insights. Men must assume a position of tutelage to women, deferring to their superior knowledge of human affairs. Because men's perceptions are clouded by the stultifying effects of masculinity, because men are desensitized by conditioning and rendered arrogant by inflated status, they need to relearn humility to the point of giving up their own masculine point of view, to feed from the feminist trough so that they may one day no longer be, as the radical coinage of the sixties put it, "pigs." Men were expected to be ready to eat a good amount of crow to help atone for the wrongs they were believed to have wreaked on the world since the dawn of history. Many feminists took delight in mocking men—and some men were suspiciously eager to cooperate. One of NOW's few male activists suggested in 1974 that

As a men's group becomes more stable, if it contemplates turning activist a *beauty contest* might be an excellent consciousness-raiser and even a fund-raiser. Every man attending the contest is carefully surveyed by the women in the audience as a possible nominee. Nominations are made from the floor, only by women. A man waiting through a half-hour of nominating without his name being mentioned will begin to feel the pressure of being a sex object—

especially an unsuccessful one. After nomination, men are paraded in bathing suits, and a group of women judges comment on the shape of their legs, their buttocks, their chest span (or lack of one), the way they walk, their posture, arm muscles, hair thickness; the women make guesses at their penis size, read waist and chest measurements, and then ask them a few simple questions to see if they are "talented."[12]

And so the New Man emerged, or tried to, eagerly hoped for by the majority of feminists who remained heterosexual despite their deference to the ideologically purer life-styles of their "lesbian sisters," his values defined in opposition to those that had been associated with men since before the dawn of civilization.

This was to be a man "freed" from the constraints of masculinity, one who was sensitive rather than aggressive, who was unthreatened by the new feminism because he was "secure in his sexual identity," who abhorred the thought of physical violence of any sort, who was, in short, safe— and consequently an utter bore. He was so boring in fact that European feminists like Germaine Greer and Lina Wertmüller recommended interludes of steamy sex with unreconstructed working class men, who posed no threat of entanglement to these upper middle class storm troopers. The new feminist man was not to mind doing half the dishes, half the cooking, half the child rearing, including bottle-feeding, changing diapers, and babysitting; he was to be "just as nurturant" as women.[13] He was to be unthreatened if his wife made more money or had more seniority than he did. He was to overcome urges to dominate. He was to be agreeable, patient, and not to obtrude himself into his woman's career, which he accepted took priority over her relationship with him—unless, that is, he was equally willing to sacrifice his own career advancement to the exigencies of her job or education. Despite all this he was supposed to be "strong," a fitting ornament for the new feminist who would then brag to her friends about how she had him doing the dishes, sweeping the carpet, and performing other domestic tricks. Many was the man who came home from work to a sinkful of dirty dishes requiring his attention, who was about to initiate sex after dinner (probably cooked by him) when it was suggested he should clean the toilet. If the two of them made it into bed with any energy left, he could then stimulate her clitoris and eventually ejaculate in her vagina (Latin was popular with feminist lovers, in an attempt to avoid the "sexism" of Anglo-Saxon) after being sure she had climaxed first.

It was a recipe for living tailor-made for masochists, but even this way out was denied the hapless feminist male. The wish to be dominated, like the wish to dominate, was a product of our "sick" society, and although his woman was in fact forcing his thoughts and actions into a predetermined mold not of his own choosing, she would never abide the thought she was dominating him: Of course he was a free agent! So even surrender was ruled out. The only real choice a feminist left her man was to leave her. Many did, sooner or later—departures the feminist rationalized as necessary to preserve her own freedom.

The other possibility, to reevaluate the ideology that was causing so much stress and so many absurd situations, was a difficult option in the prevailing cultural climate, especially since the apparently scientific validation of feminist ideology was so widely disseminated. But it was one that virtually all couples that stayed together, inevitably, took tacitly: they would continue to pretend, and often actually to believe, that they were living according to the tenets of sexual egalitarianism, but their lives soon assumed very different patterns. I see it in my friends, in my relatives, in people I meet casually, in relationships I read about in the press. Time after time, equal parenting doesn't work out, and the wife gives up her job to become a full-time mother and house-keeper. Time after time, the couple moves when the man's job requires it, not when the woman's does—she, on the contrary, gives up her job for an inferior one in the new location. Equality in housekeeping sometimes works out—until children enter the picture. And virtually no women follow Greer's exhortation to choose men who are poorer or less gifted than them-selves; on the contrary, women still want a man they can look up to.

Only the ideology of sexual egalitarianism prevents us from drawing the obvious conclusions: first, that a definite degree of male dominance is still desired by women and manifested by men; second, that the division of labor by gender which is common to all human societies is alive and well in our own; and third, that far from being a source of injustice, this state of affairs seems so congenial that the question arises, should we come to accept it?

The confusion of the ideal of sexual equality with the notion that the sexes are identical and should behave the same in all ways toward each other, that they differ only in their genitals, imposes hypocrisy on our words and actions, since we continue to be human and therefore sexually differentiated, and confuses our thinking about men, women, and society.

It is time to begin to lift the veil beneath which unisexist piety has concealed the Janus head of gender. Perhaps what we discover under the veil will not be so horrible after all: perhaps we shall like a gendered world of men and women rather better than the neutered ideal of the feminists in which "the only things the sexes can uniquely exchange are semen and transudate."

Chapter 5

Feminism and Sex

Sex as Rape

The channeling of sexuality was central to the nascence of the New Woman, in what has aptly been called the "Control Generation" of American women.[1] Sex, for feminists, is the primal means through which men oppress women. It offers a microcosm of the larger patriarchal order of society. The sex act thus assumes a central importance in the feminist scheme of things. The feminist analysis of sex follows from the feminist perspective—that the human condition is a product of men's oppression of women. Women must resist this oppression by refusing to submit to sex on men's terms.

According to the feminist analysis, rape is the paradigm for the sex act. Sex is a sadomasochistic power transaction whose sole purpose is to affirm the dominance of the male over the female. The man penetrates the woman without regard for her comfort or pleasure, thrusts until he is satisfied, and then ignores her. Women derive little satisfaction from this kind of sex. Such is the conception of the sex act that appears time after time in feminist literature.

Rape is the feminist crime *par excellence* because in it women suffer at the hands of men. There are of course no bounds to the sympathy we should extend to women who have suffered rape. We should further increase the funding and training law enforcement receives to deal with this serious crime. But we must not allow our concern to obscure the fact that feminists' outrage over rape is quite different from that of the average person. Feminists depict rape as the most horrible of crimes because of the peculiar angle of their perspective. Common crimes that are even more atrocious than rape, like child neglect and murder, but that are committed by women as well as men, or that victimize both males and females, do not receive even remotely comparable levels of feminist attention. Nor is homosexual rape—a daily event in the nation's prisons—a source of feminist concern. Feminists protest rape not as an outrage against the person but as a "political crime."

To resist rape, in the feminist view, is to resist male dominance—not simply a means of self-protection but a revolutionary act. The oppressor is not just men, but the feminine elements in oneself that make one vulnerable to men's exploitation. That is why thousands of young women in the Feminist Era followed self-defense classes with such unsmiling intensity. The characteristic goal of these white-garbed flocks was not so much self-protection (which could conceivably be achieved through other means) as the smashing of their own feminine, vulnerable self-images. The destruction of vulnerability to male aggression, if successful, should enable the feminist to refuse to interact with men in "traditional" ways.

The belief that rape is the paradigm for the sex act, that the male aggression which makes rape possible must be neutralized, led to the peculiar strategy of bedroom politics. Sex became central to a power struggle between the sexes in ways that Lysistrata never imagined.

The Rejection of "Roles"

Sex as we know it, according to feminists, is a reflection of the sick masculine and feminine roles. These roles are arbitrary impositions on a genderless "human" personality common to both men and women. Kate Millett's formulation, though extreme, is representative: "the enormous area of our lives . . . labeled 'sexual behavior' is almost entirely the product of learning."[2] As Betty Friedan explained the feminist consensus:

> What had to be changed was the obsolete feminine and masculine sex roles that dehumanized sex, making it almost impossible for women and men to make love, not war. How could we ever really know or love each other as long as we played those roles that kept us from knowing or being ourselves?[3]

As usual, "radical" and "moderate" feminism operated less as opposing camps than as different wings of a common movement. Although some "moderates" expressed dismay at the radicals' emphasis on sexuality, they lacked a separate analysis with which to combat it. They too subscribed to all the basic ideas that underlay the radicals' view, like the notion that "sex roles" are "obsolete" and "dehumanizing." As a result, they were unable to present an alternative to the radicals other than to suggest that "too much" attention was being paid to sex and not enough to jobs. This may have been true, but it was of course irrelevant to the understanding of sexuality. Because a bad idea is infinitely more powerful than no idea, the radical view soon became the universal feminist line on sexuality.

The feminist view of sex is alive and well today. It flourishes in offices and on college campuses across the land, a detritus of the sixties which remains an issue of all-too-current importance for millions of Americans.

The characteristic rationale for bedroom politics is accurately laid out in *The Female Eunuch*—indeed, it is implicit in the title. Rather than abandon sex with men, as radical lesbians like Kate Millett advocated, feminists should instead make sex their main battleground. "Sex," wrote Greer, "is the principal confrontation in which new values can be worked out."[4]

> Much lesbianism . . . may be understood as revolt against the limitations of the female role of passivity, hypocrisy and indirect action, as well as rejection of the brutality and mechanicalness of male sexual passion.[5]

By rejecting feminine modes of behavior—pejoratively cast as "passivity, hypocrisy and indirect action"—women could redeem men from their "brutality and mechanicalness." Women's rejection of femininity would save men from masculinity. Men who attempted to love feminists were thus subjected both to hostility as victimizers and pity as victims.

This approach made it possible for feminist women to continue to have sexual relations with men, while retaining intact feminism's anti-male point of view. The radical lesbian argument that to make love to a man is to make love to the enemy was not rejected but qualified. Woman would remake men so that they would no longer be the enemy.

The need to remake men imposed major responsibilities on women, the redeemers. Women were exhorted to withdraw their sexual favors from men who fitted traditional concepts of masculinity. For instance, Greer argued that women should refuse to love traditional male heroes like soldiers and sports stars.

> It would be a genuine revolution if women would suddenly stop loving the victors in violent encounters. Why do they admire the image of the brutal man? If only they could see through the brawn and bravado to the desolation and misery of the man who is goaded into using his fists. . . . We are not houris; we will not be the warrior's reward.[6]

Not only were women to change *whom* they loved; it was even more important to change *how* they loved. Sex was branded as "inauthentic and enslaving in the terms in which it is now possible."[7] The difficulty with "the terms in which it is now possible" is that men tend to act in sex, women to react; that men are initiating, women accepting; in short, that in most couples, most of the time, men are sexually aggressive and women are sexually receptive. Instead, in the feminist view, sex should be the meeting ground of two absolute equals, neither of whom feels any aggressiveness or dominance, neither of whom is "castrated" into relative passivity.

So, across the board and up to the present, feminists have shared the belief that "feminine and masculine sex roles" are "obsolete" and have "dehumanized" sex. The sex act itself is therefore invested with tremendous political resonance, for "moderate" as well as "radical" feminists. A feminist makes love as an **act** of high social responsibility. By refusing to submit to aggressive male sexuality, by banishing all dominance behaviors from the bedroom, the feminist literally believes she is helping to save the human race from nuclear Armageddon. She believes that men's "misdirected energies have now produced the ultimate weapon." Men, she thinks, equate sexuality with violence; they see penises as weapons, weapons as penises. The solution, then, is to "take the steel out of the penis," reversing the alleged "dehumanization" of men and of the human race at the same time. Since "the personal is political," this female redemption of humanity starts with the individual woman acting upon the individual man. And, fellow man, you thought you were just out on a date!

Fashion, Etiquette, and Personality

The fight against what feminists claimed was a male definition of sex assumed many forms. It affected the whole process of courtship and love, from casual glances exchanged on the street through the manner in which couples engaged in sexual intercourse.

As noted in the previous chapter, feminist fashion criticism contains an extensive set of prohibitions. The struggle required the rejection of the symbols of male dominance (or what were taken to be such), like short skirts, long skirts, tight skirts, billowy skirts, and all other clothing which through restrictiveness or lack of "practical" function caused or suggested vulnerability. Pretty clothes were severely criticized; their frequent lack of practicality suggested to feminists that women were presenting themselves as objects to men, and had acquired or were feigning the lack of serious purpose they believed was characteristic of feminine women. Although the rhetoric has softened somewhat in the past few years, in their heart of hearts feminists remain deeply suspicious of prettiness and sexiness in women—of anything in fact that suggests to them a woman may be making herself a lure for male aggression. The feminist perspective literally imposes the belief that it is wrong for a woman to be attractive to men. The only exception to this rule is for *femmes fatales* like the heroine of *Carmen,* who feminists admire as "strong" women. Since they destroy men, *femmes fatales* can be admired despite their beauty.

In addition to objects—clothing, jewelry, and cosmetics—feminism proscribes actions, starting with all men's acts of chivalry: paying for a woman's dinner, letting her pass through doors first, even walking her home at night. Such actions, to a feminist, imply a humiliating dependence on men.

But perhaps the single most obnoxious manifestation of male dominance is a man who is in fact dominant. His very personality is a source of offense, reason enough to embark on an attempt to recondition him—not, to be sure, to recondition him to recognize women as dominant, but rather to believe that dominance itself is inherently a bad thing.

The games to which these notions gave rise were played out all over America, in doorways, at coat racks, behind restaurant tables—and above all in the bedroom.

Foreplay

The politicization of sex freighted its slightest aspects with a deadly weight of self-consciousness. For example, Greer argued that men were too obsessed with women's breasts. To help them overcome this supposed defect, she proposed it would be "progress" to "remind men that they have sensitive nipples too."[8] While some men do have sensitive nipples, most do not. But with excruciating seriousness, feminist women proceeded to caress their lovers' nipples, expecting to derive an ideological benefit from the exercise. As a result of these prescriptions for progress through sex, feminist women came to approach sex as a tutelary exercise. With a veritable laundry list of things to do and things to avoid, spontaneity and real communication became virtually impossible.

Positions

The positions of lovemaking acquired ideological meanings. Rather than lie pinned under a man in the standard lovemaking position, women were encouraged to use the female superior position.

> Enlightened women have long sung the praises of the female superior position, because they are not weighted down by the heavier male body, and can respond more spontaneously.[9]

Because of this misuse of the ideal of equality, many couples in the seventies felt compelled to alternate male superior and female superior positions on a roughly equal basis, to show that neither partner was above the other, the metaphorical sense of superiority being confused with the physically superior sexual position.

Not only would a feminist woman feel uncomfortable if her man habitually assumed the male superior position, she would also feel uncomfortable if she herself habitually assumed the female superior position, for this would suggest she had been infected by the male preoccupation with dominance.

The other common position for intercourse, in which the woman presents her buttocks in the universal primate gesture of submission, is almost never mentioned by feminist writers. Its implications are apparently too horrifying to contemplate. Despite its popularity, it is literally never mentioned in the awesomely detailed feminist treatises on sex except as a physically convenient alternative during pregnancy—to the modern mind, the most desexualized of sexual contexts. The traditional feminine woman might feel uncomfortable with the primate position because it made her seem like too much of an animal; she would be preoccupied with losing the man's respect. The feminist woman would have a different but parallel reason to engage in this position only hesitantly and occasionally: with her newfound set of ideological inhibitions, it seemed to imply male superiority.

Sexual Semantics

In their mission to humanize the species, feminists did not hesitate to force men into line with their "new insights." The semantics of liberation were central to this effort. Language that distinguished between the sexes was to be eliminated as much as possible. While the substitution of "chairperson" for "chairman" posed no insuperable difficulty for most men, the feminist attempt to redefine the English intimate vocabulary was another story. Feminists were fond of telling men they felt "threatened" (another buzzword) by the women's movement. No one bothered to point out that feeling threatened is a normal response when you are in fact being assaulted.

The man who associated with feminists was constrained to act and to feel, or to pretend to feel, in certain ways. For instance, he was not to view women as "sex objects." A man who viewed women as sex objects was said to be dehumanized by his upbringing; his world had been split into unnaturally differentiated spheres of sex and emotion. No wonder feminists expressed such condescending pity for men who felt humiliated and inadequate because of the new feminist consciousness: feminism was indeed an insult to men and did indeed put men, particularly those who tried to accept its tenets in good faith, in impossible situations like trying not to feel aggressiveness or dominance toward a woman when making love to her. What am I saying, you weren't even allowed to make love "to" her in the feminist lexicon, because this construction implies a distinction between active and passive roles. The correct syntax was to make love "with" her.

Expressions of affection like "honey" and "sugar" were held up as further evidence of the degradation of women. It was asserted that "[T]he terms of endearment addressed to women are soulless and degrading." The list of words proscribed by feminists includes "terms like *honey, sugar, dish, sweety-pie, cherry, cookie, chicken,* and *pigeon.*" Pretty soon you can't call a woman anything, for the list continues indefinitely, including "*doll . . . baby . . . baby-doll . . . chick, bird, kitten, lamb.*" Needless to say there is no question, even in the heat of lovemaking, of using words like "*heifer*" or "*bitch.*"[10]

All that is required to play this game is a grasp of how to apply the feminist perspective. You simply list any word that has ever been applied to women, and then show how its meaning degrades them. Since, from the feminist perspective, any terms that are applicable to women as a category are products of a "sexist" culture, it follows that they must degrade women; at an absolute minimum, any such word will fail to take into account individual variations. Why, the feminist wonders, should it not be equally acceptable to call a man "kitten"?

The vocabulary of male sexual aggression was to be replaced with a purified, intersexual set of expressions. Obscenity was measured with a feminist yardstick.

> All the vulgar linguistic emphasis is placed upon the *poking* element; *fucking, screwing, rooting, shagging* are all acts performed upon the passive female. Names for the penis are all *tool* names. The only genuine intersexual words are the obsolete *swive,* and the ambiguous *ball.*[11]

In the feminist lexicon, it is all right to "ball" someone, because the term is (quite illogically) held to be interchangeable for the two sexes and to be free of aggressive connotations, but it is not all right to "fuck" someone because the word "fuck" evokes an aggressive action. Millions of men in the seventies struggled with the new ideological correctness imposed on them by their feminist lovers.

The process of culling obscenities for the acceptable and the unacceptable often achieved a bewildering level of exegetical subtlety. For instance, many feminists thought the word "cock" to be acceptable as a term for that part of the male body, but considered the word "prick" offensive. The extremely thin rationale for this distinction was that the word "cock" is innocuous (the feminists had obviously never seen a cockfight), whereas the word "prick" suggests a weapon and the causing of pain. The etymology involved is superficial and specious—in earlier centuries, the word "prick" had nothing to do with weaponry, but rather with shape, as in a "prick candlestick"—but, as with Millett's flaky legal history, accuracy was not the main criterion for these semantic transformations.

The attempt to establish a sex-neutral, aggression-free vocabulary served a number of valuable tactical functions for feminists. It dramatically differentiated feminist from standard social norms. It reinforced the disengagement from men embodied in the consciousness-raising groups. If it distanced the sexes, that was of little concern, for equality was expected to grow in the space between. Above all, by controlling the terms of discussion, feminists gained the initiative against men. At the same time, by being forced to apologize constantly for their inevitable verbal lapses, men were kept on the defensive, that being the appropriate posture for the suspect oppressors of the human race.

For the man who accepted these bizarre dicta, it became impossible to express love or desire with any degree of spontaneity. For desire *is* gendered, "sexist" as feminists put it (implying that to respond to sex difference is tantamount to racism). But the man who dares to express himself in gendered terms to a feminist lover opens himself to rejection, sarcasm, or simple noncomprehension.

It is time to put the matter right. When your lover lies before you, you are not exulting in some metaphorical or legal sense in which she may be equal to you. You do feel dominance—or perhaps submission. Or aching desire, eons from ideology. Or tender, merciful love. Whatever you feel, it cannot be expressed in a vocabulary acceptable to feminists. This is no time to respect her "personhood": true respect for her emotions calls for something far more primitive, far more savage, and it will come as if by instinct. . . . And the more freely your emotions flow, the more thoroughly each word you speak will offend the feminist notions of sexual morality. Will you listen to them, now, or to the deep, atavistic urges welling up inside you and she?

The Clitoral Theory of Female Sexuality

One of the most effective routes to escape male influence was the clitoral theory of female sexuality. At one and the same time it offered three advantages: first, it depicted men as superfluous to women—as one slogan expressed this idea, "A woman without a man is like a fish without a bicycle"; second, it placed men in a position of tutelage to women, since it granted women exclusive knowledge to direct the sex act; and third, it gave women a way to strike back at men. For the acolytes of the feminist perspective, independence, control, and revenge were a heady trio.

Sigmund Freud argued that women are capable of two kinds of orgasms, a clitoral and a vaginal one. The clitoral orgasm is an immature reaction that fails to involve the whole personality. It is caused by friction to the clitoris, the delicate, erectile organ over the vagina. The vaginal orgasm, on the other hand, is caused by interior stimulation of the vagina during sexual intercourse. This form of orgasm is, according to Freud, the mature sexual response of the adult female. As such, it is a sign of healthy functioning. Vaginal orgasms are evidence that neurotic conflicts have been successfully resolved and the individual is able to face life as a whole person.

In the late sixties, the sex researchers William Masters and Virginia Johnson took issue with the Freudian position. They reported that the interior of the vagina is actually rather insensitive: they found no evidence that there is such a thing as a vaginal orgasm. Their subjects did, however, respond with orgasm to stimulation of the clitoris. This finding—through no intention, it seems, of its authors—became central to the feminist account of women's sexual experience.[12]

Although Masters and Johnson's work has achieved something of a scriptural status in contemporary discussions of sex among both feminists and non-feminists, it should be noted that it is subject to the same sorts of errors, limitations, and eventual revisions as other scientific research. It does not slight their effort to point out that as in other fields, particularly those in which very little work has been done previously, there is every chance that future research will overturn initial findings, or place them in a context so altered that they appear in an entirely different light. When a field is as new as sex research, we should not be too impressed with the earliest findings, particularly when they conflict with personal experience.

But Masters and Johnson's assertion that in female sexual response the clitoris is supreme was accepted uncritically by most feminists. It fitted too well with the spirit of the feminist movement to be too closely examined.

A sexual mismatch was thereby discovered between men and women. Because stimulation of the clitoris was claimed to be the sole key to female orgasmic response, it was argued that the penis is useless in women's quest for sexual pleasure. Intercourse served only the selfish gratification of the male.

As we have seen, a minority but vocal group of feminists, like Kate Millett actively hated the penis for mutually reinforcing psychopathological and ideological reasons. They were delighted to discover a theory that seemed to make this envied and dreaded instrument, the "badge of the male's superior status," harmless by making it useless.

But though hatred of the male, transposed onto the penis, was a major theme in the feminist rush to embrace the clitoral theory of female sexuality, it was rivaled in importance by the theme of independence. The easiest way to be independent of men is to not need them, and where sexuality is concerned, the clitoral theory opens wide the door. If men are not necessary for women's sexual fulfillment, are indeed likely to impede it through their "brutality and mechanicalness," then women become free of them.

In practice, the quest for independence and the grudge match against men tended to blend imperceptibly into each other. As a direct result of the triumph of feminism as a national philosophy of gender in the seventies, it became intellectually and socially respectable to hate men. One symptom of this situation was the credulous reception of Shere Hite's best-selling *The Hite Report: A Nationwide Study of Female Sexuality* in 1976 and its sequel, *The Hite Report on Male Sexuality* in 1981.

Hite's central thesis was that women do not particularly enjoy intercourse. Intercourse was forced on them by the advent of "patriarchal society." Since women do not especially enjoy intercourse, they would, Hite asserted, rather be manually or orally satisfied. Men too, she wrote, were ambivalent about intercourse, which was to them a power play devoid of real pleasure.

Hite's method of research was to circulate lengthy, open-ended questionnaires. Such a method presents a clear danger of abuse, for it is all too easy to simply design questions that will lead to the answers desired. For example, to "prove" that men were divorced from their feelings by masculinity, Hite asked: "Do you force yourself to behave like a robot? Do you ever *feel* like a robot?" Such a question is so nonspecific as to be meaningless—but of course even a low positive answer rate allows an amateur sociologist like Hite to generalize about men's alleged emotional stunting. The *Hite Reports* are thus distinguished from the Kinsey Report of the 1950s and from Masters and Johnson's work by their disdain for standards of evidence. This did not give pause to Hite, who claimed, "My book is as good as Kinsey."[13]

Hite's rhetoric can be superficially attractive, as when she says that "We must begin to devise more kind, generous, and personal ways of relating which will be positive and constructive for the future";[14] but a careful reading of such passages reveals their utter lack of substance. The focus of her books remains the message against men. If Hite's books stand out from the feminist crowd (other than in their sky-high sales figures), it is in the insidiousness with which, behind a good deal of progressive sounding but empty rhetoric, they transmit the message that men and women are fundamentally incompatible.

Playing fast and loose with her own figures, which showed that 52 percent of women experience orgasm from intercourse *without* direct stimulation of the clitoris (a high figure, considering the bias of her study), Hite did her best to give the impression that the penis is not very good at giving pleasure to women. Now, it is certainly a good thing for men and women to discover the clitoris, if they have not already done so. But to pretend, as Hite did, that this somehow makes the penis superfluous, and that in consequence a man's main job in sex should be to stimulate his partner's clitoris, penile thrusting being strictly for his own pleasure, simply distorts the reality of everyday sexual experience, including the evidence of Hite's own respondents. Beneath their vaguely idealistic rhetoric, the *Hite Reports* represent a phenomenon of curious vindictiveness. Value-laden words are constantly cropping up in her descriptions of sex. Like Millett, Hite is ready to sneer at the penis whenever she thinks she can get away with it, as when she claims that "for a woman to orgasm during intercourse, she must adapt her body to *inadequate* stimulation," namely, that provided by penile thrusting. Again, she describes clitoral self-stimulation by hand as "the *best* way for most women to orgasm during intercourse."[15]

Predictably, men are the villains. Hite warns her male readers "how tired women are of the old mechanical pattern of sexual relations." She presents one woman who is entangled in a disturbed relationship as a symbol of the confrontation in which women, she says, must engage men:

"Cutting short an orgasm doesn't leave me frustrated, if I'm masturbating, but I am becoming more and more short-tempered about cutting sex with my husband short just because he is satisfied. Continuing along the same unsatisfying sexual patterns expresses to me a lack of care and concern for me that I am finding unacceptable."[16]

It is taken for granted, in the feminist frame of reference, that the woman's husband is typical, that the difficulty she is experiencing arises not from a bad relationship between two individuals but from a bad relationship between the two sexes.

Hite's solution for this type of situation, in which resentment on both sides is poisoning a relationship (for reasons that, as she fails to point out, probably have nothing to do with sex as such), is for women to adopt a confrontational posture. At this point, feminism degenerates into pure female chauvinism: since men have been so nasty to us, we're within our rights to be nasty to them. As Hite explains,

What if [men] still try to follow the same old mechanical pattern of sexual relations? There is no reason why women must help men during intercourse. . . . We are taught that if we are anything but helpful . . . during intercourse, it is tantamount to castrating the man. This is nonsense. Our noncooperation with men in sex is no worse than their noncooperation with us.[17]

Hite's confrontational me-tooism is typical of feminist prescriptions for how to deal with men, sexually and otherwise. This attitude is a direct outgrowth of the feminist perspective: if men really are that bad, it's understandable that the rage feminists feel against them is such that they need men to eat crow for awhile. But the results of such an attitude on the part of either member of a couple, regardless of its causes, will be predictably destructive. It is a sure recipe for either the failure of a relationship or the driving underground of its object's true feelings and opinions. The prevalence of this attitude among feminists accounted for much of the inauthenticity of the New Man as he attempted to let feminists lead him out of the "trap" of "traditional masculinity."

The vision of men presented in works like the *Hite Reports* is so close to caricature that it would be cause for amusement if it had not so recently been taken with such deadly seriousness. The "male" who inhabits these tracts is a stereotype if there ever was one. Like most effective stereotypes, he contains just enough truth to mislead the inexperienced and the unwary.

The "male" of the *Hite Reports* suffers from all the pitfalls and embodies all the worst excesses of masculinity, which is unrelieved by any trace of the female virtues and unredeemed by any virtues of its own. He has been conditioned to unyielding rigidity by his society's cramped concept of "masculinity" and is incapable of tender or inventive lovemaking.

> It is probable that what we think of as the "natural," physical, movements of intercourse are nothing more than "learned" responses. Isn't it possible that men have been told that "mounting and thrusting" is the "right" thing to do, but that they too, if allowed to experiment, would find many other ways they liked to have intercourse?[18]

Oh blessed feminists! We men can't wait to be freed to "experiment" through your compassionate intervention! But what on earth makes you think we have *not* experimented already? Is it not just barely possible, enough so that you might at least consider the possibility in passing, that we *have* experimented, and that we do what we do *because* it comes naturally and because we *do* like it?

Perhaps the most bizarre aspect of the *Hite Reports* is their not-so-subtle appeal to male masochism. Hite repeatedly describes situations in which women dominate men in sex. By experiencing their suppressed submissive side, in this view, men can contribute to the progress of humanity. *Penthouse* magazine, which sponsored Hite's book on men, became a monthly advocate of this notion through its letters section and its spinoff publications like *Variations,* which on a quarterly basis describes the wondrous improvements in intimacy achieved by couples in which the woman habitually chains, whips, or sexually abuses the man. This notion is utterly groundless in terms of human behavior. Women, for whatever reasons, rarely are interested in real control of another being, and the minority of women who are, undoubtedly choose different routes than the ones depicted in the fantasy world of *Penthouse* magazine. But Hite sensed the dialectical power of this approach: by simultaneously claiming first, that men should experience submissiveness and second, that submissiveness is a reflection of our society's sick preoccupation with dominance, you catch men coming and going. Such are the rhetorical advantages of controlling the terms of discussion.

This is a classic example of the feminist double whammy, which has been a highly popular ploy and is far from extinct. The technique is to offend a man (or men) and then to make the insult stick by persuading him that he is retrograde to feel offended. Hite is a refined practitioner of this technique. One of her shining moments is to suggest that men should perhaps give up orgasm altogether. She cites as a model the highly aberrant practices of the nineteenth-century Oneida cult, whose members actually did practice sex without male orgasm. She claims that "this concept [that is, frequent sex with suppression of ejaculation] is again being tried at present by some groups of men living in various experimental communities." (One would like to see some evidence for this assertion, but of course there isn't any.) Immediately afterward she states "there is no reason why the reintegration of intercourse into the whole spectrum of physical relationships should threaten men."[19]

What, you, a man, are *threatened* by the suggestion that you should give up intercourse? How absurd! You only want intercourse because you are unable to integrate it into "the spectrum of human relationships." If you could become whole again through feminism, you wouldn't want intercourse anyway. There's no way out of this logical trap: men are boxed in, damned if they do and damned if they don't. Like Valerie Solanis of the Society for Cutting Up Men, Hite doesn't care: it is all too obvious she is glad to see them wriggling on the hook.

Masters and Johnson pointedly refused all comment on Hite's lucubrations. This refusal to legitimate her work, which drew so heavily on theirs, did not discourage the media from lionizing Hite to the extent they could (she treated even sympathetic female reporters with extreme discourtesy[20]), nor did it prevent NOW and other feminist organizations from endorsing her compendia as a major step forward in the understanding of human sexuality. A characteristic feminist accolade describes Hite's first book as "Highly recommended. . . . The results challenge many stereotypes."[21] Like the clitoral theory of sexuality they helped popularize, Hite's books were too perfectly attuned to the spirit of the times not to be successful: women, they argued, don't need men, even for sex.

The fact that this hodgepodge of vindictiveness and naiveté has so recently been hailed as a major work demands an explanation beyond the overextended excuse that all movements are extremist in their early phases, for Hite's second book was published to widespread acclaim in the early 1980s, long after the period of early extremism should have passed. In fact, the *Hite Reports* are not works of excess compared to other feminist writings, then or now. To feminists, Hite's books are strictly mainstream. It is no coincidence that Hite's original questionnaire went out under the letterhead of the powerful New York chapter of NOW, of which she was a member. NOW has always carried the banner of "moderate" feminism. Upon publication, each of Hite's books received the endorsement of NOW as a work of the greatest importance and authority—a major advance in the understanding of sexuality.

If Hite is extremist—which she is—in what then does the "excess" of "early" feminism consist according to more recent feminists, and where is the evidence they have rejected it? Although the language today is often less virulent, the guiding assumptions of feminism have not changed. The continuing admiration for such works as the *Hite Reports* attests to the basic continuity in the feminist perspective.

The clitoral theory of female sexuality was designed to free women from men. It described the male as superfluous and the penis as an instrument incapable of giving pleasure, or at any rate inferior to a woman's own fingers. The feminist "redefinition of sexuality" proclaimed masturbation and lesbianism to be equal, indeed higher, forms of sexuality than heterosexual intercourse. Intercourse was just another option, no different emotionally from alternatives like oral sex. Not only did women not need men, it was retrograde of men not to realize they didn't need women either. According to Hite, "there is no evidence that men biologically 'need' vaginas in which to orgasm, or that there is anything hormonal or 'instinctual' which drives men toward women or vaginas."[22] Indeed, feminists sometimes reduced sex to nothing more than an expression of friendship that could with equal validity arise in any close relationship. As Hite, among others, wrote, "There need not be a sharp distinction between sexual touching and friendship."[23]

The conditions of Masters and Johnson's laboratories are one thing, human experience another. This is one of the few occasions on which I agree with Greer, the sexual revolutionary, who played Cassandra to the feminist account of sex with her remarks on intercourse.

> The banishment of the fantasy of the vaginal orgasm is ultimately a service, but the substitution of the clitoral spasm for genuine gratification may turn out to be a disaster for sexuality. Masters and Johnson's conclusions have

produced some unlooked for side-effects, like the veritable clitoromania which infects Mette Eiljersen's book, *I accuse!* While speaking of women's orgasms as resulting from the "right touches on the button," she condemns sexologists who "recommend . . . the stimulation of the clitoris as part of the prelude to intercourse, to that which most men consider to be the 'real thing.' What is in fact the 'real thing' for them is *completely devoid of sensation* for the woman. This is the heart of the matter! Concealed for hundreds of years by humble, shy and subservient women."

Not all the women in history have been humble and subservient to such an extent. It is nonsense to say that a woman feels nothing when a man is moving his penis in her vagina: the orgasm is qualitatively different when the vagina can undulate around the penis instead of vacancy. . . . The process described by the experts, in which man dutifully does the rounds of the erogenous zones, spends an equal amount of time on each nipple, turns his attention to the clitoris (usually too directly), leads through the stages of digital or lingual stimulation and then politely lets himself into the vagina, perhaps waiting until the retraction of the clitoris tells him that he is welcome, is laborious and inhumanly computerized. . . . There is no substitute for excitement: not all the massage in the world will insure satisfaction, for it is a matter of psychosexual release.[24]

Most people will find their own experience corroborates Greer's argument. Orgasms through intercourse are perhaps a bit less predictable than orgasms through clitoral massage, but they are strikingly more powerful, seeming to involve the whole person: they can be shattering, overwhelming experiences in a way that orgasms resulting from masturbation rarely or never are. Feminist writers have neglected to point out that in this regard men have the same experience as women. Were speed, efficiency, and multi-orgasmic capacity the principal criteria for good sex, men as well as women would without doubt be content with masturbation. If they are not, it is because, for both sexes, sexual intercourse is incomparably more fulfilling. Many young men in the Feminist Era wondered what could be wrong with their lovers, who seemed to respond so much less powerfully to even the most dedicated digital or lingual stimulation than to intercourse—especially to intercourse in the reviled missionary position. Not for the first time, common experience contradicted a prevailing cultural ideology.

The Masters and Johnson approach emphasized sex as a mechanical act, in which form it is doubtless easiest to observe. This has been a useful approach, but surely there is more. Through the emphasis on sex as a mechanical function, some of its most important aspects were overlooked. In particular, the sense that sex is a communion between two unique individuals was lost.

As Megan Marshall describes the results of this misplaced emphasis,

> The cult of the orgasm became part of the Myth of Independence, encouraging sex as a purely physical, even solitary act. Even with a partner, women were counselled in countless magazine advice columns and sex manuals to attend primarily to their own satisfaction. . . . The new emphasis on sexual mechanics ignored the emotional sources of sexual pleasure, and implied that women did not need a committed relationship, or even a man, to enjoy themselves in bed. While most studies showed that women usually did not reach their sexual peak until their late twenties, no one connected this with the fact that those were most likely the years of their peak emotional experiences as well.[25]

One other point is worth making about the criticisms Hite *et alia* level against men. To read these feminist theorists of sex, men are incurious and uncaring about women's response to their sexual actions. The feminist perspective leads naturally to this notion, but it is completely at odds with experience. No doubt some women have been stuck with men who are cold fish, but it is perfectly obvious that sexual mismatch cuts both ways: many men, but also many women, are incurious and unimaginative about sex, to their partners' irritation. People have different levels and kinds of sexual interest, and these do not always match up well. But a taste for variety and experimentation is certainly found at least as frequently among men as among women. Most men do want to vary their sexual routines: it is often women who insist on a predictable pattern of intercourse. The feminine complaint about men tends to be that they are if anything *too* concerned with variety in the mechanics of sex, not the other way around. Like other feminist analyses, the *Hite Reports* shrink from the complexities of reality whenever these threaten to infringe on the uncomplicated dualism of the feminist perspective.

The Assault on Spontaneity

The sex drive in humans is an imperious urge which, like women's need to have children, feminism has been unable to suppress. But to the extent these drives continued to express themselves in the Feminist Era, they did so in opposition to what had become the authoritative ideology on sex and gender. Regardless of which aspect of sexuality is considered, the conclusion is inescapable that "liberation" simply imposed a new set of constraints. The libido was as trammeled as ever.

It is tempting to speculate that women were once more played false by the evolution of industrial society: that the corporate culture, reacting to the new employability of women, found it expedient to impose a new set of linkages and blockages on women's libidos, so as to enable them to compete with men without putting them in touch with themselves in ways that would threaten their docility to corporate values. Greer had predicted such an outcome in her critique of the clitoral theory:

> The fact that [many women] have only ever experienced gratification from clitoral stimulation . . . is the index of the desexualization of the whole body, the substitution of genitality for sexuality. The ideal marriage as measured by the electronic equipment in the Reproductive Biology Research Foundation laboratories [of Masters and Johnson] is enfeebled—dull sex for dull people. The sexual personality is basically antiauthoritarian. If the system wishes to enforce complete suggestibility in its subjects, it will have to tame sex.[26]

Regardless of the causes, putting people in touch with their feelings was not the effect of contemporary feminism. Feminists were supposed to change their feelings, not accept them. Amid its zaniness and contradictions, Greer's book embodied both the liberating impulse and the constraining ideology that strangled it. As she wrote in her discussion of feminist strategy, "We must . . . refuse, not only to do some things, but to want to do them."[27]

Spontaneity thus became fundamentally suspect, despite glowing visions of revolution as "the festival of the oppressed." In sex as in other areas, feminism replaced one prescription for female fulfillment—the fifties ideal of suburban domestic happiness that Friedan attacked in *The Feminine Mystique*—with a new one that was equally restrictive. It may be sobering to reflect that such uncompromising moralism flourished in the atheistic soil of *The Female Eunuch,* which exhibits as little sympathy for religion as it does for the other institutions of society.

A new belief system is being inculcated, and its arbitrariness is such that it is clearly no unmixed blessing to its acolytes. Perhaps its most disturbing aspect is the extent to which feminists are encouraged to censor their thoughts, deny their emotions, and suppress their impulses in the interests of an ideology.

The "sexual revolution" of the sixties and early seventies has been maligned on all sides since. But it has one notable and probably lasting achievement to its credit. For the first time since the Industrial Revolution, it became possible to discuss sex without self-consciousness in public. Contrary to the assertion of some moralists of the right, this does not contribute to the destruction of the family, as should be obvious from the many cultures in which sex is discussed relatively openly and in which the family is very much intact—more intact than in our own. The positive result of the sexual revolution has been an increase in our ease with the fact of our sexuality. The unattainability of such ease earlier in the century is seen in D. H. Lawrence's inability to escape from self-consciousness when discussing or describing sex, or more drastically in Henry Miller's need to exaggerate and pervert sex in order to be able to write about it at all. Sexual honesty continued to be equally elusive amid the guilty giggles of the fifties.

Nor has this greater ease led to any decrease in the intensity of sex: sexuality is too deep, mysterious, and primeval not to survive the fears of moralists who worry that taking the figurative gauze off the statue of Venus would lead to a loss of sexual intensity. Aphrodite conquers, nude as easily as in silk stockings.

The achievement, minor perhaps but real, of making millions of people feel more comfortable with their sexuality has since come under attack by our twin puritanisms.

In the field of sex, "Women's Liberation" was anything but. American women were trapped between two competing puritanisms, a traditional one which analyzed human sexual impulses in terms of sin, and a feminist one which analyzed them in terms of patriarchal oppression. Although they could not be more ideologically distinct, one having been conceived to support the "traditional" family, the other to undermine it, the tactics of these two puritanisms are much the same. Both try to frighten women with fairy tales about the destructive effects of yielding to their sexual impulses. Each invades the marriage bed as thoroughly as the other. Regardless of whether their natural desires and fantasies are attributed to sin or to patriarchal oppression, women are told to censor their thoughts, repress their impulses, and confine their behavior within unnecessarily and often unbearably narrow limits.

Feminist sex is an impossible balancing act. Each member of a couple must give without being submissive and accept without being passive; must initiate without dominating and show vigor without aggression. The difficulty of the Freudian prescription to achieve vaginal orgasms while avoiding clitoral ones pales into insignificance beside this inhumanly difficult set of demands and taboos. Feminist sex is a tightrope—with the human emotions waiting as pitfalls on either side.

It seems likely that the incidence of orgasm and of lovemaking itself actually decreased among the "liberated" women of the 1970s. Megan Marshall has talked to such women:

> From my interview subjects I began to hear of a problem that women of the sexual revolution had never expected to confront: frigidity. Despite often prolific sexual activity, many women could not have orgasms with their lovers. It was embarrassing. Women of our mothers' generation had been frigid because they believed in sex for reproduction not recreation, and because they had not taken control of their bodies and learned to understand female sexual response—or so we told ourselves. But if we could control our bodies, sometimes we went too far in controlling our emotions. The women who spoke to me about sexual problems were unable to have orgasms because they could not submit to their feelings; they felt incapable of the trust that made passionate lovemaking safe. They could not lose control long enough to permit out-of-control feelings.[28]

It was a problem that Friedan and other feminists had attributed to "obsolete" roles which made it "almost impossible for the sexes to make love, not war." But the true source of this problem was the catastrophic emotive straitjacket imposed by feminist ideology. The political resonance with which feminism invested the sex act often overwhelmed the fragile flowers of love and desire.

Feminist sex was at best a halfway house. It encouraged women to view their desires as legitimate in principle, suspect in practice. It was useful to discover the clitoris but not at the price of alienation from other aspects of sexuality. The psychological pressure to distrust men and to deny one's feelings was often impossible to resist. Feminism supplied some useful cues to women, but interlarded them with new prescriptions and old inhibitions in new guise. To the extent that women in the Feminist Era were able to enjoy reasonably uninhibited sex, it was much less because of than in spite of the prescriptive ideology which claimed to speak in their name.

So much for liberation. For all Greer's promises of a new sexual nirvana, men in the seventies were to learn through painful experience what they continue to learn today: feminists are not sexy. To the extent that they bring their beliefs into the bedroom, feminists become impossibly tense and demanding lovers. Men who accepted Greer's dismissal of the feminine woman as a sexual bore were to discover that the feminist woman was no improvement—was if anything even more inhibited. Only the rationale for the inhibitions had changed, and it was accompanied by a whole grievance list of new demands. Thousands of mild and decent men took the brunt of the feminist supposition that men are collectively responsible for the injustices of history and for all that is wrong with the world today. And the women who accused them and tried to change their nature were, not merely necessarily ignorant, for the most part, of the nature of men, but further divorced from their own female being than any previous generation of American women. For by devaluing the feminine, feminists rejected so much of women's nature that unhappiness and confusion were bound to result—a condition that is only beginning to lift today.

Some Further Thoughts on Feminism and Sex

Will the pundits never allow us to relax with our sexuality? Perhaps feminists are right to claim that sex does contain sadomasochistic elements. If so, does it really matter? In the nineteenth century, specialists advised parents to harshly discourage the emergence of childhood sexuality, lest it lead to "perversions" such as masturbation or the sexualization of the anus. Similarly, in earlier decades of our own century, millions of Americans were terrified that they might be prone to homosexuality. Often quite unnecessarily, they went far out of their way to deny even the possibility that they might, sometimes, have some homosexual inclinations. The feminist evocation of inarticulate fears through the use of vaguely defined but scary-sounding terms like "sadomasochism" is the latest chapter in this venerable tradition of anti-sexual moralizing.

The line between aggressive male sexuality and a troubled world is direct and uncomplicated in the feminist scheme of sex. The fantasies of having power over women that are so common among men and the fantasies of being "taken" that are so common among women—as is evident, for example, from Nancy Friday's books on female sexual fantasies[29]—are usually painted by feminists as a sick reflection of the "sexist" reality they are trying to change. Eliminate dominance in human relations, they argue, by eliminating the aggressive male behavior that causes it. It is an argument of painful naiveté.

The male propensity for aggression is indeed what makes possible war and rape, but it does not follow *a priori* that we should try to change this potential. In the first place, we may not be able to do so, and, in the second, even if we could alter or neutralize it, we should not do so. Aggression serves useful, constructive purposes in human society.

Aggression is a precondition for all violence, but it is hardly the same thing. Aggression has positive as well as negative uses. Most obviously, it is necessary to defend against other aggression. But aggression is not merely the potential for violence, or the potential to counteract it. Aggression is not distinguishable from what makes us move: the force that drives us to impose our wills on others is the same force that lets us inform them of our needs and opinions.

As the work of Konrad Lorenz and every scientist who has subsequently studied animal societies has shown, aggression is the basic structuring tool of all societies. Although men are on average far more aggressive than women, women are aggressive too. (The question of whether this difference is culturally or biologically caused is outside the scope of this chapter.) As the feminist sociobiologist Sarah Blaffer Hrdy has most recently demonstrated, female aggression serves major functions. To structure a society without aggression—a countercultural Grail that continues to lurk beneath most feminist thought—is a wholly unrealistic approach to the betterment of humanity that overlooks the most irreducible constant of social organization. An aggression-free society is the most utopian of pipe dreams, which can only continue to flourish amidst the willful ignoring of obvious facts.

As Megan Marshall says,

> Power is an inevitable part of any love relationship, as indeed it is present in all relationships. . . . For [the Feminist], any power struggle implied an eventual victim, usually the woman. She fantasized an almost utopian, egalitarian closeness, ignoring the basic motivation of lovers of both sexes: to

possess and be possessed. She could not let herself be wanted, nor could she want a man as she continued to doubt her ability to survive passion. [She] was floundering in a world whose requirements for self-assertion she despised.[30]

The only thing that Marshall does not say is that men and women differ in the ways they want to possess. Regardless of whether the condition is permanent or not—a question that will be taken up in a later chapter—men and women do at present differ in their approaches to love. Men have no monopoly on the urge to possess, but they have more of it; women have no monopoly on the urge to be possessed, but they have more of it. A cursory examination of men's and women's hopes and fantasies shows as much, and it is an impression that will only be reinforced if one goes into more detailed studies. Men are more interested in power and control than women (although it is by no means clear they habitually get either in marriage).

Even the case of sexually masochistic men, sometimes invoked to prove there are no sexual differences between the sexes, reveals just the opposite.[31] Such men want *their* fantasies realized, and often despise the women who "service" them for hourly fees, whose steepness suggests just how distasteful such activity is to most women.*

Perhaps violence, which is on the whole a male preserve, can be contained by means other than drastic surgery on the human personality. Certainly in the area of sex, this is what most women want: a live wire who is capable of aggression, but not a driven maniac. It's possible. Indeed, this describes the sexual personality of most men. That is one reason why, despite all pressures, so many marriages are successful.

Men and women fit together. Their body parts fit together, whatever the specific physiological processes involved may be. Their contrasting sexual fantasies, emotions, and behaviors fit together. Heterosexual intercourse is deeply fulfilling in a way that is lacking in any other form of sexual experience. Let us begin to recover from the feminist disparagement of the sexes' relations and start to affirm that, despite

---

*Most women are allergic to masochistic men because of the built-in hypocrisy of the male masochist pose. Under the guise of offering submission such men demand total attention. Masochistic men seek not submission to the will of another but temporary regression to the condition of infancy in which they are once again the treasured objects of the all-controlling, all-providing will of a woman, and the world seems to exist to serve them.

characteristic areas of difficulty, the two sexes do indeed belong together. Not only do they belong together: they belong together as they presently exist in the here and now, not as a few misinformed utopians imagine they may become in some ever-receding future. The fit is not always perfect, but for the vast majority of people it utterly overwhelms the possible alternatives, of which it is the easiest, the most natural—and beyond question the most pleasurable.

Chapter 6

Feminism in Politics

As the 1970s advanced, the xenocentrism of the Protest Era gave way to more complacent attitudes. When contemporary feminism was new it called forth a measure of originality. Friedan, Millett, and Greer, for all their intolerance, were saved from imitative drabness by the very iconoclasm of their positions.

But the reckless creativity of the sixties generation soon waned in the seventies. The exuberance of the original bra-burning revolt, the sense that "Revolution is the festival of the oppressed," was quickly lost in the humdrum world of work amid the realization that the "women's movement" was in for a protracted and uncertain struggle.

This loss of momentum was true of the products of the sixties in general. What was gained in refinement was lost in vigor and originality. This was perhaps nowhere more evident than in rock music, the central expression of the counterculture. The arrogant virility of the early Rolling Stones and the lost-in-space wildness of Jimi Hendrix's fatal encounter with celebrity were homogenized into the smooth posing of slicker groups. Most rock no longer sought to transcend either its own format, as Hendrix did when he recorded a speaker underwater for "1983 A Merman I Should Turn To Be," or the predictable milieu of suburban living in which its fans lived. From an idealistic attempt to change the world, rock returned to its roots in teenage sex. The aspiration to affect the world's ways had gone, and with it most of the impulse to innovate.

In place of creativity came conformity. A cooling-out period was necessary, because the most pressing goals of the countercultural revolt had been achieved—and its illusions shattered. Civil rights for blacks had been obtained. Affirmative action programs were in place; they needed time to produce results. The prevailing climate of opinion had induced the Supreme Court to legalize abortion in *Roe vs. Wade.* The Vietnam War, the single greatest social irritant, was winding down, the advocates of U.S. withdrawal triumphant.

Death played its role: the shooting of student demonstrators at Kent State, bloody and unnecessary as it was, showed just how far the country was from falling to a successful social revolution, and the fatal overdoses of Jimi Hendrix and Janis Joplin broadcast the simple fact that drug abuse is dangerous. The nightmare of the Altamont rock festival vitiated the belief in a unified counterculture, while the Manson cult murders did the same for the fantasy of unstructured communal living.

Leftist pundits warned that a time of reaction was setting in, but this was hardly the case. With the Nixon administration partly unwilling and partly unable to halt the growth of the welfare state begun by Johnson and initiating a new era of accommodation with the Soviet Union abroad, conservatism was in full flight in the early seventies. The political climate of the seventies set in, not because conservatives stepped up their efforts, but because the prevailing radical-liberal consensus had used up its fund of ideas and was morally exhausted. A true revival of conservatism did not occur until the late seventies.

With no larger movement to sustain them, feminists in the seventies became increasingly isolated from the mainstream of American politics. This was seen in their increasingly inept attempts to influence public opinion on "feminist issues." Foremost among these issues were the Equal Rights Amendment, pornography, abortion, day care, comparable worth, and the vice-presidential candidacy of Geraldine Ferraro. In each case, the position espoused by organized political feminism lost. The only exception is the abortion battle—and even there, the position espoused by feminists has been steadily losing ground.

The Equal Rights Amendment Controversy

The Equal Rights Amendment to the United States Constitution, perennially proposed and never passed, reads in its essential section:

> Equality of rights under the law shall not be denied or abridged by the United States or by any State on account of sex.

After decades of dormancy, this law swept to the gates of victory in the first flush of the feminist revolt. Supported not just by feminists but by men and women, young and old, and by both political parties, ERA encountered little opposition. It was within three states of ratification when its progress was abruptly checked, reversed, as several states rescinded their ratifications, and ultimately stymied altogether. With such a popular issue and such broad support, how did feminists manage to lose?

The first and most obvious reason is that a campaign against ERA was mounted under the leadership of Phyllis Schlafly, who thereby earned an enduring place in feminist demonology. Begun as a last-ditch effort, just when the triumph of ERA seemed certain, the Stop ERA campaign organized housewives to lobby and demonstrate against ERA in Illinois. How did such a flimsy organization as Schlafly's stop a national movement dead in its tracks?

The standard answer at the time among feminists was that Schlafly was a stooge of big business, which, it was claimed, poured money into her organization's coffers. Stop ERA was quite literally believed to be a conspiracy of the military-industrial complex. This was a convenient way to avoid having to think about, or even learn about, the arguments with which Schlafly was motivating her volunteers and convincing state legislators by the scores. Schlafly exercised the same advantage feminists had had earlier in the decade when they were able to spring novel concepts like "sexism" and "male chauvinism" on unprepared opponents: she had analyzed and refuted her opponents' arguments, but they were ignorant—often willfully so—of hers.

Swept up in the messianic righteousness of their mission, feminists were unable to believe that other female voices could legitimately challenge theirs. To make matters worse, they called themselves, and believed themselves to be, "the women's movement"; yet, having triumphed in the male bastions of Capitol Hill and the nation's state legislatures, here they were opposed by a movement of women, led by a woman, which also claimed to be acting in women's interests. Worse, feminists believed that women in public life would "humanize" public affairs, bringing peace instead of conflict into the world, and here was Schlafly attacking Communism and defending the U.S. military. Didn't she know the war in Vietnam was caused by masculinity, not Communism? Schlafly was hateful to feminists: she was spoiling their party.

As for her followers, they must surely be dupes. Feminists poured forth their pity and scorn on these "transitional women" who were so weak-willed that a Schlafly could manipulate them for her own, presumably demonic, ends. The possibility that they had minds of their own was completely out of the question. Naturally, if they understood women's interests, they would be on the side of the women's movement. And so the case against ERA went largely unexamined in the feminist camp: for what does rational argument matter when a belief structure, in this case that of feminism, is at stake? While the feminists blustered and avoided coming to terms with contrary ideas, their opponents were winning votes.

To be sure, Schlafly's style of argumentation had its limitations. Combative and uncompromising, it eschewed any attempt to reach the baby boomers or the intelligentsia of the coasts. Yet these apparent defects became strengths on the ground of Middle America where the ERA battle was decided.

The Case Against ERA

The gist of the argument against ERA was that, under superficially attractive rhetoric, it represented an assault on the American family. Inflammatory but decidedly secondary issues included the arguments that ERA would legalize abortion, permit homosexual marriage, and force the military to use women in combat.

ERA, its opponents argued, would end women's legal right to be supported, along with their children, by their husbands. It would eliminate the complex web of laws that surround and protect the institution of marriage. In particular, by forbidding all differences in the treatment of the sexes, ERA would eliminate a married woman's right to be supported by her husband (making a wife, even one with young children, equally liable to support her husband), to receive alimony and presumptive custody of her children in case of divorce, and would in general impair the right of women to pursue careers as full-time homemakers.

In addition to impairing their rights in the home, ERA would impair women's rights as workers. For instance, perhaps the one aspect of ERA about which there is no dispute is its effect on existing legislation to protect female industrial workers. ERA would wipe out all such legislation as discriminatory. Feminists like Friedan argue that such protection is degrading to women. This argument, which seemed persuasive to the affluent and childless baby boomers, made a good deal less sense to blue collar mothers working at exhausting, repetitive jobs, eager for scarce time to spend with their families—as feminists who ventured into the heartland to lobby rudely discovered.[1]

Feminists were ill-equipped to deal with the argument that ERA was an assault on American homemakers, since they did in fact believe that the role of wife-mother was obsolete, that for men to support women led to destructive dependency, and that the family had to be radically changed or done away with altogether. In addition, they believed that the sexes were completely interchangeable in all occupations, including the "parenting" of young children, which was to replace mothering; in the workplace, in all respects; in competitive sports, where a "continuum" of strength was thought to best describe the sexes' abilities; and—although they did not like to think of it, because war was "obsolete"—in military combat. The notion that marriage should only happen between a man and a woman, that children might benefit in any way from having two parents of different sexes instead of having one female parent, two female "parents," or two male "parents," was foreign to the feminist mindset.

Feminists didn't know that ERA would actually at one stroke lessen the involvement of individuals with the family, mandate universal day care, legalize abortion, and sanction homosexual marriage, but they certainly hoped it would do at least some of these things. That is why Stop ERA was able to alarm so many state legislators over the potential impact of the law. At the same time feminists were busily assuring one another that ERA would underpin all the changes in society they were seeking, they were trying to sell ERA to the public as a measure of simple justice. The manipulative dishonesty of this two-pronged operation gave ERA opponents their best opening: their most effective tactic was simply to quote feminists themselves.[2]

Why did feminists feel justified in giving such an incomplete account of their support for ERA to the public and to politicians? What is the source of such a patronizing attitude toward the general public?

The tendency to patronize stems partly from feminists' belief in their messianic mission and partly from the rage retained from the sixties, continuously fed by the feminist perspective. The resulting self-righteousness and lack of realism have been severe liabilities for the feminist movement and for any cause it touches. Out of thousands of possible examples of these tendencies, let us consider the explanation for the defeat of ERA put forward by Gloria Steinem of *Ms.* magazine:

> A handful of firmly entrenched, white male legislators control enough votes in the remaining few states to keep its victory just three states away.[3]

Never mind that most of the legislators who voted *for* ERA were white, male, and presumably "firmly entrenched." Sex and race must explain opinions with which Steinem does not agree. What an extraordinary insult to all those legislators who were white and male, who did vote for ERA, and who nevertheless continue to suffer guilt by association in feminists' eyes through two things they cannot change, their race and, above all, their sex! Politicians who have tried to work with feminists, like Walter Mondale, have learned the hard way that such treatment is par for the course. The male is always guilty, since males, from the feminist perspective, are responsible for the alleged oppression of women throughout history, and consequently for all the ills of the present. The message feminists cannot help constantly sending their would-be male supporters is in effect "Take it like a man, you wimp." A man associates with feminists on the same terms as a Jew with anti-Semites or a black with white supremacists. He is condemned to a permanent and unsuccessful series of apologies for his misconduct, a perpetual shuffling of the feet. Nothing he can ever do will erase the stain of his physical being, which is responsible for an indelible spiritual pollution.

Conversely, since men are responsible for all evil, women are rinsed clean of the sin of Eve and become incapable of evil. According to Steinem, ERA was defeated not by women but by the "special interests controlling state legislatures."[4] The question "Why are women against ERA?" is therefore irrelevant, for, in the feminist frame of reference, women are not and therefore cannot be against ERA, or any other feminist cause, since feminism is "the women's movement."

This hopeless tautology results in the casting out from the female sex of any woman who does not behave as women are supposed to— in a leftist, vaguely pacifist way. Prominent non-women include Margaret Thatcher, Jeane Kirkpatrick, Nancy Reagan, and in recent memory Golda Meir and Indira Gandhi—and the list goes on indefinitely. Such female persons are not really women; they have been "co-opted by the male establishment," and are not representative of what "women," that is to say, feminists, will be like once they share public power equally with men. In effect, whenever "women" in the feminist lexicon does not refer specifically to feminists themselves, it represents an abstract, mythical category. Feminists' relation to the category "women" is the same as the sixties New Left's relation to the category "the working class": although it is the group they have dedicated themselves to working for, they have little sympathy for its members outside of that small minority which agrees with their own views. The real masses are despised and ignored, their opinions explained away as "co-optation" whenever they contradict the "revolutionary line."

The main point of the ERA conflict of the seventies, like that of most political battles, was as much symbolic as substantive. For feminists it represented, at a minimum, a necessary legitimation of women's dignity under the Constitution, whereas for their opponents it was a primary symbol of the feminists' anti-feminine, anti-male, anti-family ideology.

But an equal rights amendment, if passed, would cease to be a symbol and become a practical reality. As a law, ERA raises two very serious concerns. The first is its rigidity. ERA would prevent the United States from making useful and necessary distinctions between the sexes in law, beneficial to men and women alike. It represents the sacrifice of pragmatism to principle, of equity to equality. Of course the sexes are equal in dignity and should have equal levels of protection under the law, but the securing of equal dignity and the achievement of equal protection may at times require *different* treatment under the law. A law that forbids the mention of women is extremely unlikely on balance to improve the condition of women.

The second serious concern raised by ERA is its unpredictability. Nobody knows exactly what the overall effects of an ERA would be. The almost total disagreement which prevails among legal scholars over ERA's likely effects demonstrates the extent of this uncertainty. The one certain thing is that it would expand the potential intrusiveness of the federal government by throwing enormous discretionary powers to the Supreme Court, as the Court coped with the mountain of litigation generated by a constitutional change affecting so many aspects of American life. The ultimate effects of ERA would depend on the Court, which might respond with either a broad or a narrow construal of ERA's language depending on the sociopolitical views of its majority, who, as past experience of both conservative and liberal Courts demonstrates, would be heavily influenced by the politics of whatever president appointed them. ERA thus represents an abdication of power, and therefore of both freedom and responsibility, by the voters and lawmakers to the federal judiciary.

ERA leaves many other unanswered questions, which feminists are reluctant to discuss. Is ERA a good substitute for the inelegant, imperfect, Burkean set of laws that protect women and the family that it would invalidate? Would it or would it not mandate legal abortion, legal homosexual marriage, nationally subsidized day care, female combat service, mixed-sex football teams and choirs, and possibly co-ed bathrooms? Even if we favor all of these, is a sweeping amendment of uncertain effect the best way to achieve them? Feminists do not like to discuss these issues, but the fact is we just don't know how ERA will be interpreted by the courts. The battle for ERA may yet be refought, but however protracted the struggle, the questions over the effects of the amendment will remain unanswered—until they reach the bench.

Finally, regardless of how one assesses the merits of the ERA debate, the struggle over ERA demonstrates that feminism is not the only women's movement possible. "The women's movement" claimed to speak for "women" on "women's issues." For whom, then, did Stop ERA speak? If the right to a husband's support, alimony, child custody, the protection of women in industry, and the exemption of women from the draft and from combat are not women's issues, what are?

Of course, all these issues *are* women's issues. Why then have they been so consistently ignored by feminists? The conclusion is inescapable that either (*a*) the feminists are right and Schlafly is a harpy in the service of multinational corporations, or (*b*) feminism does not have a monopoly on issues that affect women and feminists' use of the phrase "women's issues" is really a code word for *feminist* issues; that in the final analysis the feminist movement promotes its own ideology, which sometimes happens to coincide with the general interests of women, but more often works against them.

Women Against Pornography

As the prospects for passage of ERA receded, feminist leaders began casting about for another issue to keep them in the public eye and bring in new members. The first issue tried was pornography. To this end, two new organizations were formed, Women Against Violence in Pornography and Media (WAVPM) in 1978, followed by Women Against Pornography (WAP) in 1979. Because of the central role of Women Against Pornography, the subsequent campaign can be referred to as "the WAP effort."

In 1980 a book was assembled to galvanize the campaign. Some thirty feminist writers, including Gloria Steinem, Susan Brownmiller, Alice Walker, and the rising star Andrea Dworkin, contributed to this volume, which carried as its title the WAVPM marching slogan *Take Back the Night*. From whom, one wonders.

The tangle with Stop ERA had floodlighted the gulf between feminist and "traditionalist" women. One of the chief attractions of the pornography issue was that it seemed to offer a means to bridge this gap. The Midwestern housewives who made up the bulk of Schlafly's shock troops were churchgoers who viewed pornography as yet another sign (along with permissiveness, drugs, and feminism) of the decadence of the times. They viewed pornography as not just disgusting and obscene, but as immoral and licentious. By encouraging unbridled sexual desire, pornography was seen to threaten the controls necessary to maintain the family.

The feminist objection to pornography was entirely different, since the destruction of the "patriarchal" family was high on the list of feminists' shared objectives. The leading feminist authors advocated a loosening of sexual controls precisely *in order* to undermine the family.

A sexual revolution would require, perhaps first of all, an end of tradi- tional sexual inhibitions and taboos, particularly those that most threaten [*sic*] patriarchal monogamous marriage: homosexuality, "illegitimacy," adolescent, pre- and extra-marital sexuality. The negative aura with which sexual activity has generally been surrounded would necessarily be eliminated. . . .[5]

The feminist definition of pornography follows from the feminist perspective: that evil is caused by men and takes the form of the oppression of women, who must resist the oppressor by undermining his power— in this case, by "taking back the night [from men]."

Given these goals—to undermine the family and masculinity—the feminist conception of pornography had little in common with the older definition that pornography is "material which appeals to prurient interest."

Sexual desire was in principle good. As one of the organizations proclaimed, "WAVPM has no objection to explicit sex, nor do we object to depictions of nudity per se."[6]

It was *unhealthy* sexual desire which had to be defined and repressed. The feminist perspective determined the meaning of "unhealthy": sex in which men dominate women. A distinction was drawn between "erotica," which may be explicit but respects its subjects' "personhood," and "pornography," which was defined in an ordinance proposed by feminists in several American cities (Minneapolis, Indianapolis, Suffolk County on Long Island, and Cambridge, Massachusetts) as "the graphic sexually explicit subordination of women," particularly if women are shown in "positions of servility or submission or display." In other words, explicitness is not a sufficient characteristic to define pornography; it must also show the "subordination of women."

This definition is both extraordinarily narrow and extraordinarily broad. The definition of pornography as the "graphic sexually explicit subordination of women" contains no ban on male homosexual pornography even if it is violent, nor on explicit sex acts including all forms of sodomy. And, indeed, feminist sex manuals are full of photographs of out-of-shape men and women earnestly engaged in graphically explicit acts that violate all the biblical taboos except for bestiality. Under the feminist definition of pornography a picture of, say, ten men buggering each other in a circle is *not* pornography, but Manet's "Le déjeuner sur l'herbe," the great Impressionist painting that shows two well-dressed men sitting outside with two naked women (presumably lower class, and therefore "subordinate") arguably is. Is it possible that something was just a little bit out of balance?

The Times Square Tour

The method used to promote the Women Against Pornography point of view is one we have already encountered in the writings of Millett and Greer. It involves shocking people to create a window of vulnerability, while keeping an explanation ready to exploit the resultant temporary lowering of their critical faculties. From the initial sense of horror, the goal is to build up an emotional commitment strong enough to resist future rational argument. It is something less than the coercive psychological manipulation practiced by destructive cults, but something more than the orderly transmission of objective information in a balanced framework.

For many feminists, the acquisition of "raised consciousness" had in fact resembled a conversion, as reflected in book titles like Betty Friedan's *It Changed My Life.* The goal of the WAP movement was to provide this beneficial experience to yet more women. The presentation of evidence was designed to change women's values, not to create a balanced understanding of the phenomenon of sexually oriented materials.

In pursuit of this goal, a principal tactic was to expose women to pornography stores, often for the first time. As one of the WAP leaders reported,

> New York, N.Y., 1979: Biweekly tours of Forty-second Street are being offered by a new organization called Women Against Pornography. The tours take groups of twenty women around Times Square to expose them to the thriving pornography industry. Tour leaders believe that once women see for themselves the brutality of the industry they will be better equipped to fight it. In one year over two thousand women toured New York City's pornography strip. Many later participated in a large March on Times Square.[7]

To subject women who have often had no previous exposure to pornography to the monumental sleaze of Times Square is a shock tactic *par excellence,* well calculated to produce a reaction nothing short of trauma. How, how to make sense of this dreadful experience, these horrifying extremes of degradation, the violence, inhumanity, and sheer stupidity of it? The WAP organizers were close at hand, as ready to teach as to guide.

The experience, of course, was a setup. Most men grow up with pornography. They know it is sleazy, second-rate, and overpriced. They have read in men's magazines about the sweatshop conditions under which pornographic novels are produced (virtually no such books, for example, get even a cursory re-write). They've seen the same photo angles dozens of times and have noted the photographers' typical lack of originality. They suspect most of the hard-core stuff comes from organized crime, and evaluate its merits accordingly. They know pornography is pretty rotten stuff, and as a result they have pretty low expectations of it. Any erotic charge it may contain is likely to be buried beneath a pile of sleaze. But they're just as helpless to change its level of mindless violence as they are to change the violence on the TV shows aimed at their kids.

They also know exactly what's in it from personal experience. Most pornography, contrary to the feminist assertion that "domination and torture is what it's about,"[8] consists of written, photographic, or film depictions of people making love, or of photographs of naked women (in which case the male viewer supplies the action in his own mind by imagining himself making love to the woman in the picture). The feminists claim that it is the context which makes pornography degrading to women, but pornography is on the whole distinguished by its very lack of context: you don't know who these people are, how they met, what they have in common, what the basis for their relationship may be. Some men find this direct coupling of bodies intensely stimulating, while a good many others find it arid and unsatisfactory. Pornography is sufficiently diverse that you can "prove" anything about it by citing examples—exactly what the WAP organizers did—but the fact remains that most pornography consists of glossy magazines featuring page after page of photographs of naked women, with little or no text. This same lack of context is the stock in trade of the other genres, pornographic films and novels. (Novels, well—novels, I suppose.)

In addition to these majority genres there are specialties through which the producers of pornography seek to increase their profits by appealing to minority sexual tastes, or what have traditionally been known as perversions. These exist in certain well-defined categories, which occupy discrete areas in pornography stores, making it easy for the male customer to find—or to avoid—such materials. (Not so the WAP proselytes.) The specialized materials can get incredibly, absurdly specific—Anybody for gay sadomasochistic foot fetishism? Did you want that in leather or in rubber?—but the overall categories are few in number.

The Function of "Sadomasochism" in the WAP Argument

But all this is lost on feminist ears. The WAP guide will waste no time leading her group to the "SM" section of the store, where the fun really starts.

"SM" is shorthand for "sadomasochism," a word with at least three different usages: first, that category of sexual fantasy to which the SM material seeks to appeal; second, various more or less abstruse clinical pathological categories; third, a vaguely defined semicolloquial pejorative applicable, for instance, to James Bond villains and torturers who enjoy their work. These meanings are so diverse as to be practically unrelated, but by confusing them, feminists gain a significant tactical advantage: they are able to build a conceptual link between the productions sold in pornography stores, severe forms of psychopathology, and the deadly violence that is one of the worst aspects of the human condition.

There are two misleading aspects of the WAP approach at this point. The first is that the SM section represents a discrete area of the store, and the themes to which it caters do *not* pervade the materials on sale as a whole. Having just stepped into an environment totally alien to them, the tour group members are not likely to give much weight to this fact (which would be obvious to most men). The SM rack is about half the size of the gay rack, which itself fills only about a tenth of the available display space. SM strikes many as shocking and repulsive, the very embodiment of filth, but it is important to note that it only occupies a relatively small niche in pornography and does not, as feminists claim, pervade the whole.

The second misleading aspect concerns the nature of SM materials. One can scarcely recommend these productions as a criterion of health, but the feminist description of their content makes a bad thing far worse than it is. SM productions typically show men and women—feminist literature fails to point out how often the roles are reversed—bound, dressed in bizarre costumes of leather and rubber, women in outlandishly high heels, and—relatively occasionally—individuals being "whipped" in what is obviously play-acting. Male-to-female transvestites and men and women giving each other enemas round out the category. For whatever reasons, the sex act is conspicuous in such productions by its absence. A relatively small minority of people find enough interest in such fantasies to keep these magazines in business.

What the SM material does not show, contrary to the WAP assertions, is aggravated violence. Such violence is dished around pretty evenly throughout the pornographic media, where it can be sickening, as gratuitous violence is anywhere: on television, at the movies, and in real life. Violence is not, however, the particular property of that category of pornography devoted to "SM." The feminist argument depends for its shock value on the blurring of such distinctions. Aggression, domination, sadomasochism, and killing become a seamless web, until all moral and practical distinctions between a normally aggressive man and a mass murderer are lost. At this point, the tour will have succeeded in its purpose, to convince its proselytes that pornography is equivalent to "rape, woman-battering, the murder of women by men, or the molestation of young girls by their fathers" and is therefore nothing more or less than "the acting out of male power over, and often hatred toward, women."[9] Having portrayed pornography's central concern as violence, the attack on pornography is then revealed as secondary to its underlying purpose, the attack on men. When Andrea Dworkin, the most visible leader of the WAP campaign, expressed how she hoped pornography would "raise consciousness" about the male sex, she wrote:

> Men love death. In everything they make, they hollow out a central place for death, let its rancid smell contaminate every dimension of whatever still survives.[10]

The attempt to define pornography as being mostly "sadomasochistic" is a lie, which is calculated to alienate women from men and to build the sense of rage and aggrievement necessary to create a feminist (at least as feminism is currently understood). Even if this lie were not built on a distorted and alarmist representation of SM pornography, it would be no nearer the truth. Most men are not interested in SM. The guiding force behind the WAP effort is the conviction that men hate women, whereas the truth is that even if pornography were as hateful as feminists depict it, the fact would remain that most men, although they have experience of pornography, do not frequent porn shops. Those who do so must put up with what pornographers produce—which is based on the search for easy financial gain, not on the desire off which pornography feeds. There are no grounds to assume that sex shop pornography accurately reflects male fantasies just because it is targeted at and consumed by a male audience, any more than there are to assume that television programming reflects children's tastes or current fashion women's tastes. By its very nature, commercial pornography is inclined toward sleazy, insensitive, violent, and stereotypical productions. A minority of men continue to consume these products because, like moonshine whiskey, they may be of atrocious quality, or even acutely poisonous, but they still pack a wallop. But to confuse such products with the fantasy life of most men is to yield to a facile calumny.

Sex shop pornography may not be pretty, meritorious, or necessary to social stability, but it presents a very different reality from the relentless "subordination of women" projected by WAP. The categorization of pornography by WAP is deliberately misleading. It slanders and defames an entire sex.

The driving force behind men's attraction to pornography is desire for women, not a need to degrade them. That the products which seek to profit from this desire may be degrading is irrelevant to this essentially benign fact. To conclude, as feminists do, that pornography shows that male sexual desire must be fundamentally remade is sheer folly, like claiming the human need to eat is bad because of dishonest ads that present hyperenriched bread as sound nutrition or proclaim that MSG-laden soup is "good food."

A better understanding of the phenomenon of erotic materials requires some sense of how these materials are actually used—a topic that is carefully avoided in all the feminist literature on pornography.

Men and Pornography

Upon reaching puberty, boys get very interested in girls and sex. Masturbation occurs almost universally. It is impossible for a youth to be unaware of his own erection. Either through the instruction of other boys or through simple repeated touching of this irritated area, virtually all boys learn to masturbate and do so regularly. The activity is often furtive and sometimes surrounded by considerable religiously motivated guilt, but it does not fail to occur.

Since women are unavailable to boys at this stage of life, their representations acquire a particular importance. The thing in itself being absent, its symbolic representation acquires a heightened immediacy. Furthermore, since what is desired is also unknown, an extraordinary amount of curiosity is evoked. And of course what is sought is not a textbook sketch of the external and internal genitalia, but rather a representation of the male's perceptions of the female while having sex, or something which can pass as such. The whole embarrassing, absurd, and irrepressible process is sympathetically and hilariously chronicled in Neil Simon's play *Brighton Beach Memoirs.*

This shared experience accounts for much of the social aspect of pornography consumption. By experiencing pornography together, men share a bond compounded of shared attraction and shared frustration. The widespread practice of group masturbation among adolescent boys finds a later echo in, for example, the (chaste) viewing of stag films at bachelor parties. Sex becomes an area through which men create a sense of cohesion among themselves as a group.

However, the most essential function of pornography is to stimulate the sexual imagination in order to create a masturbatory experience that resembles the sex act as closely as possible. From this arises the continuing attraction of pornography to substantial numbers of adult men who find themselves without a sex partner or who seek variety without the complications of infidelity.

Because of the universality of the experience it represents and of the needs to which it responds, the possibility must be considered that pornography—broadly and correctly defined as erotic materials which produce sexual stimulation, and which therefore should include (for instance) the paintings of Titian and the underwear ads in the *New York Times Magazine* as well as *Playboy* and the hard-core matter purveyed in urban "combat zones"—may play a useful and permanent role in male sexual development and socialization. At the very least, it possesses a permanent appeal which derives from inherent stages in the development of male sexuality which, as part of the irreducible biological core of human maturation, are immune to ideological manipulation.

The Dark Side of Pornography

Unquestionably pornography has its dark side too. This must be specified with more precision, though, than the cardboard claim that it "objectifies" women—which is just another blanket accusation of men—or that it "leads to" sex crime. Consider the latter. The claim that pornography leads to sex crime is in fact only very weakly supported by the evidence.

The WAP crusade was designed to generated outrage, not understanding. Inflamed with messianic zeal as they held aloft the torch of the women's movement, the humane movement, convinced of the curative powers of "feminist rage," the anti-pornographers were inclined to place a low valuation on mere facts. After all, the feminist perspective had shown them the way things really were—to the point that even evidence which seemed to contradict the feminist perspective on pornography only confirmed it, by showing the treacherous extent of "male-dominated culture." Expediency therefore characterized the effort.

Pornography and Violence

Does pornography cause violence? *Take Back the Night* claimed it did. Almost the only evidence presented, however, consisted in the mere assertion that pornography is about violence: "Pornography usually combines some sort of violence with sex. . . . Domination and torture is what it's about."[11] As we have seen, this is not true: pornography is first, foremost, and finally, about *sex*. The only other shred of evidence offered for the doubtful (but politically convenient) hypothesis that pornography causes sex crime was by analogy with a study of the effects of television violence on convicted criminals. As this study was described in *Take Back the Night,*

> Three out of the fifty-nine rapists (5 percent) said that they had felt inspired or motivated to commit rape as a result of something they had seen on TV; of the thirty-one men serving life sentences for murder, two (6 percent) said their crimes had been television-influenced; and of the 148 men who admitted to committing assault, about one out of six (17 percent) indicated that his crimes had been inspired or motivated by something he saw on TV.[12]

This may sound impressive until one stops to consider what these figures really mean. In the first place, there may not be a parallel between television violence and pornography. The parallel in fact does tend to break down when it is realized that the violence level in pornography, although far too high, is not its distinguishing characteristic. More seriously, the figures given indicate the opposite of what they are trotted out to prove. Given the suggestion implicit in asking someone if television influenced their actions, at least a few people are going to answer yes, even if a more accurate answer would be no. Furthermore, in a society as thoroughly permeated with television as ours, television is going to influence almost everything at some point ("Did TV influence the way you saved that child from drowning?" "Hmm, yes, I guess it did."). In light of these considerations, the influence of television on violence (at least as documented in this report) seems extremely weak. One need only turn the figures around to see that 87 percent of those committing assault, 94 percent of murderers, and 95 percent of rapists felt they were *not* influenced by television violence when they committed their crimes. While the possibility that pornography leads to sex crime is not disproved, it receives no support from the evidence rather underhandedly advanced to buttress it.

Both feminist and conservative foes of pornography, starting from a conviction that pornography is unhealthy, have tried to establish a valid statistical link between pornography and violence, without success. They have been looking in the wrong place.

The Real Ill Effects of Pornography

The real ill effects of pornography are more subtle. Pornography uses an extraordinarily powerful set of symbols to convey messages that are badly thought out or deliberately perverse because of the essentially economic motivation of the genre, its semilegitimate status, and the widespread dissemination of sexual misinformation of various sorts. Pornography represents a major stimulus in the lives of some men, and although its negative effects are poorly known, it stretches credulity to believe it may not have a disruptive impact on the vulnerable—in particular on obsessive and immature men. (And all men are immature at some point and most are virtually obsessed with sex at times.) It may even make some slight contribution to sex crime, although one would at a minimum want to know whether societies with less pornography have less sex crime and whether societies with more pornography have more sex crime (neither of which seems to be the case) before jumping to such a conclusion.

The major problem that pornography causes is something that may not be entirely amenable to legislative remedy, namely, the distancing of men and women. The feminist claim that "even the most banal pornography objectifies women's bodies"[13] is substantially correct provided it is recontextualized to remove the sense of grievance, the belief that women are the victims of a grand conspiracy of men which underlies the feminist accusation that "men see women as sex objects." It will be a sad day when men no longer see women as objects of their lust, nor is it humanly possible to socialize men not to be excited by a well-shaped thigh or a luscious mouth quite apart from the personal merit (or lack thereof) of its owner.

The problem with most pornography, whether visual or written, is that the power of its representations tends to work its way into the male psyche to the point of distorting male perceptions of women, not because women shouldn't be sex objects (they should), but because in pornography they tend to become *only* objects. The adult male user of pornography thus faces the difficulty of living in two sexual worlds, an unsatisfying, demoralizing, and alienating but titillating fantasy one, and a difficult, frustrating, uncertain, but emotionally validating real one: the first peopled by the whores of pornographic fantasy, the second by real women. The adolescent male may actually face less of a problem with pornography than the mature male, since he is in transit between the fantasy world of pornography and what is to him the incomparably more thrilling one of real sex. The sheer strength of his sex drive will usually serve to bridge the gap with ease.

The direct threat posed by pornography is to men, not to women: namely, its potential to contribute to a divorce from self, and thus from others. While providing useful information about sex, while filling a minor social role, it also tends to jam the gears that must operate to make possible the fusion of souls between men and women through love.

In this regard, the influence of pornography closely resembles the influence of feminism, as exercised through works like the best-selling *Hite Reports,* which encourage women to view men as members of a class, the impersonal category of "males," rather than as individuals. Feminist works on sex present as misinformed and depersonalized a view of male and female sexuality as pornography. By replacing the individual's inner-originated, outer-oriented system of arousal, fantasy, and performance with an external, homogenized alternative system that is outer-originated and inner-oriented, pornography and feminism cause similar alienation from one's authentic, internal sexual guidance system. Too often the words on the page raise the blood pressure at the price of obscuring the beating of the heart. In either case, one's own needs come to seem more important than those of one's lover. Instead of communication, sex becomes primarily a way to actualize oneself; even intercourse becomes colored by a masturbatory fixation or by clitoromania. It may become more important for the male heavy consumer of pornography to experience deep throat or anal sex than to find sustaining love; it may become more important for the convinced feminist to have ideologically correct orgasms through clitoral manipulation and to reeducate her lover through sex than to let herself go and damn the consequences. Such difficulties are the inevitable result of the substitution of externally generated for internally generated needs.

The picture of pornography that emerges from even a cursory examination that does not seek to use it as an ideological cudgel is thus not the simplistic view that pornography represents the degradation of women, but one that is multi-layered and morally mixed. Pornography serves useful functions in the socialization of adolescent males; it does not cause sex crime; it does make a subtle but pernicious contribution to the alienation of the sexes. It is neither the liberating source of joy naively heralded by sexual revolutionaries in the sixties, nor the terrifying incitement to destruction portrayed by feminists, but something in between: a problematic social phenomenon that feminists deserve partial credit for bringing to public notice; but that, because of the very anti-male mentality that made it a focus of feminist attention, they are unable to resolve.

A Case in Point: The Soft-core Glossies

Sex shops are not the only purveyors of pornography, however. Neither the traditional (prurient interest) nor the feminist (sexual subjugation) definitions exempt the bevy of "soft-core" magazines from the category of pornography. Such magazines are most conspicuously distinguished from the "hard-core" item sold in pornography stores by the infrequency with which they show the aroused male genitalia, the last part of the human anatomy to retain some vestige of taboo. They are further differentiated by the fact that their chief selling point, pictures of naked young women, is given a window dressing of literary respectability. In the case of *Playboy,* the sex magazine aspect has been progressively downplayed, with a consequent decline in sales (although there has been a general decline in the sales of these magazines from their peak years in the seventies, which is presumably not unrelated to the conservative trend in American life). A closer look at the covers of the flagship publications in this category, *Playboy* and *Penthouse,* suggests just how much is missed by the feminist definition of pornography.

These magazines sell by their covers: they have fractions of a second in which to catch the eye of potential purchasers. The methods used have nothing to do with the simplistic feminist notion that pornography is just about the sexual subjugation of women by men. Some years ago, an exposé of the advertising industry was published called *Subliminal Seduction,* which detailed the information advertisers imbed in their ads to be perceived below conscious level. If one can believe the critique in *Subliminal Seduction,* the cover of *Playboy* is a prime example of such psychological manipulation. Its attraction is based not on an appeal to mature sexuality, but to unresolved Oedipal urges. The cover girls are ultimately maternal and unavailable. The rabbit head with ears which is the *Playboy* motif evokes a pair of scissors and therefore castration complexes.[14]

The argument presented in *Subliminal Seduction* can be extended to *Playboy*'s main competitor, *Penthouse* magazine. The covers of *Penthouse* present women characterized by their unavailability. They are seen as "older" by the magazine's eighteen- to twenty-four-year-old primary readership: tormentingly attractive but sexually remote. The principal appeal is not to mature sexuality but to residual Oedipal conflicts. The only solution is to pick up the magazine in the hope that something will happen within: perhaps sex will become available after all. The basic ploy is to combine titillation and rejection. The fact that Shere Hite's study of men, with its convoluted message of aggravated love-hate, was heavily promoted by *Penthouse* fits with this consistent approach.

The manipulativeness of the soft-core glossies is as unattractive as the worst productions of "hard-core" pornography, and because their message is more refined, covert, and widely disseminated, it probably does more damage. What are the psychological effects of perusing these magazines month after month, particularly when one considers there is a whole stack of such magazines to read? It seems likely that they make it significantly harder for young men who are unaware of the games that are being played with their heads to cope with the emerging maturity of their sexuality. Like the equally enticing pleasures of drugs, theirs is a siren song.

But these ill effects have absolutely nothing to do with the feminist definition of pornography. Rather than encouraging men to sexual aggressiveness, the soft-core glossies probably make it harder for men to relate to women (or to themselves) in any way at all. They stimulate not aggression but regression. The immediate victims of this attempt to make money by manipulating the sexual urge are not women but men, who thus emerge not as the violent, threatening creatures of the anti-pornography crusade, but as vulnerable—to the point, where the delicate matter of their sexuality is concerned, of being almost defenseless.

Aggression by men against women is not the primary stock-in-trade of *Playboy* and *Penthouse*. These magazines have plenty of faults, but that is not one of them. Women's books, on the other hand, present a different picture.

The Romance Novel

The most ubiquitous brand of fiction in America is the romance novel. While pornography is a male world unknown to women, the romance novel is a female world unknown to men. Yet you can buy these books as readily as a newspaper: they are sold in drugstores, convenience stores, supermarkets, and airport newsstands, among other places. The standard plot of these books is that a young and innocent woman falls in love with a man who is alien to her because of differences in temperament, social status, nationality, or race; often he is a "bad guy" in conflict with society's proprieties— a pirate, outlaw, or barbarian. When she meets him, she feels weak, helpless, and confused. Although she denies and fights the urge, she wants to be carried away by him, and in due course, this actually happens. The ensuing scene, growing a little more explicit each year, gives the lie to the feminist assertion that pornography is the "sexually explicit subordination of women," for if this is so, what on earth is the romance novel?

Consider the seduction of Season, a maiden who has fallen into the hands of the Raven, a mysterious pirate captain. Ashore, the Raven is actually a very presentable young man with whom Season has recently fallen passionately in love, but she doesn't know his true identity in this scene. He in turn has been misled by one of her rejected suitors into believing she is a slut and a traitress.

The Raven enters the darkened cabin where he has confined Season and approaches her. Paralyzed with fear, she is unable to resist as he sweeps her off her feet and places her on the bed. Then,

All at once her fear was replaced by a deeper and more frightening sensation. She felt his teeth nibbling at her earlobe, causing tiny shivers of delight to skirt across her skin, and she seemed to go weak all over as he brushed his hot mouth against hers.

Season tried to remember that she was a lady, that this man was nothing more than a black-hearted pirate. She was about to voice her objections, when his hand brushed against her breast and caressed it with a slow circular motion. The only sound that escaped her lips was a low moan. . . .

Season cried out as he thrust his swollen manhood into her. . . .

"Pity you are so young and inexperienced, my lady, but I know just how to make you want me."

"No, never," she said, not realizing her passion-laced voice lent the lie to her claim. . . .

As his lips tasted the salty tears on her face, he realized he was being too rough with her, so he gentled his movements. Where was the victory in striking out at her as at an enemy? Just then his body reached the highest plane of satisfaction. He shuddered. No, he thought. I have not conquered the enemy—she now holds me captive! In truth, the Lady Season Chatsworth had answered a hunger deep inside him that he had never known existed.

In that moment she experienced a new and deeper feeling. Her body seemed to erupt, and she felt her whole being tremble. Never had she felt so at peace with the world, never had she felt so fulfilled and alive![15]

The passage just quoted is excerpted from a novel by Constance O'Banyon, but in terms of its sexual content it could equally well have come from any one of hundreds of other books that celebrate the same themes. The titles of these books are eloquent: *Savage Conquest, Escape Me Never, Captive Heart, Velvet Chains*. The cover of each of these books shows a man kissing a woman with considerably more forwardness than tenderness, while she leans back in an ecstasy of sensual delight, on the verge of swooning. Short descriptions on the cover tell of the delights within: "SHE DREADED THE NIGHT WITH THE HANDSOME BRAVE—AND HOPED IT WOULD NEVER END!" "KIDNAPPED—SHE WAS BOUND BY THE FIERCE PASSION OF HIS LOVE" "SHE WAS ENSLAVED BY DESIRE AND BRANDED BY PASSION'S FLAMES!" "FIRST HE TOOK HER BODY—THEN HE STOLE HER HEART!"[16]

Now, is this the "explicit sexual subordination of women" or is it not? If "he thrust his swollen manhood into her" is not explicit, what is, short of an anatomy text? If sexual subordination is not precisely what is occurring, pray tell what is. The theme is the conquest of a woman by a man through his indomitable will, overpowering strength, and irresistible sexual skills. The woman goes "weak all over" even though it is "against her will," and requires the man's guidance to force her to what she in her heart of hearts wants anyway, namely, sexual climax and the acknowledgment that (even though he may be a dastard) she is in love with him. Nothing brutal, nothing deadly is desired: these stories are filled with rejected male suitors whose capacity for coercion and violence causes only fear and disgust. The whole trick is to be ravished by the right man. The fact that this may be difficult to arrange takes away none of its urgency. The means is sexual subordination, but love is the end. As Season's abductor realizes after raping her, "she now holds me captive! In truth, the Lady Season Chatsworth had answered a hunger deep inside him that he had never known existed." The point of the whole process is to achieve through sexual inequality, emotional equality. The result of the woman's being sexually overwhelmed in the proper context is passionate, undying love.

Quite apart from the questions of whether this schema does or does not represent a realistic guide to love and sex, and whether it is or is not an accurate reflection of ancient and inalterable primate realities, the point remains that these are books written by women for women and produced by an industry, publishing, which is increasingly known as a "women's field." To claim that these books owe their form to coercive influence by men is utterly fanciful. For whatever reasons, women are even more avid producers and consumers than men of the "sexually explicit subordination of women." Those who are dissatisfied with the sexes' relations should therefore take the onus off pornography (which is not thereby, however, vindicated of its real faults) and place it on the human condition as a whole. Women have played a more dynamic, causative role than is allowed by the feminist belief that they have always been the helpless and unwilling victims of men. Quite the contrary: with all their faults, if men didn't exist, women would invent them.

Sex and Aggression, Once More

The feminist equation of aggression with violence is an insidious point. By failing to draw a distinction between aggressive sexuality and psychopathic violence—in fact, the whole thrust of the WAP effort is to obfuscate this real and important difference—men as a group are stamped with guilt. The married man who responds passionately to his wife's pleas to "take me, ravage me," the timid Englishman who nurtures a guilty and unrealizable fantasy to witness the caning of schoolgirls, and the rapist who lurks in a stairwell, armed with a revolver and driven by hatred—not necessarily hatred of women[17]—are indiscriminately lumped together as "the perpetrators of violence against women." The woman who breathlessly follows the adventures of Season or Modesty or any of the other heroines of romance novels is seen by feminists, and thus possibly even by herself, as a subversive agent, a betrayer of her sex to the enemy.

The WAP crusade is based on an inaccurate and unworkable conception of male and female sexuality. Healthy male sexuality is not defined by the absence of aggression. Healthy female sexuality is not defined by the refusal to submit to aggression. It may be possible to overrate the importance of male aggression in the sex act, which is nothing if not complex and varied, but it is impossible to subtract it completely.

Even if women and men were to become equally sexually aggressive, there would still be aggression in the sex act—and therefore feminists would still be unhappy over images of the "sexual subordination of women." A "woman" in the feminist lexicon is inclined neither to submission nor to dominance. Since aggression and dominance are held to be symptoms of the sickness of masculinity, it follows that women who behave aggressively or in a domineering manner are corrupted by male values—so that, contrary to appearances, they remain the victims of men. Therefore—such is the subtlety of the feminist logic—images of sexual dominance by women also fall under the category of "the sexual subordination of women." Of course what feminists really want is for all aggression, however slight, to be banished from the sex act altogether, as from all human interactions.

Since sex always contains an element of aggression, whether expressed or implied, the feminist critique of pornography contains a rationale for the censorship of all sex—not just in traditional pornographic media, but in art, literature, film, and fashion, with no end in sight until the millennium, when aggression will be banished from the sex act. The qualification "explicit" in the feminist definition of pornography is a sop to civil libertarians, expedient to help pass a law but alien in spirit to the feminist critique of pornography. For since aggression is equated with violence, and is always present to some degree in sex, it follows that *sex is violence*. This is the unvarnished logical basis for the phobia of heterosexual lovemaking that underlies the feminist critique of pornography. It goes a long way toward explaining the paradox that a movement which proclaimed human liberation became mired in a fever swamp of anti-sexual moralizing.

Not only do the feminist anti-pornographers condemn any sexual image: non-sexual images may be equally "pornographic." The feminist definition of pornography readily expands to cover all images of women that do not reflect the Graham cracker virtues of Susan Brownmiller's book jacket. The mentality of the feminist anti-pornography crusade makes no distinction between *Hustler* magazine and a department store "mannequin in spike-heeled boots," and is capable of discerning "violent pornography" in such unlikely places as *Vogue*.[18] Since violence rather than arousal defines pornography in the feminist lexicon, and since violence is defined in an extraordinarily broad sense, the category of the pornographic expands limitlessly.

"Rape in Marriage"

In fact, the repression envisaged by the WAP forces is incomparably greater than that urged by fundamentalist conservatives—so great that the only factor inhibiting a feminist Brave New World is the feminists' lack of political power. The fundamentalist goal is to restrict sexual activity to marriage, but the infinitely more ambitious feminist goal is to subject all expressions of sexuality to the control of feminist ideology.

This is nowhere more clearly seen than in the feminist attempt to invent a crime of "rape in marriage." This effort was closely linked to the WAP campaign and involved many of the same figures.[19]

A marriage in which the wife would take her husband to court over sex is clearly on the rocks. Judicial remedies to such a situation exist, namely, legal separation and divorce. But not content with these existing remedies, many feminists would place the state in the position of determining whether or not a husband engaged in legal sex with his wife. The attempt to discover a crime of rape in marriage would place the state in American bedrooms to an extent fully as absurd (and unenforceable) as the Georgia statute, upheld in 1986 by the Supreme

Court, which forbids "sodomy"—that is, oral-genital contact and anal intercourse—even between an adult man and woman in the privacy of their own home.

Like the Georgia sodomy statute, the creation of a crime of rape in marriage would impel absurdities among those attempting to comply with the law. Every man making love to his wife would be a potential victim of prosecution. The marriage bed would no longer be secure from the state. Any male approach to lovemaking other than extreme gentleness (indeed, not even that) would risk placing husbands on the wrong side of the law. Women, many feminists have assured me, would never engage in false accusations. One should consider the several rape cases that have surfaced in the past few years in which innocent men were convicted on women's false testimony before accepting such a sanguine conclusion. Even unenforceable laws have a way of being enforced: their injustice lies not in any lack of power but in their selective arbitrariness.

The law must recognize what the feminist perspective does not: that women are independent moral actors capable of good and evil, and consequently of pettiness, vindictiveness, and bringing false accusations, just like men. The law cannot assume that women operate on a moral plane superior to that of men.

Yet in the absence of any countervailing force, by 1987 twenty-five states, yielding to the steady pressure of feminist legal activists, had quietly enacted the crime of "rape in marriage" into law—eight states since 1984 alone.[20] When one realizes that these same activists define normal heterosexual intercourse as rape, one begins to realize the full intent behind this development. All such laws should immediately be repealed. The only case in which the state has any conceivable right to intervene in the bedroom of a married couple is where a legal separation already exists—a wholly different case from the "rape in marriage" laws that have recently been propounded.

Of all the feminist causes discussed in this chapter, marital rape is the only one to have succeeded unequivocally so far. This success suggests what is likely to become feminism's most effective strategy in the future: not national confrontations where its programs risk coming under public scrutiny, but quiet, steady pressure through administrative, judicial, and lobbying methods.

Conclusion

The feminist hysteria over sexuality shows how far the feminist perspective has carried feminism from the libertarian impulse that gave the movement at least part of its initial impetus. Instead of a movement to remove the constraints on women's lives, feminism had become a movement only too eager to impose its own constraints. The fight to eradicate "sexism" had become a consuming passion, and freedom be damned. Having worked themselves into a frenzy of outrage through "consciousness-raising" experiences like the Times Square tour, the feminist anti-pornographers displayed a blind eagerness to write their version of "raised consciousness" into law, indifferent to any damage that might result to the human freedoms won at such cost over preceding centuries.

In February 1986, the Supreme Court struck down the feminist anti-pornography ordinance, summarily affirming the decision of a Federal appeals court that the ordinance violated freedom of speech under the Bill of Rights. The decision described the ordinance as an attempt to establish "an 'approved' view of women" and consequently a form of "thought control." The feminist ordinance would place "the government in control of all of the institutions of culture, the great censor and director of which thoughts are good for us."[21]

The overall effect of the anti-pornography campaign for the feminist movement is difficult to assess in a positive light. If some feminists opposed the new censorship, it was not because of their feminism, but because of the persistence in their values of an alternative tradition, such as civil libertarianism. Feminism began to appear more and more as just another point of view, with its strengths, to be sure, but also with its blind spots and misplaced emphases. This newly realistic appraisal tended to undermine the fervent belief in feminism as *the* grand movement of human progress.

The alliance feminists proposed with fundamentalists bore little fruit. The incompatibility of the conceptions of "pornography" held by feminists and conservatives virtually guaranteed the failure of the Women Against Pornography effort. Predictably, most conservatives remained as opposed to feminism as ever, continuing to view feminism, like pornography, as an assault on morality and family life.

As a result of the proselytizing purpose of the campaign, its arguments were marked by expediency. Data, like those on pornography and sex crime, were commonly presented in a one-sided way. It stretches credence to imagine that this tendency went completely unnoticed by the public. If the movement acquired some new adherents and breathed new fervor into some of its veterans, if a few conservatives were very partially reconciled to feminism on this one issue, the price paid was a loss of credibility for feminism where it could least afford to lose, among its liberal sympathizers. By attacking elements in American life that were disposed to support their cause—pop culture, the fashion milieu, *Playboy* and *Vogue* magazines, and above all the extreme sensitivity to freedom of speech issues among left of center Americans in the generation after McCarthyism—feminists allowed the divisiveness of their perspective to push them into a nearly hysterical one-sidedness. Feminists seemed determined to isolate themselves from their most obvious sources of support in return for an ethically questionable and politically evanescent payoff.

Other cases of this self-defeating tendency follow, in the feminist handling of the issues of abortion, day care, comparable worth, and the vice-presidential candidacy of Geraldine Ferraro.

Abortion

Few controversies of our time have generated as much heat on either side of the political spectrum as the abortion issue.

The arguments for and against abortion are better than one could possibly guess from the mean-spirited diatribes that have been so conspicuous on either side of the issue. There is much to admire in the anti-abortion argument, in particular the idea that human life is so sacred that even its potential deserves our protection. This can be a high ideal, which merits, if not necessarily agreement, then certainly respect. Similarly, the pro-abortion vision of a world in which every child is wanted is by no means devoid of moral luster.

Unfortunately, these points of view are often presented in such a way as to vitiate the high principles from which each arises, as if all the opponents of abortion were fascists who wanted to forcibly return all women to "Kinder, Kuche, Kirche" ("children, kitchen, church") like the Nazis,[22] or as if all the advocates of legal abortion were Brave New World technocrats who wished to destroy civilization through euthanasia and genocide. An argument that is supposed to be about life and liberty is conducted in unpardonably extremist terms. By allowing its most intemperate representatives free rein, each side not only reduces the level of discussion and damages its credibility with the public, but in a quite real sense assaults society by abasing the public frame of reference.

The most basic difficulty with the anti-abortion position, even in its most enlightened form, is that it is not by any means self-evident that a human being in every sense of the word exists from the moment of conception. This is true whether in terms of common sense, of science, or of history.

As the Supreme Court pointed out in *Roe vs. Wade,* the decision that in effect legalized abortion in 1973, the generally accepted theological and legal view until about 1800 or even until the late nineteenth century was that the fetus was not a full human being entitled to protection until quickening, the moment when the fetus first moves in the womb, so that in consequence early abortion was not generally held to be a crime. Indeed, the fetus was traditionally not entitled to full legal rights, such as inheritance, until after birth, and so was not considered a "person" in all senses of that word. Maintaining this traditional distinction, the Supreme Court distinguished three distinct stages: the first, in which the fetus had few if any rights; the second, in which it had some but not all of the rights of a "person"; and the third, after birth, in which it became a person in all respects, at any rate in the eyes of the law. Whatever one thinks of the validity of this legal sequence, it must be emphasized that it has real precedents in Western societies from the start of the Christian era until the Enlightenment. The personhood of the fetus is an intellectually defensible posture, but it has not historically been a self-evident one.[23]

Nor is it now necessarily self-evident that a human being, in all senses of the term, exists from the moment of conception, when a cluster of cells comes into being scarcely more complex and certainly not more sentient than an amoeba, nor a few weeks later, when a human embryo is indistinguishable except to the highly trained eye from that of a fish, frog, or horse.

One of the most common and least impressive arguments against abortion is what may be termed "the euthanasia argument": that to permit abortion is to begin a run down a "slippery slope" on which the next stop will be euthanasia for the old and infirm, followed by the elimination of those who, for one reason or another, are judged less worthy of survival than others, leading to the eventual creation of a controlled society of nightmare proportions in which the destruction of all freedom and happiness will be fueled by the disregard for human life that abortion is said to instill. This scenario is sheer fantasy, for the simple reason that its elements don't fit together. Various antique and Polynesian societies practiced infanticide without impairing their social structures in any obvious way. That we prohibit infanticide may represent moral progress, but it is difficult to equate with any particular discovery about social stability. Nazi Germany, which rigidly prohibited abortion (for "German" women), elevated euthanasia to a principle of state and systematically planned the enslavement, torture, and murder of millions. Modern Sweden freely allows abortion—and has low rates of homicide the United States may well envy. And for better or worse, Sweden stayed out of the last European war and is at least nominally neutral in today's conflicts. Do the proponents of the euthanasia argument really understand what makes a good society?

The fact is that the human being has some ability to be selectively concerned with life and death: for instance, American conservatives tend to oppose abortion but to favor capital punishment. Conversely, proponents of legal abortion are more likely to oppose capital punishment. There is not necessarily any internal inconsistency in such sets of attitudes, nor do they indicate a lack of caring or morality.[24] Moreover, the most morally and logically consistent stances—pacifism and anarchism—are the most practically problematic. The conclusion we should draw is not that either side in the abortion debate has a monopoly on life or on death, but simply that we cannot make one issue a test for the personal or public morality of an individual. Those who accept one or another rationalization against the spirit of toleration exhibit an ignorance of or, worse, a cavalier disregard for the enduring principles on which American liberty was founded. The most visible actors in the abortion debate have tended with suspicious regularity to lose sight of the fact that most of those who oppose them are good, decent people who just happen to—in all sincerity—hold different beliefs from theirs.

Unfortunately for those of us who believe there is a concrete, humane case to be made for legal abortion, the abortion issue has been mishandled by feminists to the point where one hesitates to side with a position that leaves so little to its opponents for one-sidedness and dogmatism.

Feminists claim that a woman has "a right to control her own body" that is absolutely immune to violation by the state. This position has been advocated with consistent vehemence, as if to bring up any other considerations would betray the cause of humanity (which to feminists, acolytes of the feminist movement, the humane movement, it really would). There are few hints indeed in feminist writing that there may be moral and psychological dimensions to abortion that go beyond those of a routine medical procedure. Like so many anti-abortionists, the feminist pro-abortion forces refuse even to consider the views of the other camp, behaving like diplomats who feel no need to negotiate, either because they feel their own side is strong enough to win the war, or else because the other side represents forces so satanic that to truckle with it at all would be tantamount to acquiescing in its evil goals—respectively, to kill "unborn infants," or to destroy women's freedom by forcing them to bear children whether they wish to or not.[25]

Feminists' repetitive overuse of the slogan "A woman's right to control her own body" has obscured the extent to which at the start of the seventies the argument for legal abortion was complex and multi-layered. It was this complex argument which influenced the Supreme Court's decision in *Roe vs. Wade* in 1973—the only law that prevents a renewed ban on abortion in many states.[26]

One line of argument revolved around the alleged unenforceability of the abortion prohibition, which was said to lead to needless danger and inequity as many poor women, desperately seeking abortions, were sterilized, injured, and sometimes killed in back-alley "abortion mills," while the rich simply flew off to countries where abortion was legal.

The other principal arguments for abortion were summarized by Justice Blackmun as follows:

[The right of privacy under the Fourteenth Amendment] is broad enough to encompass a woman's decision whether or not to terminate her pregnancy. The detriment that the State would impose upon the pregnant woman by denying this choice altogether is apparent. Specific and direct harm medically diagnosable even in early pregnancy may be involved. Maternity, or additional offspring, may force upon the woman a distressful life and future. Psychological harm may be imminent. Mental and physical health may be taxed by child care. There is also the distress, for all concerned, associated with the unwanted child, and there is the problem of bringing a child into a family already unable, psychologically and otherwise, to care for it. In other cases, as in this one, the additional difficulties and continuing stigma of unwed motherhood may be involved. All these are factors the woman and her responsible physician necessarily will consider in consultation.[27]

The justification offered by Justice Blackmun—essentially, that abortion is a complex moral and medical decision which should be a private choice made by a woman in consultation with her doctor—was heard less and less often in the course of the seventies.

By reducing the complex case of the late sixties to the slogan "A woman's right to control her own body," feminists threw away some of the best arguments available to them. Having defined masculinity as a disease and the family as women's prison, feminists in the seventies followed their own advice to create a "woman-centered" perspective only too well. Often they came to seem exclusively concerned with women (as they conceived "women" to be), to the point of neglecting the legitimate and sometimes conflicting claims of men and children. The claim that a woman has an absolute right to control her own body may or may not be true, but in any case it is incapable of dealing with the anti-abortion argument that the fetus is a human being and therefore entitled to its own rights. This argument needed to be squarely faced: for if the fetus is a person in the full sense of the word, then abortion is infanticide. The claim that a woman has a right to control her own body is fundamentally irrelevant to this point.

In fact, the decision to abort necessarily involves the resolution of conflicting moral claims, whose very complexity is a potent argument for legal abortion. It is precisely the murkiness, not the clarity, of the issue which mandates that abortion should be a woman's private decision—but feminists showed little patience for such gray areas. Feminists thus impoverished the discussion of abortion rights, of which they had, through their own insistence and liberal abdication, become the principal defenders, and left the moral high ground to their opponents.

Is there a non-feminist case for abortion? We may perhaps derive one from an examination of some of the further difficulties with the "pro-life" position.

One should automatically be suspicious of those who are eager to require the suffering of others in the name of a higher moral good. Religion has the right to make such demands on those who have freely chosen it; the modern state in a free society does not. This is not a theory of secularism but a pragmatic lesson learned by the people of the West at the highest possible cost. The Wars of Religion wrought a holocaust comparable in intolerance, institutionalized sadism, and sheer numbers of dead to the political repression and megadeath of the twentieth century. During the Thirty Years' War, one third of the German population perished. Even the Nazis failed to invent tortures more gruesome than those commonly practiced on "heretics," both Protestant and Catholic. Jews and Muslims were also victims in Spain. Perhaps, as our religious right claims, religious zeal inspires morality in public life, but the record is unsettling.

We ignore the lesson in tolerance so excruciatingly learned by our predecessors at our peril. Religion may help to inspire morality, but it can never again be allowed to dictate it to society. Eschewing religiously derived views, the modern state must provide a compelling nonreligious—if possible, empirical—basis for any restrictions it places on its citizens.

In the case of abortion, such a justification does not exist. Motherhood—pregnancy, giving birth, nursing and raising a child—represents the largest commitment of which a human being is capable. Few if any activities can provide such a source of joy, none are more useful—yet what in the ordinary course of life could be more demanding or less possible to escape from than the situation of being a mother? This situation should therefore be chosen freely as much as possible—and because of its rewards, most women will choose it. Coercion is not required to ensure the perpetuation of the human race. But do we have the right to impose this commitment of confinement, risk, and the utter involvement of one's personality with another being on someone else? Can we be so fearless?

It is objected that people at least decide to have sex. Women, then, should face the consequences, namely pregnancy, of having sex. Why, however, must sex result in pregnancy? The function of sex is not just procreation, but the establishment, strengthening, and maintenance of a relationship between a man and a woman, as is attested by a growing body of scientific literature.

This view is clearly articulated in Desmond Morris's highly readable *Bodywatching,* for example.[28] Actually, sex serves functions that are more varied and complex than even these two functions of relationship building and reproduction. A recent work by the feminist sociobiologist

Sarah Blaffer Hrdy, called *The Woman That Never Evolved,* presents some stimulating ideas on this subject.[29] On a more general note, it is typical for a human activity to have varied and even conflicting ramifications. Elaboration and linkage characterize human (and often other primate) activities. People do not use clothes only to keep warm, food only to supply nutrients, or shelter only to protect against the elements. The rare exception to this rule would be an area of activity that in fact does serve only one purpose.

But in the case of sex, we need not even appeal to the complexity of human activities to justify a conceptualization of it that goes beyond mere reproduction. The significance of sexual activity in most higher primates goes far beyond the minimum copulations necessary for reproduction. Like aggression, sex is a basic social structuring force that is intimately and centrally related to the forms taken by individual relationships, to the place held by individuals in a group, and so forth. Whatever the theological basis may be for the idea that sex is for reproduction only (and that in consequence non-reproductive sex is sin), it makes no sense whatever from the point of view of the most elementary sociobiology.

It is clear that sex has functions besides reproduction which are not only legitimate but so basic to the way human relationships and societies are structured that we could not eliminate them if we tried. It is therefore very hard to maintain a rationale, without relying on faith alone— specifically on particular varieties of the Christian faith, since many Protestant churches and most of the other major faiths do not censure abortion—for the belief that sex should result in reproduction, or that "good" sex must involve the potential for conception. People have a right to have sex without exposing themselves to the enormous commitments of having children.

What, most seriously, of women who do *not* choose to have sex but who become pregnant anyway? Dare we require that women "face the consequences" of acts for which they are not responsible? Do we demand that sex must have punitive "consequences" for those who did not choose to have it, who are victims of rape or incest, or were too weak or immature to resist the psychological coercion to have sex in which some men specialize? Are we truly strengthening the family if we require a fourteen-year-old to become the mother of an illegitimate child, or a twelve-year-old impregnated by a father, uncle, or other close relative to nurse the offspring of such a union? If we encourage such girls to give away their babies, their emotional pain will be far greater than that arising from the more hypothetical separation of an abortion. Dare we blind ourselves to the plain emotional meaning of the desperate quests of thousands of mothers and adopted children for their biological families?

Let us state the truth squarely. Bourgeois, middle class values of stability, tolerance, and the right of individuals to protect their self-interest against the claims of society (which, like the Nazis, may want cannon fodder) support the tolerance of abortion. Safe, legal abortion supports the continuities of life: parental and sibling relationships unclouded by teenage motherhood, the crucial years of girls' educations uninterrupted by pregnancy or, conversely, schools' atmospheres unperturbed by the presence of unwed pregnant students. It improves the likelihood that each parental couple will be married, that each child will have two loving parents; that the care and planning responsible for the better physical and psychological health and success in adult life of middle class children can be increased within the middle class and perhaps extended to the less affluent; that, finally, we can move closer to the ideal of a world in which every child is wanted and each child has a fair chance. The option of legal abortion is an essential part of a "sexual safety net" for the inevitable failures of contraception and security against sexual violence, and for the major errors in judgment to which youth is prone.

In this regard, abortion is a men's issue as well as a women's issue. It is no accident that so many early marriages end in divorce. Boys who form families *after* they have achieved maturity will in most cases be better parents and more stable husbands.

The "bourgeois family"—controlled, self-conscious, a locus of planning, and widely reviled for all these traits—has been the greatest engine of personal satisfaction, social stability, and economic, political, and moral progress the world has ever seen. And in a variety of ways, a right to abortion is a significant contribution to family integrity and stability. Effectual compassion and the hope for human progress are indissolubly linked to the maintenance and improvement of the family; and, with a directness matched by few other rights, the right to abortion supports the family.

But this is not an argument feminists have been able to make. When one's whole philosophy, life-style, and politics are directed to undermining an institution, it is impossible simultaneously to defend it. Wishing to substitute one unfreedom for another, to liberate women from the family by forcing them onto the job market, to protect women from home life by mercilessly thrusting them into the public arena—having, in short, traded in the old mystique of femininity for the new mystique of feminism—feminists were reduced to defending the right to abortion in narrow terms, which continued to shrink in the course of the seventies as the logic of the feminist perspective sank in and undermined whatever libertarian impulse had been present in the original revolt.

As the decade of the 1980s approached its close, the moral high ground lay squarely with the opponents of abortion. The chance that, against the wishes of most Americans, abortion would soon become increasingly difficult to obtain was severely augmented by the moral weakness of the feminist defense of abortion rights. You cannot long defend freedom with intolerance, still less with a refusal to consider opposing points of view. How much longer could liberal Americans afford to leave the defense of their positions to a movement that had strayed so far from the principles on which liberalism ultimately rests?

Day Care

The feminist design to remake society requires a level of coercion irreconcilable with the respect for human liberty that is basic to the liberal spirit. The inherent radicalism of feminism is apparent in the feminist case for nationally subsidized day care.

The rationale for day care, as feminists present it, rests on the idea that "the sexes are inherently in everything alike." If the sexes are not doing all of the same things with the same frequency, it is believed that some injustice must be at work to cause this disparity. In addition, the feminist devaluation of the feminine encourages feminists to believe that all the things worth having are enjoyed by men—aggressive personalities, prestigious jobs, and freedom from child care. Sexual equality is defined by sameness of result. The sexes must be represented equally in all professions and at all levels of remuneration; or, failing that, their average rates of pay must be equalized through "comparable worth."

Feminists think the source of women's lack of "equality" (where "equal" is understood as "identical") resides ultimately in their domestic role. Housekeeping and child raising responsibilities hamper women's job performance, accounting for their lower average rates of pay. As long as women have primary responsibility for caring for home and, especially, children, they can never, it is argued, achieve equality with men.

To counteract this perceived problem, feminists propose a new norm. Men and women will both work full-time for the same average wages. Mothers will spend a few weeks or months with their infants, but will then return to full-time work. The infants will at that time be placed in full-time day care. From then on, they will spend their mothers' working days in day care until they are ready to go to school. School hours will be extended to increase the rigor of instruction so as to compete with European schools, which are imagined to be better than American schools, and to accommodate mothers' newly universal extended work hours. The young will benefit since, like Kate Millett, who argued that "the care of the young is infinitely better left to trained professionals rather than to harried amateurs with little time nor taste for the education of young minds," recent feminist writers like Sylvia Hewlett continue to argue that "education [is] a serious business to be undertaken by professionals in the schools, not by amateurs at home."[30] It would be not merely a necessary evil for some children but a positive benefit for all if they were to spend nine, ten, twelve, or more hours in day care or in school each day, so as not to inconvenience their mothers' employers.

Such a new norm, if it is ever implemented, would make it very difficult for American couples who fit the "traditional family" model to pursue the traditional American style of family life—exactly the result feminists seek to bring about. The equalization of male and female wages would make it very difficult for a man to support a family by himself and so would tend to oblige every woman to work, regardless of her wishes. Even the affluent, who no longer set the tone, might feel obliged to work, so as not to be hopelessly out of step with prevailing norms. It is easy to imagine that banks, insurance companies, credit agencies, condominium boards, and so forth, would grow suspicious of couples in which only one member worked. In addition, the tax increase necessary to implement universal day care would be substantial—4 percent of annual GNP if we are to imitate the French, as Hewlett recommends. This will be paid for, like all tax increases, by a net decrease in the overall efficiency of the economy—a tradeoff that may possibly be justified but must not be overlooked.

The inexorable effect of universal federally funded day care would be to tax families in which the mother stays home, further undermining the economic viability of their life-style choice, in order to benefit other families in which both parents have decided it is more important to work, or to benefit single mothers who have decided to bear children outside of marriage. If all the other kids are in school for ten hours a day, it is going to be very hard to keep little Johnny or little Molly at home, where they will miss whatever common experiences their friends and competitors are having. The centrality of home life will, not accidentally, be radically diminished in the American landscape. The family will inevitably come to play a lesser part in the socialization of children, and the state (which will hold the purse strings) a greater one. It is a vision that appeals to some. We may be sure it does not appeal to most Americans.

It is simply not possible to establish the feminist proposals for day care without these significant tradeoffs. Independence, with its virtues and scourges, would be traded for dependence on the state, with its virtues and scourges. The case for universal day care is anything but cut and dried. We cannot massively support all possible life-styles at the same time, and so must come to a decision: Is the standard American life-style to be the traditional family or not? The lines of battle over gender issues in the immediate future will be largely defined by the way individuals answer this question. The day care question, as feminists present it, forces us to choose squarely between a familist society and a socialist one. In effect, of course, America has already made its choice.

A more modest version of day care, though, may well prove to be acceptable. It does make sense to relieve working mothers of some of the burden of child rearing; and such work will undoubtedly be welcomed as interesting and worthwhile by many young women as the anti-feminine ethos of the Feminist Era recedes. In addition, the poverty and loneliness of a significant number of older women could possibly be alleviated and their abilities tapped as day care workers. If we are prepared to accept that women are society's primary child-rearers, new possibilities open up. Americans should begin to explore these possibilities. But the 1960s-style approach of imagining an untested solution to a hastily defined problem and then hurling billions of taxpayer dollars at it seems to have little chance of winning over the American public in the foreseeable future. The problems with the feminist proposals for day care underline the need to go back to first principles *before* trying to institute massive and expensive social reforms.

The unpleasant truth is that the real needs of working mothers will go begging until feminists manage to overcome their repugnance for the family and the free market, and so become able to imagine child care solutions that are compatible with these basic American institutions— or until the current feminist establishment is entirely replaced with a more effective advocacy that may well no longer even bear the name "feminism."

Day care presents several other problems that prevent it from being the unisex panacea that feminists claim it is.

It is now being discovered the hard way—although it could have been predicted—that there are sharp limits to the value of early education. Recent studies conclusively show that children who enter kindergarten or the primary grades when they are a bit older are far more successful. In one such study, it was found that 75 percent of children who had to repeat a year of school had begun younger, while none of those who had begun older had to repeat a grade. It is precisely an informal, individualistic setting that best nurtures young children. Day care may at times be the lesser of necessary evils; it is never the best of all possible worlds.[31]

In addition, day care centers turned out to be significant transmission sites for several minor diseases and a few major ones. A recent study from the American Academy of Pediatrics concludes that

> children in day care have higher rates of diarrhea, hepatitis A and meningitis than children who are not in day care. And there is some evidence that they are at higher risk for respiratory illness and cytomegalovirus (CMV) infection.[32]

A veritable slew of studies, rarely reported outside the medical literature, confirms that infants in day care have a higher rate of respiratory infections than infants cared for at home. Some of the "day care diseases" represent a particular threat to infants, with their immature immune systems.

Up to the late eighties, such facts remained shrouded in mystery where the general public was concerned: "Despite numerous articles in the medical journals describing significant health risks associated with group care for very young children, this issue has, up to the present time, received virtually no coverage in the mass media."[33] Anyone who brings up such considerations is quickly accused by feminists of playing on mothers' guilt—with the result that the day care diseases have remained politely unmentionable. The fact remains that any benefit middle class children may derive from day care is obscure and speculative, and in any case not the primary concern of day care advocates; while in terms of their physical health, it is clearly better for children to live at home.

Less drastic, but in the long run even more serious, is the emotional impact of day care on women and their children. Even women who have access to complete day care services usually find that having their children out of sight does not put them out of mind. While most men are able to drop off their kids at the center and get on with other things, many women find they are torn by guilt and anxiety at leaving their children in the hands of strangers. Women, but not men, can't stand to leave their kids in day care. As one mother reported of her husband, " 'Mark simply doesn't understand what it's like to drop Lisa at the day-care center and hear her start crying and begging, as she often does, 'Don't go, Mommy; don't go'. . . . And this is a *good* center.' "[34]

The psychological constellation of necessary versus elective day care is very different. It is one thing for a mother to explain to her child—and herself—"I'm leaving you because we need the money." It's quite another to explain, "I'm leaving you because I find it personally fulfilling to work." In the first case, the child is better able to perceive that he and his mother are both called on to make a necessary sacrifice. In the second, the child feels, correctly, that his mother is sacrificing his interests to hers, for no reason that is intelligible to him. With their uncanny grasp of adults' true motivations, children are keenly aware of the difference. While there is no limit to the ingenuity with which feminists explain away such genuine emotions, the fact remains that optional day care subjects the child to an early and powerful experience of systematic rejection from the one person on whom he most depends.

Reinforcing this situation, the day care environment demands a level of altruism and cooperation quite beyond what very small children are capable of. Forced to defer constantly to the needs of others before he is ready, the day care child often responds with a defensive selfishness. Young mothers have begun to talk of a visible distinction between "day care kids" and "home raised kids." The secure child, they feel, is actually better able to understand others' needs than the child who is pushed into a premature self-sacrifice whose basis he is completely unable to fathom. Adults may argue till Doomsday, but kids are unanimous: they want their own toys, their own space, and they want Mommy at home.

Mothers who do choose to stay at home find they do not undergo lobotomization. They do notice other things, though. As one young housewife in the suburbs of Hartford, Connecticut, explained to me, "By the time their father gets home, the children's best hours are over. He never gets to see them at their best except on weekends, and then we're always doing something we've planned in advance. But the best things happen spontaneously. I feel sorry for him—but of course we need the money from his job. I wouldn't miss these years for anything."

It is possible that neither the male career track with full-time day care nor the housewife pattern provide entirely satisfactory settings for either women or children. What is certain is that the virtues of the career track have been recklessly exaggerated, and its severe pitfalls minimized, in the course of the feminist devaluation of the feminine. In the meantime, the drawbacks of the housewife role have been exaggerated out of all proportion, and its major advantages for women and children disparaged and denied. The truth is that most men will be most happy with a full-time job; most women will be most happy with a modest extrafamilial commitment combined with a primary commitment to love in the family; and most children will be blissfully happy with this gendered situation.

Significantly, the day care argument is not based on children's needs, but on women's needs—as women's needs have been construed in the feminist devaluation of the feminine. It is time to go back to idealism. We must ask, What do children really need? What do women really need? What do men really need? if we are to halt the ongoing sacrifice of America's women and children to the bastard god of Success Through Stress.

Finally, day care is being promoted as something it is not. Day care is the most central issue to many feminists because they view it as the most essential step in eliminating sex roles. In practice, while universal day care would indeed force women onto the job market, it would have no effect on sex roles as such. As we contemplate the ruinous effects of past programs like Social Security, which now threatens to bankrupt the nation, and Aid to Families With Dependent Children, which has practically destroyed the family among the black poor, we may perhaps be forgiven if this time we look before we leap.

Universal day care would require the mobilization of millions of day care workers. In the absence of a drastic change in sexual personality, it is a foregone conclusion that the vast majority of day care workers will be women and that they will be paid a wage lower than the average rate for employed men. Universal day care will not equalize the sexes' average incomes—but it may well augment class disparity in America. Women will still care for children, only they will do so primarily as professionals instead of as mothers. In effect, millions of poorer women will be paid to care for the children of millions of richer women. Sex roles will be intact, though increasingly divorced from the family. The institution of universal day care will have little or no impact on the disparity between men's and women's wages for which it is being presented as a remedy. "Comparable worth" or a straightforward socialist leveling of all incomes will still be required to achieve unisex goals.

Comparable Worth

In the early 1980s, steam built up behind the issue of "comparable worth." Social liberals widely anticipated it would be a major issue of the decade.

The idea of comparable worth is fairly simple. Women are concentrated in certain occupations such as secretarial work and nursing—so-called "pink collar" jobs. By the end of the seventies, it was clear that this gendered division of employment was not on the point of breaking down anytime soon. Indeed, sometimes it seemed that no sooner was a profession sexually integrated than its gender balance radically tipped one way or the other, as happened for instance with real estate brokers. And in general the occupations primarily staffed by women were remunerated at a lower level than those primarily staffed by men. In 1955, the average female worker received fifty-nine cents to the average male worker's dollar. By 1985, the figure was only up to about sixty-four cents to the dollar—not significantly different from where it stood in the 1930s.

The doctrine of comparable worth described this pay disparity as the result of discrimination by employers, and ultimately as the fault of society at large for encouraging women, sometimes with offensive blatancy and sometimes with insidious subtlety, to pursue certain occupations at the expense of others in which they might have been more happy or at any rate better paid. Something, according to comparable worth, has been unjustly taken from women by society: it is time for society to pay it back.

This repayment was to take the form of introducing a scale of jobs rated according to their "comparable worth" to society, based on the level of education and skills required for their performance. Salaries were to be adjusted by legislative or judicial decree to eliminate wage differentials between "comparable" male- and female-dominated occupations. Secretaries, for example, were no longer to be paid less than janitors, or nurses less than sanitation workers.

Comparable worth reflected the sixties assumptions of the feminist mindset. The sixties, heyday of the Youth Culture, represented the intellectual triumph of emotional adolescence. Rage at the adolescent experience of powerlessness combined with responsibility, together with the recurring urge to slip back into the reassuring dependencies of childhood, supercharged the atmosphere of the Protest Era. The sixties protesters raged and fumed against society as against an unjust yet overindulgent parent, "proclaiming," "demanding," "declaring," always seeking a solution from an external source—the government, the military-industrial complex—which was felt to be both the cause of and the solution to whatever injustice was currently being resented. If this bad parent, society, would not lift the intolerable burden of life from their unaccustomed shoulders, they would *make* it behave and do so.

The idea of comparable worth is fundamentally bound up with this conviction of aggrievement. It is believed that a group of people—in this case women workers—have been willfully and unjustly deprived of their due, a situation they must protest so that it can be rectified through the benevolent intervention of the state. This belief had come to seem less than fully plausible by the late 1980s.

The notion of wealth was assessed from the same viewpoint of irresponsibility and aggrievement. The progressive mentality of the late sixties was inclined to view wealth as a symptom of exploitation at the same time it took its ease of creation for granted. If prosperity was not increasing, it was because exploitation had reached the point of self-defeat. Justice required the redistribution of wealth rather than its creation. There was no fear this would damage the economy, first, because it was felt the economy could easily sustain such damage and second, because the increase in justice that was expected from redistribution would, by reducing exploitation, actually have the net effect of *increasing* efficiency.

But all this could not happen without the benevolent intervention of the state, which, ironing out the kinks of capitalism into a nice uniform surface, would play the central role in this simultaneous increase of both social justice and, incidentally, economic efficiency.

In the mentality that feminists inherited as part of their sixties legacy, then, there was simply no reason not to go ahead with comparable worth. The bitterer lessons of the seventies were required to once more teach Americans the value of money.

It must be admitted that the scale of wages and benefits in our society approaches being a complete mishmash, defying any rational principle of organization including that of the free market. Local tradition and historical accident inflate or deflate the level of wages in entire industries and regions. Unskilled jobs susceptible to political patronage, like those of urban sanitation workers, or semi-skilled jobs in heavily unionized industries like auto manufacturing, may be remunerated at a far higher rate than highly skilled professions like those of military officers and college professors. What this demonstrates, however, is not that our society is unjust, and not merely that it is not a pure free economy, but that justice is not the main criterion of remuneration and that money is not the sole deciding factor in the choice of an occupation. The system brakes itself socially, since most people always have an "out" from their current status through such means as seniority, union struggle, or the accumulation of capital, and it brakes itself economically because the law of supply and demand is never so emasculated as to destroy the competitive efficiency of the economy as a whole. The result is the awesome social stability and no less awesome economic power of the United States— a unique combination in a society so diverse.

It did not take long for commentators to discover that comparable worth would pose a fundamental threat to American liberty and prosperity.

It is, for example, obvious to me that I would rather be a college professor than a plumber, even though I might be paid more as a plumber. Not all financial rewards are reflected in a salary. Pensions; use of athletic, medical, cultural, and library facilities; access to discounted housing; availability of grants, stipends, and fellowships; and frequent contacts with the powerful, who may have yet further benefits to confer, are some of the advantages which connection with a university, corporation, research institute, or government agency may have to offer. What is the dollar value of the near-absolute job security conferred by tenure, of annual vacations totaling three months or more, of assured and often high social status, to say nothing of the possibility of being one of the favored few who can do work that genuinely interests them? The overproduction of university Ph.D.s in the late seventies comes to seem less irrational, for with a bit of luck, the game could well be worth it for the individual.

The worth of a job to society cannot be measured in dollars any more than can its attractiveness to individuals. The president of the United States is paid a fraction of the compensation received by the chief executive officer of a major corporation, yet does anyone feel his job is less valued by society? What is true at the top of the ladder is true farther down. For example, one of the major attractions of secretarial work is its un-committed nature. Its temporary and episodic potential and standard-ized, readily transferable skills fit well into the life plans of many women, as does its typical lack of spillover into the non-working hours. Similarly, a major attraction of nursing is the opportunity to work with and to care for people in a structured environment in which one has a small but definite amount of authority and the unquestioned respect of society. I am not arguing that secretaries and nurses are adequately paid, nor am I arguing that they might not be well advised to seek higher pay through unionization, but simply that financial remuneration is only one aspect of the attractiveness of jobs to people. The factors that push people into one occupation or another are so complex as to defy any simple analysis, and can rarely be summarized as "discrimination."

The comparable worth argument looks worse the harder one looks at it. Are skills and education really adequate to establish the worth of a job? Even if it is assumed that non-monetary financial rewards, status benefits, opportunity for personal growth or lack thereof, and convenience could be factored into the equation determining "worth," how would one allow for such factors as boredom, stress, and danger, which are important for many jobs, to say nothing of talent, which affects skill and is important not merely for sculptors and ballet dancers but for high-rise construction workers, pilots, and urban planners, to name a few? The concept of "worth" becomes ever more elusive as one enumerates the minimal factors that must be considered to establish it, for this very good reason: economic worth is not determined by justice, but by a market, abetted by a host of additional factors.

There is simply no *a priori* standard of justice according to which jobs can be classified by their relative worth and then remunerated appropriately with money. The rule of thumb that a job is worth what someone will pay for it remains as valid, and as just, a principle as any.

Comparable worth actually threatens to radically increase the injustice of job remuneration. Because it requires the definition of what cannot be defined, namely, the financial worth of a job in non-market terms, it would of necessity create a set of arbitrary job valuations that would be unlikely to represent an increase in justice over our present messy but effective system.

Not only would such arbitrary valuations impose injustice, they would hamper economic efficiency, without which there is only uniform poverty with all its evils. One has only to look at the severe problems of "controlled" economies, whether in free societies such as Britain and Sweden or in Communist societies such as the Soviet Union and China—to compare, most dramatically, the exploding economy of South Korea with the stagnant economy of North Korea—to witness the economic strangulation caused by uninhibited state regulation of the market.

For most people, the comparable worth question—like other attempts at social leveling—thus comes down to this: Would you rather make ten thousand dollars a year knowing that everyone else with the same talents and education is also making ten thousand dollars a year, or would you rather make twenty thousand dollars a year knowing that some less capable people are making forty thousand?

Or to rephrase comparable worth specifically as a gender issue: which would we rather have, a society in which men and women both make on average ten thousand dollars a year, or a society in which women make on average twenty thousand and men thirty thousand a year? To answer that we would rather have a society in which both men and women average a hundred thousand a year begs the hard question of the crippling effect of uninhibited state interference. Others may answer that these are all excessive sums, that we should all live more simply. Tell this to the poor, after you have demonstrated a method to increase prosperity without recourse to the profit motive. This argument may make the rich feel greedy, but it can't help the poor who will still be needy.

Comparable worth has truly been dubbed "the feminist road to socialism."[35] How did such an unworkable—and unpopular—idea come to carry weight in feminist councils?

The answer lies in the continuing influence of their sixties heritage on feminists—a heritage they had yet to critically reexamine. Whatever its merits as a philosophy of gender, contemporary feminism stood revealed as a problem area of social progressivism—and a disaster area of economic theory. In light of the comparable worth flap, could one seriously maintain, by the late 1980s, that feminism is a universal theory well suited to lead humanity into a better future?

By the mid-eighties, the idea of comparable worth was effectively dead among thoughtful Americans, as the unprecedented scope of the government interventions required to implement it became apparent. Comparable worth survived only in the increasingly anachronistic platform of the national Democratic party, which had developed an intimate and little-known relationship with the National Organization for Women.

The Ferraro Fiasco

This chapter so far has examined feminist politicking on some of the major "women's issues" of the late seventies and early eighties. ERA was promoted by browbeating legislators and patronizing the public; the pornography issue was exploited as a "consciousness-raising" device to politicize women against men; abortion was defended with a clannish and counterproductive self-righteousness; day care was advocated in order to undermine the family; and comparable worth revealed the lack of hard thinking beneath the feminist conception of a "nonsexist" society. These various strands were to come together in Geraldine Ferraro's candidacy for the vice-presidency. All these individual failures of feminism ultimately derived from the feminist perspective, which defined femininity and masculinity as diseases, marriage as female slavery, homes and families as women's prisons, and men as the enemy. Just as the feminist perspective underlies the forms taken by feminist ideology, behavioral ideals, science, and literature, so it also underlies the objectives and strategies of feminist political causes. In the case of Geraldine Ferraro, the result was nothing short of a fiasco.

In July 1984, having survived a grueling round of primary and caucus fights over the previous eight months, former vice president, senator, and longtime Hubert Humphrey protégé Walter F. Mondale prepared to accept his party's presidential nomination at the Democratic National Convention in San Francisco. The question of the day, its answer eagerly awaited by politicians, reporters, and the public, was who Mondale would select as his vice presidential running mate. Various groups had their candidates, several of whom made the pilgrimage to Mondale's home in Minnesota to meet with the nominee. In the prevailing atmosphere of uncertainty and intrigue, nobody seemed to have a clue whom he would select. After several days of increasingly frenzied media speculation, the answer came: the 1984 Democratic vice presidential candidate would be a little-known congressional representative from Queens, Geraldine A. Ferraro—the first female candidate ever to run on the national ticket of a major party.

Four months later in November, the Mondale-Ferraro ticket went down to disastrous defeat in the national election, as conservative father-figure and ERA opponent Ronald Reagan swept every state in the nation except for Mondale's home base of Minnesota—which approved its favorite son by a mere five thousand votes.

Had Ferraro's presence on the ticket done anything to avert this crushing loss?

Ferraro turned out to be an extremely difficult person. A careful reading of her own account of the campaign in *Ferraro: My Story* (1985) suggests a personality that is far from unattractive but must have been hell to work with in the context of a political campaign. She had set out to be treated "like an old Southern senator" to avoid being taken for granted because she was a woman—overlooking the fact that she was a fairly junior congresswoman and that anyone in her position owed the major candidate a little dishwashing.

At the very first strategy meeting of the joint campaign, Ferraro became incensed when campaign chairman Jim Johnson produced a campaign schedule for her marked out in ink. Ferraro felt it should have been in pencil, so she could alter it.

"How come the chart isn't in pencil?" she demanded. "Evidently you do not want any input about the campaign from me."

The meeting turned into a debacle as the campaign manager uselessly protested that he "just thought the charts would be easier to read that way."

Ferraro petulantly refused to follow the schedule, claiming she needed more time to organize her staff—a point she could scarcely have made in a less tactful manner.

"I'm delighted to go to California," she said. "But I will not go on the eighth [as scheduled]."

She proceeded to lecture the seasoned pros around her, including Mondale, who had just come off a grueling nonstop year on the campaign trail: "This campaign has to be professional from the beginning," she proclaimed.

As Ferraro describes the scene, "I had had it with all of them. And Fritz Mondale [who had listened to this entire affair in silence] had had it with me. By now he was beet red with anger. 'I guess that ends the conversation for tonight,' he said. And he walked out of the room."[36]

This unpromising beginning to a joint campaign exemplifies what seems to be a characteristic pattern in Ferraro's behavior. She seems to be incapable of initiating. She waits until a situation arises in which she feels unjustly imposed upon and then energetically protests it— righting the situation, but never getting much past square one. She usually keeps her own nose clean but doesn't accomplish very much. This pattern is repeated so often—with regard to the protracted imbroglio over her finances, her difficult relations with Jesse Jackson's supporters, and so on—that it seems to represent a basic strategy in her approach to life.

The put-upon feeling to which she is prone dwells comfortably with her acceptance of the feminist perspective. Whenever she feels put-upon, she is quick to attribute her feeling to an attempt to discredit her because she is a woman. (Imagine how far Margaret Thatcher would have gone with such an attitude.) Perhaps Jim Johnson really did just use ink because it was easier to read, not because he assumed she could be pushed around because of her sex—many months after the campaign, while overseeing the writing of her book, Ferraro has yet to consider this obvious possibility.

As for the tough, vicious, and effective campaign the Republicans fought specifically against her, she is unable at times to resist a Grand Conspiracy theory, that she was savaged for being a woman. In 1972, Thomas Eagleton was removed as George McGovern's running mate after Nixon's "dirty tricks" team discovered that he had been hospitalized for depression, a fact that, like the financial irregularities of Ferraro and her husband, had been unknown to the Democratic presidential candidate. The situations present almost identical parallels. Could Eagleton have claimed he was savaged for being a woman?

Ferraro became incensed in her televised debate with Vice President Bush when, disagreeing with her interpretation of the Marine deaths in Lebanon, he said, "Let me help you with the difference, Mrs. Ferraro, between Iran and the embassy in Lebanon."

Ferraro felt this remark showed "Bush's true chauvinistic colors" and shot back with "Let me say first of all that I almost resent, Vice President Bush, your patronizing attitude that you have to teach me about foreign policy. . . ."[37]

"Patronizing" is a heavily freighted feminist signal word, intended to suggest its target is retrograde and overbearing, a "male chauvinist." Since there was nothing "patronizing" about Bush's remark (although it was aggressive in tone, as is appropriate in a political debate), the impression given was that Ferraro had been waiting to sling the charge at him all along. The incident spoke volumes for the self-righteousness to which Ferraro seems to be prone, and which the feminist vocabulary so readily complements.

It is easy to imagine the roller-coaster ride on which the Soviets and other world leaders would take a person like Ferraro. This has nothing to do with the fact she is a woman. There are more than enough tough, effective female national leaders at present and in recent history—women like Golda Meir, Indira Gandhi, and Margaret Thatcher—to confute any notion that women can't lead nations. The problem is that being a woman is not by itself a sufficient condition for leadership. Yet being a woman seems to have been Ferraro's main qualification. Time and again in reading Ferraro's account of the campaign, one has the feeling of someone out of her depth who is constantly trying to create and maintain a series of facades—of strength, of toughness, of decisiveness, of being in control of the facts—for which she feels little personal affinity.

> If the first woman vice-presidential candidate was going to be seen as weak, we might just as well stay home. I wasn't going to let anyone think I could be marched over by black, white, male, female, or anyone else. I never had allowed that impression in my entire time in Congress, and if I had to prove that I wasn't going to allow it at any point in the campaign, this was the time to start.[38]

Or again, as she prepared to debate George Bush on national television, she thought that

> I had to prove for all the women of America that I could stand toe-to-toe with the Vice President of the United States and hold my own. "There's a sense of responsibility that I have to do what I'm doing and not make a mistake," I said to columnist Ellen Goodman . . . .[39]

Ferraro's entire political career appears as a struggle engaged in always from principle, never from conviction. Ferraro's determination to prove she is up to the job of being vice president is matched only by her lack of genuine self-confidence.

Why did the Democrats pick a candidate with Ferraro's limited experience, personal touchiness, and lack of effectiveness? Beyond these problematic personal characteristics, why, when the front-runner was a left liberal like Mondale, was a second left liberal chosen, who would ordinarily be thought to appeal primarily to the same Northeast and West Coast constituencies as the major candidate?

Ferraro was selected because she was the candidate of organized political feminism. This is equally clear in her style, her views, and her previous associations. For instance, when Ferraro later told her side of the campaign, she placed NOW at the head of a list of organizations that were "involved in the campaign—and in my nomination."[40]

As the feminist candidate, Ferraro had a strong appeal to Mondale. The media at the time tended to overlook the fact that Mondale had for many years been the most consistent supporter of feminist positions among U.S. politicians; he had a near-perfect record of yes votes on "women's issues." In addition to supporting practically every piece of legislation advocated by feminists, he was the co-sponsor of the Brademas-Mondale bill on day care. Only being a woman could have made Mondale a more ideal candidate to feminist groups. Because of this record, Betty Friedan expressed high praise for Mondale in *The Second Stage* (1981); by contrast, Mondale was attacked by anti-feminists like George Gilder as early as 1973 for his support of feminist social legislation, and again by Phyllis Schlafly in 1978.[41] Mondale was accustomed to listening carefully to feminists and to taking their pronouncements seriously.

He had plenty of opportunity to do so. Mondale opened his door to feminist leaders while he was making his decision on the vice-presidential candidate. He was told in effect by feminists that a woman candidate would win him the election. As Betty Friedan reported a conversation she had with Mondale at this time,

> I told him that I had started an organization that had made history [NOW] and I sensed now that a woman on the ticket would give historic resonance to his campaign. It would mobilize the gender gap, embody the "new politics," and lead to the future. After all, women had delivered fifty-eight percent of the New York primary vote, the turning point of the campaign.[42]

This "gender gap" mentioned by Friedan was big news in 1984. Pollsters had noted that men favored Reagan by a slightly higher percentage than women. Starting from this rather isolated fact, feminists launched themselves on some free-flown flights of fancy which received massive and on the whole uncritical media distribution.

The gender gap theory is an object lesson in the self-deception encouraged by the feminist perspective. Women, it was asserted, felt uninvolved in the political process because it had traditionally been arrogated by men. The presence of a woman on the ticket would make them feel that the political process was indeed theirs, bringing them out to vote in unprecedented numbers. As we have seen, the word "women" has two meanings for feminists, first, female persons, and second, feminists. These meanings often fail to coincide. The confusion of these terms, as in "women's issues," "women's books," "women's studies," or indeed "the women's movement" provides an enormous tactical advantage to feminists, creating a rhetorical device which embodies their claim to speak for all women. Although politically expedient in the short term, this device is fatal to clear thinking. By confusing these terms in the fall of 1984, feminists convinced those who believed in their ability to speak for American women that a female candidate would result in a Democratic landslide—the opposite of what actually happened that November. Ideology had been mistaken for reality.

Feminist promotion of the gender gap idea may have been self-serving, but it was on the whole sincere. The idea of a gender gap fitted in well with the unabashed female chauvinism to which the feminist perspective had given rise. Let us recall once more the key to the feminist perspective, the idea that the ills of the world are caused by men oppressing women. Women, it is felt, are better than men, since men are the villains of history, responsible for pollution and torture, the crimes of the past and the ills of the present. In the feminist lexicon, women are the human sex. In particular, they are more humane than men, more inclined to cooperation than to competition, free of aggressive tendencies, and therefore in favor of peace and opposed to war: men embody the opposite tendencies.

The gender gap was thus believed to express women's moral superiority. Women's supposed preference for left over right policies reflected their greater acuity, a consequence of their greater connected-ness with their own beings. This moral superiority was assigned a very definite political cast: it favored liberals over conservatives, the Demo-crats over the Republicans, Mondale (as long as he picked a female running mate) over Reagan.

Opposing arguments were rarely heard. But suppose the opposite were true? Why should the masculine perspective not have something to contribute to political debate, particularly since men's experience of group power games from boyhood through adulthood is, as feminists would agree, so considerable? Suppose men's preference for Reagan over Mondale reflected *their* greater political acuity? Why should men not have a better understanding of the realities of geopolitics, if they created those politics? If men really are more oriented toward abstraction (destructively so, feminists argue), might this not have value when applied to economic matters, so crucial to the national well-being? As the architects of war, might men not have some grasp of what is truly necessary to prevent it, beyond the poorly thought out pseudopacifism of Steinem and company?

If this is true, then men's preference for Reagan over Mondale, far from reflecting the obsolescence of masculinity, as feminists claimed, can be read in a positive light. Men may have tended to favor Reagan because they have a better idea of what is involved in politics.

The female chauvinism of the gender gap theory makes no more and perhaps less sense than the converse argument: that the gender gap highlights the superior political wisdom of men. But in any case, such arguments over the meaning of the gender gap are of limited value because the gender gap is so small. Sex is a poor predictor of how people will vote.

One other reason for feminist overenthusiasm about the gender gap in 1984 was that it suggested their effort of fifteen years to split the sexes was finally beginning to succeed. At last, feminists enthused, women were voting as a group, defending humane values against men.

The gender gap was the carrot held out by feminists to Mondale and other Democrats. There was also a stick. In 1984, Mondale had some reason to listen to feminists apart from his personal support for their cause. A lot has been made of Mondale's eagerness to appease every special interest group, yet the plain fact is that the strength of other political constituencies such as labor and blacks at the 1984 Democratic National Convention in San Francisco paled beside that of feminists. The delegate selection rules adopted at the start of the seventies required that one-half of the convention delegates be women; in this case "women" tended to translate into its alternate meaning of "feminists." No less than *four hundred* delegates to the 1984 Democratic convention were members of NOW—an astronomical figure unmatched by any other organization. As a result of this strength, prior to her nomination Ferraro already chaired the powerful committee responsible for drafting the Democratic party platform.

The potential for pressure of this powerful representation was freely used, as feminist leaders pronounced dire warnings that Mondale's campaign would lose their support if he failed to select a woman as the vice-presidential candidate. More concretely, the four hundred NOW members at the convention formally resolved that if Mondale failed to choose a woman, they would force his hand by nominating their own candidate from the convention floor. What the NOW members demanded was not merely a woman, but specifically a feminist; a "woman" who was "strong on women's issues," in the language of the NOW resolution.[43] It is impossible to guess exactly what role this pressure played in Mondale's decision to select Ferraro, but it is clear that he was under the gun from feminists—far more so than from other constituencies. Such was the feminist stick.

Feminists thus secured the nomination for Ferraro through at least three routes: through Mondale's habitual support for feminist causes, which went back to his time as a member of Congress in the early seventies; through convincing Mondale and many others that women voted differently from men, and that in particular, they opposed Reagan and would flock to vote for another woman; and through political pressure on Mondale and the Democrats in general, exercised by the four hundred NOW delegates at the 1984 Democratic convention.

It is difficult not to see the 1984 election as a referendum on feminism. In Mondale and Ferraro, the Democrats had an almost perfect feminist slate. The Ferraro-drafted party platform contained most of the NOW agenda. On the opposing side, Reagan squarely opposed most of the feminist positions, including the popular ones for legal abortion and ERA. When he selected Ferraro, Mondale was fifteen percentage points behind Reagan—a lead that Ferraro's presence on the ticket did nothing to dissolve. The problem is not that Ferraro failed to swing the nation— and in particular the nation's women—behind the Mondale ticket: this would have been too tall an order for any vice-presidential nominee. The problem lies in the extravagant claims of feminists who maintained that this would indeed happen, that "women" in decisive numbers would support another "woman." Feminists misled those unwary enough to believe them—apparently including Mondale himself—into believing that when feminists speak, it is not merely as another political pressure group, but as the voice of the world's women. The extravagance of this pretension makes it appropriate—indeed, necessary—to judge them by a higher standard than we would apply to those who promote the narrow self-interest of a well-defined group like the oil lobby. The 1984 election showed the hollowness of the feminist claim to have a direct line to the thoughts of the nation's women and consequently to be able to speak on their behalf and predict their behavior at the ballot box. As one disgruntled Democratic pro carped when the lopsided election returns came in, "In the olden days of politics, the worst thing you could say about a man was that he couldn't deliver his wife. Well, these people can't deliver their sisters."[44]

Not only did feminists' confident political predictions fail to materialize: what did occur was the reverse of what they had predicted. While a slightly higher percentage of men than women voted for Reagan, post-election analyses showed that women too had voted overwhelmingly for Reagan. So much for the gender gap; so much for the idea that a feminist woman would be an irresistible advantage to the Democratic ticket.

Worse, feminist support was probably a liability for Mondale: the heavy pressure he was placed under at the convention contributed to the image of indecisiveness that dogged him throughout the campaign. At all events, feminists turned out to be highly uncomfortable, inconsiderate, and ungrateful allies. Despite his long-standing, near-perfect record on "women's issues," Mondale was treated to feminists' suspicion and hostility at a time when his campaign desperately needed to project an image of unity. Quite literally believing the feminist perspective—indeed, it was the guiding idea of their very lives—the feminists active in the 1984 campaign were unable to stop projecting the negativity of that perspective. Any man, even a feminist supporter of such impeccable credentials as Mondale, could only be accepted provisionally and continued to be the subject of scrutiny and suspicion. We have already encountered this feminist tendency to slash male allies in the discussion of ERA. The same message, "Take it like a man, you wimp," was liberally and publicly supplied to Mondale by his feminist allies. After fifteen years of taking heat from conservatives for his pro-feminist positions, little wonder that Mondale finally exclaimed in exasperation at feminists' continued sniping during his presidential campaign: "Why am I working so hard for women and everyone is still mad at me?"[45]

The lesson in this is clear: politicians had better not simplemindedly seek alliances with feminists; and they had better disabuse themselves of the notion that feminists speak "for women." The politician who declares himself an advocate for "women's issues" suggests either that, first, he supports the feminist program as it exists, including the belief that the family in its present form is "obsolete" and complete with feminism's statist, anti-family agenda, or that, second, and more likely, he is foxed by "women's issues" and has not yet discovered that most women are not feminists. Because feminist women are aware on some level that they don't really represent all women, they will react with more or less veiled derision to any man naive enough to take their pronouncements at face value—as was the case with Walter Mondale.

In 1984, the Democrats were still the majority party at the local and state levels, but at the national level this status was problematic. Under the McGovern rules of delegate selection, the national Democratic party was hostage to its left wing. How much longer would this situation be allowed to continue? For as long as it was forced to truckle to its left ideologues, the Democratic party would remain out of touch with the pulse of the American people, and consequently find it difficult to win national elections.

Feminism in Politics: Conclusion

Through the seventies and into the early eighties, American feminism presented the paradoxical spectacle of a movement that continued to grow in importance while becoming less and less effective in promoting its political ideas. After the initial legislative and judicial victories of the late sixties and early seventies, the progress of feminist political causes ground to a virtual halt. One feminist cause after another collapsed. Even the proportion of women in Congress fell. Organized political feminism, as exemplified by NOW, seemed to have developed a Midas touch in reverse.

The paradox of increasing acceptance and declining influence is explained by the nature of feminism as a program guided by an ideology. The fundamental assumption of this ideology is the anti-feminine, anti-male belief structure of the feminist perspective. The greater contemporary feminism's success, the further it was able to give free rein to its fundamental negativity. In addition, feminism's very power as a social movement gave its ideology an authority inflated beyond any reasonable claim in the emotions of its disciples. Because of the fundamentally negative and unrealistic nature of the feminist perspective, it embodied a self-defeating counterprinciple which was bound to emerge with greater clarity in proportion to the successes of the movement.

Today the feminist causes, good and bad, are in full retreat. ERA and comparable worth are virtually dead issues. The feminist anti-pornography campaign is at best becalmed. In many states, only the crumbling shield of *Roe vs. Wade* stands between legal abortion and a new prohibition. By the time the credulous Walter Mondale bowed to the pressure of NOW and accepted Geraldine Ferraro as his running mate in his disastrous 1984 campaign against Ronald Reagan, feminist support had become a liability for most U.S. politicians.

Why the pressure group that by definition should have been working to improve the lot of women became a liability to the Democrats and proved totally unable to affect the 1984 election outcome ("these people can't deliver their sisters," as the disgruntled pro carped after the election) is a question worth exploring, especially since the Democratic party still seems unable to distance itself from the influence of the National Organization for Women.

The answer to this puzzle is that contemporary feminism has never been anything so straightforward as an attempt to improve women's lot. It is a reformist movement functioning on mistaken premises about the nature of men, women, and society. It is strongly affected by a radical utopian view of the glowing future that the millennium of "women's liberation" is wrongly claimed to ensure. It was in its inception anti-male in viewpoint and out of sympathy with the vast majority of middle class American women who find fulfillment as wives, mothers, and members of a community. Contemporary feminism was tinged from its beginning with a poisonous negativity[46] that destroyed feminists' sense of proportion and made them unable to communicate effectively with individual American politicians or to carry their case to the American public.

Organized political feminism speaks neither for women nor for progress; it increasingly reflects the views of an embittered minority which has long since forfeited the respect of the "transitional" generation of its parents and has now lost the pulse of the rising generation. Feminists are currently admitting in droves that the early seventies movement was guilty of "excesses." In *The Second Stage* (1981), for example, Friedan admits that feminists "overreacted" in the 1960s and 1970s. We have recovered from the "stridency" of that period, they assure the public; you can trust us now. But the difficulty with feminism lies not in its superficial mistakes but in its basic assumptions. As long as the feminist perspective is adhered to, as long as feminists believe their enemies are femininity and men, the same self-defeating negativity will prevail. Only by going back to first principles, analyzing where they went wrong, and taking steps to correct their position, can feminists—or the Democratic party—or American liberals—arrive at a new consensus, one that will reflect the needs and aspirations of the majority of Americans.

PART III

New Perspectives in Science and Gender

Chapter 7

The Rise and Fall
of Cultural Determinism

The feminist analysis has seemed convincing because it built on a widespread belief that there are no important differences between the sexes. Each sex, in this view, shares the same perceptions and motivations, and undergoes the same maturational processes. Emotionally, psychologically, sexually, behaviorally, the sexes are the same except for the form and function of their genitals.

Therefore, the more just society toward which we are evolving will see the disappearance of sex differences, except for the irreducible constants of biology, which are limited to these differences of genital shape and pregnancy. At present this belief is the consensus view of gender in the Western world. It is shared by most educated Americans, French, Swedes, and Israelis, among others. We can term this belief "unisexism."

The most common scientific justification in America for unisexism is cultural determinism, the theory that human behavior is produced by "conditioning," which if it were stripped away would somehow leave us as more valid, unique individuals, "the way we really are"—which, it is believed, has nothing to do with gender.

Cultural determinism is the latest incarnation of the *tabula rasa* theory propounded by John Locke in the eighteenth century: that the human child is a blank slate upon which society writes to create a personality. This is a radical idea. It is also severely reductionist. To maintain it in modern times requires the argument that evolution, which determines most animal behavior, at some point ceased to affect human beings. The idea used to explain this discontinuity is the modern anthropological concept of "culture."

The culture concept is not the only version of the *tabula rasa* theory in circulation, however. B. F. Skinner's behaviorist psychology, which makes much of the presence of conditioned reflexes in animals and humans, is one alternate version. Marxist theory is another, which describes economic forces as determinative. There are two reasons for bypassing these alternate versions in order to concentrate on cultural determinism. The first is that cultural determinism, unlike behaviorism or Marxism, is a widely accepted belief in contemporary America, which prepared the ground for the rapid acceptance and continuing credibility of contemporary feminism. The second reason is that the updating of the culture concept leaves the behaviorist and Marxist assumptions in wreckage as effectively as their direct refutations would.

The Nineteenth Century

The late nineteenth century is remembered as the age of the robber barons, fabulously wealthy industrialists like Andrew Carnegie and Cornelius Vanderbilt who drove their managers like slaves, formed cartels, smashed unions, fixed prices, and built mansions of uncertain taste but unabashed opulence in Newport, Rhode Island. Following this orgy of muscular capitalism (so goes the standard historical interpretation), an Age of Reform gave rise to a mostly successful struggle for anti-monopoly legislation, protective labor legislation to prevent the exploitation of women and children, government safety standards for food and drugs, and other innovations we now take for granted.

Another way of looking at this era, though, is that the period from the end of the Civil War to the Spanish American War witnessed a totally unprecedented growth of America as a nation. The West was settled, the railroads were built, and great institutions like the University of Chicago were founded or vastly expanded. Unchecked by barriers to immigration, millions of immigrants from all over the world sought, and for the most part found, better lives in the United States. By the end of the period, America had changed its status from a minor power to the most powerful nation in the world (though it had yet to really flex its muscles). Then, as so often in American history, a period of vital change and progress gave way to a period of taking stock and retrenchment.[1] America needed a breather to recuperate and correct the abuses to which the vast changes it had so rapidly undergone inevitably gave rise.

The leading social theorist of the late nineteenth century was Herbert Spencer. Spencer was a frosty intellectual who despised businessmen and politicians. In his best-known writings he spoke out forcefully against imperialism, colonialism, militarism, and government waste and corruption. Though Spencer was primarily a political theorist rather than a scientist, his views on man in society, expressed in *Social Statics* and other works, reached a level of sophistication far in advance of his contemporaries, from Taine to Marx.

But when social reformers sought to give a scientific underpinning to their politics, they felt obliged to attack Spencer's use in social theory of the evolutionist concept of "the survival of the fittest." Spencer, the very model of the tolerant liberal thinker, a "progressive" if there ever was one, and a pacifist to boot, was subjected to one of the most thorough-going character assassinations in the history of thought. Capped in the 1940s by socialist Richard Hofstadter's masterpiece of innuendo, *Social Darwinism in American Thought,* this effort resulted in the teaching of generations of American college students to believe that Spencer advocated "social Darwinism," a philosophy which, students were told, was an apologia for imperialism, militarism, upper-class exploitation of the workers, and all the other causes which Spencer himself passionately opposed. Spencer, the quintessential liberal, who hated aristocracy, the officer corps, and established religion, was painted as a reactionary. Someday some researcher may reveal the roots of the two conflicting strands of the eighteenth century Enlightenment which were thus thrown into bold relief: the concept of society as an organism developed by Spencer, and the concept of society as a mechanism espoused by his opponents.

Biology, the reformers thought, was antithetical to the cause of reform. They advanced a variety of arguments designed to show that human behavior was in fact determined, not by universal, immutable factors, but by local, alterable ones. Accusing Spencer of "biological determinism," they proceeded to advocate the contrary, "environmental determinism."

But a new discipline, cultural anthropology, was to supply the specific theory of environmental determinism peculiar to the twentieth century, sweeping earlier versions before it. This was "cultural determinism," the creation of one of the reforming intellectuals of the time, Franz Boas, and his followers. Sociology was henceforth to rely on anthropology for its theoretical underpinning.

Franz Boas and the Culture Concept

Franz Boas is accurately known as the father of American anthropology. He was a member of the great German intellectual migration which, starting in the 1880s and continuing into the 1960s, stimulated the creation of a world class American academic culture. His students became the leading lights of American cultural anthropology. No modern scientific discipline is so specifically located in one country as cultural anthropology, or so closely associated with the legacy of one man.

Boas's work attacked the social science simplemindedness of the Victorian era. Boasian anthropology represents in part an attempt to dissect human experience down to its constituent parts—an activity not without analogy to the deconstructionism of our own day.

The views against which Boas struggled centered around "evolutionism" and "racialism." Evolutionism, best known through Herbert Spencer's work, attempted to integrate the recently formulated theory of evolution with the study of human society and behavior. Part of Boas's critique of evolutionism was merited. Evolutionist anthropologists of the nineteenth century often lumped together superficially similar traits and confidently arrayed them into grand schemes of evolution whose successive stages led in an orderly sequence from the most primitive tribe right into, as one recent observer notes, the door of the anthropologist's own study.[2]

Boas proposed that instead of taking for granted that a trait represented a similar phenomenon wherever it occurred, it was necessary to study the function of the trait within a given society. For instance, "totemism" in one tribe might mean something entirely different from "totemism" in another.

> In some cases the people believe themselves to be descendants of the animal whose protection they enjoy. In other cases an animal or some other object may have appeared to an ancestor of the social group, and may have promised to become his protector, and the friendship between the animal and the ancestor was then transmitted to his descendants. In still other cases a certain social group in a tribe may have the power of securing by magical means and with great ease a certain kind of animal or of increasing its numbers, and the supernatural relation may be established in this way. It will be recognized that here again the anthropological phenomena, which are in outward appearances alike, are, psychologically speaking, entirely distinct, and that consequently psychological laws covering all of them can not be deduced from them.[3]

In other words, similarities between societies do not provide a basis for comparison between them. It is necessary to grasp, not the statistical incidence of a trait, but its psychological essence.

All societies, therefore, require intensive and detailed study—"primitive" cultures no less than "civilized" ones. Boas doubted that societies could be classified along a straightforward continuum of development, leading from savagery through barbarism to civilization, and ultimately to modern European civilization. He argued that the change from primitive to civilized society did not, as was then believed, involve a change from simple to complex forms. For example, primitive music was often so complex it would challenge "the art of a skilled virtuoso."[4] Societies do not move from simplicity to complexity in an orderly progression; some traits may grow more complex while others grow simpler. This was the corollary of cultural determinism: cultural relativism, the idea that all societies are of equal complexity and, presumably, equal moral stature. The idea of the unilinear moral and material development of civilization, one of the basic assumptions of nineteenth-century thought, was a major casualty of the emergent Boasian paradigm. In its place came the idea of cultural relativism: that all cultures are equally valid and can be understood only in terms of the totality of their individual values and circumstances.

In addition to his conflict with evolutionism, Boas struggled against scientific racialism. "Racialism" was a respectable explanatory stance in the nineteenth century, and is not to be confused with "racism," or organized xenophobia. The two sometimes overlapped, but they are not the same thing.

Again, part of the Boasian critique was merited. Racialists argued that the "genius" of a "race" explained its level of "culture." Skulls were painstakingly measured and compared in order to determine the relative intelligence of different groups. Quite apart from their confusion of brain mass with intelligence, the level of statistical rigor of the racialist scientists was often laughable by contemporary standards. Windy speculations on the nature of different "races" were occasioned by the examination of a few skulls.

But it is all too easy (and has been all too common) to go too far in criticizing such early efforts. Boas himself practiced this kind of anthropology extensively in his early years. However naive some of their ideas may now appear, the racialists played a central role in the development of physical anthropology. Mere grace, at least, should discourage us from mocking our grandparents, for we ourselves will most certainly look as foolish to our grandchildren, and our own most fervently held notions may as miserably fail the test of time.

Most racialism was too unsystematic to qualify as a determinism. While explaining behavior in terms of "race," it was usual to identify environmental factors such as climate, diet, economics, religion, and marital customs as influences on "the genius of a race," typically within a very short time horizon of one or two generations; so that, although it is at present commonly depicted as a hideous rationalization for imperialism and racism, in practice the racialism of the nineteenth century tended to function as a neutral force, as more of a vocabulary than a theory. It is true that Houston Stewart Chamberlain, whose theories helped inspire the Nazis, used racialist concepts, but so did early feminists like Olive Schreiner and Beatrice Hale, whom today's feminists claim as their distinguished forebears. The innocence of most racialist thinking is best grasped in the still-current phrase "the human race."

Yet Boas correctly perceived that the attempt to explain differing social forms in terms of differing physical inheritance was fundamentally mistaken. His critique of racial determinism was a necessary and major advance. Boas pointed out that the barbarians of Western Europe were far from civilized at a time when other parts of the world were far more advanced. If their "genius" was so great, why had they lagged so far behind? The stimulation of the Roman Empire which gave rise over long centuries to civilization in Western Europe provided Boas with a clue to one of the most important concepts of twentieth-century thought: culture.

If biology, through "race," was not responsible for the nature of human societies and individuals, what was? The answer formulated by Boas and his followers in the first two decades of the twentieth century was: culture, used in a new sense. Culture, not inherited traits, as the racialists had thought, determined the nature of a given society and the capacities of its members.

In the nineteenth century, the noun "culture" was rarely if ever pluralized.[5] "Culture" was a state attained only by the highest civilizations, and within them only by the most gifted, best-educated, or highest-born individuals. Michelangelo, Descartes, and Queen Victoria had culture; the local blacksmith or the South American Indian imported as a curiosity manifestly did not.

In Boas's work, this concept of culture was transformed. If the music of some primitive peoples was complex enough to challenge "the art of a skilled virtuoso," could culture really be the province of just one civilization? It began to seem appropriate to speak of the "culture" of all peoples. Boas's refutation of the scientific racialists supplied another clue: if human attainment was not racially determined, but was transmissible, in the way that Rome transmitted civilization to Europe, then "culture" became separable from any specific people.

The word "culture" thus underwent a transformation. From a term for the most specialized activities of the highest reaches of European society, it became a property which all peoples possessed to an equal extent. Anthropologists began to think in terms of many widely varying "cultures." The singular "culture" of the nineteenth century became the plural "cultures" of the twentieth.

Science and Politics in the Boasian Paradigm

Boas did retain the idea that modern Western society stood at the head of the march of humanity, but his conception of its superiority was reduced to vague terms, which could easily be overlooked. Boas at times betrays an intellectual elitism, as when he says that "the average man in by far the majority of cases does not determine his actions by reasoning."[6] Most of the functions of modern society confer no special enlightenment. It is from the perspective of the scientist that the superiority of modern civilization exists. Scientists represent the next stage in the evolution of civilization, in which national boundaries will be transcended.

> A soldier whose business is murder as a fine art, a diplomat whose calling is based on deception and secretiveness, a politician whose very life consists in compromises with his conscience, a business man whose aim is personal profit within the limits allowed by a lenient law—such may be excused if they set [other considerations] above common everyday decency. . . . They merely accept the code of morality to which modern society still conforms. Not so the scientist. The very essence of his life is the service of truth.[7]

Anthropology had a major role to play in Boas's vision of human progress, by searching for principles "that have a greater absolute truth than those derived from a study of our civilization alone."[8]

Alongside the tolerance implied by cultural relativism, Boas made frequent use of a dichotomy between "modern" and "primitive" types of culture. This dichotomy predisposed him to overestimate the differences between human beings, as when he stated that in primitive society, we find an inextricable association of ideas and customs relating to society and religion. . . . It will be recognized that we have here again a type of association in primitive society which has completely changed with the development of civilization.[9]

Here Boas overlooks, first, the continuing importance of religion in modern society and, second, the extent to which the secularized ideologies of modern civilization mimic the functions of religion. I have in mind not just such belief systems as Marxism and feminism, but specifically Boas's faith in science as a transcendent value, "the ice-cold flame of the passion for seeking the truth for truth's sake" to which he liked to refer.[10] Boas believed that scientists' superior status, arising from their calling as keepers of the flame of a transcendent value, gave them the ability to generalize directly about human affairs.

In fact, Boas's cultural relativism and scientific objectivism were associated with strongly held ideological beliefs. Many of these beliefs sound like surprisingly up-to-date expressions of the American left. The main point is not that these ideas are wrong—although I think they are—but that the pose of scientific detachment never existed for Boas. Boas thought that science should play a very specific role in the political evolution of human society. He did not hesitate, for example, to use the scientific case for cultural relativism to establish a political point in a letter to the *Nation,* written in 1916 while Boas was campaigning for American neutrality in World War I:

> The American, on the whole, is inclined to consider American standards of thought and action as absolute standards, and the more idealistic his nature, the more strongly he wants to "raise" everyone to his own standards. For this reason the American who is cognizant only of his own standpoint sets himself up as arbiter of the world. He claims that the form of his own Government is the best, not for himself only, but also for the rest of mankind; that his interpretation of ethics, of religion, of standards of living, is right. Therefore he is inclined to assume the role of dispenser of happiness to mankind. We do not find often an appreciation of the fact that others may abhor where we worship. I have always been of the opinion that we have no right to impose our ideals upon other nations, no matter how strange it may seem to us that they enjoy the kind of life they lead, how slow they may be in utilizing the resources of their own countries, or how much opposed their ideals may be to ours.[11]

In this passage, Boas was arguing for American neutrality in World War I, claiming that Americans' cultural insularity prevented them from appreciating the virtues of Kaiserist authoritarianism—an argument that was to resurface periodically in the *Nation* and elsewhere. In the sixties, it was one of the main arguments against American involvement in Vietnam. Books opposing American involvement in Indochina, like Edwin O. Reischauer's *Beyond Vietnam* (1967), argued that Americans could not understand the appeal of Communism to Eastern peoples because they were ignorant of the Confucian tradition.[12] This was before the boat people and the killing fields. More recently, the same argument of American insularity has been used to explain the "irrational" distrust Americans feel toward the Soviet leadership.

Influenced by the activist milieu of Columbia University in the early years of the century, Boas went so far as to briefly join the Socialist party. From then on, he involved himself extensively in political causes. While some of these causes, notably the effort to improve the condition of American blacks, were just and urgent, we cannot overlook the fact of the pervasive pressure of politics on American anthropology in its formative years.

Human life is composed of equal parts of stability and movement, but Boas early on pledged his undivided faith to one side, that of movement—an elementary and fatal mistake for a synthetic thinker. As he wrote,

> My whole outlook upon social life is determined by the question: how can we recognize the shackles that tradition has laid upon us? For when we recognize them, we are also able to break them.[13]

That tradition—namely, the conditions of life as they now exist— might have value is an alien concept to the Boasian mindset. Progress is defined as breaking with tradition.

Cultural relativism, which in appearance leads to a value-free conception of society, in Boas's case at least concealed some powerful ideological biases. Science and politics were inextricably mixed in the genesis of cultural anthropology. Cultural anthropology developed as a science with a mission: to discover endless diversity in human societies so as to further the plausibility of social reform in America.

The Rejection of Biology

Boas was driven to reject biological explanations as a result of his conflict with evolutionism and racialism, but he also possessed an independent hostility to biology that derived in part from his absorption in the ideas of Rudolph Virchow, a fierce opponent of Darwin. Virchow argued that man is phylogenetically distinct from the rest of the animal kingdom, going so far as to dismiss the first Neanderthal fossil discovered as a pathological individual.

In addition, Boas was inspired by Kant's idea that man makes his own world.[14] Through Boas's neo-Kantism, the antique mind-body dichotomy directly entered the twentieth century. Boas's philosophical beliefs, and not merely the exigencies of his struggle against evolutionism and racialism, influenced his rejection of biology and heredity as significant factors in human affairs.

Most American anthropologists agree that theirs is a biological science. As Boas wrote, "The science of anthropology deals with the biological and mental manifestations of human life as they appear in different races and in different societies."[15] Anthropology aims to unify the "biological" and the "mental," to use Boas's categories. But in practice this is mere lip service paid to an ideal which is continuously receding into an ever-more-distant future. Biology is accepted in principle but rejected in practice.

The roots of this approach are found in Boas's work, the thrust of which was to multiply the complexity of anthropological studies. By successfully reinstating "the much-abused historical method" over the methods of the "hard" sciences as the means of anthropological investigation, Boas virtually guaranteed that his followers would be unable to create generalizations about man and society, whether true or false, hasty or circumspect. As he insisted,

> One of the fundamental points to be borne in mind in the development of anthropological psychology is the necessity of looking for the common psychological features, not in the outward similarities of ethnic phenomena, but in the similarity of psychological processes so far as these can be observed or inferred.[16]

This point seems eminently reasonable—until one stops to consider what Boas is really recommending: that similarities between ethnic phenomena be discounted unless it can be proved through a detailed study of each culture that such phenomena resemble each other from a "psychological" as well as from an apparent viewpoint. In light of his struggle against evolutionism and racialism, this emphasis on variation may have been understandable; but by forbidding comparison of the general features of societies, it deferred the goal of a unified science of man to an indefinite future. That goal was postponed to cultural anthropology's equivalent of the Second Coming or the classless society: one could not even begin to ask biological questions until all the cultural ones had been answered.

This disintegration of the conceptualization of human social life was accelerated by Boas's heavy use of the modern-primitive dichotomy, which by its nature emphasizes the alienness of primitive experience to our own. Scholars are unlikely to seek parallels where they expect to find contrasts.

Science for Boas was dispassionate in name, passionate in practice. Hostile to tradition, he founded one of the most powerful traditions of the twentieth century. Opposed to authority, he was himself highly authoritarian, to the point of arrogating the entire discipline of American anthropology as a personal fief.

The picture that emerges from the work of Boas and his followers is that of a kaleidoscopic jumble of cultures, some happy, some embittered, all uniquely interesting human adaptations to the exigencies of nature and the foibles of their own histories. It is an engaging, enormously stimulating picture. In it, the four thousand or so known societies become a grab bag of culture traits from which we can, if we are wise enough, choose the best to improve our own culture. This idea of the infinite plasticity of the human being has been singularly important to the feminist conceptualization of a remade society. But is it true?

Margaret Mead and the Return of the Noble Savage

The connection between anthropological science and social activism which lurked in the work of Boas jumped confidently into the American limelight with the work of his student Margaret Mead.

It is difficult to overrate Mead's influence on American thought. Hundreds of young Americans decided to become anthropologists after reading one or another of her many works. Although some anthropologists take her ideas for granted, and others reject them as too simple, Mead's work remains the main transmitter of anthropological ideas to the

American public. For the past sixty years, since the publication of her best-selling *Coming of Age in Samoa,* she has spoken as the voice of authority to Americans on questions of sex, gender, and culture. Mead's influence on American thought has surpassed that of any other theorist, including Freud. Quite apart from her enormous prestige within the anthropological profession, she wielded an even greater direct influence on the American public, to whom she was able to express herself without the intermediaries of professional consensus or journalists' reporting.

Mead made Boasian ideas on culture into a virtual dogma accepted by social scientists and the general educated public alike. She was the great popularizer of cultural determinism—particularly as it applied to the sexes. Mead dressed the idea of cultural determinism in vivid, unforgettable color and brought it to the non-anthropological public as a simple, irrefutable idea which promised a better society. It was quite a pitch.

> Many, if not all, of the personality traits which we have called masculine or feminine [she wrote] are as lightly linked to sex as are the clothing, the manners, and the form of head-dress that a society at a given period assigns to either sex. . . . We are forced to conclude that human nature is almost unbelievably malleable, responding accurately and contrastingly to contrasting cultural conditions. The differences between individuals who are members of different cultures, like the differences between individuals within a culture, are almost entirely to be laid to differences in conditioning, especially during early childhood, and the form of this conditioning is culturally determined. Standardized personality differences between the sexes are of this order, cultural creations to which each generation, male and female, is trained to conform.[17]

Mead's most glamorous evidence came from her studies of gender in primitive societies. In the course of a single trip to the South Seas, she discovered three primitive societies, all living close together, which showed—so she said—that the differences in temperament we associate with maleness or femaleness are arbitrary. According to her report on one of these societies, an obscure mountain tribe in New Guinea,

> We found the Arapesh—both men and women—displaying a personality that, out of our historically limited preoccupations, we would call maternal in its parental aspects, and feminine in its sexual aspects. We found men, as well as women, trained to be co-operative, unaggressive, responsive to the needs and demands of others. We found no idea that sex was a powerful driving force either for men or for women.[18]

This seemed like an impressive proof that a society could, without any serious difficulty, assimilate the temperaments of men and women to a unitary standard without contradiction from biological forces, and thereby establish sexual egalitarianism. Men could be feminine, women masculine, both sexes masculine, or both sexes feminine. These different solutions, Mead argued, had their characteristic strengths and weaknesses. It was up to Americans to choose the balance that would be best for their own society.

A grand design, indeed: what crushing responsibility, but, too, what a heady sense of power Mead gave her readers! Let us "choose" the society we wish to become, declaimed the liberals of the time; let us "re-invent" our culture, trumpeted its visionaries; let us "redefine" our sexuality, polemicked feminists. Cultural determinism's appeal was its very indeterminacy: it reduced the demands on social reformers to optimism, idealism, and imagination. Good intentions became all, while attempts to understand humanity as a unified species were despised as sour grapes, for were not all cultures "relative"? The grand idea that had informed the work of liberal thinkers from Montesquieu to Hayek—that society is a complex dynamic organism which engenders a morally mixed unity— was forgotten in the national wave of enthusiasm for cultural determinism. Cultural determinism thus became an essential part of the social liberal plan for a better society.

This accounts for the ferocity with which American leftists have defended cultural determinism in general and Mead's work in particular, even if they are neither informed nor concerned about the progress of anthropological science. Criticism of cultural determinism is not seen as an honest difference of opinion but as retrograde, a betrayal of the liberal consensus and thus of freedom and progress into the hands of fascists, racists, and other extreme right-wingers who wish to preserve the old and crush the new. Science must wait on politics.

Boasian ideas on sex and temperament were so widely disseminated that it simply never occurred to most college-educated Americans to doubt them. As of this writing, you still cannot open an anthropology, sociology, or psychology textbook without finding Mead's reports on the Arapesh, the Tchambuli, and the Mundugumor presented as definitive proof that "culture" wields absolute sovereignty over human life.[19] Mead's reports of 1925 on Samoa and 1931 on New Guinea have had a singularly long run. The textbooks are commonly sketchy on dates. You would never suspect, to read most of them, that well over half a century has passed since the grand dogmas of cultural determinism were established by Mead's field research. Yet this is an eternity in the progress of modern science. Despite the difficulties of working outside the politicized consensus on cultural determinism, American scientists have been anything but idle in the interim. American social thought in the eighties depends heavily on the social science of the twenties. It is time to catch up.

Mead was a first-rate writer whom everyone enjoys reading, but as a theorist of human personality she had severe limitations. There is no use beating around the bush in an attempt to preserve the cult of Mead, whom many Americans, including myself, read with fascination in earlier years. Mead habitually allowed her conscience as a social reformer to overwhelm her conscience as a social scientist. When the scientific evidence didn't fit the reformist point she wanted to make, she often contradicted it—or simply ignored it. Mead was an extremely strong personality with a determination to remake the world as she conceived it should be. When she wanted to see something, she tended to see it, whether it was there or not.

The tendency to remake evidence to fit conclusions, or even to assert conclusions that are flatly contradicted by the evidence, can easily be detected by the alert reader in Mead's descriptions of sex and temperament in the three societies of her often-reproduced 1931 study. For instance, Mead describes the Arapesh as a sexually egalitarian society whose "conditioning" produces a "feminine" personality in both men and women—then casually mentions "the quarrels when a woman is abducted."[20] In addition, it turns out that all the Arapesh leaders are male. Another people, the Tchambuli, are said to socialize men into femininity and women into masculinity. But as a recent critic writes, "Dr. Mead points out that the Tchambuli boy's initiation consisted of the boy's killing a [human] victim and hanging the head in the ceremonial house as a trophy; it is difficult to see this as an indication of 'male femininity.' "[21] Mead's *Sex and Temperament* overflows with such wild inconsistencies. Her readers were not getting the full story.

Mead realized she was presenting an incomplete picture to her audience. Her motivations for doing so were those of other cultural determinists: biology is too dangerous. Even though it isn't really true, we must behave as if culture determines all, because this is the most productive political route.[22]

The studies which, half a century after their publication, are still widely believed to prove sex and temperament are unrelated, in fact do nothing of the sort. This is true not just of Mead's studies of gender and temperament but also of the evidence she and other cultural anthropologists amassed to prove the larger point that the parameters of human life are limitlessly variable, "responding accurately and contrastingly" to whatever behaviors a given culture prescribes.

The same defects that vitiate Mead's studies of gender and temperament are found in her study of adolescent girls in Samoa—her first and most celebrated case of the unlimited plasticity of human beings. Mead claimed to have discovered that the stress of adolescence was not necessary, for in Samoa it was "the time of maximum ease."[23] Even the phases of human psychological maturation were said to be culturally determined. The Samoan adolescent simply flowed, as it were, from an easy childhood, unmarred by parental harshness, into an untroubled adolescence, in preparation for an undemanding adulthood. As Mead described this island idyll,

> As the dawn begins to fall among the soft brown roofs and the slender palm trees stand out against a colourless, gleaming sea, lovers slip home from trysts beneath the palm trees or in the shadow of beached canoes, that the light may find each sleeper in his appointed place.[24]

What a vision of bliss to her American adolescent readers, wracked by sexual frustration, the inability to understand the opposite sex, acne, parental pressure, and the insistent demands of adult society! No wonder cultural anthropology has been so well-liked in twentieth-century America. What other science could promise a future of love under the palm trees?

Indeed, the only wonder is that we have not all packed our bags and left for Samoa, paradise on Earth. But had we done so we would have discovered it never existed—except as the projected fantasy of Western social critics who find it expedient to cling to the idea of the Noble Savage.

An authoritative critique of Mead's Samoan reports unmasks their phantasy. Predictably, Derek Freeman's *Margaret Mead and Samoa* (1983) was attacked less on scientific than on political grounds. Freeman's debunking of Mead's Samoan research was seen as an assault on the social liberal world view. This was correct, for Mead's work had indeed provided fifties and sixties liberals with their most essential assumptions about man and society.

Freeman spent far more time in Samoa than Mead, who never learned to speak fluent Samoan. He asserted that her description of Samoan life as an idyll of parental permissiveness, peace, and easygoing sex was false. Samoan parents were harsh disciplinarians. Adolescence in Samoa was marked by severe stress, which led to frequent psychological breakdowns and high delinquency rates. Illicit sex, defined in the same ways as in traditional Western culture, was severely tabooed. Violence, including murder, was common. Rape not only occurred as often as in most Western societies, but was culturally validated by a practice called *moetotolo* in which men tried to insert their fingers into the vaginas of sleeping girls. The virginity of upper-class brides was forcibly taken in a public ceremony. And at the time Mead visited this innocent Eden, its leaders were incarcerated in colonial jails for seeking political autonomy.

Mead depicted a hierarchical society as egalitarian, a puritanical society as permissive, a violent society as peaceful, and a politicized society as a tropical paradise. Whatever the real virtues of traditional Samoan society may be—and Freeman obviously thinks they are considerable—they are different from the projected ideal of the Noble Savage into which Mead cobbled the evidence she collected during a short stay in one location.

Mead's account of Samoa is a utopia imposed on an ethnography—which is why it so thoroughly captured the imagination of the American public.

Are we ready to move beyond utopia?

Is the Family Universal? Spiro and Malinowski

While Freeman's debunking of Mead's Samoan reports[25] was creating a national furor, a more quiet but perhaps equally effective attack on culturist orthodoxy had been launched by a widely respected American anthropologist, Melford E. Spiro. In 1982 Spiro published a critique of the work of Bronislaw Malinowski called *Oedipus in the Trobriands.* Malinowski, a Polish expatriate who moved to London as a young man, played a role in Britain similar to that of Boas in America, as the founder of a national approach to anthropology. The American school became usually known as "cultural anthropology," the similar British school as "social anthropology."

In addition to the parallel with Boas, there are significant parallels between Malinowski and Mead. Malinowski exercised the same popularizing function in Britain as Mead in the United States. Malinowski's work, like Mead's, reported on the little-known climes of the South Seas, the last word in unknown exoticism to Westerners early in the century. Like Mead, Malinowski focused on sexuality, the fashionable topic of the day as the Jazz Age discovered Freud. What could have been more up-to-the-moment in the Roaring Twenties than a book called *Sex and Repression in Savage Society*? Even greater success was enjoyed by its sequel, *The Sexual Life of Savages* (1929), whose lurid title contributed to its long-lasting popular appeal. (Reader, be forewarned: anything by Malinowski is dry as dust, except for his personal diary—but that is another story.)

The conclusions Malinowski drew from his fieldwork paralleled Boasian theory. Malinowski described sexuality, temperament, and social organization as independent elements in human culture. The most outstanding characteristic of human life is a near-infinite diversity which proves that people's needs and potentials are almost endlessly mutable. Human nature does not fit any universal scheme.

Malinowski's rejection of human nature was directed less toward evolutionism than toward psychoanalysis. Freud, of course, claimed that his theory of personality was universally applicable. In his work among the Trobriand Islanders, Malinowski proposed to test one of the cardinal tenets of that theory: the Oedipus complex. If it were universal, he would certainly find evidence for it in the Trobriands.

Instead, he reported that the Oedipus complex does not exist there. The Oedipus complex is replaced in the Trobriands by what Malinowski dubbed a "nuclear complex." The male Trobriander exhibits repressed desires not to kill his father and make love to his mother, as psychoanalytic theory predicts, but to kill his mother's brother and make love to his sister.

This differing "nuclear complex" arises, according to Malinowski, from the differences between Trobriand families and the bourgeois Viennese families with which Freud was familiar. In the Trobriands, permissive child rearing allows the boy's libidinal desire for the mother to spend itself naturally before puberty. As a result, repressed incestuous urges toward the mother simply do not exist. Too, unlike European fathers, Trobriand fathers are uniformly kind, warm, loving, and patient. They therefore do not evoke their sons' hostility like the tyrannical fathers of Europe. The authority figure within the Trobriand family is not the father but the mother's brother, who exercises punitive authority over the boy. Repressed hostility is directed toward this maternal uncle. Desire for the sister is caused by a severe incest taboo, which is so pervasive that the boy is always sexually conscious of his sister.

Sifting through both Malinowski's evidence and more recent studies of the Trobriands, Spiro argues that these interpretations are all wrong. Repressed libidinal desire for the mother is pervasive among Trobrianders, as shown by the very Trobriand myths cited by Malinowski, which include an "improved" Oedipal myth in which a son who kills his father lives ever after in conjugal bliss with his mother. In fact, Malinowski's mythological evidence suggests that a particularly *strong* Oedipus complex prevails in the Trobriands. Trobriand fathers are no doubt more warm and tolerant than the average Western father of Malinowski's day, but, contrary to Malinowski's claim, they remain the primary authority figures for their children. The "jural authority" attributed to the mother's brother does exist; but, given the infrequent contacts boys have with their mother's brothers and the lack of severity with which they are treated, there are no grounds to assume "hostility" from the boy. In fact, says Spiro, a careful reading of Malinowski's works shows no evidence for this postulated hostility.

On the basis of Malinowski's own evidence, it thus appears that the structure of Trobriand families does not differ significantly from that of families elsewhere. Despite the relative prominence given the mother's brother in the boy's upbringing, the father remains the principal authority figure. The same forms of incestuous desire exist in the Trobriands as elsewhere, along with the same hierarchy of incest taboos. Son-mother incest is most severely tabooed, and occurs least frequently. Father-daughter incest is less severely tabooed, and occurs somewhat more frequently. Brother-sister incest, which Malinowski says is most severely tabooed, is in reality *least* severely tabooed and occurs most often.

In addition, Spiro argues, Malinowski's refutation of the Freudian Oedipus complex was irrelevant because it was based on a misunderstanding of its nature. The Freudian Oedipus complex is triangular. The boy wishes to make love to his mother. He hates his father as a rival for his mother's affections. In turn, the father may resent the child as a rival to his own attentions. Malinowski's postulated "nuclear complex," by contrast, is a two-way constellation, which fails to consider the relationship between the boy's desire for his mother and hatred of his father.

All this, however, is resolved in early childhood in the ordinary course of events. Spiro points out that Malinowski did not examine early childhood at all among the Trobrianders. The Trobriands "nuclear complex" alleged by Malinowski occurs not in early childhood but many years later on the brink of puberty. Malinowski's argument is thus doubly irrelevant to the question it addresses: he both misunderstood the form and overlooked the timing of the Freudian Oedipus complex.

One need not subscribe to psychoanalytic theory to appreciate Spiro's main point: the diversity Malinowski claimed to have found in family structure did not exist. The main interest of *Oedipus in the Trobriands* is not whether its implicit rehabilitation of Freud is correct or productive, but its affirmation of the universality of the human experience—in this case, the nuclear family and its emotive significance to the individual.

Despite its dubiousness, Malinowski's "proof" was widely accepted. An especially strong impact was made by the idea that some other relative, such as the mother's brother, might readily take on the functions of a parent. This often-quoted "fact" has played a major role in the devaluing of the family among "progressives" in our century. Malinowski's picture of the Trobriand "nuclear complex" was widely received as justifying the possibility and desirability of "alternative family types" in which to raise children. It was easy to cheer on the demise of an institution which seemed to be doomed by women's economic independence, sexual freedom, divorce, and single motherhood, if that institution was believed to play no essential role in the development of healthy human beings—was in fact a threat to sound emotional health by encouraging unhealthy closeness and neurotic dependency, as suggested both by the Trobriands "nuclear" complex and a (superficial) reading of the Oedipal one. If the family was so unimportant to human well-being, then who cared if its demise was imminent, except for a few hidebound conservatives and some older adults too trapped in neurotic life-styles to think freely?

On the basis of limited fieldwork, Mead and Malinowski indulged themselves in hasty generalizations about man and society that had a profound impact on following generations. Mead's *Coming of Age in Samoa* and Malinowski's *The Sexual Life of Savages* are anthropology of limited scope applied to social problems of vast implication *à outrance*. Why did it take so long to discover the mistakes in their work?

To answer this question, it is necessary to consider the enormous prestige each of them wielded in their professions. Cultural anthropology was for many years virtually synonymous with Boasianism—and Mead was the great spokeswoman for Boas's theories. She stood at the pinnacle of her profession; her early work provided the most powerful underpinning for the social liberal consensus which was dominant in academe; and by the sixties she had become a virtual living national monument, "the symbol of the woman thinker in America," as Betty Friedan wrote in *The Feminine Mystique.*[26]

An anecdote widely circulated in anthropological circles suggests something of the immunity from attack which Mead's position conferred. In the fifties Larry Holmes, a graduate student in anthropology, returned from a field trip to Samoa flushed with excitement. Mead, he had discovered, was wrong, and he, Holmes, would make his name refuting her. Back in his department, he sat down in his professor's office and poured forth his new ideas. The professor, a famous anthropologist, listened in silence. When Holmes finished, the professor looked him in the eye and said deliberately, "Don't attack Margaret."[27]

Anyone who has been a graduate student can appreciate the lack of alternatives available to a person in Holmes's situation. The university is the last surviving medieval institution in America, in which a guild mentality among the tenured elect prevails, along with near-absolute authority over the candidates for initiation. This no doubt represents the best of all possible worlds, but our admiration for the system should not blind us to its pitfalls. For a mere graduate student to attack the greatest living American anthropologist, without even the support of his professor, was unthinkable. Holmes's critique never appeared. Instead, he produced a standard ethnography in which he took care not to make waves.

Since it would have been a form of professional suicide for an American anthropologist to attack Mead—as one can readily gauge from the virulence and innuendo expended on Derek Freeman who, not coincidentally, is Australian—no professional critique of her Samoan work appeared in her lifetime; and since there was no professional critique, there was no critique at all. Samoa was remote and hard to know: terrain tailor-made for the appropriation of specialists. One could not just hop on a plane with a phrase book and go off to confirm or refute Mead's findings.

Similar considerations in Britain protected the work of Malinowski. Malinowski virtually *was* British anthropology to his students, who dominated their profession.

As we have seen, attacks on cultural determinism were seen as a betrayal of the social liberal consensus which dominated academe up to the 1980s. Cultural determinism was such a fundamental assumption of this consensus that to question it was to guarantee exclusion or expulsion from the cushy club of intellectual inquiry. Conversely, those who produced works which seemed to validate the dominant ideology could secure an easy path for themselves, and often high reputation. As Melford Spiro says, it is "remarkable" that Malinowski's report on the Trobriand family was received with so little skepticism. Spiro concludes it is a "scientific myth" which "enjoys uncritical acceptance because it serves important functions for those who believe it to be true."[28]

The Universal Nuclear Family

The radical-liberal consensus of the sixties based its goals and methods on what seemed to be definitive accounts of the plasticity of human nature in general, and of gender traits in particular. We no longer face the same intellectual landscape. Over the past decade, every one of these demonstrations of gender plasticity has conclusively been shown to be false.

The attempt to discover variation everywhere has led to widespread underestimation of the consistency of the basic elements of human society. The family is a case in point.

It is still common to encounter statements that the extended family preceded the nuclear family and is the primordial form; or that in our time the family is losing its importance in favor of the individual. Such assertions, though they may possess a limited validity as descriptions of changes in degree, obscure the readily accessible fact that *the nuclear family is the basic building block of all societies past and present.* A society such as Tibet's, which sequesters a large part of its male population in monasteries, continues to rely on the nuclear family for procreation and primary socialization. A society which emphasizes the extended family more than our own remains based on nuclear family units. It is therefore misleading to speak of the extended *versus* the nuclear family as if they were a dichotomy, or as if there were any possible choice between the two. Without the prior existence of the nuclear family, there is no such thing as an extended family.

Even in our own relatively fragmented society, individuals continue to live in families, or to wish they did. The usual response to the absence or inadequacy of a biological family is, precisely, to create a new family, either through marriage or through the development of a network of peers who are as much as possible "like a family." At an absolute minimum, it seems safe to say that virtually all members of our society have been profoundly touched at some period in their lives by a family to which they have in some sense belonged. Although the prominence of the family in the lives of individuals in contemporary America is often—though by no means always—less than in other times and places, there is no indication whatever that the basic emotions attached to the family have in any way altered, or that the indispensability of the specifically nuclear family has in any way lessened.

Yet that was precisely the impression given by standard cultural anthropology. A passage from one of my college anthropology textbooks from the seventies gives the flavor in its discussion of the family in America:

> For an older generation one important meaning for the family was stability; the unit was expected to endure. Furthermore, family life meant authority for the parents, especially for the father, coupled with lifelong responsibility for his children and wife. Today family life no longer has such meaning to many Americans; stability and authority have been replaced by mobility and equality. Of course for such a large society "family" is going to have different meanings for different groups.[29]

It is true that there had been at the time this passage was written a relative change away from "stability and authority" toward "mobility and equality," but the authors' cultural determinism has caused them to confuse relative and absolute change. The family continues to stand for stability and to represent authority in essential ways; although weakened, its function has not changed at all.

What is equally serious, this passage implies that "family" is an extremely flexible, variable social concept, which is not the case. The forms of the family may be radically different in some sectors of our society—consider the prevalence of unwed mothers among the black poor—but these differences are associated, not with instructive alternatives, and still less with heroic challenges to social norms, but with severe social pathologies. There is "a" family, whose breakdown is a symptom of a disrupted society and has serious consequences for the well-being of individuals and social groups.

The Grail of Primitive Egalitarianism

A common rhetorical trap has been to describe societies as sexually egalitarian. The ideology of unisexism made the search for a sexually egalitarian society—one in which male dominance does not exist and which has no gender roles—a sort of Holy Grail for some anthropologists. Like the Holy Grail, it can never be found.

But in the late sixties, when feminist doctrine was forged, accounts abounded of supposedly egalitarian societies. These reports carried the imprimatur of the best social science. Confusing relative egalitarianism— a society which is seen, rightly or wrongly, to be more egalitarian than another society used as a baseline, which was usually our own, or sometimes that of Freud's Vienna—with absolute egalitarianism—a society which is truly egalitarian—these accounts presented seemingly solid evidence that identical status for the sexes would be a simple thing to implement. In fact, these accounts implied, sexual equality was the state of nature of human society.

Guided by cultural determinism, a massive effort was underway, long before contemporary feminism appeared, to prove that the essential nature of the sexes in society is sexual egalitarianism and role resemblance. Those participating in this effort tended to overlook its self-contradictory nature. For if cultural determinism is correct, human beings have no nature at all, neither hierarchical nor egalitarian, similar nor differentiated. You can't have cultural determinism without cultural relativism.

Unperturbed by this contradiction, social scientists produced quantities of evidence, much of which seemed incontrovertible at the time, to prove that the essential nature of human societies is sexually undifferentiated. Primitive man was imagined to live in a condition of peace with his fellows, harmony with nature, equality between the sexes, and non-violence toward other living creatures. Hierarchy, madness, difficult parent-child relationships, dissatisfaction with gender roles, war, gratuitous violence, xenophobia, misogyny, rape, difficult births, indeed all things cruel except for disease and hunger (perhaps not even these) were unknown to humanity in its pristine state before the coming of civilization.

Mead's gentle, peaceful Samoans found their echo in Jane Goodall's reports in the sixties and early seventies on chimpanzees. Primatologists who generalize from their evidence to human behavior—which is why most of them study primates in the first place[30]—were at this time divisible into "chimps" and "baboons," according to the species they felt most accurately reflected the condition of primitive man: the peaceful, vegetarian, sexually undifferentiated forest-dwelling chimps, or the vicious, hierarchical, radically male-dominated savanna baboons. The chimp argument—inherently stronger because chimpanzees are more closely related to humans—depended heavily on the work of Jane Goodall, who has spent years observing chimpanzees in their undisturbed habitat in the African rain forest. And the chimps were everything a good social liberal could wish them to be, it appeared: peaceful, affectionate, emotional, inquisitive, almost vegetarian, and nonviolent—though it was a truism of the times that man is the only animal who kills his own kind. It was easy to argue that people are really like chimpanzees, that if civilization could be reorganized to approximate the virtues of the natural state, mankind would easily slip back into its natural egalitarianism and pacifism. Two of the most powerful and least plausible ideas of the eighteenth-century Enlightenment thus reared their heads together in the second half of the twentieth century: that man is a blank slate, but carries within him a Noble Savage. The close association of these two ideas had not weakened a bit in the intervening two hundred years, any more than had their mutual exclusivity.

This agreeable fantasy began to fall apart in the late seventies as shocking new reports began to come from the Gombe Stream Reserve where Goodall worked. Chimpanzees, it turned out, fought one another, quite violently at times. Then it was observed that groups of young males patrolled the perimeter of a chimpanzee group's territory, attacking intruders from an adjacent group. Then an actual chimpanzee war was observed, in which the patrolling males systematically killed off all the males of the adjoining group one after the other. In the meantime, a female chimpanzee was observed to make a habit of killing and eating the babies of other chimpanzee females, a habit which she passed on to her daughter, who helped seize the babies from their mothers. From Locke, the science of primatology was thrown back to Hobbes: beasts really were beastly. Could the animal element in man then be so innocent?

The early chimpanzee reports, used as an example of the innocent goodness of proto-humanity, were supplemented by accounts of many primitive and a few advanced cultures that were said to embody the same virtues of peacefulness, egalitarianism, and so on. One of the most convincing cases was that of the San and other tribes of Bushmen, a remnant of the primitive race which occupied sub-Saharan Africa before the coming of the black man.

The Bushmen were idealized in dozens of widely read anthropological reports as "The Harmless People,"[31] whose culture shared all the qualities wishfully attributed to chimpanzees. They were widely used as "exemplars of gender equality."[32] If the chimpanzees represented the conditions of human evolution, the Bushmen represented the conditions of human prehistory, the long hunter-gatherer phase of human existence.

But extended observation since the sixties has been no kinder to the idealization of the Bushmen than to that of the chimpanzees. More recent work by Melvin Konner and others has shown that, far from being the peaceful, egalitarian people portrayed in previous studies (the Bushmen's marginal habitat was often attributed to their lack of cultural aggressiveness), the Bushmen exhibit rather different behavioral features. As Konner writes,

> Some features of San life, and of hunting and gathering life in general, have been lost sight of in a wave of ethnographic enthusiasm. . . . For example, from the champions of San nonviolence we rarely hear mention of San homicide rates. These have been measured, and are comparable to those in American cities. We hear much about San egalitarianism, including the absence of sexism. But what of the observations and reports of wife-beating, and the obvious sexist ideology evident in all-male discussions? We have much talk and print about San sharing, but little until recently of the now plain fact that almost all sharing occurs only among close relatives. We dwell on the absence of war; but the San lack the manpower to mount even the simplest war, and when they talk about other tribes, even other groups of San, they make it clear they are not above prejudice. If they could make a war, perhaps they would. We speak of their "affluence" without mentioning periods of shortage, in which they may lose 10 percent of their body weight; of their kindness to their children, without mentioning childhood illness which kills half before they ever grow up; of their decency to the aged, without mentioning that only 20 percent of infants can expect to live to be sixty, leaving San society with an incomparably lighter burden than the elderly and infirm constitute in our own.[33]

Konner suggests that one reason "initial idealizations" occurred is that it is inherently difficult to study "rare events" like child punishment, rape, and homicide during a limited stay among a small group. To convey a sense of the pitfalls awaiting the field anthropologist, he points out that one can live in New York City for years without witnessing a rape— but cannot thereby conclude that rape is a rare crime there.

The restudies of the Bushmen suggest that they do not differ from other peoples in the ways that had been claimed. Among the Bushmen, contrary to earlier assertions, physical punishment of children is probably fairly common, homicide occurs often enough to raise the possibility they are as violent as most other peoples, and most intriguing, given the use of the Bushmen as "exemplars of gender equality," coercion of women by men is widespread, and rapes not only occur but may be fairly frequent.

The peaceful chimpanzees turn out to commit infanticide and wage war, the peaceful Bushmen to commit rape and murder, and the peaceful Samoans to commit violent crimes at a rate that rivals American cities'. In each of these cases, an initial idealization is giving way to a possibly less pleasing but definitely more accurate interpretation.

And these were just some of the most-cited versions of the Grail of primitive egalitarianism. The instances of sexually egalitarian societies current in the late sixties included the Alorese, Arapesh, Bamenda, Berbers, Bushmen, Red Chinese, ancient Cretans, Communist Cubans, Eskimo, Filipinos, Hopi, Iroquois, Jivaro, kibbutzim, Marquesans, Mbuti, Nama Hottentot, Navaho, Nayar, Samoans, Semai, Shakers, Soviets, Swedes, Tchambuli, Yegali, and Zuni.[34] Every last one of these reports is now known to be false. But how could the specialist, let alone the generally educated individual, possibly have taken issue with such an overwhelming list?

This plethora of false accounts bolstered the assumption of sixties and seventies social critics that it would be a fairly simple matter to "choose" whatever form of social organization was desired. All that was needed was an awareness of the limitless possibilities opened by cultural determinism and a modicum of good will. This belief encouraged the tendency of social critics in the sixties and seventies to make bombastic pronouncements that we can "choose" the sort of society we want to live in, that we can "create" a new world, tailored to whatever specifications we desire.

Painful naiveté! Age of innocence, to believe human nature so barren! Spendthrift age, to expend wealth and years of lives in the pursuit of chimeras!

The Myth of the Primitive Matriarchy

More "popular" in origin than the bumper crop of sexually egalitarian societies, accounts of alleged matriarchies were also common in the sixties and seventies. Reviving a literary tradition of the nineteenth century, in which abstruse fragments of Greek myth were interpreted to mean that the first condition of mankind was matriarchal, various feminists of a literary rather than a social scientific bent argued that matriarchy—a society ruled by women—was the original state of human society. We have already encountered this deplorable belief in Millett.

To the extent there is historical validity to such myths, they appear to represent a confusion by the Greeks of relatively egalitarian societies among their antecedents, such as the Minoans, with a condition of female rule. While the Greeks' antecedents were not matriarchal, they may have seemed to be so when contrasted with the radically male-dominated culture of Athens at its peak of civilization.

The argument for primitive matriarchy rests on extremely thin ground. There is quite simply no believable evidence for it. As one feminist social scientist notes in a review of human societies, "there is little evidence for the existence of truly matriarchal societies at any time."[35] As another critic points out,

Theories that hypothesized a matriarchal form of society that prevailed "at an earlier stage of history" made a certain, if tortuous, sense until findings gathered in the past fifty years both failed to uncover a single shred of evidence that such matriarchies had ever existed and demonstrated the inability of all such theories to deal with reality.

The myth of the primitive matriarchy represents the sort of "big lie" that is hard to refute: all the evidence for it has been wrenched out of context and is either outrageously false or impossible to verify. Few, if any, social scientists would dispute Steven Goldberg's statement of the matter:

I have consulted the original ethnographic materials on every society I have ever seen alleged by anyone to represent a matriarchy, female dominance, or the association of high-status, nonmaternal roles with women. . . . I have found no society that represents any of these.[36]

But despite the implausibility of a human matriarchal society, books like Robert Graves's *The White Goddess* (1948), which presented what can most charitably be called non-scientific arguments for the primitive matriarchy, enjoyed a considerable vogue, culminating in the publication of contemporary feminist works in the same tradition, notably Elizabeth Gould Davis's *The First Sex* (1971) and Merlin Stone's *When God Was a Woman* (1976). Because the point-by-point refutation of such works requires highly specialized knowledge in arcane areas of archeology, linguistics, and comparative literature, and in the absence of any theory to say that matriarchy is improbable or impossible, these works often seemed convincing to the general reader. Indeed, cultural determinism, with its picture of limitless human plasticity, legitimated the notion of matriarchy in a general sense: for cultural determinism cannot supply any reason matriarchy could *not* occur, apart from a specific set of social circumstances.

The sloppy use of words and concepts that led to false reports of sexually egalitarian societies could even go so far as to imply that matriarchies existed in the present. For instance, Mead described the Tchambuli as a society "where women dominate."[37] This claim at best repeats the fallacy of confusing the relative with the absolute. It is possible that Tchambuli women were less subordinate than women in certain other societies, but there are no grounds to believe they actually dominated their society—even in Mead's own evidence. As we have already seen,

> The excellent ethnographic data Dr. Mead presents enables the careful reader to see that Dr. Mead's conclusions concerning the plasticity of sex roles do not follow from the observations she describes. For example: Dr. Mead points out that the Tchambuli boy's initiation consisted of the boy's killing a [human] victim and hanging the head in the ceremonial house as a trophy; it is difficult to see this as an indication of "male femininity."[38]

Despite its fanciful character, the myth of the primitive matriarchy enjoyed a considerable vogue in the seventies, and was an important contribution to the fund of ideas available to Americans in the Feminist Era.

Human societies vary enormously, but not as much as was believed when cultural determinism held unquestioned sway. Human society has a form. Some of society's more obvious aspects are that it places the nuclear family at the center of emotive and reproductive life; it forbids incest according to a universal hierarchy of taboos; it uses gender as a means of organizing work and social life; and its leaders are predominantly male. These elements can be exaggerated; they can be downplayed; and we can imagine their disappearance in the future; but they were universal in all past societies, and they are universal in all present ones. Cultural determinism cannot explain such universals, for as sociologist Steven

Goldberg points out, to explain four thousand identical events with four thousand different explanations, as required by the Boasian paradigm, is "a logical barbarism."

Having discarded the infinite variety of the cultural determinist perspective as too simple, and as failing to fit the facts, what is the alternative? It is necessary to proceed cautiously in this investigation. We must steer clear of the idea that biology doesn't matter, but we must also avoid falling into a facile use of biology to prove the legitimacy of whatever happens to exist at the moment. Part of what exists is immutable in character, another part is not, and it is rarely easy *a priori* to tell the difference. For example, democracy might well have seemed at first glance to be biologically unworkable before the success of the American Revolution because, in terms of the biological evidence, it seemed to contradict the principle that social groups are hierarchically organized and, in terms of the circumstantial evidence, it had been rare and less than fully successful as a political system beforehand. Yet democracy, as practiced in America, does work, and in fact works far better than the other known systems of government, all of which place far greater emphasis than American democracy on one or more of the well-established human biological propensities toward hierarchy, kin-group nepotism, and the supernatural validation of existing institutions.*

So we see that societal progress can to some extent supersede biological tendency. The cultural determinist perspective at least had the virtue of not confusing what is with what could be. It is important to bear in mind that the scientific study of humans has a built-in conservative bias: since it describes the already existent, it tends to lose sight of the possible.

The problem with cultural determinism is that it ultimately fails to tell us anything useful about human beings except that they vary. This is an important piece of information, but we still need to know what the limits of this variation are. As will be seen in the discussion of "nonsexist child rearing" later on, the failure of cultural determinism to specify any such limits resulted in excessively fuzzy thinking and in predictably unworkable attempts to implement social innovations. Thus, despite the

---

*In point of fact, American democracy does not work against universals but with them: a hierarchy of merit replaces a hierarchy of privilege, nepotism is turned against itself through decentralization, and religion is strengthened by removing it from the corrupting influence of the state. Any good constitution is brilliantly pro-biological.

intellectual risks, the effort to reintegrate the biological into our conception of human affairs is urgently required in the interests of intellectual integrity and social justice.

The Fear of Biology

At this point in a discussion with a cultural determinist, the objection is commonly raised that biology is too dangerous to study. Since racialist science was sometimes used to justify the subordination of blacks in the late nineteenth century, and since the Nazis made use of pseudobiological arguments to justify the murder of Europe's Jews, any mention of biology in human affairs is suspect: it is just too dangerous politically to be acceptable scientifically now or in the foreseeable future.

Much of the American left has nourished a virtual paranoia of biology.[39] At the height of this feeling in the seventies, such legitimate scientists as E. O. Wilson, Richard Hernnstein, Lionel Tiger, and Robert William Fogel were regularly heckled when making public appearances on American university campuses. (Such incidents are still common at Harvard and other universities and are typically winked at by campus authorities.) More recently the feminist sociobiologist Sarah Blaffer Hrdy has gently chided her "sisters" for their intolerance, assuring them that "The sociobiologists were mystified to discover that feminists were demonstrating at their lectures."[40] It is possible the sociobiologists were mystified—but it is certain, and more to the point, that they were routinely heckled and harassed.

Biophobia is a prejudice of the worst sort, which deforms idealism into intolerance through the spread of alarmism and misinformation. The most elementary observation should compel us to see that the abuse of "nature" by the Nazis and other racists is paralleled by the Soviet and Khmer Rouge abuse of "nurture." The Nazis, believing heredity to determine all, tried to kill off or enslave the "inferior" races. The Soviets and the Khmer Rouge, believing man to be infinitely mutable,[41] tried to remake human nature, with even more deadly results—if indeed it is possible to speak in comparative terms of megadeath and the total annihilation of human dignity.

Since the crimes of both political extremes are hideous almost beyond contemplation, perhaps it is time we learned to distinguish legitimate science—which may include a political component—from its political exploitation, in which science is reduced to a mere servant of political ideology. The only means of doing so, fragile though it may be, is through the dissemination of information. Obscurantism—specifically, the refusal to acknowledge human behavioral biology as a legitimate area of inquiry—is not the cure.[42]

Biophobes argue that their antagonists, who see a biological component in human behavior, claim that human behavior is "determined by instincts."[43] This is a standard line, a buzz phrase intended to substitute ideology for inquiry. Entire fields of scholarship are breezily dismissed with these three words. Without bothering to consider any evidence, this phrase brushes aside the ongoing life's work of "ethologists, neuroethologists, physiological psychologists, neuropsychologists, behavioral neurologists, behavioral endocrinologists, biological psychologists, comparative psychologists, biological anthropologists, behavioral geneticists, psychopharmacologists, and others."[44]

It should be noted that "sociobiologists" happen not to appear on this extensive list. Equivalent to the canard "determined by instincts" is the irresponsible use of "sociobiology" as a pejorative umbrella under which to clump all fields of inquiry that are thought to threaten the culturist consensus. "Sociobiology" is the heir to the old buzz phrase "social Darwinism," popularized in the forties by Richard Hofstadter's diatribe against Herbert Spencer. "Sociobiologists," according to those like Stephen Jay Gould who carry on the culturist tradition, are those who believe "human behavior is determined by instincts." In fact, this claim has nothing to do with the actual theories or research of real-life sociobiologists—let alone of their hundreds of non-sociobiologist colleagues who are also engaged in the study of behavioral biology.

Sociobiology is the study of societies as biological systems. As such it is only one among dozens of currently active areas of behavioral biology. Sociobiology is an engaging and challenging field, but it is not essential to the critique of cultural determinism. If sociobiology were to disappear tomorrow, there would be little net effect on the new perspectives in science and gender that are rapidly emerging today. Nor do any of these fields rely on a concept of "instincts." As soon as the phrase "determined by instincts" appears, the reader can be sure the author using it either is ignorant of the state of research or is simply trying to mislead him.

For nobody in the latter half of the twentieth century is arguing that "instincts" determine human behavior (which does not mean that human instincts do not exist, only that they are not the primary units of behavior). Today's scientists are not studying "instincts" but far more sharply defined areas such as comparative population statistics, biochemistry, and genetics. Today's cultural determinists are still declaiming against the Spencerian evolutionism of the late nineteenth century (and a caricature of it at that), and ignoring the vastly more sophisticated evolutionism of the late twentieth.

While few biophobes have bothered to acquaint themselves with contemporary behavioral biology, which they have assimilated only through polemics against it in political journals like the *Nation,* the most sophisticated are consciously culling the evidence they know exists before offering it to the public: for they judge the public would turn against the political positions they favor if it had a more complete knowledge. The man and woman in the street, argue these new obscurantists, cannot handle the full knowledge available to specialists; let us tell them just as much as it is needful for them to know. The tradition of scientific elitism that Boas represented is thus carried on; Big Brother, the social scientist-cum-social engineer, knows best.

And so the hoary untruths of Mead's 1931 research are taught to successive generations of students, not as the result of a conspiracy but of a consensus. At every major college and university, students are trained to revere cultural determinism as a pillar of freedom and to despise behavioral biology as a naive superstition that behavior is "determined by instincts." Mead's obsolete views on sex and temperament have been virtually written into the U.S. Constitution in the left liberal mentality, while serious theorists like E. O. Wilson who argue that biology is a factor in human behavior are branded apologists for the Third Reich. A new student rebellion is needed to overturn these tired prejudices, so that the standard discourse of American intellectual life can recover a choice between Boas and Genesis: Darwin.

The attempt to define the biological limits of human variability may be hazardous and difficult, but it is urgently necessary. The potential costs are too high for each succeeding generation to make the same mistakes. The alternative—to continue to ignore the relevance of the biological to human affairs—is no longer possible, unless we are to despair completely of the quest for truth and define science as merely a branch of ideology.

Human societies are variable but not arbitrary organisms. Cultural determinism is unable to cope with their elegant regularity. It is this regularity that gives us a common humanity, that makes it possible for us to approach members of widely separated cultures with sympathy and intuitive understanding. This regularity provides a far more enduring basis for tolerance than cultural determinism, for it recognizes that all people everywhere have a great deal in common. Kaiserism was as bad for Germany as it would have been for America; communism is as intolerable to Vietnamese as it would be to Rhode Islanders. People cannot be socialized to enjoy slavery or other forms of basic deprivation. It is only because there *is* a human nature that "life, liberty, and the pursuit of happiness" are valuable to people everywhere. Let us proceed then, with due measures of trepidation and determination, to the recovery of the biological.

Chapter 8

Advances in Behavioral Biology

Interactionism

As we have seen, the most celebrated cases of social variability are flawed beyond remedy. The Bushmen do not provide an example of sexual equality, Samoa is not a paradise of adolescent free love, and Trobriand families do not differ in structure from families elsewhere. The quest for a sexually egalitarian society has borne no fruit across the four thousand-odd cultures known to science and the search for matriarchy is an exercise in charlatanism. The question arises, is there perhaps some order after all in the Boasian kaleidoscope of cultures? In fact there is: no matter how you juggle the kaleidoscope, certain patterns emerge.

Many institutions that have been described as "cultural" are universal in human cultures and have analogs in other higher primates, such as the incest taboo. It is not inaccurate to say that "war is a cultural institution," but when we have also noticed that war is a *universal* cultural institution and that it is a *male* cultural institution, we have begun to describe the phenomenon of war in terms that no longer imply that a bit of social tinkering will suffice to end it. Actually, it is quite misleading to describe war as a cultural institution, either in the context of one society in particular or of all societies in general, without taking note of the fact that war is also a biological phenomenon.

The cultural determinist looks at a human trait, such as modesty, and sees that its expression varies enormously. Modesty in one culture may require that a woman keep herself veiled from head to toe; in another it may simply be expressed by wearing a triangle of cloth over the genital region; and, in yet another, it may have to do less with what one wears than with whom a woman feels comfortable spending time alone. The cultural determinist looks at these disparate expressions and reasons that modesty is not a universal trait. Let teenage boys and girls share the same dormitory rooms and showers (as they did in the early days of the Israeli kibbutz). The interactionist, on the other hand, notes that although modesty is shown in disparate ways, it is universal; he notices that modesty appears in girls at puberty, regardless of how it is culturally expressed; and he leaves open the possibility that these disparate expressions reflect a universal need, the study of which might well be interesting and useful, and the violation of which should be approached with caution.

Similar considerations apply to all other universal human institutions, including most obviously marriage, the family, and the incest taboo. It is misleading to describe these as merely cultural institutions. The differences in form these institutions take are not independent inventions but variations on themes that pervade all human societies.

The nature/nurture dichotomy is no longer adequate to the state of our knowledge about human beings. A hint of the emerging inadequacy of this dichotomy is found in Freeman's critique of Mead, and is most clearly seen in his discussion of the polemic between Franz Boas and the eugenicist Charles Davenport.

> Here, then, in 1911, were two antithetical intellectual and scientific schools—that of Boas and that of Davenport—with neither disposed to explore, in a constructive way, the coexistence and interaction of genetic and exogenetic processes. . . . The stage was set for an unrelenting struggle between two doctrines, each insufficient in scientific terms, which had originated amid the theoretical confusions of the late nineteenth century, the one overestimating biology and the other overvaluing culture.[1]

Child psychologist Jerome Kagan is explicit about the difficulties of studying the human being under the opposed rubrics of biology and culture.

> We must never treat the biological and the experiential as separate, independent forces. The complementarity of the two is best illustrated by the early growth of the brain. Although the number of neurons a particular species will possess seems to be determined strictly by its genetic constitution, the locations of those nerve cells and the pattern of final synaptic connections in the central nervous system are influenced by both local physical and chemical conditions and experience and, therefore, are much more variable. Indeed, whether a particular cell appearing in the earliest phases of neural development becomes part of the spinal column or part of the eye depends in large measure on the cells it meets as it travels from the neural crest to its final destination.

Kagan goes on to illustrate this point by the analogy of a pond freezing in winter:

> Physicists do not explain the pond's freezing by assuming that the forma-
> tion of ice can be apportioned into one set of factors attributable to the
> inherent properties of water and into another ascribable to external change
> in temperature. Freezing is a unitary event resulting from a particular quality
> of the outside air acting upon a closed body of water.[2]

Thus not only is it impossible to treat culture in isolation from biology; the nature/nurture dichotomy was a false opposition to begin with. It is the latest version of the mind-body dichotomy so common in Western thought, and no more accurate than the original one. Human culture is biological, human biology is cultural.

This can be seen if we consider the experiment said to have been undertaken by a number of rulers in bygone centuries, in which a child or children were raised in isolation to see what the result would be: Would they speak at all? If they did, would they perhaps speak Hebrew? The experiment is permanently impossible, because an infant raised in isolation—a theoretical impossibility in any case, since an infant will die without the intervention of other humans, but never mind that for the moment—will exhibit severe pathologies; its very isolation, in proportion as it is complete, will make it atypical and thus useless as a basis for study. Other attempts to separate culture from biology run into similar, inevitable problems.

Human biology cannot function independently of culture, and in fact never does: put differently, our cultural capacity is one of the most important characteristics of our biology. Similarly, our culture, while it makes our biology more adaptable than that of other animals, cannot exist without our biology. The recognition that is now occurring is that human culture is far more biological, and human biology far more diverse and subtle, than was previously imagined. The nuclear family, for example, can be described as a cultural institution; but a universal human tendency to live in families cannot be explained in terms of the culture concept.

The belief that biology is limited to gross physical needs has resulted in a genuine impoverishment of knowledge. For example, my college anthropology textbook admitted bewilderment at the similarities in human cultural expressions:

> Anthropology cannot offer any very good answers to why man has gone to such lengths in his adaptations. Everywhere he does far more than simply to meet his biological needs. Strangely, the direction the elaborations take are generally parallel.[3]

Biology is more than a set of gross needs and motor reactions: it pervades our lives in terms of delicate perceptual frameworks and elaborate behavioral complexes. The opposed concepts of biology and culture have come to smack of a certain artificiality when applied to the human animal, and must eventually be replaced with more felicitous expressions. In the meantime, it is becoming increasingly clear that, at a minimum, we cannot profitably characterize human behavior in terms of culture alone.

A useful interim concept may be interactionism: the idea that "culture" and "biology" always operate together. In this way, the culture concept is provisionally saved, though in somewhat altered form: human culture itself is understood to have biological elements, such as a predisposition to live in families.

We are not faced with a choice between a virtuous, tolerant cultural determinism and a reactionary, racist biological one. Instead, we are challenged to move beyond this obsolete dichotomy and develop a new frame of reference in which the old conceptual wall between biology and culture is broken down altogether. This process is already underway, and it seems to be largely a matter of time before it triumphs.

Biology is not limited to the "inherent" but is subject to transformation by experience. As we stand on the threshold of a new era in which "gene surgery" becomes a reality, it would be foolish to claim otherwise. But even without going into the complexities of speculation on what future techniques may make possible, it is clear that the very genes undergo routine transformation in the course of life: for example, the release of testosterone in boys at adolescence literally modifies the genes. Experience has been shown to visibly modify the brain in rats; there is every reason to believe similar changes will be identified in humans. At no point is the biological ever beyond the reach of the environmental: not in the infant, whose behavior is affected by the care it receives; not in the fetus, which is affected by its mother's diet and moods; not in the zygote, where causes such as radiation exposure may induce mutation.

It may be tempting to arrange such events along a continuum, in which biology becomes increasingly less deterministic from conception on through the life cycle, but such a continuum fails to take into account such major biological events as puberty and childbearing as well as on-going influences such as the differing hormone levels in men and women. In human beings, the "genetic" is subject to a variety of environmental impacts, and the "exogenetic" responds to biological imperatives. Our under-standing of learning, maturation, and personality increasingly transcends the artificiality of the nature/nurture dichotomy. For instance, neither B. F. Skinner's behaviorism nor Boas's cultural determinism allowed for the fact that people learn some things much more easily than others.

"Socialization" has been a useful bin for anthropologists, sociologists, and social critics to dump unexplained aspects of behavior in. Children are said to be "socialized" through "conditioning" to learn certain behaviors—sex roles for instance—instead of others. But rather than referring behavior to something as abstract as "socialization," it might make sense to examine what actually goes on in the process of acquiring new behaviors.[4]

And here a problem with the idea of socialization is immediately apparent. It has become clear that not all behaviors are learned with equal ease. A simple, uncontroversial example is that it is easier for humans to condition themselves for long-distance running than for dancing *en pointe,* presumably because evolution has preadapted us to run, but not to do ballet.

But things get more complicated as more factors are introduced. Not only is it easier to learn some actions than others, it is easier to learn some *sequences* of actions than others. This was shown in a study of rat learning published in 1966 that has since been widely replicated.

The rats were divided into four groups. Each was given a punish-ment while drinking water, preceded by a signal. The expected result was that the rats would learn an avoidance response and stop drinking at the appearance of the signal, before the punishment was given. As Melvin Konner describes the experiment,

> So far this is all the standard stuff of the learning lab. But the special twist is this. We give the four groups of rats different combinations of two signals and two punishments. One group gets a noise-and-light signal followed by an electric shock. The second group gets a distinctive flavor in the water, followed by an artificially induced feeling of nausea (caused by X rays and having nothing intrinsic to do with the flavor).
>
> Up to this point both the experiment and the results are conventional. The rats in Group One and Group Two acquire the avoidance response—stop drinking at the appearance of the noise-and-light signal or the distinctive flavor. . . .

The surprise comes with Groups Three and Four. In those groups, the pairing of signal and punishment is reversed. Group Three gets the noise-and-light signal followed by the X ray-induced nausea. Group Four gets the distinctive flavor followed by the electric shock. *These two groups do not learn the avoidance response.*

Konner points out that, while these results initially puzzled psychologists, they came as no surprise to biologists. It makes good evolutionary sense for rats to have learned to associate noise and light with physical pain, and nausea with tastes and smells. Natural selection led to "genetically based tendencies to learn some lessons better than others."[5]
Similar evidence comes from studies of the golden hamster.

In the golden hamster a number of complex behavior patterns, such as digging, rearing on the hind legs, washing and scratching, are "instinctive" in the sense that they emerge without training, but modifiable in the sense that they can be trained to certain cues. However, if you reward all four of these patterns with food, only digging and rearing will increase in frequency; these are the patterns associated with the food quest in the wild.[6]

Some things are easier to learn than others, and some combinations of things are easier to learn than others. Learning is not a unitary process, subject to an unvarying set of mechanistic laws, but a complex, biologically mediated event.

We do not have to restrict ourselves to circumstantial evidence from observations of behavior. It is becoming possible to explain the rats' learning patterns by direct reference to the structures of the brain.

General laws of learning—laws that will apply to all stimuli and all responses—are implausible not only ecologically but neurologically. The nerve path of the taste modality, for example, has its first way station in a lower brain center called the nucleus of the solitary tract; visceral sensation from the stomach reports first to the same nucleus. Why should we expect an auditory stimulus, with an input pathway relatively isolated from these, to form an equally easy link with the visceral sensation of nausea? Similarly, there is a close central nervous system association between sound and skin-surface sensations—in the thalamus and in the cerebral cortex, far from the centers where the rat senses nausea.[7]

Clearly, we cannot choose just any form of behavior to reinforce. Different behaviors will require different levels of reinforcement to produce.

None at all will be required for a behavior that is completely unlearned, while at the other extreme no amount of reinforcement will induce an organism to produce a behavior of which it is biologically incapable. In addition, as the rat studies show, behaviors are not discrete, isolated units, but are strung together in ways that are just starting to be discovered. Although the process of discovery is only beginning, it requires no special prescience to see where it is headed: toward an understanding that learning is a more complex, and a more biological, process than was suspected in the simpler days of the mid-twentieth century. The habit of tossing around the concept of "socialization" without reference to the specific processes that are occurring will have to be discarded by conscientious social scientists and the educated public.

The narrowing gap between studies of the experiential and the biological can be seen in our ability to visually detect changes wrought by experience in the brain itself. The brain is not a computer, to be merely programmed with a variety of electrical impulses. Experience changes the brain, in minor but increasingly detectable ways.

Another rat experiment provides dramatic visual evidence for such change. As Konner relates it,

> Rat pups were raised in rich or poor environments. The favored pups, selected at random, grew up in a world full of toys and other pups. A control group grew up under ordinary laboratory conditions. A third group was impoverished; even the relatively low level of stimulation available in the ordinary laboratory was withheld from them.
> These different conditions stamped differences in the brain. In the visual part of the brain, where patterns taken from the eye are converted into usable thought, those same pyramidal cells so crucial to higher mental life appeared changed under the cold eye of the microscope. Not changed in their basic placement or overall structure; in rats as in ourselves these are determined by the genes, mostly before the time of birth. But in the finer aspects of structure the impact of experience was evident. Animals raised in a rich environment had more small branches far out along the main trunks of the dendrites.
> . . . Look, I remember thinking when I first saw the photographs, see for yourself. Experience changes the brain.[8]

"Environmental" influences do not remain separate from "biological" ones. Instead, they become *part of* the biological, which in turn again modifies the environmental. The forms that such interactions take are a complex mixture of developments that are partly necessary, partly guided, and partly mutable; and that, once having taken place, may or may not be susceptible to further alteration, in one or more directions. We may hope that the nature of these interactions will become more and more a matter for empirical determination, and less and less a matter for ideological struggle, in the same way that cosmology gradually left the province of religion to become the province of physics and astronomy. As usual, objective inquiry and tolerance are two sides of the same coin.

Our ability to trace such interactions is still very inconsistent, but it is steadily growing. Recent, tantalizing evidence has begun to accumulate from many areas: that practicing male homosexuals exhibit hormonal differences from male heterosexuals; that contact with an infant releases the hormones prolactin and oxytocin in women, absent in men, which elicit mothering behavior; that women's health is enhanced in a variety of ways by regular sexual intercourse, in the course of which women imbibe a beneficial substance tentatively called "male essence" released through the man's skin. Not all these conclusions are yet firmly established; but they will bear close watching over the coming years.

Biology and Sex Differences

The visual detection of sex differences in the brain is becoming possible. The pioneering study was published by Geoffrey Raisman and Pauline M. Field of Oxford University in 1973. Raisman and Field were able to photograph the preoptic area of the brain in rats and, by careful counting, to show that male and female brains differ greatly in the number and distribution of synapses on the dendritic spines. This was the first demonstration that there are structural differences between male and female brains.[9]

The principal agent in this process is the male hormone testosterone. The genetic blueprint of mammals is female. Male hormones act to alter a basic female mammalian plan. One could conclude from this that females are superior, since they supply the basic schema of which males are a mere variation. One could also conclude that males are superior, since they represent a higher development of the more basic female structure. It would be far better, though, to avoid such value judgments entirely and simply acknowledge the fact of *difference* when appropriate, without seeking to impose an irrelevant, chauvinistic value schema.

In 1976, Dominique Toran-Allerand was able to extend Raisman and Field's observations by culturing slices of the hypothalamus of newborn mice and treating some with testosterone, others with a neutral oil suspension. The result was that the slices treated with testosterone showed more and faster neural growth—which of course should not lead us to conclude that the testosterone-treated hypothalamus will be *better,* but that it will be *different.*[10] The results can be seen in the dramatic photographs published by Toran-Allerand to illustrate her finding.

It is striking that these differences occurred right where they should have, in a part of the brain concerned with the regulation of hormones. Testosterone, if you like, is an environmental influence that visibly changes the brain—a genetically mediated environmental influence.

Another refinement of Raisman and Field's discovery has been the finding that, not only do the density of the synapses vary in the pre-optic area, but the nucleus of the preoptic area, as observed in rats, is significantly larger in males than in females. This difference is so great that it is visible to the naked eye. This finding is so striking that it is worth emphasizing: at least in rats, the sex of the brain can be determined by examining the appropriate structure with the unaided eye. Because of the similarity of the structures and hormones involved, it seemed inevitable that comparable findings would soon be forthcoming for humans.

In the early eighties, researchers confirmed the existence of a sex difference in cell density in the preoptic area in humans. Perhaps most dramatic of all, it has been firmly established that the corpus callosum, the structure which links the two halves of the brain, differs significantly between men and women—a difference that is readily visible to the naked eye.[11]

In summary, male and female brains differ in mammals, including humans, from before birth, as a result of the higher levels of testosterone in the male fetus.

Concepts advanced by child psychologist Jerome Kagan raise further objections to the old view of "socialization" as an arbitrary, mechanical process. Kagan believes the importance of continuity in human maturation has been overrated. It has been assumed that experience is cumulative, so that learning occurs in a steady upward curve, the achievement of competence at one stage being the prerequisite for attainment of the following stage.

On the contrary, Kagan argues, experience is only partly conserved. The differing requirements of different stages of development appear in behaviors many of which are not conserved to any significant degree. The stages of maturation differ not just quantitatively but qualitatively. For example, separation anxiety, which is presumably important to protect the infant, begins to disappear around the age of three, when it becomes less functional, regardless of what actions parents do or do not take. Again, it is common to think of crawling as a stage in learning to walk; but a baby who does not crawl, for example one who is swaddled, learns to walk just the same, and nearly as soon. Similar considerations apply to other abilities, like speech. The emergence of new abilities is determined by the maturation of central nervous system structures, which bring them into being given the necessary minimum of environmental stimulation.

> Each life phase makes special demands, and so each phase is accompanied by a special set of qualities. Succeeding phases have a different set of demands; hence, some of the past is inhibited or discarded. The new pattern may contain none of the elements of the earlier, but often functionally similar, competence.[12]

The stages of development, according to Kagan, occur except under the most extreme forms of environmental deprivation—and, even then, they emerge to a remarkable extent. Instead of an abstract, formless process, socialization becomes more specific and intelligible. Socialization appears as an idea that must be applied with great conceptual rigor, rather than a convenient receptacle in which to dump problems that can't otherwise be readily explained. The idea that accretive socialization can produce any change desired in human beings—basic, as we shall see, to the feminist program of "nonsexist child rearing"—becomes extremely doubtful.

Learning in humans is a complex interactive process that occurs in the context of a biological set of predispositions according to a genetically determined timetable. One should at a minimum retain this idea: environment is not the sole factor in what people learn or how they learn it.

This brings us squarely to the question: to what extent are sex differences in behavior the result of environment? Entirely, replies the cultural determinist. So powerful is conditioning, so pervasive is sexual stereotyping, that any differences in the behavior of the sexes are due to cultural rather than biological forces.

This argument simply doesn't hold water. For the past twenty years, evidence has been steadily accumulating against it. Extreme environmental determinist beliefs are still widespread, not because of any scientific imperative, but because of a will to believe in the extreme malleability of human nature, because that belief is thought necessary to promote efforts to establish equality between the sexes, and also between races and classes.

However, the inherent differences between races and classes that have been suggested by serious researchers are minimal, poorly documented, and unconvincing in explaining any aspect of social relations as they exist. The exact opposite is true in the case of the sexes. That this idea is so novel that it will be shocking to many demonstrates just how thorough the influence of the unisexist consensus has been over the past twenty years. For though the facts are not in doubt, the issue is still alive.

It is useful to test the assumptions of environmental determinism against the evidence that has appeared over the past twenty years for the influence of hormones on human personality. For if personality isn't influenced by hormones, the converse must certainly also be true: that hormones don't influence personality. But the evidence is overwhelming that they do.

Perhaps the most striking evidence for the influence of hormones on personality comes from studies of "fetal androgenization." The basic mammalian plan, it will be recalled, is female. For years, investigators had suspected that male hormones circulating in the fetus were responsible for the emergence of male characteristics. Before Raisman and Field's direct observation of such changes in the fetal brain, various indirect means of investigation of fetal androgenization were used.

Experiments with other animals had established that castration of males at birth resulted in an absence of normal male sexual activity after maturity, even when replacement doses of testosterone were given. Apparently, something was going on early in life which had permanent effects on behavior, regardless of later hormonal levels.

Another suggestive experiment involved female monkeys who were given male hormones before birth. The result was that, "as they grew, these females showed neither the characteristic low level of female aggressive play nor the characteristic high male level, but something precisely in between."[13]

This shows that hormones influence the behavior of other animals, but do they affect humans as well? The work of John Money and his colleagues, led by Anke Ehrhardt, demonstrates that the answer is yes, they do.

The question of fetal androgenization is particularly interesting because boys and girls do not differ much in their hormonal levels. The behavioral differences that are observed between boys and girls thus cannot be explained by the hormones present, for it is only at puberty that significant hormonal differences between the sexes appear.

Anke Ehrhardt studied girls born with adrenogenital syndrome, a condition in which a genetic defect causes masculine levels of testosterone to be present in female fetuses. The result is a hermaphroditic appearance of the external genitalia and a subsequent masculinization of appearance in terms of muscle growth, deepened voice, and so forth. The condition can be corrected after birth through a combination of plastic surgery and hormone therapy. In other respects, such girls are physically normal and at maturity become capable of intercourse and childbearing.

As they grew up, the girls who had received male doses of androgens in the womb exhibited significant behavioral differences from a carefully matched control group of similar, non-androgenized girls. They considered themselves to be "tomboys." They often had little interest in playing with dolls. They tended to prefer playthings associated with boys, such as toy cars and guns. Compared to the other girls, they preferred physically vigorous activities to more sedentary ones. They were fond of competitive team sports, especially ball games like baseball and football. They tended to prefer boys rather than other girls as playmates. Such girls saw themselves and were seen by others unambiguously as girls, but they were much more likely than the other girls to think it might be more fun to be a boy. They preferred functional clothes to pretty ones and were less interested in cosmetics and hair styling.

They did not share the other girls' fascination with weddings, marriage, and pregnancy. Whereas the other girls were more interested in marriage than in careers, the fetally androgenized girls expressed equal or greater interest in careers and tended to view marriage as secondary.* Unlike the control group, who were uniformly enthusiastic about babies, they attached a relatively low priority to bearing children. They had little interest in caring for infants. Several of them feared they wouldn't know how to behave with infants, a fear that continued in at least some cases up to childbirth.

In terms of gender identity, these girls are clearly female. In terms of later sexual orientation, the evidence suggests that the great majority will be heterosexual, with possibly higher than average interest in sex. There is some indication of a higher incidence of homosexual behavior in later years, but the evidence is not conclusive on this point.

Their average IQ may be slightly higher than would be expected, an effect also documented with boys who have been exposed to excess prenatal levels of androgens.

It is possible that adrenogenital syndrome is only an extreme case of a more common phenomenon. Money and Ehrhardt point out that

> No one knows how many genetic females born with normal female genitalia might, in fact, have been subject to prenatal androgen excess insufficient to influence the external anatomy, though perhaps sufficient to influence the brain.[14]

Parallel evidence on hormones and behavior comes from androgen-insensitive males. A condition called "Turner's syndrome" prevents a genetic male from responding to testosterone. Since the basic mammalian plan is female, the result is a technical male who is female in appearance, and indeed female in all respects except for shorter-than-average stature and infertility (due to incomplete internal female genitalia). Androgens are present in human females as well as human males, though at far lower levels, and are important in certain areas of behavior, including sexual desire. Since girls with Turner's syndrome, unlike other females,

---

*This does not of course mean that there is a hormonally determined biological imperative for any culture-specific activity, such as a "career" as currently conceived in America; "career" is just the most likely screen on which currently to project a sense of one's worth and potential that revolves primarily around one's individual achievement rather than one's surrounding relationships. There is no "career gene" or "career instinct"; but testosterone has certain rather definite effects on motivation, fantasy, and action. Incidentally, it remains likely that fetally masculinized women will remain less aggressive than men; their behaviors, like those of the artificially androgenized primates mentioned above, will mostly fall in between the male and female averages.

are completely insensitive to androgens, one might expect them to be particularly feminine, in the absence of any hormonally influenced masculine traits.

The androgen-insensitive girls resembled a matched control group of other girls in all the areas in which the fetally androgenized girls diverged, such as a high interest in doll play. In fact, the androgen-insensitive girls displayed even more "feminine" emphases than the control group: less interest in athletic contests, more in personal adornment, and a lower incidence of fighting. Despite their infertility, they all reported fantasies of being pregnant and all hoped eventually to care for a baby.

Nearly all the androgen-insensitive girls (90 percent) reported themselves to be fully content with the female role, compared with less than half the fetally androgenized girls (47 percent). The overwhelming majority of the androgen-insensitive girls (80 percent) reported a strong interest in personal adornment, as opposed to a small minority (13 percent) of the fetally androgenized group.[15]

Fetal androgenization places environmental determinists in the quandary of having to argue that while sex hormones influence behavior, somehow behavior is not influenced by sex hormones. They have responded in two ways. The first is to try to explain away the findings by maintaining that the families of these girls knew about the androgenization of their daughters, and therefore elicited male-like behavior from them. This argument is hard to take seriously, since the behavioral effects of fetal androgenization were completely unknown and might have been nil, or feminizing, for all the girls' parents knew. This is an argument born of desperation.

The other tack taken by environmentalists is beyond desperation, and consists in simple denial. They admit the influence of hormones, but claim we can "choose not to be ruled by them." Perhaps. But we might also want to consider whether it is possible to live in harmony with our hormonal systems. Perhaps our biology is not all bad.

In any event, our biology will continue to influence us, whether we wish it to or not, whether we are aware of it or not. We can, of course, close our eyes to the obvious, as did Margaret Mead, who reported "male femininity" in cultures with all-male leaders, in which abduction was a standard way for men to initiate sexual relationships, and in which a boy had to kill another person to be accepted as an adult. Wishful thinking cannot be eliminated by science. There will always be a few to admire the example of King Canute, who sat on the beach commanding the tide to stop while the relentless waves crept forward and engulfed his chair.

The behavioral effect of fetal androgenization has been known since Ehrhardt's first report was published in 1967. It is no longer a new or controversial idea, but a well-established fact. The personality differentiation it causes between boys and girls receives an enormous boost with the massive release of hormones at puberty.

A striking demonstration of the relative *unimportance* of socialization in the creation of gendered temperament is the *guevedoce* or "penis-at-twelve" syndrome found in a few isolated villages of the Dominican Republic. The syndrome results from the absence of an enzyme which changes testosterone into dihydrotestosterone, a male hormone responsible for the appearance of external sex characteristics at birth. Those afflicted with this condition appear at birth to be female and are raised as girls. But at puberty, they develop masculine characteristics, including larger muscles, facial hair, a deepened voice, and a penis. Of eighteen cases of the syndrome studied, all but one adopted male roles, and without any counseling or other special assistance went on to lead normal lives as men, with typical levels of sexual desire for women. If in fact sex roles are the product of culture, and of early conditioning in particular, how can we explain this anomalous result?

Of course it can be argued that, by one means or another, culture was still responsible for the adoption of male roles in these cases. Any theory can be stretched to cover a given set of facts. Ptolemy's theory that the planets move around the earth described their motions as accurately as Copernicus's theory that the planets move around the sun. In fact, Ptolemy's theory predicted the motions of the planets *better* than Copernicus's, which did not achieve the same level of predictive accuracy until it was refined by later astronomers. The question is not which argument is possible, but which argument most convincingly explains the facts. It is certainly *possible* to construct a hypothesis that culture was responsible for the assumption of male roles by the *guevedoce*. For example, one could argue that everyone in the Dominican villages wanted to be male because men had greater cultural advantages than women. But if that were true, why would women not have sought male roles? If conditioning to gender roles is so weak that it can be easily cast aside, how can it be such a powerful determining force in all societies?

For the adaptation of the *guevedoce* was not the only conceivable response. They might have become homosexual, or they might have

become heterosexual transvestites, like some members of certain Polynesian societies and the *berdaches* of some American Indian tribes. Why
should they, in particular, choose conventional male roles in response
to the development of a male physique, after some dozen years of
socialization to be female?

As Julianne Imperato-McGinley, the director of the *guevedoce* study,
concludes,

> These subjects demonstrate that in the absence of sociocultural factors that
> could interrupt the natural sequence of events, the effect of testosterone
> predominates, over-riding the effect of rearing as girls. . . .[16]

Perhaps it will be one proof, perhaps another, that finally tips the
balance in favor of a new paradigm that allows for factors previously
dismissed as too biological, in an era that viewed biology as necessarily
inscrutable or racist. But it is not hard to see where the future lies.

Feminism Meets Sociobiology

The new direction in which the science of man is headed is apparent
in the work of Sarah Blaffer Hrdy (pronounced "Hardy"), who is one
of a number of people to occupy the anomalous position of being a
committed feminist and a sociobiologist. Because Hrdy's work, in addition
to integrating social and biological science, shows both the best features
of feminist social science and its limitations, it is worth examining at
some length.

Hrdy's work is guided by two themes: to reject a "male-centered"
explanation for human evolution and to reconcile feminism with sociobiology. She is trying to overcome an earlier, widely disseminated point
of view, which describes the adaptation of male hunting groups as the
principal driving force in human evolution. This view is particularly associated with Desmond Morris's *The Naked Ape* (1967), Lionel Tiger's
Men in Groups (1969, republished 1984), and Tiger and Robin Fox's *The
Imperial Animal* (1971). As Morris has recently restated this framework,

> When our ancient hunting ancestors switched to hunting as a way of life,
> the relationship between males and females was dramatically altered. Females,
> with their heavy reproductive burden, were unable to play a major role in

this new feeding pattern, which had become so vital for survival. A much greater division of labour between the sexes arose. The males became specialized for the chase. They became more athletic and they spent long periods of time away from the tribal home base, in pursuit of prey.

In this new hunter-role, the males were competing with the great carnivores—the big cats and the wild dogs—and they could only hold their own against these powerful killers by adopting a more cunning style of predation. What they lacked in tooth and claw, they had to make up for with their superior intelligence. This meant using weapons and developing a high level of cooperation. A solitary, unarmed male stood little chance as a rival of a massive carnivore. But a group of communicating, armed males was unbeatable. The all-male hunting pack was a powerful new force on the land and was soon spreading to cover the globe.[17]

Man the hunter is seen as central to human evolution:

First, he had to hunt if he was to survive. Second, he had to have a better brain to make up for his poor hunting body. Third, he had to have a longer childhood to grow the bigger brain and to educate it. Fourth, the females had to stay put and mind the babies while the males went hunting. Fifth, the males had to cooperate with one another on the hunt. Sixth, they had to stand up straight and use weapons for the hunt to succeed.[18]

These theories at times created the impression—probably not always intended by its authors—that men have been the principal agents of human evolution. Bearing in mind the pioneering nature of their effort to bring some unity to the Boasian kaleidoscope of cultures, it is unreasonable to be overly critical of these thinkers, who are demonstrably open to amplifications of their early work. But their primary emphasis was on men and, as a result, important parts of the story remain to be told. Both as a woman—and therefore more likely than her male colleagues to be sensitive to characterizations of women—and as a sociobiologist, Sarah Blaffer Hrdy would appear to be well placed to make a contribution to filling this gap.

Hrdy's work represents a real contribution to our ability to think about women. It is difficult to fault her when she says that

It is often assumed—most often implicitly—that only males gain an evolutionary advantage from being competitive or sexually adventurous. To the extent that female behavior contradicts these assumptions . . . , it is dismissed as merely a by-product of the masculine character.[19]

Not enough attention has been paid to the fact that females are just as marked by evolution as are males, just as subject to the effects of natural selection. Too often, females have simply been overlooked. Hrdy tries to counter this bias in the following terms:

> There has been a prevailing bias among evolutionary theorists in favor of stressing sexual competition among males for access to females at the expense of careful scrutiny of what females in their own right were doing. Among their recurring themes are the male's struggle for preeminence and his quest for "sexual variety" in order to inseminate as many females as possible. Visionaries of male-male competition stressed the imagery of primate females herded by tyrannical male consorts: sexually cautious females coyly safeguarding their fertility until the appropriate male partner arrives; women waiting at campsites for their men to return; and, particularly, females so preoccupied with motherhood that they have little respite to influence their species' social organization. Alternative possibilities were neglected: that selection favored females who were assertive, sexually active, or highly competitive, who adroitly manipulated male consorts, or who were as strongly motivated to gain high social status as they were to hold and carry babies. As a result, until just recently descriptions of other primate species have told little about females except in their capacity as mothers. Natural histories of monkeys and apes have described the behavior of males with far greater detail and accuracy than they have described the lives of females.[20]

Hrdy, whose background is in anthropology and primatology, draws her evidence from observations of non-human primates. Her viewpoint is evolutionist: characteristics that help an individual to pass on its genes will tend to be selected over time. She argues that from this viewpoint previous descriptions of female primates, including women, are mistaken. Women, she says, are not "merely passive, fecund, and nurturing." The primate evidence, although it provides "no basis for thinking that women—or their evolutionary predecessors—have ever been dominant over men in the conventional sense of that word" does provide "substantial grounds for questioning stereotypes which depict women as naturally less assertive, less intelligent, less competitive, or less political then men are."[21]

Competition between primate males has correctly been seen as a major driving force in evolution. In a typical primate situation, a dominant male will have more chances to copulate with ovulating females, will have access to the most plentiful and highest-quality food sources, will be relatively untroubled by stress, and consequently will be healthier than subordinate males. A high dominance ranking appears to be adaptive for males, since it increases the chances of passing on their genes to descendants. To the extent that competitiveness is an advantage in achieving dominance, it makes sense that competitiveness would be selected among males.

Along with competitiveness, another advantage in achieving and maintaining high status in some species, including humans, is the ability to bond, to form sustained relations of mutual support with members of the same sex. Men have been said to have a much greater propensity in this direction than women.

But, argues Hrdy, the fact has been overlooked that high rank and bonding are also adaptive for females. A high ranked female will have many of the same advantages as a high ranked male, including better access to food sources and relative freedom from attack by other group members. Relative freedom from attack leads to lower stress levels, which are linked to higher rates of fertility. In addition, there is less chance that the baby of a high ranked female will be attacked and killed by other group members—a common event in primate species. And in fact, Hrdy argues, observations of many primate species show that females can be highly competitive.

Furthermore, females, according to Hrdy, are inclined to bond in many species, usually with close relatives. In a number of primate species, the stable core of the group is composed of related females who remain in the same group and on the same territory year after year, while males may come and go as they displace one another.

In summary, there are evolutionary antecedents for a disposition on the part of women to climb hierarchies. Such climbing offers a survival advantage to the offspring of higher ranked women that will in time translate into higher survival rates, selecting for at least some measure of competitiveness. This counters assumptions that just nurturance would be selected for in women. Women's achievement of a high dominance ranking in relation to other women—and possibly also to men—would increase the viability of their offspring.

These results of Hrdy's represent an almost unadulterated contribution to the study of primates, including humans. But are they complete? Do they provide us with a good working model of the human female? I think not.

Some earlier studies may have focused too exclusively on women as nurturant and submissive. But does Hrdy's alternative really present a balanced picture? Her women are competitive, assertive, manipulative, disposed to climb hierarchies, and possibly sexually adventurous. Do these traits really adequately characterize women, are they consonant with the characteristics we may minimally expect to have been selected for in the course of evolution? Hrdy may be right to describe some earlier models of human evolution as "projections of androcentric fantasy," but has she escaped the same tendency to project one's wishes onto one's theories? If women were not biologically predisposed to be highly nurturant toward their infant children, none of the competitive qualities Hrdy enumerates would serve any purpose. Although competition with other women and to a lesser extent men was important, nurturance was (and is) probably more important for the survival of women's offspring, and therefore of their genes. This is clearly the quality that would have been most selected for among women. Presumably the persistence of this quality is the reason many women, as is pointed out in a recent book on mothering, "are so totally surprised by the intense love they feel for their babies."[22]

Furthermore, most of the competitiveness Hrdy documents occurs between females and other females. It is not at all clear that women's evolutionary interests would have been served by emphasizing competition with men. It seems likely that a capacity to ingratiate oneself with men would be more valuable than an urge toward direct competition, given male control of the high-quality food source represented by meat.

Indeed, it is not at all clear that women evolved one strategy to the exclusion of others. The overall interests of a primate group might well be served, not by a uniform personality, but by a distribution of different adaptive strategies among its members. Thus, although an individual female's interest in perpetuating her genes might be best served by a high degree of nurturance, there might be enough evolutionary advantage in having some females who were less nurturant to ensure the perpetuation of their genes. Each group, among higher primates, may have a set of behavioral "niches" that the differing personalities of individuals best fit them to occupy.

If this speculation is correct, the feminist description of the feminine woman as a lower, "biological" being and the "new" woman, who is primarily oriented to her personal accomplishments rather than to her mate and children, as a higher stage in human evolution, appears as the projection of a wish to believe in one's personal superiority. All personality types are equally the products of evolution.

The extremely complex and critical affair of nurturing the young and maintaining the emotional bonds of society can be expected to call forth what is most complex and most human in every woman involved in the enterprise. Successful human development is not an inevitable "biological" process. Nor is the feuding for position in a university department or corporation a "post-biological" process. We are complex, biocultural beings—equally so, however we are impelled by temperament to manifest our complexity.

Moreover, a diversity of strategies, while very unevenly distributed between individuals of different temperaments, is also distributed among the population at large. People have a range of capacities that they call upon to meet different situations. Women are submissive *and* aggressive, cooperative *and* competitive, nurturing *and* indifferent toward offspring, depending on what a situation calls forth in them. To reduce this range of qualities, through deference to either the feminine or the feminist mystique, is to diminish our conception of women.

Finally, it is not at all clear that bonding among females works in the same ways as bonding among males, or that the female hierarchies described by Hrdy operate on the same principles as male hierarchies. Although women can be extremely rank-conscious, the type of impersonal ordered hierarchy associated with human male groups does not have an obvious analog in female groups.

Hrdy's argument, though it threatens some aspects of the hunting hypothesis of human evolution, does not manage to replace it with a more convincing explanation. A synthesis that moves beyond the inadequacies of both the male-centered and the feminist hypotheses, using the strong points of each to cancel out the deficiencies of the other, remains elusive.

It is striking that Hrdy's attempt to show that females were of comparable importance in human evolution to males, and that they are comparably marked by evolution, takes the form of an effort to show that women possess similar qualities to men. This is not the only approach one could take to correct the incompleteness of a male-centered approach. It could also be argued, for instance, that women were of equal or greater functional importance in the evolution of human society as men, while preserving the hypothesis that evolution would have favored different levels or forms of behaviors like aggression and group affiliation. Perhaps, for instance, the long period of child rearing made it necessary for the men to be given illusory status rewards in return for the burden of the long absences, fatigue, and danger encountered in hunting, while the women continued to provide the stable core of the group.[23] It could also be argued that men and women are equally affected by evolution, in contrasting but complementary ways: for example, that women tend to respond submissively to male aggression. Such arguments will receive fully as much support from the primate evidence as will Hrdy's attempt—useful as it is—to minimize differences between the sexes.

For Hrdy downplays some of the most obvious facts that emerge from the investigation of primate society. It is true, as she details at length, that in some primate species females dominate males—but what is glaringly obvious all through her discussion is that such species are a small minority among primates and that, furthermore, they represent those species most distant from humans. Significantly, even in those species, female dominance is reversed in the mating season. Again, she says that

> In order to compete with other males for the metabolic resources marshaled by females, males were selected for large body size, strength, and aggressiveness. Bigger males became virtually—but not totally—predestined.

The same objections of infrequency and phylogenetic distance apply as in the previous example. Or consider Hrdy's assertion that "in some—but not all—cases, larger body size permitted males to dominate females."[24] In reality it is not a question of "some" primates but of the vast majority.

The overall trend of the primate evidence is clear. Among primates, with only a few exceptions influenced by unusual environmental conditions, males are larger and more aggressive than females, whom they dominate under most circumstances. To argue that this is not the case, or need not be the case, among humans requires an argument, such as cultural determinism, that the rules that govern relations between the sexes in other primates are suspended or mitigated in humans.[25]

Hrdy's work is powerful evidence that feminism as we know it, while it has led to genuine progress in some areas, is not the end of the road. Feminist science is at best an antithesis to the distortions imposed by an excessively male-oriented perspective on human affairs. An approach that is conscious of the importance and inherent value of both sexes, regardless of how much and in what ways they resemble each other or differ, may seem to be just a wish.

And yet there is cause for hope. A newly sophisticated and appreciative understanding of the sexes is brought closer by Hrdy's work and that of other sophisticated feminist social scientists—if we can move beyond the limitations of the feminist point of view.

It is striking that, although the degree of sexual dimorphism in humans is pronounced, it may be smaller than that which prevailed among our hominid ancestors. It is vitally important not to let wish fulfillment, in whatever direction it may lead us, obscure such obvious and significant facts. The overall trend of the primate evidence is clear. Males are the dominant sex. In humans, as in all our near primate relations, male dominance is a central fact of social life. This fact has now become as unmentionable as sex was in Victorian times, and the attempt to deny it generates comparable levels of hypocrisy. At the same time, this fact also requires a complex and thorough contextualization, for females are as marked by evolution as are males, sometimes to the same ends and sometimes to different ones. What individuals might like to find is diverse, but where science must go on this question is not. In the end, we will be left with neither the absolute dominance of a gelada male over his harem nor the near-egalitarian monogamy of a gibbon couple, but with something in between. That is where we will find a more lasting definition of what is human.

Chapter 9

The New Female
Psychology

The cultural determinist position is unable to cope with the gathering flood of biobehavioral evidence. The belief that gender is a purely cultural construct is fast becoming a peculiar archaism, to be ranged with such past curiosities as the Ptolemaic idea that the sun moves around the earth, the flat-earth theory, and the Victorian notion that women are uninterested in sex. Statements that were widely accepted in the heyday of feminism are now seen to be acutely, embarrassingly mistaken, like Kate Millett's claim that "endocrinology and genetics afford no definite evidence of determining mental-emotional differences."[1] This is simply not true: endocrinology and genetics, among many other fields, now offer rich and growing evidence of differences between the sexes, including mental and emotional ones. It might still be argued that such differences were overrated before the Feminist Era, but it can no longer be seriously claimed that such differences are unimportant or that they do not exist. Temperament is gendered. Despite tremendous variability within each sex, and despite a gross quantitative overlap between the sexes in many areas, there remains a qualitative difference in the sexes' experiences. Is it possible to specify what female characteristics are, and if so, can we learn to value them as highly as male characteristics?

Beneath their aggressive rhetoric, American feminists have often been struggling to overcome a fearsome inferiority complex about women. The feminist perspective is the very incarnation of the belief that the feminine is second-rate and inauthentic, the fruit of male oppression. According to Germaine Greer, for instance, the feminine virtues are the servile virtues, and as such deserve to be rejected. Femininity was seen as a liability imposed on women by men.

As a result of this view, feminists felt such intense hostility toward any attempt to explore sex differences that they virtually removed them as a topic of discussion. For instance, one day I said to the teacher of a college anthropology class, "If I follow you correctly, all societies have sex roles."

Interrupting the teacher's reply, one of the young feminist women in the class glared at me suspiciously and snapped out, "Why do you want to ask *that*?"

Such incidents were daily events wherever feminism was strong, both for women who dared to dispute the feminist line and for men who dared to obtrude their views onto the subject of gender at all. Millions of Americans can corroborate the effect of this climate. To avoid the hostility of feminists, most Americans abandoned gender altogether as a topic for intellectual debate or polite conversation. A cloud of obscurantism settled over the discussion of gender, which has only recently begun to fray at the edges.

This new obscurantism also befogged feminist writers who were operating on the edge of the unisexist consensus. Hrdy, for instance, argues that feminists were wrong to have "undertaken intellectual lobbying to exclude knowledge about other nonhuman primates from efforts to understand the human condition."[2] In the Feminist Era, men who mentioned sex differences invited hostility and ridicule; women who mentioned them provoked cries of betrayal. The humane movement had sanctions for those who broke ranks.

But alongside the belief that sex differences were the result of male oppression, most feminists, as we have seen, held a contradictory but equally strong belief: that women were superior to men, because they were less aggressive and therefore less inclined to violence and dominance. It was often said that "putting women in charge" of politics and diplomacy would lead to an end to war. The feminist movement thus became literally the key to the survival of the human race in the nuclear age. The facts that women are less likely to lead, for the biological reasons Steven Goldberg adduces in his brilliant and widely misunderstood *The Inevitability of Patriarchy,* and that to the extent they do lead, for the equally biological ones presented by Hrdy,[3] they are no less likely than men to embody the characteristics of competitiveness and territoriality that feminists hold responsible for war, suggest the depth of unrealism beneath this particular recipe for ending the human race's troubles.

Another aspect in which feminists felt women were superior to men was also rooted in their lesser aggressivity. Women were felt to be more inclined to cooperation than to competition. It was felt that women should preserve and enhance this characteristic, from which men could learn. This concept persists, for example, in the ambivalence toward hierarchy within the National Organization for Women.

From the point of view of this female chauvinism, it was possible to initiate inquiries into sex differences. Feminists tolerated such studies, provided they were engaged in by other feminists—women only, of course—and contributed to the collective platform. By the late seventies, as the maturing influence of living and the discipline of working within the professions mellowed the spitfires of countercultural feminism, some of these inquiries began to bear fruit. These inquiries are characterized by a high level of professional achievement, which exists in an uneasy cohabitation with an ongoing commitment to feminist goals and beliefs.

These neo-feminist writers often seem to be caught in a time warp between their new, relatively tolerant view of gender and the confrontational ideology of their formative years. There is often a radical discontinuity between their individual writings, depending on whether they are dealing with political issues or with their specialties. When they are addressing political issues, they tend to reiterate the old feminist line with no significant change; paradigm shift has yet to occur. But when they are discussing the questions on which they have actually been working for the past several years, a new wind is gathering.[4]

An influential early stirring of this trend was Nancy Chodorow's *The Reproduction of Mothering: Psychoanalysis and the Sociology of Gender,* which appeared in 1978. Chodorow attempts to reconcile the doctrines of feminism and psychoanalysis in order to make a case for the elimination of sex roles. Psychoanalysis is used to reveal the complex neurotic structures that she believes underlie male and female personalities. Masculinity and femininity are neurotic constructs caused by "the fact that women mother." Cultural determinism is used to present a dazzlingly simple alternative. If men and women would "parent" equally, all the neurotic dross would be stripped away, leaving men and women free to be "people," without the personality distortions represented by masculinity and femininity.

Because Chodorow has too quickly rejected biology, she is completely at sea as to what basic male or female characteristics might be, since she no longer has a basis to suppose there might indeed be any. Psychoanalysis becomes a variant form of cultural determinism, in which complex neurotic structures determine human behavior instead of simple "role-training" ones. The Freudian complexity of these structures creates an odd contrast with her often reiterated belief that, pervasive though they are, such structures are entirely mutable.

Chodorow equates "caretaking," "nurturance," "parenting," "mothering," and "maternalism."[5] Since she never inquires whether the caretaking functions of older children, men, and older people are equivalent to "mothering," or whether they might be qualitatively different in nature, she remains free to imagine that any person can give an infant the care it needs just as well as its own mother. "Nonbiological mothers, children, and men," she claims, "can parent just as adequately as biological mothers and can feel just as nurturant."[6] Showing considerable gullibility about allegedly different systems of mothering in the kibbutz, the Soviet Union, China, and Cuba, she claims that they represent "nonfamilial child care."[7] The solution to the difficulties to which "the reproduction of mothering" gives rise is for men and women to share equally in all aspects of child rearing from day one. Since she thinks that "psychic structure"[8] is determined by the child's experience of its parents (or caretakers, one supposes) in the first five years, this is a reasonable enough approach in one sense. But the effects of such a change—if implemented thoroughly enough to be effective—on the massive sex differences she describes are, it must be admitted, extremely speculative. If differentiated gender roles, epitomized for Chodorow in the institution of mothering, are so basic to the organization of society, it seems irresponsible to propose such an untested change on such a massive scale. We might not like what we would get very much, particularly if gender differentiation really is so basic to our psychological makeup.

Megan Marshall points out that, contrary to what one would think from reading Chodorow, American women of the "Control Generation" wanted desperately not to be like their mothers. A consensus is emerging that feminists went too far in the opposite direction. By rejecting female qualities along with their mothers' examples, feminists of the seventies rejected what is most positive and in any event inherent in female nature. Chodorow's solution of doing away with gender differentiation altogether is no solution at all but instead a symptom of women's ongoing divorce from self.

Chodorow exhibits all the characteristic faults of feminist thinking. Anti-male and anti-feminine biases, unquestioning acceptance of extreme cultural determinism, the caricature of behavioral biology as a naive belief in "instincts," credulousness toward reports that Soviet Russia, Castroist Cuba, and Maoist China represent improved societies, reflexive anti-capitalism, and a tone of hostile self-righteousness are all liberally represented in her book.

But Chodorow nonetheless rendered a major service by her catchy description of the differences between male and female psychology. Despite its conventional anti-male and anti-feminine biases, this description was a genuine novelty in the Feminist Era. Chodorow writes that

> The development of femininity . . . poses different *kinds* of problems for [a girl] than the development of masculinity does for a boy. . . . Externally, as internally, women grow up and remain more connected to others. Not only are the roles which girls learn more interpersonal, particularistic, and affective than those which boys learn. Processes of identification and role learning for girls also tend to be particularistic and affective—embedded in an interpersonal relationship with their mothers. For boys, identification processes and masculine role learning are not likely to be embedded in relationship with their fathers or men but rather to involve the denial of affective relationship to their mothers. These processes tend to be more role-defined and cultural, to consist in abstract or categorical role learning rather than in person identification.

Chodorow goes on to claim, in her most striking formulation, that

> Women's relatedness and men's denial of relation and categorical self-definition are appropriate to women's and men's differential participation in nonfamilial production and familial reproduction.[9]

Chodorow is disproportionately aware of the pitfalls of femininity and, as an exponent of the feminist devaluation of the feminine, she fails to adequately bring forth its real and major virtues. She repeatedly disparages masculinity, which she depicts in extreme, stereotypical form. To Chodorow, as to other feminists, masculinity is the end product of a pathological process rather than the outcome of normal male development, and invariably leads to negative and destructive effects.

But Chodorow makes a contribution if her ideological rejection of the "traditional" roles is replaced with a more tolerant approach. This was her unintentional contribution: for the notion that male and female psychologies are different, argued in a leftist and feminist context, was a powerful new idea, and that idea was the dominant impression left on many of her readers.

Chodorow's book thus had a different effect than she intended. It was impossible not to be struck by her delicate and intricate account of mother-child interaction and its consequences for the development of gendered personality—and by the too obvious contrast of that account with her blithe and undocumented claim that "Nonbiological mothers, children, and men can parent just as adequately as biological mothers and can feel just as nurturant."[10] Could relationships so deep, delicate, and universal as those she described be well explained by an abstraction called "socialization"? In effect, Chodorow's considerable descriptive talents got the better of her much weaker theoretical ones. It was Chodorow's highly resonant descriptions of maleness and femaleness, rather than her claim that gender traits could be readily and radically eliminated by "equal parenting," that were to mark the work of her successor Carol Gilligan.

Carol Gilligan's *In a Different Voice: Psychological Theory and Women's Development* (1982) shows both the increasing sophistication of feminist theory in the late 1970s and early 1980s, and the tendency of that increased sophistication to undermine the assumptions about men and women that had originally motivated the feminist revolt. The explanatory systems that fueled the dynamic rage of feminists around 1970, such as cultural determinism and the Marxian concept of men as an oppressor class, began to break down in the late seventies under the intense scrutiny to which gender issues were subjected in both private life and science by feminists themselves. The end result is starting to look very different from the feminism we have hitherto known, and perhaps from any feminism that has ever existed. It is not at all clear that this emerging philosophy of gender will be described by the word "feminism" at all, an eventuality that Betty Friedan suggested with brilliant intuition (despite a badly jumbled exposition) in her 1981 book *The Second Stage.*

Gilligan's book stands roughly in the middle of this process. She retains an unshaken belief in the tenets of 1970s feminism: that feminism represents the true route of moral progress for humanity; that men's nature is inherently suspect; and that professional careers represent the acme of fulfillment for women, as a higher order of existence than mere motherhood and wifedom. But alongside these conventional beliefs, she has constructed an alternative psychology of women that contains an implicit critique of the careerist prescription for women's lives and that, by moving toward a defense of women's nature as it is rather than as it allegedly should become, may even help open the way toward a similarly more tolerant rethinking of men's nature.

According to Gilligan, men's psychology has been used as the adult norm, making women seem inadequate or immature. But, she argues, women's psychology is distinct from men's. It is not inferior, but it is different.

> I began to hear a distinction in [men's and women's] voices, two ways of speaking about moral problems, two modes of describing the relationship between other and self. Differences represented in the psychological literature as steps in a developmental progression suddenly appeared instead as a contrapuntal theme, woven into the cycle of life and recurring in varying forms in people's judgments, fantasies, and thoughts.[11]

Men's psychological development causes them to value separation from others, hierarchy, abstract rules, logical consistency in principles of behavior, and individual achievement. In contrast, women's psychology emphasizes connectedness to others, the reconciliation of opposing points of view, and a pragmatic appreciation of what a situation means to the individuals involved rather than the imposition of an *a priori* logical structure. This is a qualitative difference, not a question of degree. Men perceive people primarily in terms of their "separateness," women in terms of their "connectedness."

Relying on Chodorow's analysis, which attributes the origins of this distinction to the differing relations of boys and girls with their mothers, Gilligan spends little time considering how or why these differences occur. Instead, she tries to document their nature and implications for older children and adults.

Her method is to interview subjects, using a format designed to be flexible enough to probe the specific and differing thoughts of each individual. There may be some doubt as to whether this method is truly empirical, but impressive patterns do emerge. Following the lead of her Harvard mentor, the late Lawrence Kohlberg, she focuses on the study of morality: that is, on individuals' responses to real or hypothetical situations that require a moral decision between competing imperatives.

Men and women consistently differ in ways that become impressive as they recur in interview after interview. Men, according to Gilligan, tend to evaluate moral dilemmas in terms of abstract rights, a tendency that, following Piaget, she thinks derives from the need to adjudicate disputes on the playground so that the game can continue.[12] This male tendency, Gilligan argues, has been defined as the norm for healthy development.

But, according to Gilligan, females see such dilemmas very differently, and have been unduly stigmatized for doing so. Girls are willing to give up the game itself rather than to allow disputes arising from it to threaten the continuity of ongoing relationships. Similarly, when confronted with a real or hypothetical dilemma, females typically try to resolve competing needs pragmatically, in terms of the specifics of the situation at hand rather than in terms of general, abstract moral principles. Women's distinctive moral point of view—and it must be understood that morality is used by Gilligan as a means of ferreting out more encompassing aspects of human psychology—has often been habitually underrated in the past, Gilligan says, most notably by Freud, who was never able to penetrate the female point of view, and more recently by feminist psychologists like Matina Horner, who contrasted the attitudes and behavior of women unfavorably with those of men, arguing that women need to overcome the societal handicap of what had been defined as feminine modes of behavior.

Horner's "fear of success" study is among those reevaluated by Gilligan. In that study (whose success played a key role in her subsequent selection as president of Radcliffe College), Horner argued that women fear to succeed academically or in the professions, an attitude that must be overcome if they are to participate equally in society with men. In fact, says Gilligan, Horner misunderstood the issues involved. Citing a more recent critique of Horner's study,[13] she argues that women only become anxious in competitive situations in which for one person to succeed another must fail. As she points out, "traditional girls' games like jump rope and hopscotch are turn-taking games, where competition is indirect since one person's success does not necessarily signify another's failure."[14]

The masculine bias that has prevailed in the social sciences has obscured the distinctiveness and worth of the female perspective.

Women's deference is rooted not only in their social subordination but also in the substance of their moral concern. Sensitivity to the needs of others and the assumption of the responsibility for taking care lead women to attend to voices other than their own and to include in their judgment other points of view. Women's moral weakness, manifest in an apparent diffusion and confusion of judgment, is thus inseparable from women's moral strength, an overriding concern with relationships and responsibilities. The reluctance to judge may itself be indicative of the care and concern for others that infuse the psychology of women's development and are responsible for what is generally seen as problematic in its nature. In contrast to the moral absolutism of many adolescent male judgments, women display increased sensitivity to the context of individual situations.[15]

Maturity, she argues, entails the capacity for balanced judgment, which requires the discovery of the other sex's perspective and the recognition of its validity.

The divergence in judgment between the sexes is resolved through the discovery by each of the other's perspective and of the relationship between integrity and care.[16]

But the sexes come to this understanding "from different angles" and must overcome different sets of problems to attain it. Women must not become so wrapped up in "connection" that they fail to distinguish and value their own legitimate needs, losing sight of their separateness, and men must not become so removed by "separation" that they lose the ability to evaluate the needs and feelings of others, failing to grasp the interdependence of human beings.

Gilligan's work points to a renewed acceptance of gender as a positive and necessary force in women's lives. It is an important step toward the revalidation of the feminine. The words "masculine" and "feminine" have even begun to creep back hesitantly into her vocabulary as something other than impediments to "personhood," as when she speaks of

two different constructions of the moral domain—one traditionally associated with masculinity and the public world of social power, the other with femininity and the privacy of domestic interchange. The developmental ordering of these two points of view has been to consider the masculine as more adequate than the feminine and thus as replacing the feminine when the individual moves toward maturity. The reconciliation of these two modes, however, is not clear.[17]

That there does remain a provisional, transitional character to Gilligan's thought is shown by her treatment of men. With Gilligan, the great feminist putdown of women's characteristics begins to recede—but the revalidation of the masculine has yet to begin. Even while arguing for an acceptance of feminine values as they actually exist, Gilligan often seems blind to the need for an equivalent acceptance of masculine values. Rather than remaining with her insight that it is worthwhile for each sex to take cognizance of the value structure of the other, she seems to think that men and women must adopt each other's insights to the point where the sexes become psychologically and behaviorally indistinguishable. This is particularly incumbent on men, for Gilligan has not shed the anti-male bias of her predecessors.

One can trace the lessening of the anti-male rage that was at its most virulent around 1970 in, say, Kate Millett's *Sexual Politics,* into a conventional perspective, elaborately defended and yet not deeply felt, by the mid-seventies as seen, for example, in Nancy Chodorow's *The Reproduction of Mothering* in 1978, until by the publication of Carol Gilligan's book in 1982 it is scarcely more than a habit of mind—but still pernicious. It is inexcusably poor thinking to assume that what men do is bad and must be explained in terms of pathology with a view toward changing it for a better future. Such a view is sure to constrain the thought of those who hold it, and Gilligan is no exception.

Thus according to Gilligan, the male point of view gives rise to "stereotypes" that "reflect a conception of adulthood that is itself out of balance, favoring the separateness of the individual self over connection to others, and leaning more toward an autonomous life of work than toward the interdependence of love and care."[18] This postulated "separateness" that human males, and young adult males in particular, feel impelled toward is seen in primarily negative terms as a problem to be overcome. "Although aggression has been construed as instinctual . . . , the violence in male fantasy seems rather to arise from a problem in communication and an absence of knowledge about human relationships."[19] Because she is unable to accept men (or boys) as they are, Gilligan attempts to impose a female point of view on their actions, even going so far as to see "the origins of aggression in the failure of connection."[20]

Normal male activity appears threatening and unbalanced to Gilligan, as it does to other feminists—and to many men of the Vietnam era. Many male fantasies and behavioral modes are left unexplained by the dogma with which Gilligan is familiar, and therefore seem alien and frightening to her. Like Millett a dozen years before, she finds it easiest to deal with masculinity by categorizing it as abnormal:

The prevalence of violence in male fantasy, like the explosive imagery in the moral judgment of the eleven-year-old boy and the representation of theft as the way to resolve a dispute, is consonant with the view of aggression as endemic in human relationships. But these male fantasies and images also reveal a world where connection is fragmented and communication fails, where betrayal threatens because there seems to be no way of knowing the truth.[21]

Ironically, Gilligan is repeating from a female point of view the mistake she attributes to male theorists like Freud, whom she criticizes for failing to understand and value women in their own terms. Having defined a female perspective that differs from the male perspective, she then wants to impose it as the only right way:

To admit the truth of the women's perspective to the conception of moral development is to recognize for both sexes the importance throughout life of the connection between self and other, the universality of the need for compassion and care.[22]

On one level this is true; mature development probably does involve the recognition by men of the importance of these values which, according to Gilligan, come more easily to women. On another level, though, it is highly misleading. Gilligan gives the impression that the mature development of the sexes causes their perspectives to converge to the point that they become indistinguishable. This notion defies common sense and experience. Gilligan has been proving women's needs are not men's. Why then groundlessly assert that men's needs are the same as women's? The answer, of course, has to do with the anti-masculine tradition out of which Gilligan comes and which, at least at the time of writing this book, she has not altogether escaped. She still has only one ideal of adulthood, even though she thinks that men and women must approach it from different angles.[23] The possibility that the masculine and the feminine might both be permanently valid and different has yet to occur to her.

The extent to which Gilligan is still steeped in the "old feminism" is perhaps even more apparent in her descriptions of the goals and processes of maturing in women. Gilligan has not fully escaped the feminist preconception of women's development, with its consequent suspicion of feminine ways. For example, she says of one of her subjects, who is struggling with a decision over whether to have an abortion, that

> Seeing the pregnancy as a manifestation of the inner conflict between her wish, on the one hand "to be a college president" and, on the other, "to be making pottery and flowers and having kids and staying at home," Ruth struggles with the contradiction between femininity and adulthood.[24]

Gilligan implies it is somehow more adult "to be a college president" than "to be making pottery and flowers and having kids and staying at home." To see a conflict between femininity and adulthood in this context implies a pretty dim view of femininity and suggests that, to become fully adult, women must "grow up" so that they can be, not merely mothers, but full adults. Passages like this show that Gilligan has yet to overcome the artificial opposition between femininity and adulthood that she is herself trying to counter.

The persistence of such contradictions in her work is the secret of Gilligan's acceptance by feminists. Her theorizing accords with the life experience of her feminist readers, which inclines them to tolerance and tradition, while the rhetoric with which she surrounds her theories faithfully mirrors the intolerant utopianism of their guiding ideology. Gilligan has yet to work out the contradictions between her psychology and her ideology. When she does so, it seems likely she will move even farther from feminism as we have known it.

Gilligan has begun to move beyond the feminist devaluation of the feminine, but it continues to inform her judgments. She does not consider the probability that if women are psychologically different from men, as she maintains, they are also likely to be behaviorally different; and that these behavioral differences will have societal consequences of some sort.

Gilligan's "old feminism" is especially evident in her descriptions of positive maturational progress in the young women she has studied. Megan Marshall has described the vicissitudes of the "Control Generation" of American women, those women who graduated from college in the late sixties and the seventies and whose lives were mediated by "a code made up of feminism, professionalism, and philosophies of self-fulfillment in roughly equal parts."[25] This "Control Generation" has lost the capacity for trust in an adult heterosexual relationship. The recovery of trust, according to Marshall, requires lowering the high value placed on controlling one's own life, and one's relationships with men in particular. It is therefore disquieting—if one accepts that Marshall is even partly right—to see Gilligan describing maturational progress in terms of "taking control." A serious philosophical quandary exists over whether it is possible to literally control one's destiny. But even if it is possible, is it desirable? Gilligan seems to be advocating the very trap Marshall has identified.

Gilligan's conception is that, through confronting "choice," women come to "a new understanding of relationships and speak of their sense of 'a new beginning,' a chance 'to take control of my life.' "[26] For instance, one woman who has passed through this process says that "now she feels 'really connected with my insides, really good. I just feel strong in a way I'm not aware of having felt, really in control of my life, not just sort of randomly drifting along.' "[27]

Another of Gilligan's subjects reports that, in the time elapsed since a previous interview, she had "thought 'a lot about decision-making, and for the first time I wanted to take control of and responsibility for my own decisions in life.' " An improved self-image resulted from these reflections: " 'Because now that you are going to take control of your own life, you don't feel like you are a pawn in other people's hands.' "[28]

Gilligan says of yet another interviewee that "realizing that 'it was too easy to go through life the way I had done, letting someone else take responsibility for the direction of my life,' she challenged herself to take control and 'changed the direction of my life.' "[29]

In a final example, when "a recent college graduate" is asked, "Thinking back over the past year, what stands out for you?" she replies, to the author's obvious approval, "Taking control of my life."[30]

I do not question the authenticity or the importance of these women's experiences. "Taking control," in the sense of taking responsibility for one's actions, is a prerequisite for a fully adult relationship. But it is only a way station on the road to such a relationship. The next step is to be able to truly give of oneself, which requires not "taking control" but giving up control. Yet Gilligan never looks beyond this way station, this halfway house for "wounded women,"[31] to the definitive step in achieving maturity—a step well within the reach of the majority of women.

But despite these shortcomings, Gilligan's work remains in the forefront of an incipient post-feminist effort to define the differences between the sexes in a systematic and reliable manner. The fact that Gilligan sees the sexes as different and complementary is a tremendous step in the right direction, however pitiable the need for such a step may seem a few years from now. No doubt her sample is inadequate, as she herself admits,[32] and her focus on moral dilemmas too narrow. But the idea that the differences between men and women are positive and complementary is of the greatest importance, and is almost ready to emerge from the cocoon of her book.

Toward a Revalidation of the Feminine

There is a world of difference between Gilligan's portrayal of women's psychology in 1982 and Friedan's in 1963. Friedan equated the housewife in her home with a prisoner in a concentration camp. Traditional female modes of behavior were obsolete and should be dispensed with. *The Feminine Mystique* made "femininity" a dirty word. The image of the middle-aged housewife as a mindless frump, devoid of interest and initiative, was widely accepted as accurate by feminists in the seventies— whereas Gilligan argues that "the image of women arriving at mid-life childlike and dependent on others is belied by the activity of their care in nurturing and sustaining family relationships."[33] This is moreover unquestionably a virtue, a strength of women which they must respect in themselves and from which men can learn, according to Gilligan. "Since the reality of connection is experienced by women as given rather than as freely contracted, they arrive at an understanding of life that reflects the limits of autonomy and control."[34]

Gilligan at this point begins to sound indistinguishable from Steven Goldberg, who defends "the positive, power-engendering aspects of femininity," and argues for the centrality of "woman's universal role of creator and keeper of society's emotional resources."[35] Equally significant, she also begins to sound like pre-feminist psychoanalytic writers such as Helene Deutsch. Such parallels are important in order to understand what has and has not changed in the era through which we have just passed.

History does not move like a Colorado superhighway, a broad and obvious route that proceeds without detour or hindrance between two predetermined points, but like the Mississippi River, a meandering progress of vague and mixed origin that turns, twists, and doubles back on itself, leaving in its wake wasteful loops and dry oxbow lakes, to lose itself in a near future as murky as the mud of the Delta.

Was the feminist ferment necessary to reach a higher plane of insight, or was it to some extent one of history's wasteful detours? If one agrees that Gilligan is even partly right, it must be acknowledged that her work represents a return to previous insights that were prematurely abandoned as much as it represents an innovation. Gilligan's psychology of women is not a refinement of the feminist perspective but its reversal.

The contrast between Gilligan's model of female psychology and Friedan's allows us to assess more precisely the value of the contemporary feminist movement. A minority of feminists now freely admit there were "excesses" in the early movement. This conventional interpretation of the history of contemporary feminism is as follows: Women were severely oppressed in the fifties. Responding to this oppression, they revolted at the end of the sixties. Because their oppression had been so severe, there was naturally some excess in their reaction against it, but the early excess has since been outgrown. The feminist revolution was necessary and noble, a wholly admirable cause that today could move ahead unimpeded were it not for the vicious opposition of a "right-wing backlash" which, like an echoed wave, flows mindlessly against the tide of history.

This reassuring view forestalls any need on the part of feminists to uncover the roots of their ideas. But the difficulties with feminism arise neither from its "early excess" nor a "right-wing backlash" but from its basic assumptions. Once it is realized that Friedan used a male model for female psychology—specifically that of the neo-Freudian Erik Erikson—the whole basis for her critique of femininity collapses.

It is simply not true, as Gilligan and every other feminist psychologist has asserted at some point, that psychology was once a field so male-centered that it invariably took male development to be the only adult model. The claim that only the liberating influence of feminism made possible a distinctive female psychology is a deceptive exercise in self-congratulation. Long before the feminist revolution, powerful voices spoke up for women's point of view, including those of Anna Freud and Helene Deutsch. It was feminists themselves who discredited what had previously been a widely respected view of feminine temperament. The feminist discovery of a feminine psychology smacks more than vaguely of a reinvention of the wheel.

Among the various psychologies of women available to her, Friedan chose one which argued that women and men undergo identical developments which lead to identical results. Friedan has no use for feminine qualities, for to be feminine is to be less than human. She holds up to ridicule

The sex-directed educator [who] equates as masculine our "vastly overrated cultural creativity," "our uncritical acceptance of 'progress' as good in itself," "egotistic individualism," "innovation," "abstract communication," "quantitative thinking". . . . Against these, equated as feminine, are "the sense of persons, of the immediate, of intangible qualitative relationships, an aversion for statistics and quantities," "the intuitive," "the emotional," and all the forces that "cherish" and "conserve" what is "good, true, beautiful, useful, and holy."[36]

After Gilligan, Friedan's scorn rings hollow. It does not take any very great insight to see the direct parallel between qualities such as "egotistic individualism" and Gilligan's account of male psychology, nor between qualities like "the sense of persons" and her account of female psychology. It is not the woman she quotes, held up for the ridicule of Friedan's readers, who appears to have misled her readers through a deliberately one-sided account of female psychology, but Friedan herself.

Femininity was equated by Friedan with a brainwashed condition of infantile dependence and servitude. The sexes had only one psychology that mattered, a "human" one. Jettisoning the various versions of a female psychology that were available to her, Friedan argued that the model for men was the only accurate model for both sexes. To imply that women were at all different was to belittle them.

Once these ideas were accepted, a divorce from self became inevitable for feminists, regardless of the level of success or failure of their movement. And because the sexes are engaged in an intricate minuet that constantly plays on the alternating themes of their difference and their similarity, it guaranteed a high level of difficulty and *de facto* hypocrisy in relations with men.

Was it really necessary to pass through all the storm and stress of the Feminist Era in order to arrive at ideas that were generally available forty years ago, as if these were new insights?

Gilligan's work, like Chodorow's (or Hrdy's), has an additional major conceptual fault, and it is an ideological rather than a scientific one. Having documented with care and elegance significant and universal differences in the makeup of the sexes, they disown this, the most important aspect of their own work, by falling back on a vulgarized cultural determinism and arguing that the deep and significant differences they have just described are in fact superficial and inconsequential. When it is time to sum up their work and assess its implications for human beings, their feminism preempts their professionalism. A further step is required.

For there are no grounds to assume that the discovery by each sex of the virtues of the other's perspective—of separateness by women, of connectedness by men—leads to an androgynous personality, as Gilligan claims. Temperament remains gendered—as is in fact clear from her own argument, when she is not busy directly asserting the contrary. For example, when she says that "the image of women arriving at mid-life childlike and dependent on others is belied by the activity of their care in nurturing and sustaining family relationships," she is clearly assuming that the feminine temperament she has described does in fact persist in women throughout the life cycle. The discovery of the perspective of the opposite sex—which Gilligan seems to locate around the late twenties— helps individuals to balance the excesses of their own sex, without in any way reducing the importance of their primary gender identification and personality. Men and women do not become psychologically genderless "persons" as a result of maturity, they just become wiser men and wiser women.

Two points then remain to be addressed. First, could, as Chodorow asserts, innovations in child-rearing practices change this situation and eliminate gendered temperament? Second, if the physiological and psychological differences that have been documented by thinkers as diverse as Goldberg and Gilligan exist, can we come to terms with them? Can we perhaps even come to value them, without rejecting the validity of the experiences of either sex?

These questions touch on the malleability of human beings. As we have seen, this is substantial but not infinite. This is, however, a rather abstract formulation that does not convey much of a sense of real possibility. The next chapter will examine two well-documented cases that address the question of human malleability directly. Each of these was an effort to translate unisexist ideology into social reality. These cases are the experience of the Israeli kibbutz and the attempt in America at "nonsexist child rearing."

Chapter 10

Kibbutz and Kindergarten

The Kibbutz

The Israeli kibbutz represents an "experiment in reality" that, as Lionel Tiger and Joseph Shepher note, could not have been devised by any social scientist.[1] Back in the sixties, Israel seemed to be a prime example of a society that had achieved sexual egalitarianism, or was at least well on the way to doing so. Life on the kibbutz seemed to epitomize that egalitarian spirit.

The kibbutz was a radical attempt to break with European society, in particular with the culture of the *shtetl,* the Jewish ghetto of Eastern Europe. The kibbutz sought to abolish private property among its members, who were to live in common, close to the land. This new form of settlement owed part of its inspiration to the agricultural village in which most of humanity has lived since the Neolithic period, and part to an idealization of the virtues of living in a "camp," a popular idea in the early decades of this century. German youth in particular, but also youth elsewhere in Europe and in the United States, were attracted to the camp ideal, which spawned such intriguing forms as the kibbutz and such inconclusive ones as Camp William James in America,[2] and played some as yet unexplored role in the conceptualization of the horror of the Nazi concentration camps. (Concentration camp survivors avoided the kibbutzim: the similarities were too unsettling.) The ideology of the kibbutz can be described as "communitarian socialist." It links the back-to-nature tradition that goes back to Rousseau, the German Romantics, and in America to Thoreau with the socialist tradition as epitomized by Marx and Engels. About half the kibbutzim are explicitly Marxist; the others are not.

In the area of gender, the kibbutz sought to implement a unisexist conception of equality between the sexes. The actual conditions of life in the kibbutz closely parallel the changes feminists advocate to eliminate gender distinctions in America.

Like virtually all activities in the kibbutz, with the exception of sex, traditionally female work was communalized. There was a communal kitchen, a communal laundry, and a communal child-rearing facility, the "babies' house," where a professional nurse provided most of the child care. Marriage, after a few initial experiments away from it, was retained but downgraded in importance: social norms frowned on couples spending much time together. Politics, too, was communalized: the kibbutz makes, or at least legitimates, its major decisions in a general assembly in which all members are free to participate. The general assembly is the source of authority and government in the community. It elects necessary officers and hears their reports.

Unisexism prevailed, to the point that teenage girls and boys showered together and slept in the same bedrooms. But a strong puritan streak underlay the insistence on unisexist arrangements. Tiger and Shepher report the case of an adolescent boy who could not sleep because he was consumed with desire for the girl with whom he shared a room. The kibbutz response was to send him to a psychiatrist.

Kibbutz life thus aimed to take the onus out of being a woman, as it was perceived by the kibbutz founders. No other society has gone so far toward approximating the feminist ideal in its institutions. If we are going to expend enormous effort to change our own society according to the prescriptions of feminism, it makes sense to examine similar experiments that have already taken place. Their successes and failures surely have much to teach us. So it is particularly interesting to discover that the kibbutz, though it has enjoyed success in implementing some of its ideals, has failed to establish a culture of sexual equality—at least in equality's unisexist meaning. This failure is complete and unequivocal. Its immediate cause, interestingly, was the women.

One might have expected that, once the ball of sexual egalitarianism was given a decisive push, it would have kept rolling until a point was reached where the sexes no longer exhibited any significant differences in ambition or social function. This was in fact precisely the expectation of the kibbutz founders.

Instead of this result, predicted by environmentalist theories, including the Marxism that influenced the kibbutz founders, a countertrend began, once the harsh life of the earliest settlements began to be moderated by economic success, and once the number of women in the kibbutz population came to approximate the number of men. It would be naive to overlook the fact that the kibbutz ideology rested on a base conceived almost exclusively by men, such as Marx and Engels, and implemented primarily by men, who far outnumbered women in the early kibbutz settlements.

In the second generation of the kibbutzim, a reaction set in. Women began to resist the life-style dictated by kibbutz ideology. They demanded more time with their children than was allotted under the work rules, which were designed for productive efficiency, not for babies—or for mothers. After a long struggle, they won the right to be with their children for a period of time at the beginning of the day. So incongruous was this development in terms of kibbutz ideology that it was thought necessary to dignify this time with a special name, "the Hour of Love."

The Hour of Love was part of a general push that women initiated for what has aptly been described as "familism."[3]

> Women sparked and sustained the process of change in every kibbutz where familism had been introduced. The women started with informal discussions, brought the question to the agenda of the education committee, where they usually constitute the majority, then created pressure to bring the problem before the General Assembly (which is a legitimate form of preliminary lobbying) for a positive vote; where they had to, they resorted to propaganda, and even threats within their families. Most of the men who were leaders in the process were husbands of the most forceful women advocating change.[4]

As a result of women's efforts to restore the family to its central role, by the 1970s the kibbutz had in many ways come to epitomize the reverse of the feminist ideal. Bouncing back from its earlier devaluation, marriage became the central institution of kibbutz society and acquired an even greater importance than in the rest of Israeli society. Couples were expected to be together much of the time: for example, on weekends, at kibbutz social events, and at General Assembly meetings. They were also expected to perform the periodically assigned duty of night watch together. The marriage rate in the kibbutz soared to ninety-eight percent. Today, virtually all adults in the kibbutz are married.

With marriage once again recognized as the foundation of society, the main locus of life began to shift away from communal facilities and activities, back to the home and family activities. Apartments grew in size. They became centers for a renewed family life—even though parents were still not allowed to keep their children home overnight. Family teatimes and baking by the women became central events in daily social life. Since unmarried people were in effect excluded from much of this new family-centered activity, there was additional incentive to marry. The new, larger apartments also required more maintenance and took more effort to furnish and decorate, leading people to become even more involved with the home.

Within the home, clear sexual divisions of labor prevail. The feminist perspective dictates that such divisions are imposed by men and are inherently exploitative. In the kibbutz, at least, this is not the case (unless one postulates, as feminists do, that kibbutz women are unknowing pawns of an oppressive culture—an argument we will examine shortly). Women do most of the housework, but want their husbands around doing something. Their presence is what seems to matter most: women want to do this work, but expect it to be appreciated. A man who does not participate in housework is derided by other kibbutzniks as an "effendi," Arabic for "lord"; but women seem to push their men out of a great deal of cleaning and decorating work, claiming their husbands don't do it properly. Men, on the other hand, are expected to take responsibility for different categories of housework, such as electrical wiring.

The picture of kibbutz marriage is one of mutual help and joint decision-making. Clearly, kibbutz marriage and the roles it involves afford considerable satisfaction to women. To use Gilligan's vocabulary, the women are embedded in a context of relatedness, yet have considerable scope for autonomy. So, for that matter, are the men. It seems probable that dissatisfaction with life in the kibbutz is likely to arise from women's desire for even greater relatedness and from men's desire for greater autonomy.

The sexual polarization of labor in the kibbutz became pronounced. While in principle virtually all jobs in the kibbutz are equally open to men and women, the practice contradicts this ideal: men work at certain jobs, women at others. In the cases where they work together, there is typically a division between men's and women's tasks. For example, women run the food preparation facilities assisted by a "male of the kitchen" to do the heavy lifting work.

In the political sphere, men participate far more actively than women, although women have the same opportunities for participation as men. Indeed, the communities would like women to participate *more* in public life, and are periodically bemused by their inability to motivate them to do so. Men continue to attend the General Assembly more frequently, to speak far more often once they are there, and to fill by far the majority of administrative and executive positions—particularly the higher ones that involve the most authority over people, money, goods, and land.

The rule that the higher the status of a position, the more likely it is to be filled by a man, holds good in the kibbutz. The only exception to this rule in the kibbutz involves the leadership of committees dealing with education and other aspects of child rearing, which are often headed by women.

What are we to make of this evidence? The kibbutz can be ignored as just one more society that fails to conform to the ideal of sexual equality, as that ideal is defined from a unisexist standpoint: identity between males and females in all aspects of thought and behavior. But in the sixties, when feminist ideology was being formed (or recovered from earlier thinkers like Engels), the kibbutz was a major example of a sexually egalitarian society—egalitarian, that is, in the unisexist sense. Since the sixties, the kibbutz has fallen the way of all such examples. A closer look shows that this egalitarianism is relative and superficial— or simply a mistake, made by hopeful investigators on the basis of inadequate evidence.

The kibbutz evidence can also, of course, be explained away. Feminists have in fact tried to do this. They have argued that subtle cues and pressures forced women out of the supposedly more satisfying arena occupied by men. The result of this sex-typing, it is claimed, is that "women's self-confidence and self-esteem are undermined and their participation in the decision-making of the kibbutz and in the more powerful and prestigious offices is inhibited." It is asserted that women adopted familism as a compensation for this alleged exclusion.[5]

As usual, the feminist argument assumes that what men are doing is more rewarding than what women are doing—a highly debatable assumption. It also assumes that the kibbutz women are dumb victims, whereas the whole history of the familism struggle shows them to be highly self-aware motivators who are perfectly capable of bending the kibbutz political process to their purposes when they wish to. Only the scorn feminists feel for women who value femininity forces them to invent such a tortured explanation.

Why, indeed, should gender distinctions not progressively disappear once an impetus is given away from them, as was initially the case in the kibbutz? Why should they be so tenacious? We are thrown back on two possible explanations. The first is to assume, as feminists do, that the form of human society is vicious, and that a revolution in all aspects of life is necessary and possible to correct this fault. The assumption that human life is corrupt because society differentiates the sexes requires either the denial of evolution or the postulation of a feminist Garden of Eden in which sexual egalitarianism prevailed or in which women ruled. But, as we have seen in considering this hypothesis in earlier sections, there is no fall from a feminist Eden in human history or prehistory. And if evolution is irrelevant, if men and women are completely alike, why is it so hard to get them to behave as if this were true?

The alternative is to recall that humans, like other animals, do not learn all things with equal ease. While it is possible to temporarily neutralize some aspects of gender, if sufficiently effective restrictions are imposed on their expression, gender will always tend to reassert itself as soon as the restrictions are removed. In the real world, the condition restricting the expression of gender is likely to be ideology. Once the initial period of ideological fervor winds down—as it must—society will tend to revert to its natural and unconstrained form. Nothing will have changed in the human being.

And, as Gilligan shows, women are less likely to be impressed with, or bound by, ideology than are men. In this the kibbutz provides us with an object lesson, and although the kibbutz differs in many ways from the environments in which most Americans live, the underlying similarity between the relations of kibbutz and American women to their dominant cultural ideologies suggests that feminism is not to be the last way station on the march of American women.

Nonsexist Child Rearing

Perhaps nothing shows the continued importance of the nature/nurture controversy to our time as much as "nonsexist child rearing." Millions of parents have been encouraged to alter their children's behavior, and through it society, by a philosophy of child rearing based on extreme cultural determinism.

Nonsexist child rearing is an attempt to bring up children in a way that will free them from sex stereotypes that are thought to inhibit their ability to develop as individuals. "Free to be, you and me" is the goal.

Nonsexist child rearing's reason to be, and the rationale for believing it can work, is the belief that masculinity and femininity are arbitrary constructs that are unjustly imposed by society on the individual.

Many feminists agreed with Millett that sex differences were limited to the form of the genitals. But a good number of feminists and non-feminists alike who did not explicitly subscribe to quite such an extreme view agreed broadly on vaguer formulations that had much the same effect, such as "we must do away with the limiting effects of traditional sex roles." Gender was seen purely as limitation. If there were any real differences between men and women, it was impossible to guess what they might be, anyhow: as Millett said, "Whatever the 'real' differences between the sexes may be, we are not likely to know them until the sexes are treated differently, that is alike."[6] Having denied the possibility of empirical inquiry (a serious mistake, by which the possibility of discovering any knowledge except through trial and error was rejected), it became that much more imperative to institute an experiment-in-reality, using children as its subjects. As so often before, children became pawns in the political disputes of adults.

The National Organization for Women summarized the nonsexist child rearing argument in an official encapsulation of its policies published in 1973 entitled "Revolution: Tomorrow is NOW." According to this document,

> Realizing that each individual child has the capacity for the full range of human characteristics, the child should not be channeled into a role based on sexual stereotypes.[7]

The assumption is that the acquisition of gender is a transaction between the child and society to which the child brings nothing. Individual temperaments, it is believed, are distributed along a continuum that is unrelated to biological sex—or, if there is a relation, it is too weak to serve as a useful guide for bringing up children.

The key concept here is "role": children acquire "stereotypical" gender orientations through precept, which may be conscious—"Girls don't do that"—or unconscious, and through imitation. By defining certain ways of being as masculine and others as feminine, adults induct children into sex roles. At the same time, children observe the adults around them: if these adults behave in sex-typed ways, the children conclude that certain activities are male, others female, and try to adjust their dispositions accordingly. The outcome of these influences is the sexual polarization of society into two artificial and unwholesome divisions, masculine and feminine, which bear little relation, or even none at all, to individuals' personalities. The result is conflict and tension.

Because femininity is an artificial imposition on women, they react to it negatively. They become depressed, anxious, irritable, and suffer from low self-esteem, a torture to themselves and those in their lives. Worse, femininity, with its emphasis on interpersonal relations, has stultified their ability to establish independent personal goals; it mires women in relationships while robbing them of the capacity to benefit from them. Similarly, because masculinity is a comparable imposition on men, men react to it negatively, through misogyny as they attempt to deny their softer side, and through violence because of the arrogance masculinity encourages and the frustrations it creates. Each sex, caught on the treadmill of its alienation from self, transfers its values to children, perpetuating the misery of sexist society into succeeding generations. Nonsexist child rearing proposes to break the cycle. We now begin to see why feminists made "sex roles" a dirty word.

Sex roles are responsible, not merely for the misery of individuals, making it impossible for them to lead authentic, productive lives, but also for the great calamities that bedevil the human race. War, for example, is attributed to masculinity, which feminists think of as a "deformation" that is "marked by a certain predatory or aggressive character."[8] As the NOW declaration put it, "war is the expression of the masculine mystique that historically has used violence as a solution to problems." Nonsexist child rearing thus emerges as an urgent and noble enterprise: it is being undertaken, not merely for the good of individual children, but also to save humanity from the inhuman effects of sexism, of which the scourge of war is only one of the most conspicuous. Indeed, sexism lies at the root of the threat of nuclear annihilation. It is because of men's alienation from self that "their misdirected energies have produced the ultimate weapon."[9] New parents face a daunting task: not merely to bring up Johnny, but to bring him up to save humanity. This is one reason the feminist generation produced so few children. And somewhere along the line, the progressive education concept of the "self-directed child" went out the window, under the powerful influence of the highly prescriptive feminist ideology.

Individual children, therefore, are to be treated equally, that is, identically: boys are to play with dolls and girls with trucks. They are to be spared the influence of "role models" whose behavior suggests any difference between men and women. They must see Mommy leaving for work and Daddy cleaning the kitchen. By establishing an ambience of equality in the home, parents will ensure that their kids do not grow up with reductive conceptions of masculinity and femininity.

These children will, it is expected, behave in ways that are human, not masculine or feminine—indeed, it is assumed that to behave humanly means *not* to behave in ways that have been labeled "masculine" or "feminine." Boys will play with dolls to the same extent and in the same ways as girls; girls will display the same enthusiasm as boys for building things, forming large groups, and engaging in rough-and-tumble play. Our children will begin to see one another as strictly unique individuals, whose gender is one relatively unimportant fact about them, like their hair color. Their behavior will no longer be differentiated by sex.

By now, millions of American children have been exposed to nonsexist child rearing. While the effort has no doubt been imperfect and uneven, it has also been intensive, strenuous, and committed. Hundreds of thousands, perhaps millions, of parents have devoted enormous effort to producing nonsexist children. If nonsexist child rearing is a well-conceived idea, some positive results can be expected by now: children who, at least in some cases in some places, are less "sexist" than children brought up under the old regime. The results are in, and they are unambiguous: nonsexist child rearing is a total failure. The problem isn't the ideology, which is no more cockeyed than many other schemes that have been foisted off on the human race for its misery. The problem is the kids.

As is reported in a recent book by Sara Bonnett Stein, author of over a dozen books on children, "Boys are not dressing baby dolls. Girls are not playing with trucks. . . . The problem is baffling to those who have devoted themselves to eradicating sexism and sex stereotypes in their families."[10]

The evidence mounts:

Jenny, whose mother is a doctor, believes only boys can be doctors. She plays at being a nurse. Sarah's parents are both full-time professionals. When she grows up, she plans to be a bride, or maybe a princess. . . .

How come Jerry, who has heard only nonsexist stories, himself relates to tales of risk, collision, and disaster—with all male characters? Why don't girls enliven their play with siren wails, engine revs, and crashes?

. . . Even the most scrupulous parents still find their efforts frustrated.

> The Jacobsons tried very hard to bring out Kenneth's gentleness. When Kenneth's mother gave him his first baby doll, he pulled it out of the box by one arm and then crammed it into a dump truck for a wild ride across the kitchen floor.[11]

Of course there have always been gentle, quiet boys and girls who have been tomboys. But there is not one shred of evidence that the distribution of temperament is any different among children who have been raised in a "nonsexist" manner from children raised in "traditional" ways. Children continue to be just as polarized by temperament as ever— and just as rigidly self-segregated by sex in their play groups. If adults won't segregate them by sex, children will do so themselves, as in our progressive kindergartens—perhaps a protective reaction on their part. The conspicuous differences in temperament that are universal between boys and girls remain universal, which should not be surprising, considering that these are exactly the same differences in gendered temperament that exist among all our close biological relatives.

Given the persistence among children of gender as a source of personal identity, a means of social organization, and a valid predictor of behavior, despite the best of efforts to eradicate these, is the cultural determinist, unisexist view of "roles" justified? Do children acquire these behaviors through instruction and imitation? If not, how do they acquire them? If these roles turn out not to be artificial impositions, can we dismiss them quite so readily as superficial? If they are not superficial, but ineradicable, had we not better learn to live with them? If they are ineradicable, do they perhaps deserve a second look; are they perhaps less threatening and more valuable than had been thought? Can we perhaps even come to value and enjoy them? Do we in fact do so despite an ongoing ideological alienation from our nature?

Is it possible that mothering, in the sensitive early months and years of a child's life, causes gender difference? For such difference appears very early:

> Even given the same "neutral" toys, you can look in on any group of three-year-olds in preschool and see that the boys are building long roads and the girls are making rooms and houses—if they play with blocks at all.[12]

More likely, the girls are mothering their dolls.

Clearly, by the time children are three it is too late. They are firmly launched on the "sexist" path. The behavior of boys and girls by this age is already conspicuously differentiated by sex in just the ways feminists deplore—a differentiation that will relentlessly accelerate over the coming years.

This differentiation by age three is universal. It can be observed, as Stein says, in "any group of three year olds." Not only does it occur universally, it also occurs in the same ways: girls play with dolls, boys embark on building projects, to cite only one important and obvious contrast. Given the fact that children experience diverse levels and forms of care, the universality of this differentiation and of the forms it takes suggests that some factor or set of factors is at work to produce this invariant result.

Can the factor be culture? Is it possible that socialization, with no reference to biology, could produce such unvarying results in billions of individuals among thousands of societies across hundreds of generations? Let us examine this possibility. It defies every known law of logic and every intuition of common sense, but incredible though it seems, many apparently rational men and women have believed in it recently. Perhaps they are right.

If culture is responsible for gendered temperament, there must be a point at which boys and girls are identical, since culture cannot possibly influence temperament in relation to gender before birth, when the sex of the child is usually unknown. We have already seen that by age three the sexes diverge markedly, showing "sexist" behaviors in profusion. Perhaps culture begins to create gendered temperament even earlier. Let us examine this hypothesis.

As we move back to a yet earlier phase in the life cycle in our attempt to find a point at which culture might cause boys and girls to become masculine or feminine, we discover that there are valid generalizations that can be made about the differentiated behavior of boy and girl babies.

Feminists have insisted that the difference in boy and girl babies' responses occurs in reaction to stereotyping by their mothers. It is well established "that mothers touch and hold their newborn sons more than their newborn daughters but talk to and smile more at newborn daughters than newborn sons."[13] There are two objections to the claim that this behavior by mothers causes gendered behavior. The first is that these differences between boy and girl babies are measurable literally from birth—before the mother's intervention could possibly have any effect whatever. The baby will of course be profoundly affected by its mother's care, but he or she is not a blank slate.

> Each baby has an individual style, too, and also a tendency to behave according to gender. Girls, more physiologically mature at birth, tend to be more organized than male infants. Their movements may be smoother, they remain alert for longer periods and also sleep a little longer. Girl babies vocalize more than boy babies but cry less. Many are more responsive to sounds than are boys and more sensitive to touch. Charmingly, newborn girls frequently smile—a reflexive expression once thought to be a mere grimace caused by gas pains but now known to be the fleeting precursor of the true social smile. Newborn boys show fewer reflexive smiles.[14]

Thus we see that a baby has a "style," the core of a personality, with which it comes into the world, which is determined in part by its gender. This style proceeds to interact with the mother's: the mother does not *act upon* the baby, she *interacts* with it. The trouble with the claim that a mother directs her baby's responses is that it is one-sided. It overlooks the fact of "baby power." The participation of babies in their own care has been overlooked until recently, according to Stein, because "First, it is technically difficult to record interactions in enough detail to see what is really happening. Second, we simply didn't know the system existed because it is almost entirely unconscious." The discovery that a mother and her baby are better thought of as an interactive system, rather than in terms of a subject-object relation, represents a major conceptual advance.

The development of a gendered personality has now been traced back to birth. Culture, operating through parents, does not impose masculinity or femininity on children. Girl and boy babies elicit different responses, to a great extent through their own measurable actions: "The recipe is concocted by the parent and the baby, not by the parent alone."[15]

Moreover, the differences embryonically present in boy and girl babies will persist through life: like other physical and psychic aspects of babies, they will grow and develop according to an orderly timetable. These differences are the precursors of later developments: girl babies already seem to exhibit more of the "connectedness" that Chodorow and Gilligan describe in older girls and women, boy babies more of the equivalent "separation." That boy babies fuss more and sleep less accords with their later higher levels of energetic and aggressive behavior. The evidence of fetal androgenization supplies a mechanism that explains these differences. When facts are this glaringly obvious, it requires all the tenacity of the human capacity for self-deception to avoid facing them. We must no longer do so.

We must no longer do so, because children, although they are astonishingly resistant to adults' foibles, have limits beyond which they cannot be pushed without damage. The feminist preoccupation with eliminating gender has already produced its own crop of horror stories.

> As I write this, my three-year-old daughter is with another child and a babysitter at the home of a friend. Casey didn't want to go there—she has had four consecutive mornings and afternoons of babysitters and not enough mama. This morning she climbed into her bed, pulled up the quilt and announced: "I can stay here with you if I take a nap."
>
> Her crying and wanting me gets me in my gut—that part of me that was taught to believe that mama should always be there. So I spent extra time talking and snuggling and planning the playing we will do later. I am resolved about the kind of parenting I want to do, so I did take her to the babysitter and returned to work. But I am still torn by her pain and by my own conditioning.
>
> It is of paramount importance to me that I set a good example of what a woman is—someone committed to work and ideals in addition to child, husband, and home. But at the same time my training tells me that my child should come first, that my primary job as a mother is to serve my child while she is young. I and so many other feminist mothers I have talked with need to remind ourselves that the conditioning is wrong.

Is it really the "conditioning" that is at fault?

Another feminist mother has been successful in her attempt to "save" her five-year-old son from masculinity—too successful.

> When he lies on the floor at night, drawing or watching TV, quiet as he often is when he is alone, dressed in one of the long nightshirts he likes to wear around the house so that the elastic of his pajama pants won't hurt his stomach, I am acutely conscious of my desire to feminize him, to protect him from masculinity, to keep him from moving out of my world. Only rarely do I give in to this subversive urge—I have a fear of his losing his bearing altogether; that without masculinity in its most conventional sense, at least a part of it, he will falter, stay so close to me that he will not be able to walk away at all. Now he is passionate about dolls and cooking, delicate drawings, flowers and imaginary stories about winged swans

who carry little boys to magical lands above the clouds and bring them home in time for dinner.

Violence is being done to this child. Yet there is nothing in the ideology of nonsexist child rearing, not a thing in all the allegedly universalist feminist literature, with which to oppose it.

Finally, let us consider a case approvingly described by Carrie Carmichael, one of the leading advocates of nonsexist child rearing. One wonders just where these people's humanity has gone off to.

> This couple has given their school age son a thorough education in feminism, why there is a need for a women's movement, and how he can aid women's fight for equality and justice.
>
> "We've explained to him how the bad men through the ages have hurt women, and at the same time hurt men by telling them what kind of men they should be. Our son knows he's in the vanguard of being a different kind of man. . . ."
>
> Sometimes his resolve to be one of the vanguard, one of the "good men who help women," weakens and he is wracked with tears and sobs that he's afraid he won't be good enough. He fears the "bad men will get him."[16]

In each of these cases a child is being needlessly hurt. If the pain of these children is needed to accomplish the aims of the feminist movement, then clearly it is time to reconsider those aims.

If applied in a principled, consistent way, as in these three cases, nonsexist child rearing is destructive of children's identity. More sensitive parents, less dogmatically committed to their principles and more ready to listen to their children, will yield so much ground that their efforts will be ineffective. Jack *is* going to insist on trucks, guns, and policeman caps, or their equivalents. Molly *is* going to insist on party dresses and orderly tea parties for her dolls—and no boys allowed, thank you. Boys *will* play in large, hierarchical groups. Girls *will* play in smaller, more personal groups. Over all this characteristically human sex-differentiated behavior, nonsexist child rearing will persist—if at all—as a veneer of ideal culture, what parents and teachers *think* kids should be doing, without the slightest effect on the substance of their behavior. It is possible that nonsexist values will be transmitted to some of these children. But no less than previous generations, they will stubbornly continue to manifest their gender in the way they move, the way they fight, the things they value, and the expectations they bring to their relationships with each other—a list that could go on indefinitely.

If gender will not go away, can we learn to live with it? Is men's aggression synonymous with destructiveness? Is women's relatedness synonymous with victimization?

Vivian Gussin Paley, a teacher at the University of Chicago Laboratory Schools, brings some interesting insights to bear on what the sexes contribute to each other. One clear implication of her observations of kindergarten children is that boys and girls want to participate in well-defined same-sex activities, and that if these are not supplied they will create their own. But at the same time they have a healthy complementary influence on each other.

Paley describes a day on which, in an unusual move, she let the boys and girls play dodge ball in the gym without the other sex. She found the boys too energetic to control in this setting and the girls too hard to motivate—but the children themselves felt thoroughly satisfied with the experience.

> After the girls' reaction to the boys on the classroom track, I begin to wonder if they feel intimidated in games such as dodge ball, where the boys throw harder and behave more competitively. . . . The next day, there is the same inattentiveness from the girls and combativeness among the boys. I cite the incidents that prove my point, but no one is listening.

Paley finds mixed-sex groups easier to manage: when competitive physical activity is involved, the girls are hard to motivate without the boys' presence and the boys are hard to control without the girls' presence.

> The boys quicken the pace and help the girls concentrate on the game, while the presence of the girls serves to mitigate the competitive furor. Playing together makes the girls livelier and the boys more agreeable.
>
> I must be careful: So eager are the boys and girls to have separate play worlds that I am almost fooled into believing they don't need each other.[17]

I wonder if the boys' and girls' strong enthusiasm for what is in the context of a progressive kindergarten a rare opportunity for same-sex activity does not represent an impulse that should be heeded: with the right activities and organization, I'm sure it would work out very well. But of course Paley's main point stands, and after a generation of feminism it is a radical one: males and females make different but equally crucial contributions. In due course we shall inquire whether this point can be generalized: whether it holds good, not only for the microcosm of a kindergarten, but also for the destiny of the human race.

The Meaning of the Two Sexes

If the boys and the girls in Paley's account could have what they wanted, they would choose an environment in which there is a good deal more separation by sex than there is in the Lab School at the University of Chicago where Paley works. But they would, at the same time, want to have a lot of contact with the other sex. And they would benefit from both forms of structure. Indeed, to miss one or the other set of experiences—with one's own sex and with the other—would be a form of experiential impoverishment. Yet this is exactly the direction in which nonsexist child rearing pushes American parents and teachers: away from a recognition of the validity and importance of same-sex activities. The fortunate children will be precisely those whose parents and teachers temper the rigidities of nonsexist child rearing with an intuitive acceptance of their children's real needs—or who explicitly reject nonsexist child rearing altogether, as the set of half-baked notions, incompatible with reality, that it is. Precisely because they respect their children's personalities, such parents will encourage their children's wish and need for differentiation by gender.

Nonsexist child rearing is an absolute, not a relative failure. Boys and girls exhibit exactly the same gender traits they did before the whole misconceived effort was begun. The entire attempt to socialize boys and girls into the same modes has made no impact on personality whatever. There is no evidence to indicate it is on the right track, or that more of the same will eventually produce results. It is not working, and if it is not working, something must be wrong with the assumptions that underlie it.

The environmental determinist view of inherent traits has been far too narrow. First, inherent traits were confused with biology, whereas they are just as likely to involve the interaction of biological and non-biological forces. Second, this reductionist view was made even narrower by defining as biological what are in fact only biology's crudest and most visible manifestations, such as the needs for food and sleep. This extreme viewpoint has been so widely accepted that feminists have been able to base the most farfetched claims on it and gain more converts than critics, as when Millett, Chodorow, and scores of other writers claimed that there is virtually no biological component in sexual desire, which was described as a cultural need.

In consequence of this description of human behavior as a kaleidoscope without rhyme or reason, the danger we now face is not that some band of anti-Semites or white supremacists will creep out of the woodwork and seek to overturn civilized society. This is a nightmare, but in modern America it is only a nightmare—except when it is invoked in an attempt to cut off discussion of questions that feminists would rather we didn't ask. It may well be less of a real threat than the converse possibility that, in seeking to perfect human society, we will smother the exercise of human freedom and individuality. In any case, the immediate danger is far more modest, and it has already happened: that we lose sight of the elements that make up the continuity and unity of the human species. In the final analysis, when we deny our gender we deny our individuality; and when we deny our individuality we give up the basis for tolerance. For if we accept that people are infinitely mutable—or as close to mutable as never mind—we no longer have any philosophical basis to deny the competence of society to mold all individuals according to a preconceived pattern.

If it were true that temperament is so arbitrary, socialization so powerful, things might work out: like the genetically engineered people of *Brave New World,* we could be dumbly, blissfully happy in our manipulated adjustment on our climate-controlled planet. It is because temperament is not arbitrary that all such schemes are doomed to failure. Because they are based on false premises which misconstrue vital and inalterable aspects of the human being, defining healthy aspects, such as our children's sex-differentiated behavior, as signs of sickness, they will conflict actively with human nature—for there is such a thing— for as long as they have any influence over people. These schemes cannot triumph over human nature, but they can misdirect our energies and cause conflict and suffering. The misery they cause will be limited only by the power they wield.

The problem of the sexes in America has been misconstrued by the feminists. Justice, in the feminist lexicon, consists in the sexes becoming ever more similar, until it is a matter of indifference to all people in all circumstances whether a person is male or female, married or single, homosexual or heterosexual, and so forth. Now, these things may be given more or less importance or different forms of importance, but they do matter. The problem that has been lost sight of by the feminists is central: it is that men and women need to be together, and they need to be apart. How, or even whether, this translates into social policy is an involved and difficult question, but it is highly unlikely that we can arrive at just social policies if we fear to address such a basic need.

The nonsexist child rearing experiment shows the impossibility of changing as basic and complex an aspect of human life as gender through conditioning or role-training. In order to change the meaning of gender in a constructive way, we would have to engage in deep surgery upon the human psyche. Assuredly, we do not have the wisdom for such a task.

American children, after a decade in which millions of them have been exposed in varying degrees to nonsexist child rearing, continue to show the same enthusiasm for sex roles as ever. Totally oblivious to the efforts made to "free them of the tyranny of socio-sexual stereotype," they continue to form the same kinds of play groups, to play the same kinds of games, and to dream the same kinds of dreams as all children everywhere. Their notions of gender are relentlessly stereotypical enough to stand a feminist's hair on end. They expect Mommy to stay home and Daddy to go off to work, regardless of what their parents believe or do. The boys want to race cars and organize wars, the girls want to mother dolls and hold tea parties. The less rowdy boys and the tomboys form minorities of exactly the same size and inclination as before the "role revolution." Such less typical children remain obdurately masculine or feminine even as they ring the changes on their sexes' more standard characteristics. Gender is alive and well among our youngest citizens, and is clearly destined to thrive from the crib to the kindergarten and beyond, and then to play its part in bringing forth a new day.

Summary

Feminists believe that sexual identity is the result of "role-training," a cultural process. Biology, in this view, has no significant implications for human behavior. This idea, far from being a feminist innovation, was the standard social science viewpoint in the 1950s and sixties. Behaviorist psychology, popular at the time, is predicated on the idea that human behavior is a product of conditioning. Even psychoanalysis, because it identifies parental behavior as the determinant of neurosis, could be recast to support the idea of human mutability. But the most powerful influence in this direction was the Boasian paradigm which came to dominate American cultural anthropology between the two world wars.

Guided by these viewpoints, scientists produced reams of evidence purporting to show that the conditions of human life are almost infinitely variable. The difficulty of adolescence was not universal, claimed Mead's study of Samoa. The form of the nuclear family was not universal, claimed Malinowski's works on the Trobriand Islanders. Marriage was not universal, according to Spiro's first, widely reprinted report on the kibbutz. Human emotions, human behavior, and human institutions were all arbitrary historical constructs, proclaimed the voice of wisdom of those days. Sexual desire? A product of culture. To use the phrase "human nature" in a sophisticated setting was unbearably gauche. Human nature did not exist.

Since human nature did not exist, it followed that gender was arbitrary. False cases of sexually egalitarian peoples abounded in reputable scientific literature: the Alorese, Arapesh, Bamenda, Berbers, Bushmen, Red Chinese, ancient Cretans, Communist Cubans, Eskimo, Filipinos, Hopi, Iroquois, Jivaro, kibbutzim, Marquesans, Mbuti, Nama Hottentot, Navaho, Nayar, Samoans, Semai, Shakers, Soviets, Swedes, Tchambuli, Yegali, and Zuni. These instances of egalitarian human societies were supplemented by reports on our close biological relatives, especially chimpanzees, which stressed the similarity in size and behavior between males and females, implying that our own ancestors were similar. In the seventies and eighties, more thorough studies showed that none of these egalitarian characterizations of human and ape societies could be sustained on the basis of the evidence.

Alongside these scientific reports of egalitarian societies there flourished unscientific accounts of matriarchal societies, including the ancient Cretans (also claimed to have been egalitarian), the ancient Celts, and of course the Amazons. The frequency of such accounts increased in proportion to the lack of verifiable evidence to support them.

Feminists thus stepped right into Boas's vacant shoes. That is why, in the space of months in many places, feminism was able to demand conformity to its beliefs. It simply added another layer to the unisexist beliefs which were already so widely disseminated. What it proposed seemed possible; its methods of implementation, sound; its grievances, justly founded. Even those most opposed to feminism usually admitted the justice of its cause. It was common to hear objections to feminist positions prefaced with the remark, "Of course, I don't question the vicious oppression of women throughout history. . . ." No one questioned the belief that women had been oppressed by men throughout history, or that this condition was about to change in America through the new feminist movement.

But while feminism triumphed in the seventies, its intellectual base was being eaten away, first, by the progress of scientific knowledge along established lines, and second, through a process in which, led by feminism to intensively explore the nature of gender, scientists like Chodorow, Gilligan, and Hrdy began producing evidence that increasingly contradicted the feminist line. By the mid-eighties, it was clear that biology has massive and complex implications for human emotion and behavior which are just beginning to be well understood.

The results of large-scale experiments designed to eliminate the social expression of gender came in during the mid-seventies and early eighties. In the mid-seventies, the attempt to eliminate or at least reduce the importance of gender in the kibbutz was revealed to be a complete failure. In the early eighties, similar dismal results were reported for the American effort at "nonsexist child rearing." Analyses of these failed experiments showed that the premises upon which they had been based were simplistic and incomplete.

Thus, although unisexism remained the standard, consensus ideology on gender up to the mid-eighties, the American landscape was beginning to flicker with the beginnings of a new acceptance of gender. The implications of this change, which reflected a considerably more sophisticated viewpoint than the various environmental determinisms it superseded, remained to be seen, but they boded a considerable impact on American intellectual and political culture, and seemed certain to affect social norms and the lives of individuals.

PART IV

Beyond Feminism

Chapter 11

The Revalidation of the Masculine and the Feminine

Social Gender

As we have seen, the nature/nurture dichotomy is false and obsolete. Culture does not return us to the primordial clay, to be reshaped in whatever image we choose. It is instead a flexible way of responding to universal imperatives. Many needs that in other animals are met primarily through direct biological stimuli must, in humans, be met in part through culture. Yet culture does not change these needs themselves. It is thus an inherent characteristic of our culture that it is partly arbitrary. This arbitrariness cannot be eliminated without undermining the very function of culture, badly damaging individuals and societies in the process.

Such considerations are particularly applicable to gender. Children, driven by biopsychological need to establish a distinct gender identity, seek external clues to meet this internal imperative. Social gender is a universal grammar of human perception. Much of this grammar is for all practical purposes inherent.* We may, for instance, be sure that people in all cultures asked to match "hard" and "soft" with "masculine" and "feminine" will pair "hard" with "masculine" and "soft" with "feminine." Part of social gender is totally arbitrary: that men wear pants and women skirts, that blue is male and pink is female. But many aspects of social gender fall in between the comfortingly abstract extremes of inherency and arbitrariness.

---

*As distinguished from the literally inherent promptings of biology.

The underlying imperatives of biology confer genuine meaning on these variable expressions of gender. To return to Boas in a more profitable context, the critical point is not a trait's outward form but its perceived meaning. To visualize this, we can mentally reverse the gender associations of pink and blue, imagining pink as the masculine color, the blood of the hunt, and blue as the feminine color, the wide sky of feminine serenity. The symbolic shifts endlessly; the symbolized does not.

Gender, then, is only partly deterministic: it is also a means of organization, with which no society can afford to dispense. Sex roles can be roles yet remain perfectly genuine. The issue is primarily one of optimization: first, to utilize human capacities efficiently and harmoniously; second, to meet universal physical and emotional needs with a minimum of friction and wasted effort. At times, encrusted layers of tradition may develop, which under novel circumstances it may become necessary with great effort to peel away; yet every changed society that so results will continue to organize itself through gender, whatever the expectations of its founders, mixing the inherent and the arbitrary into a meaningful synthesis.

Culture does not supersede biology; culture completes biology. It does not confer the power to change our needs, but it does confer the power to overlook and trample on them. Only a cultural animal can invent torture, the ultimate violation of the integrity of an organism— culture used to turn biology against itself. Yet there are also social forms of torture, more subtle but in sum scarcely less cruel than judicial barbarity. Culture can perhaps raise us above animal nature; it can unquestionably degrade us beneath it.

Gender is a biological necessity, but it is in part a social construct, determined by tradition, accident, and historical circumstance. To insist that the expression of gender be limited to the strictly invariant is thus to deny gender's very purpose and nature. If we accept the desirability of gender in principle but deny it its cultural means of expression, we will indeed maintain the general form of human society, but it will be a singularly joyless and insecure version.

To avoid this fate, worthy of the most rigid of ascetics, we will have to consciously relax our ideological vigilance. We must allow our tolerance of gender to expand beyond its minimal, constrained expression, into its development and flowering. It is not enough to tolerate gender; we must celebrate it.

Yet even if we ignore the nature of the human being as a cultural animal and acknowledge as legitimate only those aspects of gender that are biologically determined, the strictly biological component of gender, which has emerged through the new perspectives in science and gender of the past twenty years, remains great enough to overwhelm the simple schema of unisexism—an idea whose time has passed. We are no longer living in the age of Margaret Mead but in that of Anke Ehrhardt.

No doubt there is a tendency to exaggerate the inherent differences between the sexes, to suppose, because one sex is less likely to engage in a given activity at one moment in time, that it is permanently disabled from pursuing that activity. But this argument is practically irrelevant to the discussion of gender in America today, where the opposite tendency has dominated debate for the past generation: namely, the claim that there are no significant differences between the sexes, and that to the extent such differences can be found, they are evidence of injustice, and must be rigorously eliminated.

Regardless of whether the focus is on males, as with Konner and Goldberg, on females, as with Hrdy and Gilligan, or on both, as with Anke Ehrhardt, it is clear there are significant inherent differences in style and orientation between the sexes. Inherent sex differences are not the sole determinants of behaviors, emotions, or physique, but they represent extraordinarily powerful influences that are operative in all males and all females from the womb until death.

It is wholly implausible that the major and consistent differences in aggressiveness, motivation, perception of relationships, and even values that have been documented by thinkers as diverse as Goldberg and Gilligan have no behavioral results, or that the broad outlines of these behavioral differences cannot be known. If we retain the current societal goal of achieving absolute equality in all professions, and will not rest until each sex is equally represented in all occupations, and within those occupations at all levels of status and remuneration, we will condemn ourselves and our descendants to an endless and futile task, since to achieve an ungendered society would require the biological elimination of gender.

Are we prepared to take such a step? We cannot, should not, and dare not. Cannot, because our science does not make this possible, and assuredly will not for generations to come; should not, because to give up gender means giving up much of what is best in the human race; and dare not, because the level of biological social engineering needed to eliminate gender would make such totalitarian nightmares as *Brave*

New World and *1984* look tolerant and humane by comparison. We are faced, then, with only three approaches to gender in society: the nightmarish dystopia of a genetically engineered society that fails to work even in its own terms; the hypocrisy that is required to claim the sexes really don't differ at all, and that a gender-blind society is possible without genetic engineering; and, finally, what is clearly the preferable and humane choice, to accept that our society is going to remain gendered, and that any constructive approach to the problems we face must take that fact into account.

This does not mean that the current typing of occupations by sex will remain stable. Sex role is universal; many sex roles are not. Some occupations that are now largely male may become equally or even wholly female, while some occupations that are now female may become male. Indeed, nothing is clearer than that such ferment has occurred and will continue to occur. The result, however, will always be a society in which gender plays a massive role in determining both our occupations and our fantasies, motivations, and relationships, and thus, what is equally important, how we perceive our occupations.

The human condition destines us all to live as gendered individuals in a gendered world. Is it possible to come to terms with this fact— perhaps even to value it?

For the past few generations, the thrust of American social philosophizing has been to emphasize the liberation of the individual from the constraints of membership in a group. In line with this tradition, the fact of belonging to one sex or the other has been seen primarily as a limitation. Rather than paying attention to a person's sex, we ought instead to appreciate him or her as a unique individual.

But what happens to this view when it is shown that temperament is intimately and indissolubly linked to gender? It then becomes apparent that, far from paying too much attention to gender, we have not paid it enough. Not, on the whole, in our private behavior, but rather in the public interpretations we put on that behavior, we have been led to vastly underestimate the centrality of gender in human life.

Women's possession of such male-identified traits as aggressiveness, competitiveness, and a will to power has sometimes been underestimated; and similarly, men's possession of such female-identified traits as nurturance and a tendency to defer has sometimes been underestimated. This said, there remains an enormous quantitative difference in the extent to which these traits are present in either sex, and even more important, there is a yet greater qualitative difference. For instance, it is not merely that the vast majority of men are far more aggressive than the vast majority of women, but that the ways in which aggressive behavior is perceived, the forms it takes, and the goals it is intended to achieve differ qualitatively between men and women. It is true, as Nancy Chodorow claimed in 1978, that "men can be just as nurturant as women," but this represents just another misleading generalization unless we add that the vast majority of women are far more nurturant than the vast majority of men, and that the ways in which men and women nurture show major and consistent differences. Men and women do not talk to a baby in the same way, or play with a child in the same way. Men tend to care for children in a way that is more episodic and physically vigorous, while women are less intensely stimulating but more consistent caretakers. Gender colors our slightest actions. These facts are well established, and further research is certain to make them more so. Socialization reflects inherent differences between the sexes,[1] but it does not cause such differences unaided. Indeed, as shown by the kibbutz experience, even socialization away from gender roles will fail to eradicate them. Women, given free choice, will opt for feminine norms by an overwhelming majority once feminine behavior ceases to be seen as a liability.

Men and women are different in ways that are glorious, irritating, and worrisome, but in any case inevitable. To the extent that we recognize this fact, we will do a somewhat better job of planning for the future as individuals and as a society. Belonging to each sex involves certain characteristic vulnerabilities, which it may be possible to mitigate, but which do not justify abandoning a gendered society.

The Revalidation of the Masculine

Looking ahead, it seems clear that the fear of masculinity of the Vietnam War era is eroding in this country. The sense of American omnipotence of the early sixties was shaken by the war and the cultural challenge of the counterculture, but the succeeding sense of impotence has since been undermined too by the march of events. As we become more realistic about both our limitations and our strengths, it is time to learn to value the sexes, equally.

And here we run up against the limitations of our scientific knowledge and must switch to poetry or science fiction. Because I am a lousy poet, I hope I will be forgiven for choosing the second alternative.

Beyond the concerns of the present era lie hundreds, perhaps billions, of years in which humanity has the opportunity to flourish and prosper. This will only be possible if we properly value the resources of our temperament. Yesterday long-distance communication, an hour ago flight, today microchips, tomorrow who knows? The revolution in science and technology continues, making a mockery of the seventies' notion of an end to growth. If we can avoid nuclear annihilation, it will be to face other dangers. Climatic change will endanger human life on earth. We will be threatened with destruction by an alien species. A comet will come hurtling from the depths of space to pulverize our planet. Our sun will die. Our universe will become so big or so small that life becomes impossible within it.

To each of these threats there will be an appropriate response—if we have the values, the drive, and the imagination to meet it. It is said that with the human race, nature opened its eyes to itself. Other species have come and gone: saber-toothed tigers, dinosaurs. We are a new experiment of nature: the experiment of intelligence. It is our responsibility to make the experiment work.

And in this connection, the values traditionally associated with masculinity have a powerful role to play. They are not washed up, as was believed under the daily shock treatment of watching the Vietnam War on television in the late sixties. The values of impersonal ambition, group cohesion, and aggressiveness, the eagerness of young men to look death in the face and spit in its eye—all these will matter as much in the future of humanity as they did in the days of the caves. Without them, the species—who knows, perhaps someday the universe— will have a shorter life span than if it retains the ability to protect itself, to meet new challenges because it seeks them. When that comet comes hurtling from the depths of space, the feminine values of relatedness are not going to be of much use. The appropriate, life-saving response will be precisely that of the five-year-old boy on the playground: smash it to bits. If the nuclear bomb does not first destroy humanity, it will thus one day save it. To think these things are not going to happen is simply a failure of imagination.[2]

It is easy to make an evil fetish of the atom bomb and to overlook the fact that the future is likely to place sources of even vaster power under human control. Sooner or later, if our civilization and our species are to prosper and simply to survive, this power will be necessary

In the meantime—and this is so obvious it should never have been necessary to state it—the technological impulse that once developed better spear points has already, in those parts of the world with reasonably efficient economies, nearly eliminated the once universal specter of hunger; has wiped out smallpox, diphtheria, tetanus, polio, and scores of other once dreaded diseases; has learned to mitigate dozens of chronic ailments from diabetes to schizophrenia; has drastically reduced the danger of childbirth, the incidence of infant mortality, and the prospect of early death; and has in general, in ways too numerous to mention and too basic to require a defense, made the world a better place for vastly greater numbers of people.

The female chauvinism that became normative in the Feminist Era sees only danger in power. But power in and of itself is neutral. It is neither good nor evil, but it increases the scope of each. It is needed to destroy, but also to protect; to kill, but also to sustain and heal. Thus if men are to be blamed for evil, they must be at least equally praised for good.

The Pandora's box of the bomb is open, and it cannot be shut again. The solution, therefore, must involve the continued exercise of male values. Men and women have much to learn, as Gilligan says, from each other's values. But men are the prime recipients and conservers of masculine values, as women are of feminine ones. We forget this at the risk of becoming both trivial and dangerous.

More immediately, though lesbian separatists, who dream of a world without men, have been conspicuous in the feminist movement, they represent a tiny minority of women. Women like men. They especially like masculine men. If American women could buy tickets for a date with either Alan Alda or Robert Redford, who do you think most would pick? Having constrained her man into a reasonable simulacrum of the New Male, the feminist woman invariably found out this wasn't what she had had in mind after all. She wanted someone who was, well, *tougher*—someone who would speak his mind regardless of her beliefs, who was more sure of himself even if he was less solicitous of her, who would drag her into bed rather than politely wait for her to "initiate sex" on a fifty-fifty basis or even worse. If the opposite sex did not already exist, women, or men, would reinvent it, warts and all.

Clearly, the masculine qualities entail the potential for immense excesses. Physical strength confers the capacity for its abuse. Male levels of aggression include the potential for violence. Masculine separation can go so far that empathy becomes difficult. All these pitfalls of masculinity, however, have known or possible remedies, most of which are built into the fabric of any society, while others, like democracy, have been invented relatively recently in human history. Some, like a permanent cure for nuclear war, remain to be discovered. The pitfalls of masculinity, however, give us no reason to declare it obsolete. It will be easier to deal with its excesses if we first accept it is here to stay. At that point, we will start to rediscover its virtues.

The Revalidation of the Feminine

Similarly, the feminine qualities are as vital as they ever were. Men are the motor of humanity; women are humanity's emotional glue. Our world needs more diffuseness, sensitivity, prettiness, softness, tolerance, giving, caring, accepting, and so on. It is sheer delusion to imagine these qualities will ever come equally from men. Anyone who expects them to do so will still be waiting come Doomsday.

Like the masculine virtues, the feminine virtues have their pitfalls. Some of these are practical. Women's respect for others' needs can make it hard to adequately value their own—for instance, to ask for a raise. Some of them are moral. Taken too far, women's tendency to include others' judgments in their own can result in an inability to make sharp distinctions. Others are psychological. Deference can lead to victimization. In many cases, the male pitfalls involve giving too much weight to one's own point of view, and the female pitfalls involve giving too much weight to the point of view of others. Yet such pitfalls can be learned, and avoided—in a society that is basically "gender-friendly."

We must remove the taboos that have been placed on masculine and feminine behavior over the past generation. Only when our culture fully accepts the qualities that are basic to men and women will individuals be truly free both to live in harmony with their natures and to feel accepted and valued by the larger society. The revalidation of the masculine and the feminine demands a conscious and sustained effort, because of the somewhat greater level of sophistication which the intensive discussion of gender issues has now brought about.

Exceptions and Qualifications and Their Limits

Does this mean that a man or a woman who exhibits less of some of these characteristics is less of a man or a woman than one who exhibits more? Yes, it does. When we say "What a woman!" or "What a man!" this is exactly what we mean. On the other hand, there is no cause for complaint. Practically everyone can find some grounds for dissatisfaction with themselves: height, weight, hair texture, intelligence, athletic ability, social skills, and so forth. Most of us do feel good about ourselves most of the time because we make up in one area for anything lacking in another. In addition, a person who is less heavily freighted by the baggage of his or her own sex can often benefit from some of the virtues of the other sex. As long as a core of identity is present, there is no real difficulty.

Within each sex, some members will be more masculine or more feminine than others—a fact that has absolutely no bearing on the accuracy of general descriptions of the sexes. Gender is deterministic, but diffusely so where individuals are concerned. Even when we have stripped off the ideological blinders, truth still depends on one's point of view. Think of a picture of the Earth from outer space: a glowing blue ball with green and brown patches, covered with white streaks. There is no detail, but there is a "cosmic picture," a revelation of the Earth as a unitary organism. Think of the view from an aircraft: patches of field, grids of road. Unity has disappeared, but the life of a civilization becomes intelligible. Think of the view from the ground: the leather of your shoes, the cracks in the soil, blades of grass. The big picture is lost, but the details emerge. With a deep space probe or a microscope we can go much further in either direction. In the same vein, what is true for men or women in general may be less true for individual men or women. Our point of view shifts depending on whether we are talking about all women in all times and places, all American women, middle-class American women, or individual women. A woman, for example, may be extremely aggressive without changing the correctness of the general identification of aggressiveness with men.

Finally, it is important not to lose sight of the fact that masculinity and femininity, although they inform what each one of us is, do not exhaust the range of human characteristics. Many traits are not sex-typed, or may be found with equal strength in some members of each sex even if they are more prevalent in the other. Women are not exactly strangers to competitiveness, ambition, will to power, political skill, ruthlessness, tenacity, and so on. Each sex has avenues of influence open to it that the other does not, but shares a great many common ones in addition.

The relation between femininity and power is problematic, and needs to be explored. Femininity is not about impersonal power, but it is hardly an obstacle to acquiring or exercising it—rather the contrary. The belief that this is not the case is simply a projection of the feminist belief that women are always victims. The intense resentment many successful career women feel toward feminism and feminists becomes intelligible: if they had allowed themselves to become bogged down in the poisonous negativity of the feminist perspective, they would never have succeeded as well in their chosen professions. It seems likely that feminism is now acting as a brake on women's extrafamilial advances. By painting women's advance as a confrontation with men, feminism may actually be hampering women's ability to freely participate in the public sphere. It is presumably no accident that so many of the women recently elected to political office are from conservative districts hostile to feminism.

We should tolerate diversity where it does in fact exist. This must be true tolerance, however, not the idealization of women who fit a masculinized culture's preference for women who behave in a masculine manner. Sara Bonnett Stein argues that the revalidation of femininity doesn't mean that little Sarah may not still become a college professor.[3] That is certainly true, but if we persist in rating men and women according to the same sex-blind scale based on male needs, drives, and values, we will have missed the point altogether. True gender freedom requires that Sarah be as free to be a housewife as to be a professor—to be, in fact, whatever she really wants to be, free from needless pressure to conform to any uncongenial ideal. If the main thing we value about women is their capacity for extrafamilial achievement—to earn university degrees and make money— we will have failed to escape from a cultural viewpoint heavily biased toward masculine values. In these dying days of the Feminist Era, there are plenty of influences encouraging women to externality, independence, self, and competition with men; but very few to home, family, children, and cooperation with men. The cultural climate has changed completely since the early marriage days when Friedan wrote *The Feminine Mystique,* when an extrafamilial bent in women, however slight, was often disparaged. Today it is femininity that is ignored, distrusted, and suppressed—and so has come to seem inordinately precious. The grim statistics on the marriage market for older single women can't hide the fact that younger women who are unreservedly feminine are at a premium.

Similarly, many women are starved for masculinity. The complaint most often voiced by young women these days about men is not that they are too aggressive, overbearing, or prone to "objectifying" women sexually, but that they don't show enough of these masculine characteristics: that they are insufficiently decisive, self-assured, and sexually demanding. The contemporary young woman fears much less she will draw an abuser than a "wimp."

Betty Friedan expressed the feminist consensus in 1974 when she wrote that

> What had to be changed was the obsolete feminine and masculine sex roles that dehumanized sex, making it almost impossible for women and men to make love, not war. How could we ever really know or love each other as long as we played those roles that kept us from knowing or being ourselves?[4]

This consensus prescription for sexual harmony was a hundred and eighty degrees wrong. Masculinity and femininity call for tolerance and admiration, not rejection. It is only when men and women cease trying to neutralize and start trying to understand their own and each other's natures that they will find it easier to live together. After the premature devaluations, the unhappy reversals, and the normative hypocrisies of the Feminist Era, we must recover for each sex the values proper to it, for these values are necessary to each individual's well-being and growth, and to his or her ability to enjoy and when necessary to deal with the opposite sex.

Unisexism as Misogyny

A great deal of feminism's appeal to men arose from the fact that it seemed to place so few demands on them. If "being a woman was no more and no less than being human," as Betty Friedan claimed in *The Feminine Mystique*,[5] it exempted men from having to learn anything about women as women, or for that matter about themselves as men, since "being human" was all that mattered. Acceptance of feminism was an escape route for some men, saving them the weary trouble of finding out about women—or themselves. "I see it!" thought Greer's male reader in a blinding flash of insight, "Women are just like men!"

Unisexism is singularly reassuring to many men. "I never understood what all this fuss was about with women before, but I see it clearly now," thinks such a man. "Really, they're just like us—people. Just give them the same rights and responsibilities as men and all this fuss will cease (and I can go back to the infinitely more interesting world of particle physics, corporate law, or the Sunday crossword puzzle)."

Our culture's unisexism tends to leave men in ignorance of women—when it does not leave women in ignorance of themselves. Millions of young and not-so-young Americans are condemned to flounder about, unsure of how and to what extent men and women are similar and how and to what extent they differ. What should they ask of themselves as men or as women, what should they expect of the opposite sex? Whether in the sex act, in planning one's life, or in raising one's children, the answers continue to be obscure to many people. This obscurity creates a continued window of opportunity for the false reassurance of feminism's easy and misleading answers.

The devaluation of femininity too often began with men. Many women were pushed into feminism or the Myth of Independence by men who were unsympathetic to or ignorant of female needs. For many women, acceptance of the new feminist conformities was a response to a culture which had failed to validate their femininity. Feminism exploited women's resulting insecurity about the worth of their contributions. Because their culture, and often their men, failed to value female needs and strengths, it seemed a natural strategy to repudiate those qualities. Women's strengths were redefined as women's weaknesses.

A story told in an early issue of *Ms.* magazine in 1971 had all too much resonance for many women. In this story, a husband doubted that a wife, his own in particular, was making an important contribution to their household unless "the wife is really contributing something, brings in a salary."

His wife's reaction was that

> For ten years, she had been covering furniture, hanging wallpaper, making curtains and refinishing floors so that they could afford the mortgage on their apartment. She had planned the money-saving menus so they could afford the little dinners for prospective clients. She had crossed town to save money on clothes so the family could have a new hi-fi. All the little advances in station—the vacations, the theater tickets, the new car—had been made possible by her crafty, endless, worried manipulation of the household expenses. "I was under the impression," she said, "that I was contributing something. Evidently my life's blood is simply a non-deductible expense."[6]

Of course, in addition to their element of truth, such stories served a didactic function for feminists, cautioning young women against men, the oppressors. Their ceaseless repetition in feminist literature presents a distorted picture of relations between the sexes, which are portrayed as hopeless unless the feminist revolution succeeds in remaking men's nature. The link between the message against men and the devaluation of femininity thus appears with peculiar sharpness. If men cannot be counted on, then femininity is of little use as a strategy.

This viewpoint was articulated to millions of women in Colette Dowling's colossal 1981 best-seller, *The Cinderella Complex*. Dowling's motivation to write the book goes back to an extraordinarily happy year she spent living in effect as a housewife with a boyfriend in a house in the country, at the end of which he confronted her brutally:

> "What if you keep on like this?" he finally asked, after a year had gone by. "What then?"
>
> The "What then?" was chilling. To me it seemed proof that his care was not very deep, or else why would he be pushing me like that? Why would he be saying, in effect, "I don't *want* to take care of you?"[7]

It is likely that Dowling's initial reaction was right, that in fact her boyfriend didn't love her and was just trying to ditch a commitment he felt unable to sustain. But lacking a secure basis to justify her behavior, Dowling set out on the long effort to become financially and above all emotionally independent that is chronicled in her book. Guided by *The Feminine Mystique* and other feminist writings, she was unable to defend herself against this rejection of her desirability as a lover, disguised as an assault on her worth as a human being. Instead, she internalized her lover's message that something was wrong with her and tried to change.*

In this quest, Dowling made all the mistakes encouraged by cultural determinism, unisexism, and feminism. Most disturbingly, she rejected her female nature as an atavistic source of pain useless as a guide for a modern woman.

---

*The account in Dowling's book is partly fictionalized. In real life, Dowling was under immense pressure from the two most significant men in her life, her husband and her psychoanalyst, to defeminize her personality. The thoroughness with which she eventually yielded to this pressure is a poignant comment on the state of gender understanding in America today. In her preface, Dowling admits she is puzzled that no women played a part in her particular quest for "freedom" from "traditional femininity."

Everything about the way we were raised told us we would be *part* of someone else—that we would be protected, supported, buoyed up by wedded happiness until the day we died.

Dowling has internalized the feminist message in radically pure form:

Our old girlhood dreams were weak and ignoble, and . . . there were better things to want: money, power, and . . . freedom. . . . Freedom is better than security . . . ; security cripples. . . . Why, when we have the chance to move ahead, do we tend to retreat? Because . . . *we were not trained for freedom at all, but for its categorical opposite—dependency.*[8]

Rather than drawing the reasonable conclusion that femininity is a condition like any with its pitfalls, which must be learned and as much as possible avoided, Dowling has thrown out the baby with the bath water, concluding that woman's whole way of being is wrong and that she must completely remake herself. As Greer had written over a decade earlier, what had to be changed was "women's souls."[9] But what Dowling mistakes for unhealthy "dependency" is in fact the positive, life-sustaining "embeddedness" in tangible relationships which Gilligan identifies as a fundamental, positive element of femaleness.

In the early 1980s, *The Cinderella Complex* broadcast the message against marriage, the message against men, and the feminist devaluation of the feminine to millions of women too young to remember the days of rage of the New Left. *The Cinderella Complex* was often not even identified as a feminist work: such ideas had become strictly mainstream.

How far had we come in the intervening decade? Feminism had not abandoned its early excesses; indeed, it had scarcely evolved at all. Instead, it had entered the broader culture—had, as the new national philosophy of gender, *become* the culture. The "progressive" ideas communicated to young women in the early eighties were the same ideas their older sisters had received in the late sixties, warmed over and served in a more careful manner, but fundamentally unchanged.

The problem Dowling encountered with her lover in *The Cinderella Complex* is the same problem Friedan encountered with the culture at large in *The Feminine Mystique* (to the extent these books do not simply represent their authors' railing against the fact of their femaleness). How is a woman to cope with a society so ambivalent to the value of her contribution, regardless of whether she tries to make it in the home or in the workplace? Two distinct strategies suggest themselves.

In the first place, there is that of the many women who are temperamentally unsuited to feminine modalities. Many such women will sympathize with the remark of the feminist who recalled of her attempts at dating, "I always felt as if I were in drag, a female impersonator in my heels and makeup and earrings, trying to be a good listener to some self-important jerk."[10]

Even more to the point, women less given to feminine modalities will tend to have a more independent life orientation, which will translate into a focus on careers under the conditions of current society. Whether the main long-term expression of the capabilities of such women, who do not define themselves primarily through their personal attachments, but through their personal strivings, as do men, will be as minority participants in predominantly male corporations, in female-typed occupations, or in integrated circumstances remains to be seen; it will involve all three to some extent.

Such women have arguably benefited most from feminism, used as a tool to help pry open the gates of male exclusivity. Contemporary feminism would seem to make most sense as a guiding ideology for such women. On the personal level, though, self-identified women who accept feminism as a belief system probably suffer in ways that may be immensely significant. Even if feminism appears to some as a satisfactory resting-place, it at the very least obscures the motivations and possibilities of the rest of humanity. The feminist perspective inculcates a distrust of men, of feminine women, and of feminine elements in oneself. Indeed, feminism may be a particular threat to women who are temperamentally at odds with some aspects of femininity, endlessly postponing an already difficult accommodation to human complexity.

The position of the feminine woman—who represents the vast majority of the female population—is actually more difficult at the moment, given our current ideological presuppositions. Deprived by the culture of many of the ornaments and pleasures of femininity, its higher refinements and its uncomplicated rewards, she must assert herself as best she can against a culture that often doesn't seem to know or care about her needs and abilities. Perhaps ironically, given the long association of femininity with sweetness and compromise, it is feminine women who currently need the most independence and strength to stand up for themselves against women who are hostile to their nature and men who are ignorant of it.

Feminism is thus doubly the cry of the excluded. On the one hand, it represents the struggle of a politicized minority of those women who by virtue of temperament do not feel sympathy with femininity. In some ways feminism was an advantage to such women, and in others it was not. On the other hand, it represents a misdirected attempt by feminine women to cope with a culture which has failed to accept and provide for their nature.

Too many American women have been obliged to view their sex as a handicap. Feminism was in part a reaction against this gender inferiority complex.

It need not be so. Hints of a better way abound both worldwide and in our own culture, examples overlooked in the flush of ideological impatience, traditions ignored by a generation that could discern no charm or value in the past. You have only to travel to a country as closely related to ours as France (or any other Latin country) to realize that women's relation to their femininity can be completely different from the tense uncertainty that prevails in America. French women face many of the same problems and pressures as American women, yet somehow this has not upset the ease they feel with the fact they are women. The lack of envy most French women feel for men—the sense of a difference accepted, and thoroughly enjoyed—is far too rare in America at the present time. Few young American women dare let themselves take the intense, almost continuous pleasure in their feminine beauty and significance that is common among French women of the same age. It is a contrast with the potential to continue into later life, when women's difference, rather than being their weakness, can become a major source of strength.

Other examples will suggest themselves: remnants of behavior from family, ethnic, and regional traditions; one's own hopes and fantasies, at last cast in a positive light; and all the continuities of life which feminism has failed to destroy, from fashion to the family.

Gender Education

A serious need exists for "sex education" broadly conceived, for the transmission of information about the natures of maleness and femaleness. There is no point in censuring men, or women, for not understanding everything about themselves right off the bat, let alone everything about the other sex. People do not know everything automatically. Even the so-called lower animals rely heavily on the transmission of knowledge between generations, like bears, whose cubs must learn to fish from their mothers. How vastly richer is the amount of information people need to function with any degree of confidence! People require information about many things lest they flounder about in an unsuccessful attempt to reinvent the wisdom of generations in a few short years. Yet as matters stand, men and women reach their twenties with little useful information about their own sex and even less about the opposite one. Only a newly informed commitment of our culture can prevent the situation that trapped Colette Dowling, in which she was made to feel lost and worthless for no other reason than that she was a woman.

Any culture has a responsibility to provide the minimum of accurate and useful information to its young men and women about themselves and each other which they need. Yet in America today, young people reach puberty and adulthood with an ignorance of gender as complete as the ignorance of sex with which proper Victorian girls entered marriage. And when there is any information at all, it is likely to be partial and biased. The predictable results are confusion and trauma. Regardless of whether one envisages a greatly expanded concept of "sex education" or more modestly hopes for the diffusion of more and better information through families, peers, books, and the media, there is an obvious need for improved "gender education."

Each generation must learn life's lessons anew, and the process will always be a challenge fraught with aspects of pain and risk. But the process need not be as haphazard and drawn out as the endless adolescence of the baby boomers. In the world in which we live, there are any number of more productive battles to fight. Individual self-discovery may be an endless process, but simply growing up should not be—and for the great majority of people it need not be.

Every week I meet couples suffering from the absence of information about the other sex which is all the guidance unisexism has to offer. In such couples, one member is engaged in a constant diminishment of the other's humanity and self-respect by insisting the other's personality and actions are valid only to the extent they conform to the pattern of the opposite sex. The woman is unable to recognize her mate's need to validate his identity through external personal achievement or to admire his capacities for abstraction and aggression; or the man is unable to recognize his mate's need for warm intimacy and validation through the eyes of others—most of all, through *his* eyes. Each sex needs to be both admired and left alone by the other. While this may be ancient wisdom, it is not getting through at present. There is a serious need to ensure that each succeeding generation will not have to reinvent this lesson, so slowly and painfully learned by the baby boomers.

Neither sex has come as far from the Old Stone Age as is commonly believed. Men need to go off and achieve. Women need warm personal connections to feel right about themselves. Men and women who aspire to live in harmony with the opposite sex must acknowledge these basic facts, in order to overcome the judgmentalism of each sex's unalloyed perspective. The alternative is to crush a person's potential, as many individual men and women have historically done to their spouses and children. Although men also need personal connections and women also need a level of independent personal achievement, there remains a readily discernible difference in the level of these needs that is both quantitative and qualitative. This basic difference in style between the sexes is great enough to call both for understanding and forbearance and for admiration and appreciation from each sex for the other.

Past investigations of gender difference have often been tainted by an implied critique of one or the other sex. Freud claimed that a woman makes and nurtures a baby as a substitute for the externality symbolized by the possession of a penis. Stung by this argument, Margaret Mead came up with the counterproposal that men suffer from "womb envy": that, condemned by biology to be mere witnesses to the miracle of life, men engage in impersonal achievement as a form of compensatory behavior.[11] I would prefer to think that sex difference can be explored without either male or female chauvinism; that instead of devaluing the behavior of one sex by establishing the other as the "human norm," we will open ourselves to the idea that each sex, precious in its own right, establishes its own norm.

Feminism and Virism

To grasp the inherent inadequacy of feminism as a universal philosophy, it is helpful to consider its mirror image, a point of view that can be termed "masculism"[12] or, with greater etymological precision, "virism." "Feminism" is derived from the Latin *femina,* woman; "virism" from the Latin *vir,* man or hero, which has given us such words as "virtue" and "virility." Where the feminist perspective is that social ills are caused by the dominance of masculine values, the virist perspective is that they are caused by the decline of those values. What ails society is "effeminacy."

The improvement of society requires that the influence of female values be decreased and the influence of male values increased. This point of view was widespread in classical times, when it was a standard attitude of the greatest Greek philosophers, such as Pythagoras and Aristotle, and the best Roman writers, including Cicero and Caesar.

The parallel association of Hellenic virism with a cult of homosexuality and modern feminism with a cult of lesbianism is not accidental. Both ideologies are heavily commingled with self-serving and vindictive efforts by sexual minorities to remake the world in their own images.

Virism is unfashionable today. Its public expression now occurs largely outside the citadels of established culture. Classical virism represented a majority, respectable point of view. In contrast, contemporary virism is a defensive phenomenon. Unlike the ancient variety, modern virism does not aspire to social dominance, that is, to undermine the feminine, but simply to preserve the masculine. Contemporary virists perceive themselves to be fighting a last-ditch action against a neutered or feminized society, of which feminism is merely one recent expression.

It is tempting to see organized sports in viristic terms, as an attempt to preserve a set of values that are shunned in the gray world of corporate life and media values.[13] Heavy metal rock contains a strong viristic component.

The clearest and most visible type of contemporary virism, though, is found in the movies starring Sylvester Stallone, Arnold Schwarzenegger, Clint Eastwood, and Charles Bronson. While some of these films have been major money-makers, they retain an underground quality in terms of mainstream media culture. In these films, like *Rambo* and *Commando,* the world has gone soft. The protagonists struggle to avert dangers caused by society's loss of the masculine principle. They epitomize the virtues of independence of mind, physical strength, and fighting skill that, though rejected by corporate society, paradoxically are seen to embody its sustaining values. Unlike classical virism, which associates women with evil, Hollywood virism depicts women as tangential to the main business of life.

Another form of contemporary virism is found in the best-selling but unmentionable novels of John Norman, which describe life on a planet called Gor where men have reduced women to slavery. Gorean society achieves a balance impossible for Earth cultures, which are corrupted by the loss of the masculine principle. It is instructive to contrast this vision with the man-free utopias of feminist fantasy.

Can one seriously maintain that the feminist identification of masculinity with the worst aspects of humanity is more enlightened than the virist equation of masculinity with the best? Is not contemporary feminism's denial of any legitimate role to masculinity as shortsighted and perverse as classical virism's blanket hostility to femininity? Finally, can any philosophy that fails to respect both masculinity and femininity possibly be adequately grounded in human experience?

It would make more sense to share virtue between the sexes: to accept that each sex has always made a contribution, has always had power for good and for evil, and that it is perverse and futile to try to quantify which sex is more or less worthwhile than the other.

The solution to the devaluation of masculinity of the Vietnam War era, and to the more persistent problem of our cultural ambivalence toward femininity, lies neither in the facile equation of unisexism—to assimilate both sexes to a single "human" standard—nor in the rejection of either sex as a valued part of the human experience, but in the restoration of maleness and femaleness to their rightful place in the human scheme of things: no more, but no less. A better future lies neither in masculinity nor in femininity alone, nor in their homogenization, but in the acceptance and equally high valuation of both.

Chapter 12

American Women: The Immediate Future

If the experience of the past generation has taught us anything, it is that one cannot simply extrapolate present trend lines into the future. Young middle class women entered the salaried work force in large numbers in the forties only to flee from it in even larger numbers in the fifties. Hesitantly reentering it in the sixties, they flooded it in the seventies. The U.S. economy, buoyant through the sixties, pedaled into reverse in the seventies—only to confound the resulting predictions of "limits to growth" in the eighties. India, which seemed destined to remain a permanent basket case in the sixties, as its exploding population outstripped its limited food supply, is now a net agricultural exporter—without any halt in its birth rate. On the other hand, sub-Saharan Africa, which seemed to many observers to be poised for a period of rapid modernization at the end of the sixties, in fact saw its per capita agricultural production *decline* during the seventies. All trends are subject to countertrends, and one cannot well evaluate the prospects for continuity, or for change, by looking at raw figures alone.

It would thus be much too easy to assume that American women will continue indefinitely in the same directions as those of the past fifteen years. The current work environment in America is mixed in results and highly uncomfortable to many.[1] The tensions it generates, not purely a result of "the conditioning" we are encouraged to fear and distrust, seek a resolution. These dynamic, continuing tensions will inevitably have societal consequences—exactly which, remains to be seen.

What has changed is well known: the occupational barriers that kept men and women from doing the same jobs have been breached. What has yet to be worked out is a comfortable accommodation to this fact in the lives of individuals. The feminist answers don't work. Feminism played a role in showing women's *capacity* for all sorts of activities. The argument is not over capacity but over motivation. The new challenge is to be true to oneself.

A number of conflicts bedevil this period of transition. A good deal of hostility may develop between the sexes on the job. For example, many women feel that their male co-workers are too competitive, too subservient to the hierarchy; that, in short, their jobs mean too much to them and that this gives them an unfair advantage. Because of the persistence of the feminist perspective, it is often vaguely felt that this indicates there is something wrong with these men (or perhaps with men in general), that they are somehow prehistoric (unlike the women, who have evolved). At the same time, many women feel artificial in the job roles they have taken on, as if they are playing a game whose rules are obscure and whose purpose they don't understand, which, despite their best efforts to master it—indeed, sometimes despite real success—doesn't feel real or important to them.

Are such feelings retrograde remnants of "the conditioning," or do they deserve attention and respect as valid expressions of differing psychological imperatives of the sort described by Gilligan? Can we dismiss all our feelings as the result of "conditioning" when they don't happen to fit our current notions of political progress?

It would be hazardous to predict the exact form the resolution of the current tensions will take over the coming generation. Certain points, though, are reasonably assured.

Society is *not* evolving toward the disappearance of occupational distinctions. They have become weaker in many cases. In general, women now have a choice between the private world of home and the public world of paid work. But a society in which gender typing disappears from all, or even most, occupations is destined to remain pie in the sky. One has only to compare the high number of female college students majoring in English with the low number majoring in physics or political science to see that each sex continues to train itself in different ways. Other factors play a part. An "aggression advantage" probably gives men a real advantage in certain circumstances—starting with boys' far more frequent participation in classroom discussion in mixed-sex groups.[2] Too, the psychological imperative of maleness—that men have no alternative to achievement[3]—is so widely validated by experience and common sense that it must be accepted as a permanent advantage to men in the public sphere. Career success is an option for women, for men it is a necessity; men's motivation to succeed at work will therefore on balance tend to be greater than women's. Finally, there is the major consideration that millions of women *don't* work: to oblige all these women to work would remain a huge task of dubious moral legitimacy.

The resolution of the family versus career conflict is still unclear, but the fact that it is being thought about at all by young women represents real progress over the seventies, the period of the Myth of Independence, when millions of women literally never thought about organizing their lives to include a family until they ran up against the biological limits of the age of childbearing. Too, the terms in which this conflict is being considered have a chance of becoming more realistic, as the new female psychology comes to replace the feminist devaluation of the feminine.

The immediate future will be characterized by diversity. In the fifties, a wave of conformism caused the marriage age to drop steadily toward the upper teens, the employment rate for young women to decline, and sent the birth rate soaring to rival that of a Third World country. In the seventies, a second wave of conformism sent the marriage and birth rates down to historic lows. The number of women on the job market rose. The birth rate fell to replacement level and beneath.

The eighties are witnessing the beginning of a meaningful diversity, in which it will be somewhat easier for individual women to follow their own lights. Women will divide their efforts between paid work and domesticity—in what proportion remains to be worked out. It seems likely that we are not headed back to the fifties—but it is certain that we are not going to see the neutered norm which in the seventies was the only acceptable notion of a just society.

The new life plan for American women will be distinguished, not by the steady sweep of the male career and family paths, but by its division into distinct stages. The first third of a woman's life (roughly speaking) will typically be spent in educational and maturational experiences of various sorts. The next third will be characterized by intense involvement in family life, which will be the major locus of both affectional and work life for most women. If a career is pursued, it will be downplayed relative to the demands and fulfillments of family life. In either case, paid work will not be the primary determinant of identity or the most powerful source of fulfillment for most women. The following third, after children are grown, will see an increase in women's extrafamilial activities, which will in many cases involve a full or part time return to the world of paid work. The numbers of middle-aged women in the work force will be further swelled by the greater numbers of widowed and divorced women at this time in life.

This tripartite model confounds the nearsighted careerist track of the Myth of Independence and, unlike the feminine mystique, allows time for maturation in early adulthood before marriage and for meaningful and remunerative activity after children have left the nest. It is compatible with both interdependence and individuation, and is the only conceivable realistic model for the majority of women under the conditions of current civilization.

Women's characteristic needs will differ from stage to stage, and will at every stage differ from men's. Any viable female advocacy must address these concrete realities of women's lives.

Older women will need opportunities beyond the family, but it's not as if all twenty-year-old women were going into careers. It's a different type of problem than if that were the case. For instance, relatively few women in the post-child-rearing years will compete for executive positions in banking, law, and so forth.

Some feminists have taken to pointing out that "Women are not· cloning the male model." While this statement is intended as an attack on maleness, it does contain a grain of truth. Women really are not duplicating men's approaches to work—quite apart from the allegedly determinative issue of housework. For instance, the numerous businesses women have started in recent years tend to be small, personal affairs which, it can be expected, will give many women a work environment more congenial to them, will permit women greater economic security, and will increase the diversity of our culture, but will not compete with the world of large corporations.

American women in the mid-eighties are presented with three life paths: the careerist, housewife, and superwoman models. Each of these has its characteristic difficulties. Day care is not a panacea, for the high octane professions that the feminist mystique prescribes as the acme of female fulfillment inherently require unreasonable amounts of effort over a period of years. These years of flat-out effort usually coincide with the period in which a woman is raising a family. Even if her husband is among the few who are willing and able to contribute fifty percent or more of child care, she makes an extreme sacrifice—the experience of raising her own children—in return for a problematic reward, namely the sort of professional recognition whose value many *men* (who have no choice) came to question in the sixties. The superwoman must cram all her personal relationships into the few exhausted hours left over from work, commuting, shopping, making appointments, and so forth. The result may be worth the price this exerts on her relationships, but it is necessary to recognize that there is a price. Too, unless this life-style is a mutual decision, it seems likely that many men will be severely frustrated by a wife who is rarely home, and is constantly exhausted or busy when she is. Because modern fields change so fast, the strategy of educating oneself for a profession and then putting it on hold for five, ten, or twenty years to raise a family often doesn't work out or, if it does, mandates a lower status position than would have been the case had there been no interruption. And it is not possible to cut back work effort beyond a certain level without falling behind others. There is no way a person working eight hours a day, and subject to interruptions, can compete with a person working fourteen hours a day without interruptions. Prestige professions are inherently the most difficult form of paid employment to integrate into women's life cycles.

Yet the price of sacrificing family life to job is one that most women shy away from in horror. Most people, men and women, will in the long run make almost any sacrifice necessary to marry and have children, both for the positive reason that they wish to participate in love relationships and to avoid loneliness. As the Me Generation discovered the hard way, singleness is a miserable way to live for most people once they find themselves beyond the communal settings of youth culture.

In comparison with the careerist and superwoman tracks, the housewife alternative offers real advantages. But in any case, women are not "going back" to the fifties. To be a housewife in the late eighties is not the same thing it was in the late fifties. Women who choose the housewife option today are doing so with their eyes open, not because they have no other choices. Because they are making an informed, self-affirming choice, very few of them will be prone to the sense of entrapment against which Friedan revolted. In addition, the whole cultural context has changed, and we may expect that they will reinvent many aspects of the housewife role to their personal benefit and that of their families. The end result of the fifties and seventies excesses—if we can learn the lessons of each—is that at long last women will be free to follow their own lights, and that in consequence the misdirection of vast numbers of women into uncongenial life tracks will finally come to an end.

Indeed, the dividing line between women who "work" and women who "stay at home" may be blurred. It would be an advantage to all concerned if more jobs became available that would not require a forty-hour work week. The productivity of women who work, say, only twenty hours a week is probably far higher on average than those who work full time. It is mostly a timorous clinging to a misunderstood work ethic that delays the development of more such jobs, like that of the employers who once felt that to oblige any worker to toil for less than fourteen hours a day, six days a week, would sap the national character. Flexible work hours, which have gained considerable favor in some quarters, are another useful innovation.

The housewife role does have its pitfalls. It can be wearing to be constantly attending to others' needs. Housewives are subject to isolation from other adults. Above all, they must at the present time function in a culture that still retains a good deal of misogyny. The old view that women's roles must be second-rate persists, aggravated by the newer feminist disparagement of female activities and values, the feminist devaluation of the feminine. Housewives are in a position of vulnerability with regard to difficult husbands, which can sometimes be reduced with the bargaining power of a separate paycheck. In addition, there comes a point during her children's adolescence when the demands on a mother radically diminish. What women do at this point will be a matter of personal inclination and initiative, but for many the best solution will be to reenter the world of paid employment on one basis or another. But all the potential difficulties that beset housewives are matched or exceeded by the difficulties facing women in other life tracks, and each problem housewives face has a potential solution—unlike the superwoman model, which tends to require that women (and their husbands and children) cease to be made of flesh and blood.

The important point is that women do face real choices, each of which exerts its price and bestows its rewards. We must stop pretending that any one of these three paths presents a panacea for all women, as surely as we must resist efforts to close the door on any one of them. A more realistic life plan than those of fifties or seventies women must be made available to the girls who are now growing up, one that offers real choices, without obscuring or exaggerating either the difficulties or the fulfillments of any one of these paths.

Panaceas do not exist. Every life-style has its drawbacks and dangers. Masculinity and femininity impose their difficult aspects along with their advantages and pleasures. Masculine separateness exerts its price. Feminine connectedness is inseparable from feminine vulnerability. The careerist and wife-mother life orientations both present real, though differing, problems to women—and the attempt to combine these two life tracks is usually even more fraught with pain, anxiety, and missed nights' sleep. Even the most comprehensive day care is a very inadequate solution for a woman or her children if she must put in the kind of hours required of aspiring investment bankers, professors seeking tenure, or medical interns. And to somehow force competitive men to slow down would pose insuperable problems of oppression, anomie, and civilizational decay.

But we cannot go back to some balanced, related world of the prehistoric past, for life has always had its areas of difficulty. Even if we could go back to the Neolithic village or yet further back to the camps of the mammoth hunters, we would find sources of joy and difficulty equivalent to those that confront people in our own culture. We must recognize that life presents certain imperatives and certain choices. The nature of both the imperatives and the choices has been almost impenetrably obscured for the past twenty years, under the prevailing influence of cultural determinism, unisexism, and feminism. It is time for Americans to start educating themselves about these matters, unlike the sixties generation which crashed through life like a blindfolded driver trying to negotiate a twisting road with a guide shouting false directions in his ear.

Progress, we are told, grinds inexorably forward. As *The Female Eunuch* informed its readers, "The family is already broken down: technology has outstripped conservatism."[4] More and more women are having babies out of wedlock. Fewer than 6 percent of American families, it is said, still adhere to the standards of the "traditional" family, with a father, mother, and children. This ideal has now become "nostalgic."[5] The divorce rate is so high that marriage is a lousy bet for any woman. Men are undependable as providers, and there is no way to make them more dependable. Besides, it's degrading to depend on someone else's paycheck. Therefore, since it is obsolete, men's role as primary providers must be decisively ended by equalizing men's and women's take-home pay, by hook or by crook. Women's best and only strategy is to embrace the corporate structure, leaving their kids in day care for nine, ten, or more hours a day. This is all in women's best interest, because it is more exciting to work than to care for home, husband, children, and community: such a life-style is a sure-fire recipe for alienation and bored childishness. In short, regardless of what anyone does or does not do, traditional male roles are entirely obsolete, and the occupation of housewife, a remnant of the "retrograde" fifties, is about to be relegated to the scrap heap of history—and good riddance. The need for sensible and just policies requires that we do everything possible to hasten this process. So awesome are the inevitabilities of social evolution. We poor individuals, with our hopes, dreams, fantasies, and personalities, to say nothing of our convictions, can do nothing to halt, reverse, or prevent the imminent blitzkrieg of the juggernaut of history.

Men who cherish the retrograde wish for a wife who will tend their home, care for their children, and support their career, and women who retain the illusion that they have a right to be economically supported in marriage, who cherish the delusion that a happy home life can ever supersede the need to win professional spurs, or that their activity within the family is deserving of society's support or approval, are in for early and embarrassing disappointment. Far better that they free themselves as rapidly as possible from the "socialization" that pushes them into these "traditional roles," and embrace the self-evident truths of cultural determinism, nonsexist child rearing, and the de-gendering of all behaviors and occupations. History marches on. If we don't march with it, we are told, or at least get out of its way, it will crush us.

Contemporary feminism, in short, is still contemporary feminism. It continues to mandate one life-style for all women, professional and working class, married and single, which continues to be based on the anti-feminine vituperations of *The Feminine Mystique, Sexual Politics,* and *The Female Eunuch.* It is time to reveal these claims for what they are.

The "inevitability" of which feminists warn us is an illusion wrought by an ideologically motivated attempt to cut off the discussion of potentially awkward facts. The shoddy statistics with which feminists seek to convince us must be understood in terms of feminists' ideological prejudice against "traditional" society in all its phases—in particular, against the family. There is an urgent need for a readable book-length statistical exposition of the true state of the family and gender in America. It is to be hoped that a competent sociologist will soon fill the need for a study of the family in America that is realistic enough to be optimistic. In the interim, certain broad facts are evident which could not be guessed at from the feminist argument.

The family is not breaking down in America. Divorce does not doom the family with a male breadwinner. The self-evident solution to the financial problems of divorced and single women is not the imposition of comparable worth pay scales. Let us consider these points one by one.

1. The family is not breaking down in America.

Americans continue to live in families. And when they cannot, they continue to wish that they could.

Single motherhood is not becoming a major trend. We are given a false impression that women everywhere are having babies out of wedlock because of the highly publicized cases of a few Hollywood stars who have done so, like Farah Fawcett. The truth is that single motherhood is a class phenomenon, a symptom not of the evolution of the family but of its pathological breakdown. The illegitimacy rate among the middle and upper middle class is negligible. It is the poor in general, and the black poor in particular, who are having babies out of wedlock. This is evidence not of social progress, but of social pathology. It is cause not for celebration at the destruction of patriarchy but for despair at the disappearance of fatherhood. It is a severe social problem that desperately cries out for a solution, not for more encouragement. Once we take the elementary step of correcting the illegitimacy figures for class and race, the problem of the breakdown of the family—or the "progress" it represents—is suddenly radically diminished. We are being misled.

Americans will continue to live in families. "Alternative living arrangements" are a sheer myth perpetrated by wishful feminists and a credulous media. The vast majority of American children are born into and continue to live in homes with two parents, one of each sex. Single parents—almost invariably mothers—are largely a phenomenon of poverty, where their numbers are great enough to skew the statistics for the population as a whole. Statistically, single mothers are a sign of the breakdown of the most basic human institutions, not of liberation.[6]

It may be true that "most families don't fit the Norman Rockwell model" of Mom, Dad, and three kids, but this figure too is presented grossly out of context. In the first place, the late marriage age and low birth rate of the baby-boom generation mandate a low incidence of young married couples with children relative to the general population. Our current statistics on family types are distorted by the influence of feminism and the 1970s cult of singleness. It is likely that the 1970s extremes in marriage age and birth rate are temporary phenomena. In addition, much of a population at any given moment is either too young or too old to be numbered among young parents and their children. Much of the current "low" incidence of nuclear families is therefore expectable in *any* society. Such elementary qualifications are totally absent from the arguments of feminists, as they struggle to convince America that "the family is broken down: technology has outstripped conservatism." Feminists' habitual distortion of the family statistics inevitably calls to mind the remark attributed to Mayor La Guardia, "Figures don't lie, but liars figure."

America showed its extraordinary responsiveness to social trends in the fifties, and again in the seventies, as we ricocheted from the cult of domesticity to the cult of singleness. As we finally move toward a sensible balance, what does seem inevitable is not that the trend lines of the Feminist Era will continue indefinitely into our future, but that they will change along with our evolving social consciousness: that the marriage and birth rates will rise, and the divorce rate will fall; and that as a result, a more normal distribution of family types will appear. And if the high incidence of single motherhood among the already poor can be reduced—an urgent national need that is beginning to receive some of the attention it deserves— the number of intact families will rise even further.

2. Divorce does not doom the family with a male breadwinner.

Similar objections apply to the divorce statistics. It is true that the incidence of divorce has risen dramatically since the "retrograde" fifties (when it fell)—but when the divorce figures are corrected for class, race, and age, they begin to look less hopeless. As George Gilder pointed out in *Sexual Suicide* in 1973, marriage was (and still is) actually a rather good bet for many people: specifically, couples that are over twenty-five and have a middle class income have five chances out of six of never divorcing.* Few careers can offer such a likely margin of success.

To this must be added the fact that, while it is statistically more difficult for divorced women than divorced men to find a new mate, many do eventually remarry. Marriage remains a viable economic institution for the vast majority of middle class American women. And it is from this middle class that most feminists come and to which (despite much xenocentric adulation of the working class) they speak.

In addition to these considerations, the divorce rate, which seemed destined to rise relentlessly in the sixties and seventies, is stabilizing. It is not too much to hope for a countertrend, in which the divorce rate

---

*Louis Harris, one of America's most respected pollsters, might view these figures as too pessimistic. Harris concluded in 1987 that the popular media notion that "one out of two new marriages will fail" was based on a false reading of the data. In reality, according to Harris, almost nine out of ten American marriages survive.[7]

actually falls over a period of years.

Furthermore, women do better for themselves in marriage—unless they are willing to forgo having children, which over 90 percent of American women are not. It is at last becoming widely known that the influx of women into the labor force over the past fifteen years has not resulted in any reduction in the levels of occupational sex segregation or in the average difference between male and female incomes. Women's wages still average about two-thirds of men's.[8] As a result, it makes not just emotional or practical sense but also good economic sense for women to marry, and for married couples to treat the husband's income as primary.

The more than 90 percent of women who will bear children are better off married than single. A husband is usually capable of at least some child minding, and typically makes the heftier contribution to the family budget. If a married woman with children works and places her children in day care, she is obviously better off paying for it with her husband's help. What is true for women is equally true for men. Single men are the most unstable and least healthy major category of the adult population. Marriage supports the well-being of both men and women—to say nothing of children.

The pitfalls of the housewife role were recklessly exaggerated in feminists' devaluation of the feminine. Similarly, feminists have sold women a bill of goods with their exclusive emphasis on careers. Working class women with children would in general be happier *not* to work at jobs that are typically something less than the fulfilling careers recommended by feminists. Middle class professional women occupy only a small percentage of the high-status managerial positions that the media have taught us to associate with women and careers. Too, many of the few women who do occupy such positions find that their jobs lose meaning by their late twenties compared to their family lives—or to their wish for family lives.

In short, marriage remains on the whole a good deal for women, which is one reason (economics not being the sole fount of human motivation) women still want to get married.

3. The self-evident solution to the financial problems of divorced and single women is not the imposition of comparable worth pay scales.

The current situation has a certain rough justice to it. Men are paid considerably more than women, on average, allowing them to support families. Adult men are typically in the situation of supporting two adults and two or more children, whereas even single mothers do not support more than one adult. Until our norms change (if they should indeed ever do so), our current system is therefore more just on balance than any other conceivable system. This does not mean it does not need to be improved, perhaps radically so in some areas, but it does mean that *our current sex-based division of labor is fundamentally sound and just.* For to equalize male and female average rates of pay through comparable worth, as American feminists propose, or through leveling all incomes, as the Soviet system does, means that the breadwinner role is undermined and ceases to be viable. The practical result of this situation is that women work two jobs, one in the workplace and the other at home.

The only way around this quandary is the Swedish model of universal day care in a welfare state context, which presents its own severe problems of economic inhibition, personal anomie, and loss of freedom. These problems have major human consequences for the people of Sweden, and are inexorably implicated in Sweden's unusually high rates of illegitimacy, alcoholism, and suicide.

The Swedish model does not supply an acceptable means of equalizing the sexes' incomes. The Communist method is out of the question entirely. The comparable worth method—if applied generally throughout society, as it would have to be to achieve its aims—would have almost as bad a strangling effect on the economy. In addition, the Feminist Era has failed to change the basic American social norms: however we explain this, men and women still respond to different motivations. It will thus be far cheaper in both human and economic terms to retain our current system, pragmatically correcting its defects where necessary, than to set forth on a destructive quest for unisex utopia.

It is bad enough that feminists have been unable to face the real problems of working women, of which the most urgent is the difficulty of bearing children while continuing to meet the demands of a full-time job. As Sylvia Hewlett notes, American women are being urged to work full time and to have children in their spare time. But contemporary feminists' insensitivity to the real needs of working women pales beside their dismissal of the needs of housewives, who they think are about to disappear. After all, if housewives are about to disappear as a profession, why bother about their needs?

Is the cup half full or half empty? You would never guess from feminists' selective presentation of statistics that almost half of married American women do not work for wages at all. Are these women retrograde "transitional women," whose life choice is about to be consigned to the scrap heap of history? Can feminists, who are supposed to be "for women," find no compassion for their problems, and no admiration for their contributions?

Feminists like to assert that "48 percent of mothers with children under twelve months are already in the work force, and most of them work out of economic necessity."[9] Not only are almost half of all mothers with young children in the work force; they are "already" there, implying that some inevitable logic of history will impel the few holdouts to soon follow. The juggernaut rolls on. But the most striking aspect of this figure is passed over in silence: that *over half of mothers with young children are* not *in the work force, and most of them are supported by working husbands.* So much for the "traditional" family being "nostalgic."

Even more tendentious is the claim that "most" women "work out of economic necessity." Obviously many do—but it is equally obvious that many do not. It is of course true that many women must work—but most American women can and should have a choice between home life and paid employment. If they can choose to have both, so much the better: but they must at least be able to choose one or the other. America is a far richer nation than it was in the fifties, when middle class women stayed home in droves. Since America is far richer per capita than it was in the fifties, clearly the money is there to support families through male breadwinners. We should not confuse our life-style choices with historical inevitability. As Gloria Steinem correctly pointed out in the late seventies, when feminists viewed it as a sign of their movement's success, it is actually those women who *least* need to work who are most likely to do so.[10] Whether most women work, and if so whether they work full-time, part-time, or somewhere in between, is a choice, made in part by individuals and in part by the society at large, which received two very different answers in the fifties and the seventies.

All the talk of historical inevitability is so much stuff and nonsense. Americans have a choice. After having been pulled one way in the fifties and pushed the other in the seventies, it is high time we began to exercise it once more.

A satisfactory solution has not yet been found for the gap in meaning and the new possibilities opened in women's lives by the decline of universal full-time motherhood and wifedom. What is clear is that the solution to this problem lies neither in the feminist rejection of femininity nor in the careerist attempt to follow a masculine life pattern. For the vast majority of women, these are two non-solutions, which cannot work under any circumstances because they are hopelessly at odds with women's psychology and the female life cycle.

Because women's motivations and life cycles differ from men's (among other reasons), they are not going to join all professions in similar numbers to men. The work force will continue to be divided in multitudinous and complex ways, some geared to economic efficiency, some to the abstract principle of sexual equality, while others will be totally arbitrary. The literally equal society envisioned by those who devised the affirmative action programs of the seventies is simply not going to develop. This will lead to perennial cries of injustice from that know-nothing left which, like the reactionary noblemen of the French Restoration, will have "learned nothing, forgotten nothing, and forgiven nothing." Such concerns will be increasingly irrelevant to the majority of Americans, who will accept a gendered society as a major good that easily justifies a minor level of inconvenience.

A number of developments have conspired to undermine the uni-sexism of past decades. New perspectives in science and gender have steadily eroded the culturist consensus on which feminism built. Gender difference is becoming newly acceptable among the young. Marriage and family have become of central importance to most of the baby boomers. Their marital arrangements, their sexual lives, and their children's gendered behavior all confound the expectations of the unisexist belief in which they grew up. Millions of young women on the job market would like nothing better than to get married and have children, even if—often especially if—this would mean staying home. The quest for independence, for "self," has given way to a quest for interdependence, for permanence. There are even some flickers of acceptance of the idea that the majority of men most truly find themselves in an extrafamilial struggle while the majority of women most truly find themselves in a relationship. There are even cautious whispers that this difference may be positive and complementary, that the difficulties it can cause are less important than the fulfillments it brings.

The rejection of marriage and the family is being reversed at the present time. The sexes are drawing closer together, each somewhat more sure of itself and its value than was possible during the shell-shocked days of the Vietnam War and the subsequent Era of Feminism.

This development is taking place amid hopeful signs for the American family. For the first time in a quarter century, the divorce rate is stabilizing.

The rate of marriage is up, and climbing. Young Americans are falling in love and getting married, and staying married.

And many of their slightly older sisters are rejecting the Myth of Independence and getting married too, and, often at the last biologically possible moment, having babies. Both groups of women, the survivors of the feminist generation and the rising cohort, are opting for family life as a choice. They will be fierce defenders of the dignity of the life-style they have chosen. The new familism in American life precludes the revival of mass feminism over the coming generation.

However, the problem of feeling good about one's femininity in a culture that gives it precious little recognition or dignity remains acute for millions of American women. The slowly dawning recognition that gender difference exists, and is valid, is a badly needed advance, but by itself it is pitifully insufficient to lay a groundwork for human happiness. It tells women it is all right to be feminine, but nothing about what it might mean to be feminine. Women are thus thrown back on their own individual resources, which are by definition inadequate to sustain the well-being of a cultural animal. Ironically, it is the culturists, who argue that gender is a purely cultural construct, who wish to limit its expression to the merely biological. In the final analysis, unisexism is thus a denial not just of our biological nature but of our cultural one as well. Precisely because we are in part cultural animals, our biology needs to be carried forward and completed by our cultural traditions. In this regard, a young woman who makes up or puts on high heels (or a young man who pumps his biceps at the gym) is performing a socially responsible act. Masculinity and femininity only achieve their full meaning when they can develop and flourish in the matrix of a rich culture. If we are to recover gender in its fullness and promise, we must allow ourselves to bathe luxuriously and exorbitantly in it, free of worry as to its price or function; we must treat our sex not as a finished product but as a mere ledger line on which we can, if we have the confidence and the wisdom, construct serenades and symphonies.

Can a solution to our culture's truncation of the experience of being female arise from the ashes of feminism? There is reason to hope that a new confidence in self arising (but at what a price!) from the experience of the Feminist Era will enable American women to recover the lost dignity of the feminine, to the benefit of the whole culture.

Chapter 13

The Failure of Feminism

In its best sense, "feminism" signifies a broad concern with the well-being of women. The conditions of women's lives are to be improved through social activism of various sorts. This approach raises serious questions. The improvements in American women's (and men's) lives over the past hundred years are due mostly to economic progress and the consequent emergence of a post-industrial middle class society, not to social activism. All the feminism of the past century has not done as much to increase women's choices as the invention of the washing machine. But it is hard to quibble with the fundamental decency of the social activist impulse, or to deny that it has accomplished significant good in some areas.

Contemporary feminism, though, retains this humane approach only in the imaginations of its more distant supporters. Feminism today is a narrowly ideological movement, the last survivor of sixties leftist politics to retain any major influence in American life. A product of the radical rage of the sixties, it remains mired in the quicksand of that era's unwinnable causes.

It is very tempting to take a positive view of the accomplishments of this feminism, to continue to believe it was the "most humane revolution of all,"[1] a pure net gain for all concerned. Can such a view be sustained?

Feminism has real and significant achievements to its credit. Feminists have played a major role in opening doors to women in employment, education, and sports. Feminism has provided a guiding philosophy to many women in their prolonged and bruising penetration of the corporate and academic worlds.[2] Feminism has provided enough of a supporting framework to sustain many women through a difficult period of complete uncertainty about their sex roles. Feminists formed an important part of the constituency for abortion rights at the start of the seventies. They were responsible for desperately needed attention given to the crime of rape. They have thrown the spotlight on the syndrome of battered women. Feminists have played a highly effective role in the grass roots attempt to introduce humanity and common sense to medical practice in America. They have relentlessly hammered home the inadequacy of all intellectual disciplines that fail to take into account a female point of view. History, anthropology, sociology, psychology, sociobiology, primatology, and literary criticism will never be quite the same. Feminists have destroyed the plausibility of oversimple explanations for our partly arbitrary sex roles. Perhaps above all, feminism has helped to tear open the deceptively uniform surface presented by the mystique of femininity to reveal the cornucopia of needs, talents, and aspirations within.

Another major accomplishment of the Feminist Era was a significant shift in cultural misogyny. When you open a thriller or view a movie from the sixties or early seventies, it comes as a shock to confront the really mindless, empty disparagement of women that was often taken for granted before the Feminist Era. In an early James Bond film such as *From Russia With Love,* the heroine's role is reduced to virtual meaninglessness: scarcely vital enough to be a sex object, there is almost nothing for the actress to do. She is merely there to be fought for, fucked, and flung aside. Such was all too often the fate of the "groovy chick" of the 1960s, epitomized in a soft-core porn film like *Autumn Melody* in which a young woman is brainwashed into a literal state of mindlessness.

By the mid-eighties such images had become increasingly scarce in popular literature. While a sort of pornography of violence against women continued to be common on television and at the movies, the overall level of free-floating misogyny had fallen drastically from its peak around 1970. While various factors were involved, including the conservative resurgence and the increased life experience of the baby boomers, feminists could take pride in the central and crucial role they had played in producing this result.

These positive changes of the Feminist Era have had a generally beneficial effect on women's perceptions of themselves and the possibilities open to them. In the first place, the sense is now widespread that what women do is significant: women feel important. In the second place, women no longer feel significantly constrained in their life choices. They readily imagine themselves in any occupation, and can reasonably aspire to practically any ambition open to men (as well as to some that are not).

It would be highly unwise to reject these accomplishments. Indeed, it is probably not possible to do so. Future generations will be in part the children of feminism. Feminism has advanced the cause of humanity in important ways. However, we cannot afford to spend all our time eulogizing past accomplishments. We must also cope with the new problems facing us today, which have been brought about in great measure by feminism's very successes. Beside its real accomplishments we must place the failures of feminism.

The first of these lies in the ambiguous nature of all its successes. When one rereads *The Feminine Mystique* a generation later, one realizes how thoroughly feminism replaced the feminine mystique with its own mystique in all the areas Friedan examined: education, psychology, advertising, journalism, and so forth. Feminism successfully took over the cultural loci that were its main targets. It is now ensconced as the official philosophy of America's leading women's colleges, such as Smith, Radcliffe, and Barnard. Universities, corporations, professional associations, and departments of government are committed to enforcing its worldview. In place of the feminine mystique, it supplied its own warnings against men, marriage, spontaneity in love, and femininity. Young women in the eighties received a message as uncompromising as any the fifties had devised.

It was not worth opening the door of the workplace to women at the cost of shutting the door of the home. The message against marriage contributed heavily to the formation of an entire cohort of single women. Statisticians concluded in the middle of the eighties that many of them would be unable to marry unless they drastically lowered their standards for husbands (which, moved by the biological imperative to mate with a dominant male, they were not about to do). No amount of ideological apology can undo the fact that many women were marooned in the public arena, some for years and some forever, and denied the equal or greater fulfillments of home and family. Too, as Greer had at one point predicted, women were granted "admission to the world of the ulcer and the coronary" as, along with their increased participation in the work force, women's rates of cancer, heart disease, and the other great scourges of male occupational stress rose to rival those of men. The feminist attention to rape does not validate the analysis responsible for that attention, that rape is a political crime, or the destructive model of sexuality from which that analysis arises. Nor can the push to include women's points of view in the social sciences conceal that most of the resulting efforts were dogmatic and unimaginative, resulting in at best a marginal advance to human understanding.

As a guiding philosophy for women, feminism makes all relations with men difficult, and good relations virtually impossible. In the words of one disillusioned feminist, a leading exponent of Women's Studies, "For a long time, I thought feminism explained everything. It taught me how to analyze what was going on between me and the men I lived and worked with. But now it's left me out on a limb, feeling angry with nowhere to go and no way to turn back."[3]

Feminism is a failure as an explanation for male psychology and behavior. It is totally unworkable as a guiding philosophy for men, as shown by the rapid fizzling of the men's "consciousness-raising groups" of the early seventies. Feminists claimed to have the real goods on women. If men wanted to learn about women—how to please them sexually, for instance—they would have to passively accept the feminist insights. Men who believed this claim put themselves in the false position of the "New Man." The demands of feminism destroyed authenticity of emotion and behavior in the men who tried to comply with them. Unable to please either himself or women, the New Man, like the New Woman, was left to the cold comfort of envisioning himself as a pioneer of human progress. Feminism's inhibition of relations between the sexes leached joy from the lives of millions of young people whose youth would not come again. It was not at all clear that the thrill of having imagined oneself to be a pioneer of human progress could compensate for this permanent loss.

Feminism is a failure as an intellectual approach. The feminist perspective imposes a one-dimensional interpretation on all aspects of human life, namely, that the evils of the world can all be traced to men oppressing women. This view forces its scientifically minded acolytes into denying the most obvious facts of human biology and psychology. It generates female chauvinism and the sex-hate mongering seen in *The Color Purple,* in which tearing a newborn baby from its mother's arms is presented as typical, everyday male behavior. Not only is the feminist perspective anti-male, it also devalues female experience by denying the authenticity of women's experience under "patriarchy," that is, before the Feminist Era. After her consciousness is raised, the feminist looks at her mother and sees a victim instead of a person.

Feminism exploits women in a particularly insidious way. Many is the feminist mother today who imposes feminist goals on her feminine daughter, who tries to accept them out of deference toward a perceived cultural consensus. Feminist teachers, employers, and counselors all pressure young women to live by their tenets. Olive Chancellor is engaged in a ceaseless struggle to remake Verena in her own image. Why a movement so hostile to the feminine should have become known as "feminism" is far from clear.

The feminist revolution never took into account the fact that millions of American women would continue to choose to be housewives. In consequence, feminist policies ignored or, more often, worked against the needs of these millions of American women. Feminists could not help to stabilize "traditional" marriage while they were calling for its destruction.

As a political force, feminism's philosophical reductionism has been reflected in a pattern of self-righteousness and irrealism when faced with the hard realities of electoral politics. This led to a "Midas touch in reverse" which has damaged every cause endorsed by organized political feminism.

The assault on the misogynist trivialization of women was in some ways a success. Yet like the other works of feminism, this accomplishment was not to be the end of the road. The misogyny of the Feminist Era was of a different sort. Where before wifedom and motherhood had been presented as the only route to female fulfillment, now they were disparaged as obstacles to progress or more subtly denigrated by redefining them as "spousehood" and "parenthood." Where before women had sometimes been limited to the role of sex objects, now they were denied validation as sex objects. Where before the main actors in devaluing the feminine had been men, now they were women. If the old enemy was sexism, the new one was unisexism.

The failures of feminism are in proportion to its pretensions. Feminism in the seventies aggressively presented itself as *the* movement to liberate humanity. Instead, it now appears that feminism embraces only a small corner of the human experience, which it addresses with a point of view capable of shedding some light, but at the price of severe limitations, including a characteristic set of distorting effects which it cannot correct by itself.

As a universal philosophy, feminism is a dismal failure. Feminism cannot supply a reason why an abstraction called "freedom of the press" should be allowed to stand in the way of censoring the "sexual subordination of women." It is unable to acknowledge the psychological damage being inflicted on defenseless children in Sara Bonnett Stein's horror stories of nonsexist child rearing, for their parents are acting according to the best feminist principles, which are by definition the most advanced that exist. Indeed, such is the strength of their messianic belief that feminists frequently claim their principles are right in a pure, universal sense.

Even the idea of "liberating" women implies that they must be enslaved: enslaved by men and by masculinity in all its pernicious guises. The very words "Women's Liberation" thus represent an assault on the necessary relational bases of human existence. Contemporary feminism is a philosophy based on resentment, and while one certainly wishes the situation were different, the conclusion is inescapable that feminism as it exists is one of the most negative world-views to have emerged in recent years.

For all these reasons, it is impossible to sustain the 1970s characterization of feminism as a universal philosophy with a messianic mission. A better future will come from men and women, not from women alone; and will come from men and women practicing the traditional virtues of masculinity and femininity, albeit sometimes in new contexts, not from a neutered New Woman and New Man whose gender is limited to their genitals. Feminism is not the end of the road.

Were the Fifties All Bad?

The feminist mind-set has a great deal of trouble with the fifties rush into domesticity. The influx of young women into the labor force in the forties, under the stimulus of the American war effort, is seen as a pure gain for women that was unaccountably reversed in the following era of the fifties. Feminists are prone to inventing Grand Conspiracy theories to explain this perplexing retrogression. A common argument is that "the male military-industrial complex" schemed to force women into the home to guarantee their subordination. The feminist perspective readily leads to an effectual paranoia in historical explanation, like any attempt to blame the world's problems on a biologically defined group of people.

In fact, the evidence for such a conspiracy is extremely thin. The historical record actually tends to bear out the exact opposite. As Walter Karp writes in a recent review of a book by John Costello,

> Far from picking up rivet guns with joy, American women had to be exhorted, cajoled and browbeaten to take traditionally male jobs. The Roosevelt Administration carried on a relentless campaign of factory recruitment. Through every avenue of mass propaganda women were urged to "do your share," to "help save lives," to "release able-bodied men for fighting."
>   . . . It seems readily understandable that after being pushed and prodded into brutish factories and dreary assembly lines, American women retreated,

in Mr. Costello's phrase, into "postwar domesticity."[4]

It is an article of faith among American feminists that the subsequent era of the 1950s was a low point in the history of women. The fifties, they believe, witnessed the closeting of women in suburban homesteads *en masse,* leading to the "the problem that has no name," and to the harnessing of men to the oppressive financial service of their dependent wives, while a relentlessly conformist peer culture forced their children into stereotypical, loveless relationships with the opposite sex. In the dozens of books and scores of articles by feminists that I have read, and in the course of hundreds of conversations with old, new, and ex-feminist women, I have never heard this belief questioned. But is it true?

The best aspect of the advance of our civilization is that, century by century, it gradually reduces the need of man to exploit man. It is not merely our political systems that have become increasingly democratic, but our social arrangements as well. Each of these trends has its limits. Political democratization in America has reached its fullest development, beyond which it cannot go without losing both its form and its benefits. Social democratization, however, still has a long course of evolution before it. Socialism is a premature attempt at social democratization, which is an entirely different phenomenon—a civilizational stage rather than a means of economic organization.

When the Egyptian kings built the Pyramids, the Chinese dug the Grand Canal, or the Athenians enfranchised a small class of male citizens on the backs of millions of slaves and subjects, there was no alternative to the maintenance of a small but highly concentrated civilizational nucleus through exploiting the sweat of the many. Later civilizations were held to the same imperative. The Roman Empire was a slave empire. Through the long years of the medieval period in Europe, a small aristocratic and clerical class husbanded the thread of civilization.

With the development of a commercial middle class at the end of the Middle Ages, the torch of civilization passed to a broader constituency. There, predicted François Guizot in the nineteenth century, it would remain. On the contrary, wrote Karl Marx, the process is not over: industrial workers form a new class, the proletariat, which will seize the torch of progress from an increasingly small and exploitative middle class, which it will destroy, bringing forth a new, communally organized and socially leveled world order. They were both wrong—Marx, it is true, far more than Guizot.

Neither the bourgeoisie with which Guizot cast his lot nor the proletariat with which Marx cast his was to retain for long the form in which their champions knew them. Neither was to exercise hegemony over modern society. The story of the early modern era up to the time of Guizot and Marx was the story of the decline of the aristocracy, which despite its still-brilliant glory had become progressively less important to the affairs of society. The story of our times is above all the story of the decline in the importance of the bourgeoisie and the proletariat. The old commercial and industrial classes are being absorbed into a new, expanded middle class, which sets the norms of society like royalty in Egypt, the aristocracy in the European Middle Ages, and the bourgeoisie in nineteenth-century Europe. The process is farthest advanced in the United States, followed closely by the other Anglophone countries of the former British Empire, including Canada, Australia, and New Zealand, and at a noticeable distance by the nations of Western Europe.

This development has major behavioral consequences. Its most important consequence is usually misunderstood and diametrically misstated. It is true that professional activity becomes increasingly specialized, but this development is counterbalanced by another. This is *the decreasing specialization in the basic spheres of human life.* Political democratization gave all people the vote, but social democratization gives ever more people the ability to participate in the diverse aspects of human life. Education, opening the door to intellectual life and upward mobility, has become almost universally available. Public sports competition, once reserved to a tiny minority of citizens, gladiators, or aristocrats, is now experienced by practically everyone before they leave high school. Home ownership has become the prerogative of the majority. Even capital has been considerably democratized: neither Guizot nor Marx could have anticipated the enthusiasm with which ordinary Americans play the stock market and engage in a multitude of small and large investments. Fashion, once the preserve of a tiny minority in capital cities, is now practiced to some extent by most women—and to a lesser extent by men also.

The decrease in specialization of modern times carries with it the threat of anomie, as the interdependencies that formerly bound people together weaken. It has been said (perhaps with some exaggeration) that in the eighteenth century you could tell an unmarried man by his smell. Today, all but the most shiftless bachelors can cope with their own laundry. A woman may not make as much on average as a man but she no longer needs a man for her literal economic survival. What is lost in interdependence is gained in independence. The practical result is that modern people are obliged to define their life activities less and less in terms of what they must or can do and more and more in terms of what they wish to do. This is a daunting task, and the results are far from in. Contemporary feminism was in part a premature attempt to cope with this difficult effort to define the human animal, which sought to avoid the pain of the process by ending it with a definite set of answers. But we need more time than we have yet had.

Was the fifties glorification of domesticity another such premature answer? In some ways, it was. The conformist culture of the fifties protected individuals from the lonely uncertainties of a world without clearly fixed external imperatives. Men and women knew their place. Non-conforming individuals at least knew what they were up against. This situation may possibly have been unfair to some of those individuals, but at least it provided a concrete set of options.

In the maelstrom of the sixties this cozy world blew apart. Searching for the elements of a new cultural edifice in the debris of the fifties and sixties, we may yet find pieces of value in the earlier decade that were too quickly tossed aside amidst the reckless vandalism of the sixties.

Feminists' fixation on the destructive effects of the cult of domesticity has overshadowed the positive aspects of the fifties. These have to do, not with the traditionalism of fifties America, but with its innovativeness. We have overlooked the extent to which the fifties were a profoundly and radically progressive decade. To understand this, we must refer to the concept of the ongoing democratization of human life. It is perhaps easiest to proceed by example—specifically, the paradigmatic case of child rearing.

The mind-body dichotomy which Western Civilization received from the Greek philosophers split the world into two spheres of soul and body, thought and feeling, male and female, good and evil. "There is," wrote Pythagoras, "a good principle which gives rise to order, light, and man, and a diabolic principle which gives rise to chaos, darkness, and woman." As we have seen, cultural determinism, the offspring of the neo-Kantian Boas, is the latest variant of this ancient dualism.

This belief was highly adaptive for the small high cultures of old Europe. The mind was superior to and separate from the body. The superior functions were to be executed by the upper class, the inferior functions by the lower classes. The good was aristocratic or "noble," the bad was peasant or "villainous," from the medieval French *villein,* a peasant. The upper class ran the church, wrote the books, decided on peace or war, and upheld the social order. The lower classes plowed the fields and suckled the children.

This dualistic belief is no longer functional under the conditions of social democratization. The decline of specialization means that all people will play all roles to some extent. The emphasis on home life of the fifties was an effective protest against the affront to human dignity which the unnatural, but formerly necessary, dualization of human experience had always represented.

In the field of child rearing, it represented a total break with the past.

The utter self-confidence which his unquestioned high social status gave the aristocrat was paid for with a distant emotional life which originated in the aridity of parent-child relationships. Babies were typically removed from their mothers at birth and placed under the care of peasant nurses or *nourrices.* The bare majority that survived this treatment were then put under the control of stern tutors, placed in monasteries or convents, or sent off to live as strangers with relatives, allies, or indeed with enemies as hostages. It is possible to overdraw this picture—as do those historians who argue that the nuclear family was structurally and emotionally unimportant at this time—but there is no doubt that the conditions of life were far harsher than any we now know (except for out-and-out cases of child abuse).

Following this tradition, the bourgeoisie continued to view the child-rearing function as a lower, bestial activity. Contact between parents and children was limited and discouraged. The *nourrices* continued to ply their deadly trade in France well into the present century. Childbirth was the province of midwives, lower class women who trained on the job and contributed to a frightful infant mortality rate.[5]

Bourgeois families turned those children who survived childbirth and the nursing years over to nannies, who were as often as not out-and-out sadists. In the nineteenth century, it was common for the children of normal, well-to-do families to spend entire days locked in dark closets, to be starved as punishment, and to bear the permanent physical and emotional scars of frequent sessions with the birch, cane, or martinet—instruments lavishly chronicled in the baroque pornography of the time. The long orgy of sadism directed to "improving the character" of children received sanction from the most respected medical authorities of the pre-Freudian era, and epitomized the institution of lovelessness as the ideal of enlightened child rearing.

Despite this, the bourgeois ideal represented progress over its aristo-cratic predecessor in that a new emphasis on family togetherness surfaced in the wake of the Reformation. The Puritan father may have been stern, but at least he was present. He may have wielded unquestioned, and therefore inevitably abused, authority over his wife, but at least he was expected to find and keep love and sexual gratification within marriage, as opposed to the noble tradition that defined love as an emotion that could only develop outside the family.

In the fifties, the inhumane aspects of these traditions were explicit-ly rejected by mainstream American culture. The tradition of emotional distance between family members, with its associated harsh child discipline, was completely overturned. The dividing line between the higher and lower spheres of experience was called into question.

Certain new developments encouraged this trend. The middle class was becoming the numerically dominant class. The new middle class families could not afford, or if they could afford could no longer find, the servant staffs that had swelled Victorian houses to such agreeably, and today impractically, large dimensions. The logistics of suburban living dictated that virtually all daily contacts would occur between socially equal, or very nearly equal, members of the middle class.

These conditions, while they were not without areas of difficulty, had on the whole highly positive effects. They had the practical result of causing Americans to question whether the "higher" and "lower" functions were quite so separate as had earlier been assumed. Freud's influence is often invoked to explain why Spock and others became newly interested in the emotional dynamics of motherhood, but the plain fact is that the conditions of suburban life made every woman her own cook, ladies' maid, housekeeper, gardener, decorator, laundress, seamstress, nurse, nanny, tutor, secretary, and chauffeur. The attempt to glamorize these functions was sometimes taken to absurd lengths—but the impulse to elevate formerly despised areas of life was fundamentally sound.

This was nowhere more true than in the case of child rearing. After centuries of neglect, the 1950s witnessed at long last the dignification of the biological nature of women.

This development was profoundly democratic. Although she was obliged out of biological necessity to bear her children, the aristocratic, and often the bourgeois woman often saw little of them afterwards. It was as beneath her dignity to nurse or raise them as it was beneath her husband's to spend much time in their company (or, sometimes, even in hers). Under the new domestic ideal of the fifties, the nuclear family was revalidated as the basic unit of human society. And when the evidence is finally sifted, this development will be seen to produce happier children and happier adults.

One of the unanticipated results of the feminist revolution was to threaten the social democratization of American family life. Motherhood was disparaged as "merely biological" by Friedan, Millett, Greer, and every other major feminist writer. Traditional feminine roles were condemned as "soulless and degrading." Professional careers were glamorized to an extent fully as extreme as the fifties' admiration for motherhood and femininity. It is extraordinary that in a country with the egalitarian tradition of America "nannies" suddenly became chic in the early 1980s after a lapse of half a century. The practical result of the Feminist Era's skewed beliefs on the relative worth of the private and public worlds in women's lives is that, in many circles, upper class women now pay lower class women to perform the "soulless and degrading" tasks of home and child care that the fifties, in their retrograde innocence, had thought worthy the attention of all women. Motherhood becomes a nuisance from which society must relieve women. So long as feminism remains our consensus philosophy of gender, women will be obliged to flee from or apologize for the pleasure they take in domesticity. In the meantime, home and child care will be "professionalized" by paying the poor to perform them.

The fifties went too far. Men, women, and children alike were expected to become so involved in family life that their scope for individuation was limited. This was one common impulse behind the divorce, countercultural, and feminist revolutions, which came in rapid fire succession at the end of the sixties. The first was in part a cry for autonomy by men; the second by adolescents; the third by women. Yet though it is possible to sympathize to an extent with the motivations for these revolts, it is far more difficult to sympathize with their result, the cult of singleness and independence aptly described as "the culture of narcissism" of the late seventies.[6]

In the eighties it became obvious that the flight from the family had reached extreme lengths. It is now easier to see that the original impulse behind the fifties celebration of domesticity was sound, even though its expression was too constraining. It is time to strike a balance. To do so we must consult our own needs. Those needs will take most of us back to the family, not away from it.

It is tempting to view the fifties as the feminine decade, with the emphasis on interdependence, and the seventies as the masculine decade, with the emphasis on individuation. We must search out and accept the positives of each: and, by doing so, there is a chance that future generations will be spared the almost irresistible pressures to conform to those eras' utterly different but equally restricting ideals.

The Non-achievements of Feminism

But it is all too easy to overdraw the contrast between fifties "conformity" and seventies "liberation." In addition to its real achievements, feminism is often popularly credited with victories it did not win, or did not win alone. The belief that women were enslaved but feminism has made them free involves at least three basic errors. First, women were not enslaved to anything like the extent feminists would have us believe. Second, the positive changes in women's lives that have occurred were not primarily the result of feminist agitation. Finally, the effect of feminism has been less to free women than to impose a new set of constraints.

The Fallacies of "Women's History"

Feminists find it expedient to draw a radical line through history at the point of emergence of their movement. The fifties are the feminist Dark Ages, but around 1969 the Age of Enlightenment begins.

The truth is different. The feminist revolution conferred no special dispensation on its acolytes to understand women. If anything, the feminist perspective impoverished scholarly perceptions. The earlier history of the social sciences is littered with works that make a mockery of the claim that the study of women begins in 1969.

In anthropology, one such work is Elizabeth Warncock Fernea's *Guests of the Sheik,* a conspicuously feminine, sensitive ethnography of an Iraqi village from the early sixties. Conscientious, sympathetic, and evocative, *Guests of the Sheik* shows just how much of the human experience was obscured by the "male oppression" model of human society.[7]

The non-achievements of feminism can be traced in all the social sciences. Every discipline was subjected to false or wildly overblown charges of gender bias, since quite naturally it failed to conform to the feminist perspective. A major example is the field of history.

Historians, feminists soberly assure us, ignored women before the feminist revolution. We are told that until feminist historians recently began to remedy the defect, "half of human history" had been overlooked by the historical profession. It would be difficult to think of a more self-serving or less justified assertion.

In the first place, feminist history has benefited from the trend toward social history of the past generation. For better or for worse, the new historical emphasis on the lives of the humble—which is what makes feminist history possible—is largely the creation of those much-reviled "entrenched white males."

It is true that in the past the study of major figures and events tended to eclipse the study of more prosaic matters. However, what has changed should not be overrated. "Traditional" history is often used as a misnomer for *narrative* history. In fact, conceptual and other forms of history have been widely, if less self-consciously, practiced in the past, whether by Hegel, Guizot, Tocqueville, Marx, or Max Weber, but never mind that.

The fact that narrative historians have more often written about men than about women has nothing to do with "male chauvinism" or any form of gender bias, but with the fact that most of the major histori-cal actors have been men. Whenever women have played major public roles, they have received as much, or perhaps even more, attention as men in equivalent positions of power or influence. "Traditional" narra-tive history is the story of Julius Caesar, Louis XIV, and other men, to be sure, but it is also the story of Cleopatra, Livia, Boudicca, Queen Mathilda, Joan of Arc, Elizabeth I, Catherine of Aragon, Madame de Maintenon, and thousands of other women. If there has never been much of a specific "history of women," there has never been much of a specific "history of men" either. Indeed, it is not clear that a historiography of just one sex is either possible or desirable. Yet feminist historians claim that history has "excluded women."

Even if one demands a specific history of women, an impartial observer cannot fail to notice that there was actually a good deal of material on women in circulation well before feminists chose to make an issue of "women's history." The assertion that women's history began with feminism overlooks the considerable body of publication specifically on women by historians that existed *before* the Feminist Era, including work by such American scholars as Clarke Chambers, Jill Conway, Allen Davis, Eleanor Flexner, Aileen S. Kraditor, Christopher Lasch, William L. O'Neill, Anne

Scott, Paige Smith, William Taylor, and Barbara Welter.[8] Feminists simply did not invent the idea that historians should pay attention to women. The historical profession was never so benighted as to ignore them.

Most serious of all, even if one were to concede that historians in earlier decades should have paid even more attention specifically to women—a debatable point—feminists are not helping to remedy the defect, except in a highly equivocal fashion. "Feminist history" is not the same thing as "the history of women." To illuminate the past circumstances of women's lives and to explore the activities of interesting women in earlier periods is a praiseworthy goal, capable, as in the recent work of Steven Ozment on the Reformation family, of stimulating fascinating accounts and original scholarly conceptions. But this is not the goal of the feminist historian. Feminist history has a far more specific agenda. Its goal, instead, is simply to document the feminist perspective: to prove, through the endless multiplication of examples, that men are the principle of evil in human society. As a feminist author recently explained to readers of the *New York Times Book Review,*

> Researching and writing about women do not make the researcher a feminist. Nor is "integrating the history of women into the standard account of politics, economics and diplomacy" a feminist historian's goal.
> . . . Feminism has a point of view that involves a radical analysis of institutionalized gender relations in terms of power and subordination. . . . Feminist history by definition rests upon an analysis of the oppression of women. For this reason feminist historians do not limit [*sic*] themselves to seeing "women of the past as they saw themselves, to comprehend and analyze them on their own terms."[9]

Feminist historians are thus not primarily interested in "women of the past as they saw themselves," but rather in using them to prove the validity of the feminist perspective. The results are invariably tedious, as in any scholarship where ideology supplies all the answers before research has even begun. Like Marxist and structuralist approaches, feminist social science in the end usually tells us very little about its subjects. Research and writing become simply a means to rehearse the ideology of the writer.

Feminist historians did not invent women's history; they do not even practice it. A long-term effort will be required to rescue the histories of women, sex, gender, and the family from the ideological reductionism to which they have been subjected over the past generation.

The self-serving claims of feminist historians reflect a wider tendency to overrate the extent to which feminism is responsible for positive changes in American life. The social developments of the past hundred years are common to all Western societies and were caused by titanic macrohistorical forces beyond the reach of any social movement. With or without a national feminist movement, similar developments have occurred universally. Developments as diverse as granting the vote to women and the acceptance of trousers for women were spearheaded by feminists, but were not feminist movements as such. These trends flickered first on the flaky, innovation-hungry fringes of society, but only became important when accepted by the mainstream. The general evolution of society, not feminist agitation, opened education and the professions to women. Most of the women who pioneered in the previously male fields of law, medicine, and science in the late nineteenth century were indifferent or opposed to the feminist movements of their day. (This indifference is nowhere better captured than by the character of Dr. Prance in Henry James's *The Bostonians.*) Feminist movements are themselves as much a symptom as a cause of social evolution and its attendant dislocations.

If men were constantly driven by some mysterious imperative to oppress women, women would never have obtained the vote in the first place. When feminists like Gloria Steinem revile anti-ERA state legislators as "entrenched white males," they ignore the obvious fact that most of the legislators who *did* vote for ERA were white, male, and "entrenched." The image of heroic feminists bravely battering down the walls of oppression is false. Men, not women, voted to enfranchise women three generations ago. Men, not women, admitted women to their clubs, colleges, and professions—usually as a matter of practicality and principle, not in response to feminist pressure. The Supreme Court decision to legalize abortion in *Roe vs. Wade* was based on philosophical and legal arguments largely conceived, drafted, and presented by these same reviled "white males." To the extent that legislation has truly opened new opportunities to women in America, equal opportunity laws were drafted, voted for, and implemented primarily by "entrenched white males," not by feminists. Feminism's positive effects have been far more limited than is generally imagined, while the movement is often credited with vast powers and a monopoly on good intentions which it has never possessed.

Many of the positive changes commonly attributed to feminism were actually outgrowths of the despised era of the feminine mystique. Uncongenial as it was in some ways, the feminine mystique had a good deal more in common with the irreducible constants of female life needs than the radical ideology which replaced it, which "liberated" women from men, children, family, and home.

The challenge to the medical establishment view of women and medicine, the breastfeeding movement (opposed by many feminists, like Friedan), and the refusal of women to submit as passive objects to the superior wisdom of psychologists, gynecologists, and obstetricians all predate contemporary feminism by decades. People in the fifties were able to accomplish good in certain areas precisely because they were comfortable with a high valuation of women's biological role.

In addition, the role of men in the feminist revolution is often overlooked. Without the promotion of unisexism by thinkers like Franz Boas and Richard Hofstadter and the hippie rejection of traditional masculinity, feminist arguments would have found singularly little purchase in American thought. Feminists were often simply acting out a program already laid out for them by John Stuart Mill, Friedrich Engels, or their own fathers, husbands, or lovers. Without the active encouragement of men such as Kate Millett's dissertation adviser or Shere Hite's long-suffering editor, contemporary feminism might well not exist at all in its present form. Were these the "oppressors" against whom feminists heroically revolted?

The picture of heroic feminists battering down the walls of male oppression also conceals the tremendous extent to which feminism has benefited from male chivalry. "Since the family represents slavery for women," declared one widely circulated feminist manifesto, "it is clear that the Women's Liberation movement must concentrate on attacking this institution."[10] Even in the xenocentric sixties, no other group could have routinely made such outrageous declarations and still increased its outside support. Men's mistaken notion that gender issues are "women's issues" reflects in part a distaste for "all that emotional stuff" and is in part a craven reaction to feminist aggressiveness, but it also owes a good deal to misplaced chivalry. Many men feel that to critically evaluate feminist positions would be a bit ungallant. Misplaced chivalry is a major reason there has been so little critical discussion of feminism outside the movement itself. The Feminist Era witnessed a veritable abdication of masculine responsibility for gender issues.

One should not dismiss feminist arguments as manifestations of psychopathology. If they are wrong, they can be shown to be wrong on their own terms—as I have tried to do. But in seeking to understand feminism as a total phenomenon, it becomes relevant to discuss the relationship of feminism to the personal lives of the individuals who have been most attracted by it.

It is written in the Bible that "by their fruits ye shall know them." We have seen something of the unsatisfactory and often acrid fruits of feminism in this book. But there is no need to wait on results when there are many other means of evaluating a movement. It is possible to tell something of a cause from the personalities it attracts. From Jesus to Joan of Arc, from George Washington to Gandhi, from Martin Luther King, Jr., to Lech Walesa, the leaders of just causes have shown a certain clean self-confidence, an uplifting of the spirit. By contrast, it is remarkable how many of the feminist leaders display the quality of poisonous negativity, leading to a self-defeating approach to the causes they espouse, a Midas touch in reverse: Kate Millett, Gloria Steinem, and Andrea Dworkin are only a few of the more conspicuous examples of this mindset. It may be impolite to call attention to the extraordinarily vociferous personalities of the feminist leaders, but the facts are not exactly hard to document. Is the usual feminist explanation, "If you'd been oppressed for centuries, you'd be angry too" really satisfactory? Could not Joan of Arc, Martin Luther King, Jr., or any of the leaders just mentioned have said as much to justify outrageous statements and behavior? The fact they chose not to do so is eloquent. They understood that their opponents had to be countered with arguments and example, not with self-righteousness and abuse.

In a remarkable book called *The Wounded Woman,* Jungian psychologist Linda Schierse Leonard argues that our culture has often acted as a bad father by failing to understand or value femininity.[11] Feminism is partly a reaction to this cultural devaluation of the feminine. Feminism is capable of providing an explanatory system to women who are marked by difficult relationships with their fathers. This is not the whole story on feminism—but it is an important part of it. It is my personal observation that every feminist I know has two predictable elements in her life history, the first of which is an unusually strained relationship with her father. The feminist perspective has often given such women an easy way out. Their personal traumas and tragedies become intelligible as part of the great tragedy which, according to the feminist perspective, men have imposed on women throughout history. Feminism has often given such "wounded women" a way to strike back at the oppressor—superficially a less demanding route than to confront the reality of their frayed personal lives.

There is a silver lining to this cloud. To the extent that the political *is* personal, and the culture, not an individual, is the "bad father," the feminist movement may be a hopeful sign: that women are standing up for themselves.

But what is the ultimate end of such self-defense? Can women ultimately be supported through attacking men? The argument that the male principle is obsolete, recently put forward in all seriousness in a bevy of tamely accepted books like *The Feminization of America,* verges on the blasphemous. The female chauvinist version of feminism scarcely improves on the unisexist version. Sooner or later there must be a recognition that the defense of the female principle requires an equivalent acceptance of the male principle.

Feminism legitimizes the particular sickness of some women—but this cuts both ways. Many women have identified with feminism from a more positive aspect rooted in their fundamental health. The second predictable element in every feminist woman I have known is that as a girl she was a tomboy. Many women found that feminism validated aspects of their personalities and ambitions that did not fit majority norms of femininity, and consequently acquired an exaggerated respect for a movement that offered them a liberation they would have acquired in any case. No, you're not weird or crazy, feminism assured them—in fact, you're the way all women soon will be. While this was a healthy development as a personal validation for some women, it tended to build their self-esteem at the price of devaluing feminine elements in themselves and other women—to say nothing of the poisonous negativity it instilled toward men. It imposed a false collectivism on what would have better remained a genuine individuality.

Self-assurance should not have to be bought at the price of intolerance. Strong women who do not fit the standard feminine mold have never needed such false reassurance and are able to accept the distribution of human personality types for what it is, taking pride in their very difference. To return to the Jamesian metaphor: Olive and Verena must see each other for what they are, and decline to change each other. Otherwise all the lofty rhetoric about creating "more positive, generous, and personal ways of relating" will merely serve to conceal a permanent reservoir of deep ill-will.

There is a widespread belief that feminism was a movement to better the condition of women; that feminist leaders just want to give women a better deal. One looks in vain for this sort of feminist leader. Political activism is of course one aspect of contemporary feminism, but it has never been the central one. Contemporary feminism is also a literary movement, a movement of lesbian advocacy, and, above all, a vast effort of cultural propaganda directed against what are usually viewed as the positive bases of the human condition: family, motherhood, gender, and the love between the sexes. If feminism were primarily the positive attempt to improve women's condition that most Americans think it should be, and that some still imagine it is, it would never have occurred to me to write this book. Instead, I would be on the barricades with the feminists.

Feminism took a wrong turn at the very beginning, with Betty Friedan's anti-feminine complaint in *The Feminine Mystique,* and went completely off course just as it emerged from sixties radicalism as a national movement. What should have been a movement to uplift women, and men, bogged down in a fever swamp of dogma and intolerance.

The "women's movement" based its strategy to uplift women on severely flawed analyses. It took its conception of women from the simplistic tenets of cultural determinism, the facile abstractions of unisexism, and the implicit misogyny of psychologies which assumed that women's patterns of development would simply follow those of men. Its notions of social justice were based on the reductionism of the feminist perspective, which defined human society as the product of male oppression of females. It planned to "liberate" women from some of the most important constants in life: home, family, love.

As the eighties advanced and feminists nationally continued to hew to the same fundamental line, it came to seem less and less likely that this movement, which had set out to reform society, would be able to successfully reform itself. Could the many issues of family and gender be safely left to the initiative of a movement so dogmatic, uncompromising, and out of sympathy with the reality of Americans' everyday lives?

The real achievements of feminism must be admired and preserved, yet the ideology which has brought us this far can take us no farther. It is equally incapable of serving as a constructive guide to women or to men, to intellectual inquiry, social policy, or individual choice. Feminist ideology in any of its current forms is demonstrably misleading as a guide to the human condition. It is true that men have individually and collectively oppressed women at times, but women have also on their own initiative oppressed men and in any case this is not the central force in the human dynamic. The hallmark of the sexes' relations has always been cooperation more than conflict. The form of society is not and has never been determined by men oppressing women. The problems of the human race consequently cannot be solved by homogenizing sexual temperament or eliminating sex roles. Men and women are equally important to the future of humanity; the feminist hypothesis that masculine values are now obsolete because there are "no bears to kill"[12] is not just vindictive but naive. Feminism is a disaster as a universal philosophy, for even if feminism is able to reform itself to better reflect women's points of view, it will still fail to reflect men's points of view.

Because humanity cannot be understood in terms of either sex alone, even the most enlightened feminism is inherently incapable of providing a balanced understanding of gender issues. This is nowhere more glaringly apparent than in feminists' treatment of the issues surrounding divorce.

Divorce

Recent feminist writings describe divorce as a "golden parachute" for men, overlooking the enormous price paid by divorced men, who usually lose child custody and who commit suicide at a rate five times higher than divorced women.

Even a Sylvia Hewlett has yet to escape the feminist perspective when it comes to men and divorce. Hewlett writes that "*49 percent of children in the custody of their mothers do not see their fathers at all*" (her emphasis), while glossing over the fact that women are awarded custody in the vast majority of cases. She piles up mounds of additional statistics, which have all the seemingly irrefutable weight of Millett's or Greer's "science," to prove "the low priority . . . divorced men attach to their children."[13]

Feminists routinely paint men as the heavies in divorce, emphasizing how few divorced men continue to see their children on a regular basis, presenting the figures at their most damaging to men without bothering to ask whether any mitigating factors might be at work. For instance, some women do not *allow* their ex-husbands access to the children—whose custody the courts usually leave to their mothers. Yet one recent poll suggests that most divorced fathers not living with their kids would like to see them more but can't because of custody arrangements or because they live too far away.[14]

Even if the man does care for his children he cannot win, for he is then accused by feminists of "buying" the children away from their mother (who is presumably the only one to really care). It is considered outrageous that children may elect "to spend most of their vacation time with their dad."[15] The male is always guilty, the villain of history, the villain of divorce. Now of course this is sometimes true; but equally often it is not.

Feminists picture divorce as a tragedy for women and a triumph for men. Sylvia Hewlett presents as typical a woman who says that "My ex-husband is going to get richer and richer and will spend his middle age in comfort surrounded by a growing family. I, on the other hand, am going to get poorer and more lonely. I've lost my partner, my house, my friends, my status, and even my children. . . . I guess I feel cheated."[16]

The picture of divorce feminists paint is true, though it is largely their own creation: the problem of divorce for women has been severely exacerbated by the cult of singleness, and by the reduction in alimony caused by feminists' promotion of "no-fault" divorce laws. It is also hopelessly one-sided. Divorce is difficult, often tragic, and the financial costs are only part of the story. We are not going to find a painless way to end marriages any more than we are going to find a good substitute for motherhood.

You would never guess from feminist writers that men as well as women are divorce's victims. As one recent article, a rare male critique of feminist orthodoxy, points out,

> The suicide rate of ex-husbands is reported to be five times higher than the rate among the wives they've left behind, or that of virtually any other segment of the population. Among those men who supposedly leave their wives for another woman, fewer than 20% end up marrying her. And in those marriages, the men are burdened by guilt over spouses and children left behind. Many fathers find, to their frustration and fury, that divorce courts still regularly grant the mother custody (if she wants it, of course), taking away any of his say in how his children are raised and then forcing him to be, in essence, an absentee banker.
>
> Despite much publicity about a trend toward joint custody decisions, the woman still holds most of the cards; often in order to get his ex-wife to agree to joint custody, the man has to offer a sizable support package. And, of course, many male judges retain their overwhelming instincts for protectiveness toward the "little lady" and the sanctity of motherhood.
>
> . . . Studies show that a man who marries for a second time is soon under immense pressure from his new wife to spend his income on her and her children, rather than on his original brood. Often a "deadbeat dad" is

a guilt-ridden chump who's spending his paycheck in a desperate try for some woman's approval. And that can cost a bundle.[17]

The problem is not restricted to the middle class. Most "deadbeat dads" are working class men who must get by on very modest incomes to begin with—usually under $15,000 a year. And at the other end of the scale, affluent men often pay through the nose upon divorce. It is hard to make a commonsensical case for the successful claim of Johnny Carson's ex-wife that she couldn't maintain her accustomed life-style on less than $200,000 a month (or was it $200,000 a week?). The middle class, incidentally, is the group least likely to divorce, in which marriage remains a surprisingly good bet for both men and women. Although current divorce practice may on average favor men (in the current state of the debate, this is far from clear), we must not overlook the fact that divorce practice is also unfair to men in a significant number of cases. The law needs balancing, not feminist vindictiveness.

Disregarding the pleas of homemakers, feminists in the seventies forced through "no-fault" divorce laws that trampled on homemakers' hard-earned rights to share in the fruit of marriages on which they had long worked. The actions of feminists led to real suffering for hundreds of thousands of women with little or no compensating benefit. Today, feminists stand ready to punish men for their movement's own errors. The net result, if they succeed, will be to distance men further from marriage, leading to a further breakdown of the family. The divorce rate will actually *rise;* divorced fathers will evade their families more; and families, consisting increasingly of single mothers with children, will be thrown more and more on the mercy of government—as will the resulting single men, who, devoid of family emotional support or impoverished by alimony and child payments, will be forced to turn to the state for counseling, detoxification, and other services. Single mothers will increasingly become normative, as they already are among the black urban poor; and single mothers are inherently needy. This will then redouble feminists' cries to institute universal day care and open-ended maternity leave, and to increase welfare payments to single mothers.

It can readily be seen that every feminist "solution" generates in turn worse problems than those it was supposed to solve, requiring yet more socially costly "reforms" to make it work. The immediate result for society will be severe, and the end result catastrophic, if feminists are allowed to propound their fantasies unchecked. This is the inevitable result of trying to apply any philosophy that is radically false. The old saw turns out to be true after all: you can't change human nature.

The wonder is that anyone would want to try. If we discount the (significant) factor of sheer ignorance, I submit that anyone who actually wants to change human nature suffers from, first, a severe neurotic divorce from his own emotions, second, the hatred of those who do not share his truncated condition, and third, the confusion of free will with willfulness—that fatal disorder which the Greeks called *hubris*. We can wage this endless battle against the human condition indefinitely, but the result will never be other than destructive.

Or we can simply give it up. We could instead decide to trust our emotions and the people around us. The choice is ours; the choice is yours.

The End of the Feminist Era

The arguments presented in this book are directed to contemporary American feminism, which is in some respects a phenomenon of a particular place and time, but they also point to the limitations of any feminism as a universal philosophy. Either a feminism or a virism may be justified as a short-term response to particular historical conditions, but no feminism or virism can supply a long-term philosophy adequate to guide human thought and action. "Feminism" cannot possibly cover the spectrum of needs and abilities that must be addressed and reconciled in the coming era, some of which are male, some female, while others are common to both sexes; in addition, the needs of some women conflict with the needs of other women.

For once we discard unisexism, female chauvinism, feminist messianism, and the feminist perspective, what is left of feminism? The answer is, very little. Feminism becomes simply a commitment to the well-being of women. And here a national consensus may be possible in many areas. However, such a new, open-ended meaning is incompatible with the dogmatic movement we have known; and it may well be simpler to let the term "feminism" fall by the wayside along with the movement to which it currently refers.

Neither "feminism" nor "virism" can supply an adequate guide to matters human. If our society's discourse on gender is to progress further, men must reenter the discussion on an equal basis with women. It is time to move beyond feminism.

In its current heavily ideological, anti-male incarnation, feminism is now clearly untenable. If feminism is to survive in the Post-feminist Era, it must be separated from the ideology of alienation which it has represented. Yet if feminism is to mean simply a concern for the well-being of women, we are all feminists. Just as Kate Millett is a Marxist feminist and Betty Friedan a left liberal feminist, we must be prepared to accept that Phyllis Schlafly is a traditionalist feminist and Midge Decter a neoconservative feminist. Women's needs are diverse and we may legitimately imagine different ways to meet them. Moreover, women's needs cannot be divorced from the needs of the rest of humanity. Gender issues necessarily evoke our overall vision of the most desirable future society. The major battles over gender issues in the Post-feminist Era will therefore not be fought between feminists and non-feminists but between more standard political groups: socialists, liberals, and conservatives. The Feminist Era is over.

Chapter 14

An Open Letter to American Men

American men today face an unexpected salvage job, which cannot safely be postponed and will demand a sustained effort.

Feminists have been all too successful in their efforts to create a "woman-centered" point of view. Freed from the check of men's input— just as misogynists in past centuries spouted their nonsense without fear of women's objections—they arrived at a view of men and masculinity that parallels the worst misogyny.

The qualities feminists impute to themselves are perversely reflected in their descriptions of men. Each female virtue is counterbalanced by an equivalent male vice: cooperation by competition, connectedness by separateness, pacifism by aggressivity, intuition by logic, until finally the feminist lexicon becomes a mirror image of the very prejudice against which it allegedly revolted.

There are two feminist mistakes here which it is important to explicitly refute. First, human temperament, though gendered, is not nearly as polarized as the feminist perspective requires it to be. Men and women resemble each other far more than one would expect from the feminist railing against the masculine traits. The second and more insidious mistake, because it jibes so neatly with the still-fashionable culturism of our time, concerns the exaggerated, stereotypical form in which the masculine traits are depicted in feminist texts: for these traits are in their real forms valuable and desirable, and are of basic importance to the emotional well-being and social utility of men.

But such caveats could not be made in the Feminist Era, when men learned that to express an opinion about gender to a feminist was to guarantee swift and shrill assault—not so much because of the specific opinion offered as because a "male" dared to offer an opinion at all. Poor shrimp! Didn't he realize that "feminism is humanism"?

Their opinions rejected, and being both despised and desired for their aggression and brawn, men were in a real sense reduced to sex objects. The man actually sought by heterosexual feminists is a brilliant provider and an aggressive but considerate lover who doesn't think too hard, at least not about matters of gender. He must combine the irreconcilable ideals of traditional masculinity and the New Male. He is expected to be dominant, but to believe he is living in sexual equality; to be rugged and independent, but to defer abjectly to feminism, no matter how completely feminists disagree with one another; to have a Stone Age sex drive and a modern age sense of guilt.

The objectification of men was reinforced by the use of "male" as a pejorative, and of "male" as a noun to be used in preference to "men," "husbands," or any less impersonal, distancing expressions. For instance, feminists criticize "*male*-centered" views in social science, but recommend "*woman*-centered" views as the alternative. Feminists prefer the word "male" to the word "man" because it is abstract and impersonal: it dulls the awareness in feminist proselytes that those being reviled and ridiculed are their fathers, brothers, lovers, and husbands.

This usage of "male" drove home the perception of men as an "oppressor class." While complaining ceaselessly that men stereotyped women, feminists proceeded, with virtual unanimity, to stereotype men. Subtleties, qualifications, and diversities were ignored as feminists engaged in a general condemnation of "male aggression," "male dominance," "male violence," "male insensitivity," "male chauvinism," and so on. If it was true that "feminism is humanism," then women were the human sex; men, the inhuman one.

There are of course tactless, insensitive men who are inherently difficult to live with, who make distant fathers and infuriating husbands. But the feminist perspective bloated the numbers of such types beyond all reasonable measure. Feminists typically came to believe that this stereotype applied to most or even to all men.

Heterosexual feminists are constantly surprised that the particular man they love doesn't fit this repellent image. They describe him as a miracle, the one man among millions with whom they could bear to spend their time. Perhaps the most poignant comment on this belief is Nancy Chodorow's tribute to her lover in *The Reproduction of Mothering*:

Michael Reich has been throughout this project unendingly encouraging. He has read and discussed with me at length countless drafts of sentences, paragraphs, and chapters, and the final product bears the mark of his careful and critical intellect. His supportiveness and nurturance undercut one main argument of this book.[1]

They do indeed. What wistfulness, what unintended pathos is here as this major feminist theorist approaches the unbridgeable gap between feminist ideology and a woman's life.

Men in general continue to be lambasted by feminists without pity and, indeed, without any awareness of excess. It is commonly argued that men are "divorced from their emotions," that they find it hard to talk or even think about themselves or others except in abstract, impersonal terms. Yet this image, widely accepted in feminist writing, is no more than a caricature.

Men are said to have difficulty talking about their feelings, but in general they know quite well what their feelings are. Men are equally as competent about human emotion as women, they are just less interested in spending equally large amounts of time bathing in it. The endless agonizing that occupies the diaries of adolescent girls seems incomprehensible and absurd to most men, who would rather be engaged in more productive, and to them more interesting, pursuits: Who is to say they are wrong?

The impersonal ordered hierarchies that men instantly establish in a group, which are so denigrated by feminists, present considerable advantages over the more personal groups in which the majority of women feel most comfortable. There is a real freedom in *not* caring about someone else's feelings, his opinion of you, and his relationships in general. "What does he think of me?" becomes much less important than "What can he do?" It is possible to concentrate on the task at hand, and actually, quite often, to "be oneself" far more than is the case if one must be constantly, primarily, concerned with the moment-to-moment evolution of emotional nuance.

Women do not understand themselves better than men. Nor are they more open. As a recent article points out, "Those supposedly open windows into the feminine heart are usually covered with drapes, curtains, fans, shades, gauze, screens, fog from fog machines and scrims of many colors."[2]

Perhaps the supreme irony of feminism is that it led to a new exaggeration of gender difference. If women were to be praised for their sensitivity, men were to be condemned for their lack of it. Condemned to "insensitivity," the New Man was to passively await knowledge from feminists. "Sensitivity" became a patronizing compliment bestowed by feminists on men who submitted to the divorce from authenticity; it was passed off as the newest innovation for men. What about, one wondered, a Tolstoy? How could an "insensitive male" develop female characters with such deep resonance for so many women? What about the Jungian perception that insight into both sexes is inherent in the nature of each?

In the endlessly conflicted amalgam of unisexism and female chauvinism that is feminism, one thing is consistent: the male is always guilty, and must change. But have women really changed, and should men change?

The Feminist Era left a whole cohort of women unmarried in their late twenties, thirties, and forties. Women, it was said in the seventies and early eighties, had become newly selective about men, who could not meet their justly high standards. By 1986, it had become apparent the tables were turned: that many women who were still unmarried by their late twenties were not going to find mates even if they wanted to. Men, it turns out, prefer to marry women who are younger than themselves; and a woman is at her peak of marriageability in her early twenties.

But as usual, feminists call on men to change. In the seventies, men were too "insensitive" for women to marry, in the eighties they are marrying the wrong women. If men are more attracted to younger women, there must be something wrong with them, since this preference is inconvenient for the acolytes of the role revolution. Why, though, should men change? Why shouldn't *women* change—change, that is, their life plans to include an earlier marriage, at the time when women are at their most powerful in sociobiological terms, the top echelon of society's "sexual aristocracy"?[3]

Each stage of life should be accepted and enjoyed for what it is. But as usual, feminists prefer to advocate a wholesale remodeling of the human being, rather than to admit they have been in error, and seek simpler, more workable solutions to the adjustment of the sexes.

Feminists have endlessly condemned "male sexual aggression." But what really goes on in most sexual activity bears little relation to this blanket condemnation of men. The man initiates only after the woman has signaled that his advances will not be rejected. This simple, basic distinction is understood and respected by most people except feminists and rapists. Most male sexual aggression consists in taking the initiative, not in imposing one's will, and certainly not in a lack of consideration, let alone in violence: it is a matter of directing the show, not of engaging in either coercion or brutality (although a little symbolic coercion is keenly appreciated by most women, to feminists' perennial horror).

Given the tremendous ease with which men function as initiators in sex, and the satisfaction that women take in their reciprocal pattern, are we justified in changing so basic and congenial a modality? Do women really want men to change? In the case of lesbians, is it really appropriate that they concern themselves—as radical lesbian feminists endlessly have—with men's and heterosexual women's sexuality?

Men are criticized for their "separateness," which is unfavorably contrasted by Chodorow and others with women's "connectedness." But separateness and connectedness each have their advantages and pitfalls. Men's separateness appears to explain why, to their despair, most gay men are unable to form viable love relationships. Women's connectedness appears to explain why lesbians have no such difficulty. Lesbians' problem is different. A whole body of feminist literature has grown up around the theme of women's *inability* to separate from lesbian relationships, and from unsatisfactory relationships in general. The obvious conclusion is not that there is something wrong with either men or women, but rather that men and women function best together: that, for all the possibilities of misunderstanding which exist between men and women, heterosexual couples operate at a considerable advantage over homosexual ones; in short, that *men and women belong together just as they are.*

Men should not change: should not try to stop being men in order to become people with penises. It is not wrong for men to be masculine any more than it is for women to be feminine; it is not unnatural but natural. It is a waste of time to struggle to understand the New Woman for she does not really exist (not as she is supposed to be respected, at any rate). But men should study women as women, for the sexes are not alike and the understanding of each requires an effort from the other. Once women's general needs are grasped, most men are well able to meet them, for their own tendencies, while different, are complementary.

For example, feminists and other moralizers often claim that men initially perceive attractive women as sex objects and that women initially perceive attractive men as potential partners in intimacy. This contrast is wildly exaggerated. But even if it were completely true, would it really matter? If men come to intimacy through sex and women come to sex through intimacy, that they travel by different paths is not important if they reach the same destination.

In fact, to the extent the sexes are different, they need each other's difference to become whole. It seems that every time a social critic, whether of the left or the right, notices yet another difference between the sexes, it is held up as yet further evidence of the fundamental incompatibility of men and women. The opposite would be far closer to the truth: that sex difference is apt to be a source of *compatibility* between men and women.

No doubt sex difference can also be a source of conflict and misunderstanding. But the difficulties caused by sex difference must not obscure its benefits. In their difference, the sexes do not conflict with so much as complete each other. The roots of this difference are set before birth and while men and women can and must learn from each other, there are sharp limits to the ability of any individual to assimilate both male and female styles. The attempt by either men or women to take over the other's frame of reference results in a sort of graceless behavioral transvestitism whose practitioners are constantly groping for elusive cues they don't really understand. It is a symptom of the impaired sexual constitution of our society that these facts, which are obvious, should seem outrageous.

A better consensus on gender must start from the premise that neither sex has anything to apologize for. In the Feminist Era, men and women were endlessly warned against the "traditional" characteristics of their sexes. Such pressures were misconceived at the outset and must be stopped. Boys at Concord Academy and young women at Barnard College don't need to hear yet more propaganda directed against the influence of biological gender, they need support for the gender they already have.

The focus for many years has been on women's alleged oppression and feminists' attempts to change society. Yet men too have a right and may well have a need to force society into the shape *they* want.

The society that most resembles the feminist utopia, combining free sex with sexual egalitarianism enforced by a welfare state, is Sweden. America is sometimes contrasted unfavorably with Sweden, whose lower rates of violent crime are said to be caused by its benevolent welfare system, the world's most generous. Yet the advantages of Swedish society arise not from its current welfare system, but from its more general nature as a society. Sweden's relative prosperity and freedom from crime are due, not to its welfare system, but to the fact that it is a religiously, ethnically, and racially homogeneous society which (unlike America) has had centuries to settle in with itself. Another critical factor is that, despite massive government interventions, the ownership of most enterprises is still in private hands. In addition, Sweden is a neutral country with a modest defense budget. Sweden thus has many parallels with Japan on the one hand and Switzerland on the other. It starts with so many advantages that it can well afford to impose a certain level of social and economic inefficiency and still maintain an impressive per capita income. Yet the results of the system are decidedly mixed.

The burden of the Swedish experiment is borne disproportionately by men. The Swedish system is literally fatal to men. Sweden's high suicide rate, over twice that of the United States (though still little more than half that of Communist states like Hungary), is concentrated among men over forty-five. The radically diminished career horizons imposed by the combination of a cozy but rigid European class society with a socialist welfare state seem to be the principal causes of this phenomenon. Men cannot live without ambition. Colonized like Indians on the reservation, they fall prey to depression, drink, and despair. In its own way, the fate of Swedish men is one of the silent tragedies of the twentieth century. This was once the land of the Vikings.

There are two possible conclusions to draw from the Swedish experience: that there is something wrong with men, or that there is something wrong with the Swedish system. There is no doubt which conclusion feminists draw. Who will draw the other one?

Feminist women have been so spottily challenged in their female chauvinism that it has become an offhand habit with them. "Well, of course you'd think like that, you're a *male*" is an ever-serviceable putdown. (Any feminist who has read this far should stop and consider what her reaction would be to an equivalent statement about "females.") Yet it is not particularly difficult to defend oneself against feminist assault once the nature of the feminist perspective is grasped. Men must repudiate the doctrine of collective male guilt that underlies the feminist perspective. Instead, they should habitually assume that whatever men in general do, is right and good. Any general complaint about men is an expression of female chauvinism, a prejudice like any other. Are men "insensitive"? Now there's an insensitive assertion. Do men rely on abstract logic? It's not inferior to intuitive logic. Do men fail to understand female sexual response? What women mainly need from men is not empathy but masculinity. Did men invent a bomb with the power to destroy humanity? Someday its power may save humanity from certain destruction by a comet or asteroid. Men must refuse to be placed on the defensive any longer. Let them be never so independent, abstraction-prone, aggressive, competitive, driven, hierarchical, and dominant: they are creatures of value not despite but because of these traits, which may require tempering but should neither be altered nor replaced.

One of the greatest misconceptions to arise from unisexism is the notion that the sexes are "progressing" by becoming ever more similar, until their natures come to coincide completely. "Traditional" men and women are described as if they were vanishing species. This is seen in the discarding of gendered terms like "motherhood" and the substitution of neuter terms like "parenthood." But "parenting" fails to take into account what men do, and do not do, in child rearing.

There is a great deal of talk in the media these days about "the new fatherhood." One enduring result of the feminist revolution is said to be that men today are spending more time with their children than did their fathers. To the extent this is true, it is far more a result of a positive impetus from the pre-feminist counterculture, with its rejection of the success-at-any-price ethic, than of the constraining influence of feminism. On the whole, the new fatherhood is a favorable development, yet it is easy to misstate and misunderstand its significance.

In the first place, the stereotype of the distant, driven fifties father is severely overdrawn. The pre-feminist male ideal gave pride of place to the role of the "family man." Most men in the past expected their family lives to be a major source of involvement and gratification. Men in the fifties, like men in all times and places, were intensely interested in their offspring and expended large amounts of time and energy on their upbringing. The unaccustomed sight of young parents with children in our nation's cities, after the extended childless adolescence of the baby boomers, gives an impression that fathers' roles have changed when in fact there are simply more fathers to be seen.

The second way in which the increased involvement of men with their children is commonly misunderstood lies in the unisexist assumption that if men are spending more time with their families, their roles must be converging with those of women. Nothing could be farther from the truth. Every young couple which expects to raise its children without parental sex roles discovers the same thing: that Mommy's relationship with her baby is utterly different, and incredibly more involving, than Daddy's. In post-feminist America, women remain the primary nurturers of children to exactly the same extent as in all other times and places. Take a walk past any urban playground: you will see women with children, but no men—except on weekend mornings. Despite the alleged "role revolution" and all the hoopla over "househusbands," virtually all infant care is still performed by women.[4] The unisexist tenets of past decades cannot cope with this fact. Women mother. If this makes us uncomfortable, the fault lies not with our biology but with our ideology.

American men's somewhat greater involvement with their children's upbringing is a positive development: but to believe it is neutering society is to severely misunderstand the nature of this highly individual, diffuse, and decisively gendered movement.

Indeed, the erosion of separate spheres may in the long run have unanticipated consequences for the sexes' relations. In one standard conception of the traditional American family, Dad ran the world, but Mom ran the household. Male authority was counterbalanced by a sphere of female authority which, since it arrogated emotional relations to women, created a female power base that gave women a means of manipulating and even bullying men. The "entrenched white male" so feared by feminists spent a good many of his nights sleeping on the sofa. By contrast, in the European cultures so admired by such neo-feminists as Sylvia Hewlett, Papa runs both the world and the family. The masculine "aggression advantage" documented by Steven Goldberg is given freer rein when both parents are equally involved with the family than it is in the traditional American model. The greater involvement of men in family life may well result in an eventual reemphasis on male authority within the family. Future feminists will carp against men's invasion of the family. But that is looking far ahead—beyond the near-term focus of the present chapter.

As we have seen, men are humanity's driving force; women are society's emotional connective tissue. When both sexes rejected these necessary, positive roles in the sixties and seventies, they forced each sex to study the emphases of the other. And, very gradually, American men are becoming more sophisticated about the relational matters that are primarily women's responsibility.

The outcome of such increased sophistication, however, is not feminism, but anti-feminism. This is best seen in the sort of simple, concrete cases that matter most in people's everyday lives.

What happens to the sex life of superwoman's husband? As we saw in the discussion of feminism and sex, feminist consciousness ruins the sex life of women who fall under its sway. It makes them incapable of either submission or dominance and, because its depiction of men as oppressors destroys trust, of equality. But the feminist prescription for women's lives, the vastly influential "new life plan for women" that Betty Friedan outlined in *The Feminine Mystique*,[5] has an equally deadly effect on lovemaking to that of feminist ideology. Not having devoted any time to reflecting on these matters, millions of men are rushing into relationships that are going to severely disappoint their expectations, and that will fail to meet their legitimate needs.

Consider a day in the life of a typical superwoman. Let's assume she is one of the few whose husbands actually makes a serious effort to do half of the home and child care. She must rise in time to wash, dress, and make up. Then she must eat and drink something. At least half the time, she must deposit the children at the day care center. Hastily, she scans the day care personnel, hoping the children are safe and happy, not sure they really are. Then it's the commute, an hour or more, arriving in time to show her best face to her boss. Eight or nine hours later (more at peak times of the year), she returns home. The evening commute takes longer than the morning one. Half the time she picks up the kids. Half the time she makes dinner. After dinner, there is washing up to do and "quality time" to be spent with the children, tired from their day—or worse, still full of enthusiasm, jumping around her in circles. The kids in bed, there is just time to lay out her suit for the next day before falling exhausted into bed—if by now she is not too tense to sleep. The sixteen-hour day may be illegal in her workplace, but it is a fact of her life nonetheless.

Nor is this all. A superwoman is not just a working mother but an ambitious professional. She must find time, though where, nobody has told her, to study for her doctorate; to put in extra hours so her superiors will promote her; or to work on her avocation, be it literature, art, or whatever. She is never really "off-duty." Far more than the housewife, she is the creature of others' needs. She will not have time for herself; she will not have time for her husband, who will get little from her he couldn't get from a male roommate.

On the weekends, there is shopping, bill-paying, and more "quality time." In addition, appointments must be made; girlfriends must be chatted with; and somewhere in there, she needs ten minutes off for herself. Sex? You must be kidding. When could it happen? Sex became a major problem for women in the seventies and eighties, simply because there was no time or energy left for it in the "new life plan for women." Falling back on the old Victorian claim that women don't really enjoy sex, feminists began to argue that sex didn't matter that much to women; other things were more important and could be more fulfilling. This argument didn't seem likely to wash with men.

The superwoman routine is corrosive of a woman's libido for a number of reasons. Far more than the housewife, the superwoman is constantly scurrying to meet other people's needs. The time and relaxation needed for the gathering of sexual fantasy and response just isn't there. The longer rhythms of female sexuality simply don't fit a harried lifestyle. Male sexual rhythms are somewhat more compatible with stress and compartmentalization (though this too has its limits).

This lifestyle grinds down women more than men. Mothers, despite their most dutiful efforts, don't become neutered "parents" either in their own perceptions or in those of their children. Their feelings remain strictly paleolithic. Mothers still feel primarily responsible for caring for their infants—and all concerned quickly discover that mother can shush baby, while father can't. It is a wrench to drop off the kids at the day care center. And even when her husband is making an effort around the house, most women find it very difficult to give up control in the domestic sphere. They feel a need to supervise. When her husband begins to cook like James Beard and starts in on the bathroom wallpaper, some women are gratified. Many more are puzzled and saddened to find themselves suddenly viewing their husbands as domestic competitors. The new possibilities for conflict are limitless, and are being richly explored at present. The new familism of the eighties is seriously threatened by unisexism's potential to contribute to the divorce rate of the next generation.

It is no wonder that, as a recent Rutgers University study reveals, the mental health of the husbands of working women is worse than that of the husbands of housewives. This holds true regardless of the husbands' age, income, educational level, or approval of their wives' working. The husbands of working women in all categories were found to be far less satisfied with both their home and work lives than were the husbands of housewives.[6]

There is something to be said for self-abnegation, and something to be said for delayed gratification. There is not, however, much to be said for naiveté, except perhaps that it's "cute." Before men rush into a unisexist relationship, they should seriously examine their own needs, capabilities, and ambitions, and ask themselves whether they are prepared to accept its usual implications: to work hard to support a family without getting proper credit for it; to watch the woman you love falling prey to stress; to listen to your children complain that they want Mommy at home; to lose them nevertheless in case of divorce or separation; to give up the hope of a satisfying sex life—and despite your earnest sacrifices, to be alternately reviled in women's publications as a dinosaur and a wimp.

We live in a culture in which it has become intellectually and socially respectable to hate and disparage men and masculinity. Tina Turner saunters across the video screen heaping insults and blows on the "Typical Male." A recent best-seller discusses "Men Who Hate Women and the Women Who Love Them." Imagine the fuss if a book were to appear about "Women Who Hate Men": it is quite unlikely such a book would appear, or that if it did it would be sympathetically reviewed in all the right places and go on to climb the best-seller lists. A careful reading of *Men Who Hate Women,* in fact, shows that in this case female chauvinism has triumphed yet again over the most elementary logic and sense of fairness. The abusive men described are habitually abusive to the people in their lives in general, not just to women. Most of them are simply difficult people, not misogynists. It is in fact extremely difficult to find a real dyed-in-the-wool misogynist in America today. And men have no monopoly on the emotional abuse of other people. Most of the abusive behaviors described in the book can be found in women as well as in men. A more balanced, less sensationalist title might possibly have led to reduced sales, but at least it would not have carried the not-so-subliminal message that "men hate" whereas "women love."

"Feminism is humanism" proclaims *The Feminization of America,* which goes on to explain that the yang, the ancient Eastern concept of the masculine principle, is inferior to the yin, the feminine principle. Male "yang thinking" is blamed for "competition, material growth at any cost . . diminishing natural resources, serious ecological disruptions . . . the threat of thermonuclear power games." By contrast, female "yin thinking" is "an essentially humanistic consciousness [that implies] a holistic creativity which is sensitive, above all, to the requirements of life-oriented growth and progress." There is an aura of blasphemy to these so-very-confident declarations that half the universe is wrong. "Men left to themselves are going to engage in almost endless ceremonial acts," the reader learns, in a section on politics. By contrast, "The women in Congress work." If the men of Congress had their way, he is told, they would just sit around engaging in endless ceremony and never get anything done.[7] With all its faults, the United States Congress has done rather better than that over the past two hundred years. Why is it not enough to defend the principle of women in politics simply because some women are first-rate politicians and leaders, without this compulsive seeking to belittle men?

Seeking mainstream feminist support, even relatively progressive neo-feminists like Sylvia Hewlett routinely swipe at "the male" to prove solidarity with their "sisters." "Women," proclaims Hewlett, "are not going to clone the male competitive model." This is an astonishingly backhanded defense of femininity. By using "male" as a pejorative, Hewlett hopes to legitimate women's feminine qualities by contrast. The principle involved is exactly the same as the ritual in *Lord of the Flies,* in which each boy in turn stabs the victim to show his submission to group norms.

American men have supinely accepted such abuse for the past generation. They owe it individually to themselves and collectively to their civilization to stand back up. Feminists engaged in considerable bluster to win acceptance for such abuse. Post-feminist men and women must be prepared to engage in equivalent bluster to consign the fashionable male hatred of our time to the dark recesses of all prejudice. Feminists have had the field to themselves for so long that they now spout their anti-male rhetoric quite unconsciously. They take this rhetoric so much for granted that most of them are genuinely bewildered when it is contradicted: it has literally not occurred to them that they may be drastically wrong. Yet like Rip Van Winkle, while they have been lost in dreams the world has changed.

The Feminist Era is over, the world-historical moment for women passed. It is no accident that women's magazines over the past few years have taken to running countless special issues on "today's men." While the reporting is often superficial, it reflects an underlying sense that something important is missing from today's gender discourse: nothing pieces is a function less of the magazines' usual tone than of the fact that post-feminist masculine views exist in print in such small quantities.

Men's magazines are just beginning to catch on to this lack. Some are desperately eager to be up-to-date, and still think feminism is the latest thing. Others are primarily oriented toward a readership which is not especially interested in men's relations with women (although gays should take note of feminism's generalized androphobia). *Playboy* and *Penthouse* have begun a promising series of columns, but the sex magazine context presents its own severe and probably insurmountable problems.

An outlet like the *New York Times's* "About Men" column has been of little help, for its very reason for existence rests on the feminist perspective. It is not designed to encourage the expression of genuine male views, but to condition men to a softer, more feminine style of discourse. Consequently, while its writers are occasionally allowed to have minor difficulties in their struggle to accept the "new" feminist norm, they are never allowed to criticize the norm itself. The "About Men" column is concerned with men's emotions—especially those of weakness, vulnerability, and defeat—but has little use for their ideas. But intellect and emotion are inseparable. No recent development has affected American men to the extent of feminism. If feminists cannot be openly discussed, how genuine is a column "About Men"?

Women cannot summon a male point of view like a genie from a bottle. Of necessity, the initiative must come primarily from men. If the ideologies of the Feminist Era are to yield to a more workable gender paradigm, men must participate equally with women—no, more than equally because, having largely abandoned gender discourse in the Feminist Era, they are now coming from behind.

But if men are to lead the way out of the Feminist Era, as the state of the debate demands, they must take the trouble to inform themselves more thoroughly about gender issues. They must assign a higher priority to "all that emotional stuff" than has previously been the case. They must in a word *educate* themselves and one another about the nature of gender.

Women will continue to be the prime conservers of society's emotional resources, but this presents no barrier to men's competence in gender issues. What is called for from men is not a revised emotional style, as was widely and mistakenly believed in the Feminist Era, but simply the acquisition of knowledge about the nature of men and women and their relationships: still not an easy task, and it is not too soon and their relationships: still not an easy task, and it is not too soon to start. We must search for such knowledge wherever we can hope to uncover a few scraps, even in the female chauvinism of neo-feminist psychology and the despised virism of popular culture.

Our interpretations of post-feminist masculinity may range all the way from Sylvester Stallone's bravado and brawn to Robert Bly's gentle tale of Iron John.[8] But the search for an authentic modern male point of view inevitably places us in conflict with feminists' claim to speak for all humanity. If we wish to be authentic as men, we have no choice but to reject feminism.

But the feminist rejection of men's points of view must not be echoed back. We must always listen to women. We must learn to recognize and cherish the female "voice"—to view its limitations with tolerant amusement, and its irreplaceable wisdom with deep respect. And we must establish the point, and over the coming years make it stick, that women must also undergo an equivalent learning process toward men and masculinity. What is called for is not a male point of view in isolation but the maintenance of distinct male and female points of view in mutual sympathy and tolerance. By refusing to allow our male identity to be crushed or belittled, we are in fact helping women. And we are doing so in a way in which they cannot help either themselves or us.

It is time to lay the foundations of deep traditions that will spare future generations the anxieties and absurdities of unisexism and gender chauvinism. Or else our culture will remain eternally out of balance, and the future of humanity will be even less assured.

For every feature on feminism that appears, there are literally hundreds on the Soviet threat and the transitory state of the economy. Yet an impaired sexual constitution has the most serious consequences for a society. Despising the male virtues—like courage, honor, and strength—societies lose the very will to defend themselves, like the English-speaking nations in the thirties which, yielding to female activists who claimed "women understand peace," dismantled their militaries while the Axis powers and the Soviets began the enslavement and slaughter of millions. The Holocaust is only one of the resulting monuments to the cowardice of Western politicians and their public. Female values have no place in national defense. Most women are able to enter far enough into masculine modes of thought to understand this (indeed, to understand it far better than many men); and the minority of women who cannot, have no business making public policy. Sexual equality must be sought, not in every sphere of life, but in a fair and functional overall balance throughout society. Or else, despising female values, societies simply cease to breed, like the militarist Spartans who conquered their external enemies only to perish from a low birth rate—despite harsh laws requiring husbands to periodically sleep with their wives. Finally, as in Indian reservations, Sweden, and Eastern Europe, it is possible to so constrain male ambition that even secure, well-fed, married men come to see no alternatives to drink, despair, and death. Men who dismiss gender issues as "all that emotional stuff," interesting to other people but of little importance to them personally, are making a serious mistake. It is late in the day, but not too late, to stem the consequences of the abdication of masculine responsibility.

Chapter 15

Toward a Post-feminist Agenda

The program presented in this book is not a social but an emotional one. It is neither possible nor necessary to present a finished philosophy right away that addresses all the questions related to gender whose discussion feminism has monopolized over the past generation. What is important is that we begin to rethink all such questions with the awareness that our past solutions have not worked—that we acknowledge the failure of feminism.

The progressive consensus of our recent past pictured gender as an archaic opposition, a source of injustice. Gender, it argued, must be transcended, diminished, and eliminated as much as possible. This view is no longer tenable. The new consensus that is beginning to emerge emphasizes complementarity: the two sexes can and must learn from each other, but this interchange depends on their very distinctiveness and does not lead to a unitary identity which somehow cancels out masculinity and femininity. In other words, *Vive la différence!*

What are the societal results of this view? What consequences does it have for the organization of society, what political causes will it sponsor, to what future does it lead? These are fascinating and important questions, but they are an ending rather than a starting point. The crushing responsibility imposed on personal relationships by feminism must first be cast from our shoulders. One of the lessons of the Feminist Era is that to internalize the slogan "the personal is political" in practice simply destroys the personal. No human being owes his society such a debt, nor can he possibly pay it. It's time to relax. After the bruising politicization of every aspect of life in the sixties and seventies, the first order of business is to quietly, personally, rediscover ourselves for ourselves and for those around us.

The movement of our time is a movement away from ideology. When young women in their late twenties and early thirties like Megan Marshall decided to marry and bear children in the early eighties, theirs was a movement of instinct, which required a series of leaps of faith that could be neither guided, explained, nor justified by the belief system with which they had grown up. To act as they did demanded the belief that their impulses and emotions were right, were something better than products of "the conditioning." The revalidation of the feminine was above all the recovery of instinct as a valid guide—more valid than ideology. It was a sign that American women had finally outgrown both the feminine and the feminist mystiques and were able with increased confidence to assert themselves directly for their own benefit.

Feminists argue that if we lose sight for one minute of the great transcendent ideal of sex-balanced employment in all occupations, we will perpetuate injustice through a lack of pragmatism. It is easy for them to be pragmatic: their ideas were worked out years ago. In order to overcome the alienation from self imposed by feminist ideology, we must dare momentarily to be impractical, to refuse to worry about the long-term social consequences of our most personal actions. The recovery of the personal is necessary to forge any new consensus. If we were to follow the advice of the feminists who cry pragmatism, the coming change would be stillborn: exactly what they hope for, as they struggle to prop up the dead hand of the past.

In fact, the question "What does all this have to offer women who *must* work?" is a singularly graceless argument coming from people who hope to force *all* women to work, because they view paid employment as the only acceptable source of personal identity. Feminists hope to alter laws and customs to force all people to cooperate with their particularistic vision. They seek to bring about a society in which all women are forced into paid work through a combination of normative and economic pressures. Instead, the argument presented in this book is that *women should have a choice.*

If we cast the issue in terms of the grand ideals which have guided thought over the past two centuries, we can say that the challenge of gender today is to achieve a viable balance between the demands of liberty, equality, justice, and tolerance. In the sixties era and its feminist aftermath, equality eclipsed all other ideals—in particular, the ideal of tolerance. Only through a new emphasis on tolerance can we hope to transcend the polarization of the current Age of Ideology, of which the ideologies of the Feminist Era are just a symptom.

The sensible policy approach to gender today is thus neither uni-sexist "equality" nor a return to radical sexual separation, but the sharing between men and women of all basic rights, combined with a legal and cultural recognition of gender difference in need and motivation that is adequate to maintain the dignity and well-being of each sex in its own terms—and consequently of society as a whole. This is the basis for the new consensus on gender that is rapidly emerging.

One inevitable result of the new consensus will be a significant rearrangement of current political divisions. Post-feminist America will not display the same political landscape as the period it succeeds. In the coming years, old foes and old allies will be mixed together in unexpected combinations, as individuals work out a balance between the varied demands of the new consensus.

The Feminist Era was sparked by young single women. The Post-feminist Era will also involve millions of young single women, in revolt against the unisexist expectations they encounter. But, unlike the Feminist Era, it will involve the cooperative participation of all social groups. Indeed, it is hard to think of a single major group whose interests do not oppose it to the feminist orthodoxy: feminine women demeaned by the feminist devaluation of the feminine; ambitious women hampered by the feminist politicization of personal achievement; all men; children in quest of the basic need for a definite gender identity—in sum, the vast majority of people; so that the early demise of the feminist perspective as a significant social force begins to seem not just possible but likely.

But feminism will not crumple up of its own accord. Entrenched in the most powerful centers of influence in our culture, from academia and journalism to Hollywood and the publishing industry, feminists today are positioned to wield a massive long-term influence on our culture, regardless of their success or failure in the market of ideas or at the ballot box. They must be fought every step of the way, from our political parties to our cocktail parties, if they are not to prevail through the sheer lack of resistance that has often been their greatest asset.

One of the lessons of the Feminist Era is that women at present do have considerable collective power in society. It seems unlikely, though, that women will long allow feminists to wield this power for them. Some of the most effective shock troops of the Post-feminist Era will be American housewives. Having begun this inquiry with an exploration of Betty Friedan's attack on housewives in *The Feminine Mystique,* it is appropriate to return to the same subject in closing.

We are coming out of a period which severely overrated the advantages of professional careers and severely underrated the fulfillments of family life for most women. But women are not "cloning the male model." Their lives are not following the masculine path—and while their earning power in the aggregate suffers as a result, most women feel the tradeoffs are more than worth it.

It is not "nostalgic" for a man to wish for a wife who will tend his home, care for his children, and support his career. It is not out-of-date for a woman to seek personal fulfillment and economic security within her family. Society cannot guarantee any of these things, but it can and should guarantee that people have a chance at them—that they are not socially or economically penalized for choosing the marriage option.

"The family," feminists continue to wail, "is already broken down: technology has outstripped conservatism." If the family is broken down, it must be repaired, not discarded. We must maintain women's right to be economically supported by their husbands. It will be far cheaper in both human and economic terms to preserve American women's rights as homemakers than to bring about the wholesale overhaul of human nature and economic reality that feminists advocate. Even if we institute every feminist proposal—if we spend more on nationalized day care than on national defense; if we tailor our children's gendered personalities from birth to maturity on the Procrustean bed of "personhood"; if we abolish the housewife role through economic legislation and cultural pressure; if we restrict men from competition to give women equal average results; if we set the rates businesses must pay workers through "comparable worth"; if we turn our society and our lives upside down, trampling in like measure on past tradition and future ambition—it will make no difference in the end. We are not going to find a good substitute for motherhood.

That many women must work to support their families is a reason for regret, not a cause for celebration. It is a woman's right to stay out of the job market if she so pleases, provided she can induce a man to support her—something that most women have historically been able to do. On what grounds dare we try to take this right from them? We must seek to extend this option to as many women as possible, through supportive laws and a growing economy, not to cut it off from all women just at the point it is becoming increasingly practical in terms of national prosperity. As a result of massive economic growth combined with a modest population increase, America is a vastly richer country today than it was in the fifties, when most women were full-time wives and mothers. The number of women who "need" to work has been radically inflated, not by financial necessity, but by feminist ideology, which taught that a husband is an exploiter, marriage a trap, the home a prison, motherhood obsolete, and professionalism the only healthy source of female identity.

As Sylvia Hewlett discovered when she tried to have babies while pursuing tenure at Barnard College, today's trendy people can be callously indifferent toward the needs of working mothers. What she experienced is even more true for couples who dare to offend the reigning norm of unisexist careerism by having the man continue to work and the woman give up or reduce her work responsibilities to care for home and children. Couples who choose this arrangement often endure repeated jibes from coworkers and acquaintances, as if the man were an egomaniac who wanted to keep his wife "barefoot and pregnant" and she were a dupe to let him "take advantage" of her—projections that bear absolutely no relation to the reality of such relationships. Even when both parents work, the mother typically reduces her work load—if she can—when she has children. This untrendy arrangement is in fact the route being taken by the majority of young couples today. Since neither the old nor the new feminists are speaking for them, they are going to have to speak up for themselves, and they had best do it loud and clear, defying a corporate culture delighted to use women for its financial advantage and a feminist establishment eager to exploit them for its political ends.

Feminists want you and me to believe that any concrete steps to revalidate family life (as opposed to some pretty but ineffective rhetoric about the family) will lead straight back to the most limiting aspects of the fifties. It is a short step, we are warned, from the questioning of ERA back to fraternity pins, from the rejection of comparable worth to the reimprisonment of women in the home, "the comfortable concentration camp." This is so much hot air. Women today are not choosing family life because they have no alternatives, but because they have tried the alternatives and these don't measure up. They are reasserting their femininity, and looking for masculinity in their men, because they, or their older sisters, have tried, and hated, the nonsexist approach. American women are not regressing back from feminism but progressing beyond it. They are moving beyond feminism to a world in which their hopes, fears, desires, and instincts are no longer distrusted or rejected as the destructive shreds of "conditioning" but welcomed and accepted as the positive, life-giving, inherent womanly attributes which they are. The result is something both old and new, as predictable as tussling boys and as unpredictable as the effects of the next technological innovation. It is a world forever beyond the reach of the feminist leaders, and they will hate you—and me—for it. We can let that stop us as individuals—or we can not. In either case a new struggle is opening.

Today's post-liberated men and women must stand together to fight for the things they need to raise their families properly: for society's tolerance, respect, and support. What is called for is not feminism but familism, not confrontation but cooperation between the sexes. Not the destruction of gender roles, but their dignification; not the ruin of the family, but its restoration. *Vive la différence!*

Appendix

Appendix:
Countering Feminist
Verbal Tactics

Feminist activists don't fight fair. They are not interested in intellectual speculations or in acquiring new knowledge, for the feminist perspective has already answered all their questions. Legitimate discussion of gender issues can only take place between members of the in-group, who share a common belief structure. This eliminates most women from the discussion: non-feminist women are seen either as potential adherents to be manipulated into a correct understanding or as enemies to be outmaneuvered. It also excludes all men. Men's role in feminist discourse is limited to the role of not-quite-legitimate spectators and, above all, of targets. The structure of feminist belief makes it extremely difficult for feminists to admit the possible legitimacy of points of view which do not arise from their own ideology. Like other convinced believers in search of proselytes, they engage in argument only for the purpose of winning people over.

To this end, they have made a sustained effort to develop and disseminate rhetorical shock tactics designed to confuse, overpower, and humiliate their adversaries. These tactics were popularized through essays like "Verbal Karate" in the influential *Sisterhood Is Powerful* (1970). The mentality of this effort is nowhere better expressed than in the title of Gloria Steinem's *Outrageous Acts and Everyday Rebellions* (1982), which is laden with more such advice.

Shocking people into awareness is supposed to be fun, creating an enormous sense of superiority over the unreflective masses of "males" and "transitional women." Steinem advises that

> I now often end lectures with an organizer's deal. If each person in the room promises that in the twenty-four hours beginning the very next day she or he will do at least *one outrageous thing* in the cause of simple justice, then I promise I will, too.

Feminists should be aware that such "outrageous acts" can cut both ways. It might be amusing to imagine "outrageous acts" directed against feminist orthodoxy: writing in protest to the campus paper when it calls the university "fascist, racist, and sexist"; sending a copy of *The Inevitability of Patriarchy* to a feminist acquaintance; enjoying sex in the missionary position. The revolutionary act for today's woman is not to demand pay equity on the job. It is to go out on a date and leave her wallet home.

It takes little courage to run with the prevailing wind. In an era in which feminism has been adopted as the official philosophy of Radcliffe, Barnard, and Smith, and the *New York Times* promotes the unlovely epithet "Ms.," outrageousness and rebellion clearly lie on the anti-feminist side in the world of Acamedia, although less so in the American heartland.

"Chauvinism" and "Sexism"

The feminist buzzwords which substitute a predigested ideology for independent thought have had far too long a run. It is time they were tossed out of polite society. The most important of these buzzwords are "chauvinism" and "sexism."

Chauvinism originally meant exaggerated patriotism. Chauvin was a Napoleonic soldier whose jingoism and xenophobia gave rise to the expression which bears his name. By extension, a "male chauvinist" is someone who believes men are superior to women—and since society in its "present form" is thought of as "patriarchy," it follows that any man so retrograde as to oppose any aspect of the feminist program is a male supremacist and a misogynist. The feminist perspective, the belief that men's oppression of women is the source of the world's problems, made "chauvinist," an abbreviated form of "male chauvinist," the standard put-down to be hurled at men who dared disagree, however timorously, with any aspect of feminist dogma. In short, "[male] chauvinist" is an insult—and should be treated as such.

Contemporary feminism, though, represents an authentic *female* chauvinism. Since men are responsible for all the evil of the world, women are responsible for all the good. The Pythagorean principle that associates men with good and light and women with evil and darkness is stood on its head; men are seen as the villains, women as the redeemers of humanity.

Yet feminists continue to accuse any male opponent of "chauvinism"—little suspecting that the word applies far better to themselves.

The most popular feminist buzzword of all is "sexism." The expression "sexism" was coined in the sixties to suggest that distinctions based on sex are as pernicious as those based on race. "Sexism" is said to be a system which oppresses women in order to preserve the hegemony of men—what feminists believe is the essential principle of human society and history. In other words, "sexist" is a pejorative way of saying "gendered." Since it is men who are held to be oppressing women, sexism also equals male chauvinism. Women are therefore rarely accused of being "sexist," for who would accuse blacks of being racist? But men are almost invariably "sexists": it is indeed the rare male who has escaped a conditioning so crippling to the decent side of his character. "Sexism" is the leading weapon in the feminist rhetorical arsenal for belittling, besmirching, and befuddling their "enemies"—"traditional" society and men.

It is time to recognize this word for what it is: a rhetorical tactic, not a reality. What began in the sixties as an agreeably outrageous neologism has been reified to the point where feminists now believe there actually is such a thing as "sexism." To use this word as if it referred to a factual reality indicates that the user believes our society is built on the basis of male oppression of women and must be overturned in its essential institutions and replaced with a better order. The casual usage of "sexism" should therefore be avoided, for it tends to co-opt the user into a point of view that he or she in all likelihood does not espouse, or in many cases even understand. In reality, a good society does and must make distinctions on the basis of sex. The expression "unisexism" consequently has considerable shock value at the moment against feminists.

Whenever a feminist uses the expression "sexism," she should be challenged, and pressed: As she struggles to justify this term she has long taken for granted, the feminist perspective will out, in all its poisonous negativity. One should always remember in a public discussion with a feminist that she is the one with something to hide: namely, the true nature of feminist ideology.

The Tactic of Outrage

Holier-than-thou approaches have been the daily currency of believing feminists. One should of course refuse to conduct arguments in such debased coin whenever possible. But if it is necessary to do so, take the high ground. The most common such feminist approach is *the tactic of outrage,* used with regard to day care, pornography, etc., etc. You've got to have your facts straight and be quick on your feet to combat the two-tiered assault inherent in this technique, which seeks first, to overcome facts with emotion, and second, to discredit the non-feminist individual attacked by making him appear to lack moral compassion, thoughtfulness, and so on. Ideally, the assault actually discredits him in his own eyes so that, confused and stuttering, he is reduced to the apologetic vulnerability required in the New Male.

I say "him" advisedly in this discussion: the tactic of outrage works poorly against women because, as Carol Gilligan explains, they tend to be "morally pragmatic" in the first place. Men's tendency to abstraction and generalization makes them vulnerable to this technique, which turns that tendency against them by making it seem pompous and "insensitive." A good antidote is therefore to claim compassion yourself (because it is too complicated to explain the virtues of abstract reasoning in the context of a heated argument over, say, federally funded day care centers): the anti-feminist position is the *really* compassionate one—to say nothing of being the fair one, the just one, the practical one, the cost-efficient one, and so forth. The fact that all these things probably really are true of the anti-feminist position won't hurt your case at all.

Another way to combat the tactic of outrage is to undercut it by refusing to speak to the arguments presented (which are just a smoke-screen anyway for forcing us all to accept a neutered society). For men, this requires that they discard the out-of-place chivalry which inhibits them from using their full aggressiveness and intelligence against feminists. (It may help to think of oneself as a defender of the majority of women.) For instance, an acquaintance of mine was recently attacked in a public gathering for referring to prepubescent females as "girls." Since they can be beaten and raped, he was informed, all females are "women." Unfazed, he shot back "Do you spell that with an 'e' or an 'i'?" (Some radical feminists spell "women" as "wimmin," to avoid the hated syllable "men.")

Compliments to Avoid

There is a set of expressions which feminists use to encourage men to conform to their notions of nonsexist conduct. These should be avoided and resisted just like the pejoratives. The pejoratives are the stick, the compliments the carrot. Both represent attempts to divorce you from your authentic perceptions by people who don't know any better.

Words like "sensitive," "caring," "warm," "feeling," and "related" all represent perfectly valid qualities for a man to possess, but in the feminist lexicon they have acquired special meanings. From girlhood on, many women periodically wish human males were more of these things. Here's the rub: the feminist usage blends this ubiquitous and ungratifiable female wish with the implication that the recipient of these seeming compliments either lacks or doesn't care for the reverse virtues of toughness, independence, and so forth, and consequently is less able to stand up for himself than he should be. Many men wonder why they feel threatened by such apparent compliments. You *should* feel threatened: these "compliments" carry the implication that the psychological distance with which each man must surround himself for his basic well-being (*passim* Gilligan, for instance) is unnecessary. Like a stranger standing close to you on an empty bus, they represent a violation of personal space. Preserve your right to be distant, skeptical, and unemotional: these are qualities too, if not carried to excess.

"Sex Objects"

One hardy perennial is the claim that "men see women as sex objects." Of *course* they do. What sort of woman would not want men to see her as a sex object? When feminists attack routine aspects of the human condition which they find offensive, it is often effective to point out that your views are those of the majority. Ah, says the feminist, but the problem is that men *just* see women as sex objects. This is a curious proposition, as science has yet to uncover a single case of this bizarre delusion.

Arguing in Front of a Group

You have one enormous advantage if you are arguing in front of a group. Because feminism is the reigning orthodoxy, you will often generate sympathy, interest, and covert admiration as the underdog. Even more important, your arguments will have the virtue of novelty. Many people, including most of your adversaries, will literally never have heard them before, and even if they have, the impact of hearing a fellow student, employee, family member, colleague, or other personal acquaintance make points they had only heard in passing on TV will make them sit up and take notice. Of course, all the above points continue to apply even if you *are* talking on TV. Good luck.

Further Reading

General critiques of feminism:

Michael Levin, *Feminism and Freedom* (New Brunswick, N.J.: Transaction Books, 1987)

George Gilder, *Men and Marriage* (Gretna, La.: Pelican, 1986)

Steven Goldberg, *The Inevitability of Patriarchy* (New York: William Morrow and Co., 1973)

Arianna Stassinopoulos, *The Female Woman* (New York: Random House, 1973)

Midge Decter, *The New Chastity and Other Arguments Against Women's Liberation* (New York: Coward, McCann and Geoghegan, 1972)

Of closely related interest:

Yves Christen, *L'égalité des sexes: l'un n'est pas l'autre* (Monaco: Editions du Rocher, 1987)

Ellen Hawkes, *Feminism on Trial: The Ginny Foat Case and the Future of the Women's Movement* (New York: William Morrow and Co., 1986)

David L. Kirp, Mark G. Yudof, and Marlene Strong Franks, *Gender Justice* (Chicago: University of Chicago Press, 1986)

Lionel Tiger, *Men In Groups* (Second edition; New York: Marion Boyars, 1984)

Megan Marshall, *The Cost of Loving: Women and the New Fear of Intimacy* (New York: Putnam, 1984)

William and Wendy Dreskin, *The Day Care Decision* (New York: M. Evans and Co., 1983)

Sara Bonnett Stein, *Girls and Boys: The Limits of Nonsexist Childrearing* (New York: Charles Scribner's Sons, 1983)

Carol McMillan, *Women, Reason and Nature* (Princeton, N.J.: Princeton University Press, 1982)

Melford E. Spiro, *Gender and Culture: Kibbutz Women Revisited* (New York: Schocken Books, 1980)

Phyllis Schlafly, *The Power of the Positive Woman* (New York: Jove/ HBJ, 1978)

Lionel Tiger and Joseph Shepher, *Women in the Kibbutz* (New York: Harcourt Brace Jovanovich, 1975)

John Money and Anke Ehrhardt, *Man and Woman, Boy and Girl* (Baltimore, Md.: Johns Hopkins University Press, 1972)

Notes

Chapter 1

1. Aileen S. Kraditor, *The Ideas of the Woman Suffrage Movement, 1890-1920* (New York: Columbia University Press, 1965), 5.

2. See, for example, Paula S. Fass, *The Damned and the Beautiful: American Youth in the 1920s* (New York: Oxford University Press, 1977).

Chapter 2

1. Betty Friedan, *The Feminine Mystique, With a New Introduction and Epilogue by the Author* (New York: Dell Publishing Co., Inc., 1982; orig. ed. 1963), 336, 337.

2. Ibid., 351.

3. Ibid., 77.

4. For this use of "feminine," see for instance, Friedan, p. 77. For the other quotes, see pp. 72 and 80.

5. Ibid., 324.

6. Ibid., 325, 361.

7. Ibid., 360.

8. Ibid., 76.

9. Ibid., 300.

10. Ibid., 367.

11. From "Sex, Society, and the Female Dilemma: A Dialogue Between Simone de Beauvoir and Betty Friedan," *Saturday Review,* June 14, 1975; quoted in David L. Kirp, Mark G. Yudof, and Marlene Strong Franks, *Gender Justice* (Chicago: University of Chicago Press, 1986), 20.

12. Betty Friedan, *The Second Stage* (New York: Summit Books, 1981), 74.

13. Friedan, *The Feminine Mystique,* 351.

14. Ibid., 353.

15. The reevaluation of this idea is the central theme of Megan Marshall's *The Cost of Loving: Women and the New Fear of Intimacy* (New York: Putnam, 1984).

16. These characteristic plaudits were reproduced on the outside of later editions of Millett's *Sexual Politics* (New York: Ballantine Books, 1978; orig. pub. 1970).

17. Ibid., 33-34. My analysis of *Sexual Politics* is based largely on Millett's second chapter, pp. 31-81 in the 1978 edition; references that are not otherwise identified are from this chapter, which, as Millett says in her preface, is "the most important in the book."

18. Ibid., 131.

19. Ibid., 86.

20. Ibid., 93-94.

21. This hatred of soldiers reflects the delegitimation of the military in the eyes of the American left that resulted from the Vietnam War.

22. Millett, 93.

23. Ibid., 506.

24. Ibid., 178-179.

25. Ibid., 86.

26. Ibid., 179.

27. Ibid., 87.

28. Ibid., 507.

29. See Germaine Greer, *The Female Eunuch* (New York: Bantam Books, 1972; orig. pub. in Great Britain by MacGibbon and Kee Ltd., 1970), 109, 335-337.

30. In *Blues Guitarists: From the Pages of Guitar Player Magazine* (Saratoga, Calif.: Guitar Player Productions, 1975).

31. Joseph Sobran, to whom I owe the concept of xenocentrism, suggests the word "Alienism." "Xenocentrism" is, of course, an antonym of "ethnocentrism." See Joseph Sobran, "The Natives Are Restless," *National Review,* February 22, 1985.

32. Greer, 250, 305, 306, 345.

33. For Greer's ambivalence toward children, see *The Female Eunuch,* pp. 245, 249-251. See also her more recent *Sex and Destiny: The Politics of Human Fertility* (New York: Harper & Row, 1984).

34. Greer, 65, 74, 108, 148, 208, 303, 336. My apologies to those using different editions.

35. Ibid., 308.

36. Ibid., 62, 66.

37. Ibid., 65, 109, 337.

38. See, for example, Greer, 9.

39. Greer, 23.

40. Ibid., 21.

41. Ibid., 102-103.

42. Ibid., 66.

43. To be honest about sex differences, according to this point of view, we must pretend they do not exist. This notion was to become the central ingredient of the Feminist Era's unisex sexology and role-reversed grade school texts. Michael Levin presents a devastating indictment of the latter in *Feminism and Freedom* (New Brunswick, N.J.: Transaction Books, 1987).

44. Greer, 348.

45. Ibid., 21, 284.

46. Millett, 39.

47. Greer, 11.

48. See, for example, Greer, 352.

49. Greer, 308.

50. Ibid., 340-341.

51. Ibid., 343.

52. Ibid., 239.

53. Ibid., 252.

54. Ibid., 249-253.

55. Ibid., 350.

56. Ibid., 351.

57. Ibid., 272-273.

58. This underlying unity of feminist thought has been noted by every critic of feminism. It was first pointed out by Midge Decter in *The New Chastity and Other Arguments Against Women's Liberation* (New York: Coward, McCann & Geoghegan, 1972), p. 178.

59. Friedan, *The Feminine Mystique,* 92.

60. Millett, 35.

61. Shulamith Firestone, *The Dialectic of Sex* (New York: Bantam Books, 1971), 69; quoted by Decter, p. 175.

62. Friedan, *The Feminine Mystique,* 324.

63. Ibid., 360, 172.

64. From "Excerpts from the SCUM (Society for Cutting Up Men)

Manifesto" in *Sisterhood Is Powerful: An Anthology of Writings from the Women's Liberation Movement,* Robin Morgan, ed. (New York: Vintage Books, 1970), 583.

Chapter 3

1. Susie Orbach, *Fat Is a Feminist Issue: The Anti-Diet Guide to Permanent Weight Loss* (New York: Paddington Press, 1978).
2. As Alexis de Tocqueville discovered in the Jacksonian era.
3. Simone de Beauvoir, *The Second Sex* (New York: Vintage Books, 1974), 115.
4. Millett, 37n.
5. Ibid., 153.
6. Ibid., 156.
7. *New York Times,* Monday, November 23, 1981, and Beauvoir, 115.
8. Henriette de Witt, *Monsieur Guizot dans sa famille et avec ses amis de 1787 à 1874* (Paris: Hachette, 1880), 47.

Chapter 4

1. See Greer, p. 344, for the rationale of the consciousness-raising groups.
2. This was the title of Betty Friedan's second book (New York: Dell, 1977).
3. Both quoted in Marshall, pp. 24-25, 45.
4. Greer, 5, 26.
5. Valerie Steele, *Fashion and Eroticism: Ideals of Feminine Beauty from the Victorian Era to the Jazz Age* (New York: Oxford University Press, 1985), 243-245.
6. Susan Brownmiller, *Femininity* (New York: Linden Press/Simon and Schuster, 1984).
7. Ibid., 102.
8. For Brownmiller's criticism of skirts, see pp. 80-86.
9. Marshall, 29-30.
10. Greer, 342.
11. Burt Avedon, *Ah, Men!* (New York: A & W Publishers, Inc.,

1980), 7.

12. Warren Farrell, *The Liberated Man: Beyond Masculinity: Freeing Men and Their Relationships with Women* (New York: Random House, 1974), 331. This is in principle "moderate" feminism, and as such it shows the increasing irrelevance of the distinction between "moderate" and "radical" feminism in the early seventies. In fairness to Farrell, it must be noted that his views have undergone a considerable evolution since that time. In his most recent book, *Why Men Are the Way They Are* (New York: McGraw-Hill, 1986), he attacks feminists for promoting "a new sexism."

13. Nancy Chodorow, *The Reproduction of Mothering: Psychoanalysis and the Sociology of Gender* (Berkeley: University of California Press, 1978), 29.

Chapter 5

1. By Megan Marshall in *The Cost of Loving,* pp. 24 ff.
2. Millett, 44.
3. Friedan, *The Feminine Mystique,* 371.
4. Greer, 316.
5. Ibid., 311.
6. Ibid., 337.
7. Ibid., 316.
8. Ibid., 27.
9. Ibid., 36
10. Ibid., 281.
11. Ibid., 35.
12. See for instance *The New Our Bodies, Ourselves* (New York: Simon & Schuster, Inc., 1984), 196.
13. Interview with Shere Hite in the *Boston Globe,* Wednesday, June 24, 1981, 65-66.
14. Shere Hite, *The Hite Report: A Nationwide Study of Female Sexuality* (New York: Dell Publishing Co., 1981; orig. pub. 1976), Preface.
15. Ibid., 274, 291. (Emphases added.)
16. Ibid., 529.
17. Ibid., 549.
18. Ibid., 546.
19. Ibid., 551.

20. As documented in the *Boston Globe* interview cited above.

21. *The New Our Bodies, Ourselves,* 195.

22. Quoted in the *Boston Globe* interview, p. 66.

23. Hite, 527.

24. Greer, 36-38.

25. Marshall, 102-103.

26. Greer, 37-38.

27. Ibid., 351.

28. Marshall, 28.

29. Nancy Friday, *My Secret Garden: Women's Sexual Fantasies* (Pocket Books, 1974), and *Forbidden Flowers: More Women's Sexual Fantasies* (Pocket Books, 1975).

30. Marshall, 85.

31. See Gini Graham Scott, *Dominant Women, Submissive Men* (New York: Praeger, 1983), for an exposé of a complex gendered reality that belies the facile equations of unisexism. Better yet, read the last two chapters of *Harriet Marwood, Governess* (New York: Grove Press, 1986).

Freud understood quite well that the development of adult sexuality imposes different requirements on men and on women.

Chapter 6

1. See, for instance, Sylvia Hewlett's account in *A Lesser Life: The Myth of Women's Liberation in America* (New York: William Morrow and Co., 1986), 202-203. For Phyllis Schlafly's statement of the issue, see *The Power of the Positive Woman* (New York: Jove/ HBJ, 1977), 145-146.

2. See, for instance, Schlafly, pp. 121-130.

3. Gloria Steinem, *Outrageous Acts and Everyday Rebellions* (New York: Holt, Rinehart and Winston, 1983), 342.

4. Ibid.

5. Millett, 86.

6. *Take Back the Night: Women on Pornography,* Laura Lederer, ed. (New York: Bantam Books, 1982; orig. pub. by William Morrow & Co., Inc., New York, 1980), 13.

7. Ibid., 1.

8. Ibid., 12.

9. Ibid., 3.

10. Ibid., 141.

11. Ibid., 12.

12. Ibid.

13. Ibid., 10-11.

14. Wilson Bryan Key, *Subliminal Seduction: Ad Media's Manipulation of a Not So Innocent America* (New York: Signet, 1981; orig. pub. by Prentice-Hall, New York, 1973), esp. pp. 118 ff.

15. Excerpted from Constance O'Banyon, *Velvet Chains* (New York: Zebra Books, 1985), 150-159.

16. Janelle Taylor, *Savage Conquest* (New York: Zebra Books, 1985); Sylvia Grieg, *Escape Me Never* (New York: Avon Books, 1986); Phoebe Conn, *Captive Heart* (New York: Zebra Books, 1985); and O'Banyon, cited above.

17. See, for instance, Eldridge Cleaver's explanation of his motivation to rape in *Soul on Ice* (New York: McGraw-Hill, 1968), or Desmond Morris, *Manwatching* (New York: Harry N. Abrams, Inc., 1977), 125, 182-183.

18. See Lederer, ed., *Take Back the Night,* pp. 4, 318.

19. One of these figures is Diana E. H. Russell, whose *Rape in Marriage* (New York: Macmillan, 1982) is the essential work of this effort.

20. J. C. Barden, "Marital Rape: Drive for Tougher Laws Pressed," *New York Times,* Wednesday, May 13, 1987.

21. *New York Times,* Tuesday, February 25, 1986, 1.

22. See, for instance, "If Hitler Were Alive, Whose Side Would He Be On?" in Steinem's *Outrageous Acts,* 305-326.

23. The Court drew heavily on two highly erudite articles by Cyril C. Means, Jr., in *New York Law Forum:* "The Law of New York Concerning Abortion and the Status of the Foetus, 1664-1968: A Case of Cessation of Constitutionality," in vol. 14, no. 3, pp. 411-515 (1968), and "The Phoenix of Abortional Freedom: Is a Penumbral or Ninth-Amendment Right About to Arise From the Nineteenth-Century Legislative Ashes of a Fourteenth-Century Common-Law Liberty?" in vol. 17, no. 2, pp. 335-410 (1971).

24. As Thomas Sowell points out in *A Conflict of Visions* (New York: William Morrow and Co., 1987).

25. Typical of the hysterical atmosphere prevalent in both camps is a feminist accusation hurled against the National Right to Life Com-

mittee: *"Their goal is compulsory pregnancy."* (Emphasis in original.) *The New Our Bodies, Ourselves,* 314.

26. One of the myths surrounding the abortion controversy is that abortion was legalized in response to feminist pressure. In fact *Roe vs. Wade* was a response to two separate trends, neither of them inspired by the feminist movement: first, the general social liberalization of American mores and laws through the fifties and sixties; and second, the related growth of judicial activism over the same period. *Roe vs. Wade* was decided on historical and constitutional grounds, and owed little to feminist activity. As a result some feminists were incensed at the decision. It has been reported that "the feminists would rather have lost on feminist grounds than won on constitutional ones" (Cyril C. Means, Jr., personal communication).

27. Justice Blackmun, in the majority opinion of *Roe vs. Wade,* cited in Kenneth Davidson et al., *Sex-Based Discrimination: Texts, Cases and Materials* (St. Paul, Minn.: West Publishing Co., 1974), 356.

28. Desmond Morris, *Bodywatching* (New York: Crown Publishers Inc., 1985), 218.

29. Sarah Blaffer Hrdy, *The Woman That Never Evolved* (Cambridge, Mass.: Harvard University Press, 1981).

30. Hewlett, 126.

31. "Starting Kindergarten a Bit Older and Wiser," *New York Times,* Thursday, November 20, 1986, C1.

32. Reported in *To Your Health!: The Lahey Clinic Health Letter* (Burlington, Mass., Fall 1986).

33. William and Wendy Dreskin, *The Day Care Decision* (New York: M. Evans and Co., Inc., 1983), 42. Concerned parents may wish to consult Chapter 5, "Health and Your Child," and Appendix I, "The 'Day Care Diseases,' " in the Dreskins' carefully researched book.

34. From Diane Baroni, "Sex and the Working Mother," *Cosmopolitan,* November 1986, p. 326.

35. Michael Levin, "Comparable Worth: The Feminist Road to Socialism," *Commentary,* August 1985.

36. Geraldine Ferraro, with Linda Bird Francke, *Ferraro: My Story* (New York: Bantam Books, 1985), 148-150.

37. Ferraro reports her version of the exchange on p. 260.

38. Ferraro, 145.

39. Ibid., 241.

40. Ibid., 325.

41 By George Gilder in *Sexual Suicide* (New York: Quadrangle/
The New York Times Book Co., 1973) and by Phyllis Schlafly in *The
Power of the Positive Woman.*

42. Quoted in Ferraro, 106.

43. Ferraro, 95.

44. Frank Mankiewicz, quoted in Maureen Dowd, "Women Assess
Impact of Mondale Loss," *New York Times,* Wednesday, November
14, 1984.

45. Quoted in Ferraro, 95.

46. The young and talented writer Squire Babcock is responsible
for the phrase "poisonous negativity," which for me sums up all that
is wrong with the contemporary feminist movement.

Chapter 7

1. If I may be permitted to recast the interpretation offered by
Arthur Schlesinger, Jr., in his intriguing *The Cycles of American History*
(New York: Houghton Mifflin, 1986).

2. George W. Stocking, Jr., *Race, Culture, and Evolution: Essays
in the History of Anthropology* (Chicago: University of Chicago Press,
1968), 203.

3. Quoted in George W. Stocking, Jr., ed., *A Franz Boas Reader:
The Shaping of American Anthropology, 1883-1911* (Chicago: University
of Chicago Press, 1974), 246.

4. Quoted in Stocking, *Race,* 228.

5. Ibid., 203.

6. Stocking, *Reader,* 254.

7. Ibid., 336.

8. Quoted in Stocking, *Race,* 231.

9. Stocking, *Reader,* 251.

10. Stocking, *Race,* 274.

11. Stocking, *Reader,* 332.

12. Reischauer's book had a number of unique virtues; this argument
was not one of them. It should be noted that it never descended to
the "Ho, Ho, Ho Chi Minh, NLF is gonna win" mentality of a large
segment of the anti-war movement.

13. Quoted in Stocking, *Reader,* 42.

14. Derek Freeman, *Margaret Mead and Samoa: The Making and*

Unmaking of an Anthropological Myth (Cambridge, Mass.: Harvard University Press, 1983), 26, 22.

15. Stocking, *Reader,* 243.

16. Ibid., 247.

17. Margaret Mead, *Sex and Temperament in Three Primitive Societies* (New York: Morrow Paperbacks, 1963; orig. pub. 1935), 280.

18. Ibid., 279.

19. A characteristic example is the widely used *Sociology* by Donald Light, Jr., and Suzanne Keller (New York: Knopf; most recent ed. 1984).

20. Mead, 137.

21. Steven Goldberg, *The Inevitability of Patriarchy* (New York: William Morrow & Co., 1973), 43-44.

22. For a highly nuanced discussion of the relationship between politics and science in Mead's thought, see her daughter's account in *With a Daughter's Eye: A Memoir of Margaret Mead and Gregory Bateson,* by Mary Catherine Bateson (New York: William Morrow and Co., 1984), esp. pp. 128 ff.

23. Quoted in Freeman, 255, 268.

24. Mead, *Coming of Age in Samoa* (New York: Morrow Quill Paperbacks, 1961; orig. pub. 1928), 14.

25. There is, of course, a good deal more one can say about Margaret Mead, who was anything but a simple person. Anecdotes are rife among anthropologists about how Mead would walk into a room and take over, reducing grizzled old professors to shuffling boys. From her submissive first husband whom she overwhelmed, to her domineering second husband whom she battled, through her passionate lesbian affair with Ruth Benedict, to her standoff final marriage with Gregory Bateson, who always retained a slight ascendancy over her—the only marriage to produce a child—and through the endless liaisons of her later years, Mead was determined to see and do it all. Driven partly by scars inflicted by her difficult father but mostly by sheer zest for life, Mead never fails to fascinate and is one of the true originals of the twentieth century.

The ready brilliance with which Mead dazzled the American public and overwhelmed professional colleagues is nowhere more clearly seen than in the contrast between *Coming of Age in Samoa* and her technical monograph on Samoa, *Social Organization of Manu'a.* The popular book is translucently written, a masterpiece of clarity and accessibility, whereas the technical monograph is a morass of obfuscation in which Mead the high-spirited student trots out every self-important cliché of academic writing. Vague, pretentious prose alternates with the confusing introduction of undefined native words like *fono,* giving the reader the impression the writer must really be an expert since he has absolutely no idea what she is trying to say.

Mead was something of a chameleon, adept at presenting different facets to different audiences. Mead the cultural determinist of *Sex and Temperament* (1935) threatens to mutate into Mead the sociobiologist in *Male and Female* (1949), a work that Betty Friedan blasted in 1963 as "the cornerstone of the feminine mystique." Throughout it all, Mead never apologized or retracted anything she wrote, so that one is at times tempted to say, "Will the real Margaret Mead please stand up?"

These characteristics explain both Mead's longevity in the public eye and the fact that she has been roundly attacked from so many different sides at one time or another; why, for instance, Betty Friedan could blast Mead for supplying the foundation of "the feminine mystique," and at the same time use her ideas as the foundation for *The Feminine Mystique.*

The contradictory ideas in Mead's work have played a major role in confusing Americans' thinking about gender, underlining the need to uncover the intellectual bases for our guiding assumptions, and, where necessary, to reject them.

26. Friedan, *The Feminine Mystique,* 130.

27. I do not know whether this anecdote is precisely correct or not, but it captures to perfection the atmosphere of things. What seems certain is that, as Derek Freeman reports, quoting from a letter Holmes wrote him in 1967, "although, after his return to Northwestern University from Samoa, he [Holmes] was 'quite critical' of 'many' of Mead's 'ideas and observations' about Samoa, he did 'not believe that a thesis was quite the place' to expound these criticisms, and that he was, furthermore, 'forced' by his 'faculty advisor' to soften his criticisms." Letter by Derek Freeman, in *Anthropology Newsletter,* v. 25 (1984), no. 6, p. 2.

28. Melford E. Spiro, *Oedipus in the Trobriands* (Chicago: University of Chicago Press, 1982), 179-180.

29. Ernest L. Schusky and T. Patrick Culbert, *Introducing Culture,* Second Edition (Englewood Cliffs, N.J.: Prentice-Hall, Inc., 1973), 83-84.

30. Hrdy, 9-10.

31. *The Harmless People,* by Elizabeth Marshall Thomas (New York: Vintage Books, 1959), was one of the most widely read accounts of the Bushmen.

32. As Melvin Konner notes. His views on the Bushmen are taken from his book *The Tangled Wing* (New York: Harper Colophon, 1983; orig. pub. 1982) and from my notes of remarks he delivered to the 1983 American Anthropological Association Convention.

33. Konner, 9.

34. Much of this list is borrowed from Goldberg's *Patriarchy*, 372 ff.

35. Charlotte G. O'Kelly, *Women and Men in Society* (New York: D. Van Nostrand, 1980), 6.

36. This and the preceding quotation are from Goldberg, pp. 54 and 55n. For another well-documented refutation of the idea of primitive matriarchy, see Hrdy, pp. 10-11.

37. Mead, *Sex and Temperament*, 259.

38. Goldberg, 43-44.

39. Mead shared this fear of biology; see Bateson, chapter on "Sex and Temperament."

40. Hrdy, ix. See also, for instance, *The New Republic*, November 18, 1985, p. 9.

41. Marxism is a form of environmental determinism. See Engels's *The Origins of the Family, Private Property and the State* for the standard Marxist view.

42. This discussion of the abuse of scientific doctrines to justify genocide is indebted to the ideas put forth by Melvin Konner in *The Tangled Wing*, pp. 418-419.

43. See, for instance, Millett, Chodorow, or more recently (and regrettably) *Gender Justice*, by Kirp, et al., for some examples of this facile putdown of entire fields of scholarship in books devoted to gender issues.

44. Konner, 16.

Chapter 8

1. Freeman, 32-33.

2. Jerome Kagan, *The Nature of the Child* (New York: Basic Books, 1984), 10.

3. Schusky and Culbert, 100.

4. The following discussion is indebted to Melvin Konner's accessible and accurate summary of work in this field in *The Tangled Wing*.

5. The quotes are from Konner, pp. 27 and 28. For the original experiment report, see John Garcia and Robert A. Koelling, "Relation of Cue to Consequence in Avoidance Learning," *Biological Boundaries of Learning* (New York: Meredith, 1972), 10-14.

6. Konner, p. 29. See Sara J. Shettleworth, "Reinforcement and the Organization of Behavior in the Golden Hamsters: Hunger, Environment, and Food Reinforcement," *Journal of Experimental Psychology: Animal Behavior Processes,* 104, 1 (1975), pp. 56-87.

7. Konner, 28.

8. Konner, 60-61. See Mark R. Rosenzweig, "Effects of Environment on Development of Brain and Behavior," *The Biopsychology of Development,* ed. E. Tobach, L. R. Aronson, and E. Shaw (New York: Academic Press, 1971), and Mark R. Rosenzweig, Edward L. Bennett, and Marian Cleeves Diamond, "Brain Changes in Response to Experience," *Scientific American,* 226 (1972), pp. 22-29.

9. G. Raisman and P. M. Field, "Sexual Dimorphism of the Preoptic Area of the Rat and Its Dependence on Neonatal Androgens," *Brain Research,* 54 (1973), pp. 1-29. See also Konner, pp. 121-122, 125-126, and Goldberg, pp. 89-90.

10. As Konner rightly cautions.

11. Recent evidence for cerebral differentiation in men and women is admirably summarized in Chapter 8, "Le cerveau a-t-il un sexe?" in Yves Christen, *L'égalité des sexes: l'un n'est pas l'autre* (Monaco: Edition du Rocher, 1987).

12. Kagan, 91.

13. Ibid., 121.

14. John Money and Anke A. Ehrhardt, *Man and Woman, Boy and Girl* (Baltimore: Johns Hopkins University Press, 1972), 17.

15. This discussion is based on Money and Ehrhardt, Chapter 6, and on Susan W. Baker, "Psychosexual Differentiation in the Human," in *Biology of Reproduction,* 22 (1980), 61-72.

16. Julianne Imperato-McGinley, "Androgens and the Evolution of Male Gender-Identity Among Male Pseudohermaphrodites with 5a-reductase Deficiency," in *New England Journal of Medicine,* 300, 22 (1979), pp. 1233-37. Imperato-McGinley's report is discussed by Konner, pp. 124-125.

17. Desmond Morris, Foreword to the Second Edition of Lionel Tiger, *Men in Groups* (New York: Marion Boyars, 1984; orig. pub. by Random House, New York, 1969).

18. Desmond Morris, *The Naked Ape* (New York: McGraw-Hill, 1967), 53; quoted by Hrdy, 140.

19. Hrdy, 11.

20. Ibid., 13-14.

21. Ibid., 1.

22. Kaye Lowman, *Of Cradles and Careers: A Guide to Reshaping Your Job to Include a Baby in Your Life* (Franklin Park, Ill.: La Leche League International, 1984), 158.

23. This is in fact argued by George Gilder, drawing on Mead, in *Sexual Suicide.*

24. Hrdy, 33.

25. Hrdy is too sophisticated to fully accept the Grail of primitive egalitarianism or the myth of the primitive matriarchy, but the suspension of biology remains a necessary part of the feminist point of view. The problem, of course, is where to locate this fictitious, but conceptually necessary, event. According to Hrdy, the suspension took place with the development of "standards of morality . . . set down in the form of legal systems" and the gradual extension of "the rights of 'man' " to women also. Thus, after millions of years of evolution, suddenly the development of "legal systems" cancels out biology—an assumption that, if correct, renders all biobehavioral studies (including her own) irrelevant.

She glosses over the fact that "females have adapted" to the form of human society by claiming that "little is known. . . . the matter of their legacy will not be soon resolved." Hrdy's extremely brief treatment of the suspension of biology is found on pp. 187-188.

Chapter 9

1. Millett, 39.

2. Hrdy, 184.

3. Ibid., 190.

4. See, for example, the contrast between Carol Gilligan's path-breaking *In A Different Voice: Psychological Theory and Women's Development* (Cambridge, Mass.: Harvard University Press, 1982) and her uncritical acceptance of Susan Brownmiller's rehash of Greer in *Femininity,* reviewed by Gilligan in the *New York Times Book Review,* January 15, 1984.

5. See, for example, Chodorow, *The Reproduction of Mothering,*

pp. 28-29.

6. Ibid., 29.
7. Ibid., 216.
8. Ibid., 219.
9. Ibid., 176-178.
10. Ibid., 29.
11. Gilligan, 1.
12. Ibid., 9-10.
13. By Georgia Sassen in 1980. See Gilligan, p. 15.
14. Following an idea of Lawrence Kohlberg's. See Gilligan, p. 10.
15. Gilligan, 16-17.
16. Ibid., 165.
17. Ibid., 69.
18. Ibid., 17.
19. Ibid., 45.
20. Ibid., 173.
21. Ibid., 45.
22. Ibid., 98.
23. This view is also Chodorow's.
24. Gilligan, 96.
25. Marshall, 10.
26. Gilligan, 94-95.
27. Ibid., 122.
28. Ibid., 133.
29. Ibid., 138.
30. Ibid., 145.

31. For the origin of this term and the concepts that underlie it, see Linda Schierse Leonard, *The Wounded Woman: Healing the Father-Daughter Relationship* (Boulder, Colo.: Shambhala Publications, Inc., 1983).

32. Gilligan, 126.
33. Ibid., 171.
34. Ibid., 172.
35. Goldberg, 27, 24.
36. Friedan, *The Feminine Mystique,* 151.

Chapter 10

1. See Lionel Tiger and Joseph Shepher, *Women in the Kibbutz*

(New York: Harcourt Brace Jovanovich, 1975), 5. Other important follow-up studies of the kibbutz are the late Yonina Talmon's *Family and Community in the Kibbutz* (Cambridge, Mass.: Harvard University Press, 1972) and Melford E. Spiro's *Gender and Culture: Kibbutz Women Revisited* (New York: Schocken Books, 1980; orig. pub. 1979). Spiro, whom we have already encountered as a critic of Malinowski's interpretations of the Trobriand family, supplied one of the key cultural determinist studies which in the fifties purported to document that the kibbutz had done away with the family and instituted a unisexist culture. Spiro now completely repudiates this view. *Gender and Culture,* besides updating the kibbutz evidence, provides an exceptionally lucid critique of the assumptions of feminist ideology.

An interesting statement of the challenge Tiger and Shepher, Spiro, and Steven Goldberg together pose to the social science consensus of the 1960s and 1970s was published by Percy S. Cohen in *The British Journal of Sociology,* v. 32, no. 3 (September 1981), pp. 411-431.

2. The Camp William James experience involved a group of upper middle class American youth who felt that the Civilian Conservation Corps, a Depression-era stopgap program to temporarily relieve unemployment, had something to offer all youth, not just the indigent to whom the program was restricted. Camp William James was inspired by Eugen Rosenstock-Huessy, one of the many German intellectual emigrés of this time. Typical of these refugees from Nazism, Rosenstock-Huessy was brilliant and authoritarian, of Jewish origin, and an academic of such range that he taught in five Harvard departments. Camp William James, established in the Green Mountains of Vermont in the late 1930s, was an attempt to develop "the moral equivalent of war" which the American philosopher William James had called for at the turn of the century. In the event, most of its members were soon fighting a real war, and their youthful idealism underwent various permutations under the pressures of the Normandy beaches, the nuclear bomb, and a world suddenly dominated by America and Russia.

3. Tiger and Shepher, *Women in the Kibbutz.*

4. Ibid., 226.

5. O'Kelly, *Women and Men in Society,* 314.

6. Millett, 39. The origins of this notion may be traced to John Stuart Mill's "Essay on the Subjection of Women." It is a really peculiar conceit, which downplays the human capacity for rational inquiry to an alarming degree.

7. Reprinted *in toto* in Phyllis Schlafly's *The Power of the Positive Woman.* For a sample feminist child rearing manual, see for instance Selma Greenberg's *Right from the Start: A Guide to Nonsexist Child Rearing* (Boston: Houghton Mifflin Co., 1979).

8. Millett, 59.

9. Greer, 9.

10. Sara Bonnett Stein, *Girls and Boys: The Limits of Nonsexist Childrearing* (New York: Charles Scribner's Sons, 1983), 1.

11. Stein, 1-2.

12. Ibid., 2.

13. Ibid., 51.

14. Ibid., 51-52.

15. Ibid., 54.

16. Ibid., 5, 6, 146.

17. Vivian Gussin Paley, *Boys and Girls: Superheroes in the Doll Corner* (Chicago: University of Chicago Press, 1984), 36-37.

Chapter 11

1. Steven Goldberg presents an impressive case that socialization *must* conform to biological reality, in *Patriarchy,* pp. 108-110.

2. As Joseph V. Smith, a physicist at the University of Chicago, where the nuclear age began, writes: "On at least a dozen occasions, according to the fossil record, many species of animals have disappeared from the face of the earth. The cause of these 'major extinctions' is the subject of intense controversy, but one favoured explanation is that the Earth periodically collides with an asteroid or a swarm of comets. The blast and consequent changes in the climate as these bodies crashed into the Earth may have seen off the last of the dinosaurs and many of their predecessors. Few people seem to have realised, however, that this is not merely an historical curiosity. If it happened again, the human race might follow the dinosaurs into oblivion" ("The Defence of the Earth," in *New Scientist,* April 17, 1986, pp. 40, 44).

In an article on the dangers posed by meteors in its June 9, 1986, edition, *Time* asked the question "What if a large asteroid or comet is discovered heading toward the earth?" It is hard to quibble with Alan Harris of the Jet Propulsion Laboratory in Pasadena, who answered that "the more prudent solution is to burrow a substantial charge into the object and blow it to smithereens."

Incidentally, astronomers currently favor the theory that the moon was formed as the result of a collision between the earth and another planet. See for instance the *New York Times,* Tuesday, June 3, 1986, C1.

3. Stein, 12.

4. Friedan, *The Feminine Mystique,* 371.

5. Ibid., 141.

6. Decter, *The New Chastity,* 120.

7. Colette Dowling, *The Cinderella Complex: Women's Hidden Fear of Independence* (New York: Pocket Books, 1982; orig. pub. 1981), 10-11.

8. Dowling, 2-3.

9. Greer, 352.

10. Marshall, 81.

11. See "Even-handed, Money-minded, and Womb-envying Patterns," in Margaret Mead, *Male and Female: A Study of the Sexes in a Changing World* (New York: William Morrow, 1949).

12. Warren Farrell suggests "masculinism." See Farrell, *Why Men Are the Way They Are,* p. 196.

13. George Gilder alludes to this possibility in *Men and Marriage* (Gretna, La.: Pelican Publishing Co., 1986).

Chapter 12

1. Anyone who doubts this should consult the picture of misery in *Unnecessary Choices: The Hidden Life of the Executive Woman,* by Edith Gilson with Susan Kane (New York: William Morrow and Co., 1987). See especially pp. 48-49 and 61-63.

2. See Goldberg for an exposition of this concept.

3. The anti-feminist classics of the early seventies by George Gilder, Midge Decter, and Steven Goldberg espouse this concept; so did Margaret Mead in her less radically cultural determinist moments; Chodorow and Gilligan also contribute to this view.

4. Greer, 252.

5. See Hewlett, pp. 135, 228, and 274 for the 6 percent figure and "nostalgia."

6. For evidence of this, see Charles Murray, "Poverty in the

Heartland," *National Review,* March 28, 1986, pp. 30-34.

7. Louis Harris, *Inside America* (New York: Vintage Books, 1987), 86.

8. Exact estimates vary, but not widely. Most fall between 61 and 64 percent.

9. Hewlett, 273.

10. See, for instance, Steinem, 169.

Chapter 13

1. Marshall, 69.

2. See, for instance, Marshall, 71-72.

3. Marshall, 87.

4. Walter Karp, writing in the *New York Times Book Review,* August 17, 1986, on *Virtue Under Fire: How World War II Changed Our Social and Sexual Attitudes,* by John Costello (Boston: Little Brown & Co., 1986).

5. Feminists often glorify traditional European midwives as hold-outs against a male dominated society. Sylvia Hewlett (37-38) trenchantly punctures this myth: "Traditional peasant societies are seen through a rosy, nostalgic haze as cultures where women, supported by a midwife and a community of other women, dropped their babies simply and easily on the earth. . . . An appealing image, but unfortunately historical reality was a good deal less attractive.

"For example, in seventeenth- and eighteenth-century Europe not only was infant mortality appallingly high—children had only a 50 percent chance of living until they were twelve months old—but women had a 10 percent chance of dying in childbirth and a 20 percent chance of being perma-nently injured by the incompetent interference of untrained midwives."

6. Christopher Lasch, *The Culture of Narcissism: American Life in an Age of Diminishing Expectations* (New York: Norton, 1978).

7. Elizabeth Warncock Fernea, *Guests of the Sheik: An Ethnography of an Iraqi Village* (New York: Doubleday, 1965).

8. This list—which could be considerably expanded—is largely borrowed from a letter by William L. O'Neill written in reaction to an article called "Is Clio a Feminist?" in the *New York Times Book Review.* The article appeared in the April 13, 1986, issue; O'Neill's letter was published the following May 11.

9. From a letter by Martha O. Avery in the *New York Times Book Review,* April 13, 1986.

10. Sheila Cronin in *Notes from the Third Year: Women's Liberation* (1971), reprinted in Kenneth M. Davidson et al., eds., *Sex-Based Discrimination: Texts, Cases and Materials* (St. Paul, Minn.: West Publishing Co., 1974), 180.

11. See Leonard, *The Wounded Woman* (cited above, p. 365).

12. Friedan, 372.

13. Hewlett, 69, 63.

14. *USA Today,* June 13, 1986, 2.

15. Hewlett, 53.

16. Ibid.

17. Brux Austin, "Men, fantasy and infidelity," in *Texas Business,* June 1986.

Chapter 14

1. Chodorow, viii.

2. Asa Baber, quoted in "Men, fantasy and infidelity."

3. The expression is George Gilder's.

4. See, for instance, Hewlett, 398-399.

5. "A New Life Plan for Women" is the title of the concluding chapter of Friedan's *The Feminine Mystique.* On the absence of sex, see for instance, Anne Taylor Fleming, "The American Wife," the cover story of the *New York Times Magazine,* October 26, 1986, p. 34. Typical of the negative media image of wives at this time, the cover photo shows a tired, bleary-eyed woman: clearly, she is "exploited" by the husband who looms darkly behind her, invisible except for his heavy, encircling hands. According to Fleming, "That absence of sex is another one of the little secrets of young, upscale postliberation wives." Rationalizations for this situation are not far to seek: "Bright-eyed young women would lean forward and in a soft voice confess to me not that they were having affairs, but that they weren't having much sex at home because they were all tied up with their babies, or, in some cases, their work."

6. This study, by Kathleen Pottick, Graham Stines, and Deborah Fudge, was reported in *Gannett Westchester Newspapers,* Sunday, April 6, 1986, p. E2.

7. Elinor Lenz and Barbara Myerhoff, *The Feminization of America:*

How Women's Values Are Changing Our Public and Private Lives (Los Angeles: Jeremy P. Tarcher, Inc., 1985), 235, 242.

8. Keith Thompson, "What Men Really Want: A *New Age* Interview with Robert Bly," in *New Age,* May 1982.

Index

See also Freud, Sigmund
psychology, 13, 169
 new female, *215-231,* 279, 333
Ptolemy, 205
puritanism, 7, 10, 88-89
Pythagoras, 275

race, 201
racialism, 160, 161-163, 166, 167
racism, 47-48, 161-162, 186
 feminism as a form of, 48, 100
Radcliffe College, 31, 222, 295, 344
Radical Chic. See Wolfe, Tom
radicalism, 11, 26, 35, 131, 312.
 See also revolution, rage
rage, 12, 22, 24, 44, 81, 99, 138,
  293
Raisman, Geoffrey, 198-199, 201
Rambo, 275
Ransom, Basil (Henry James
  character), 32
rape, 35, 69-70, 108, 111-112, 117-
  118, 129, 172, 179, 181-182,
  293, 295
"rape in marriage," 120-121
rapists, 26, 119, 323
rats, experiments with, 195-199
Reagan, Nancy, 100
Reagan, Ronald, 143, 147, 148,
  150, 151
Rebel, The. See Camus, Albert
Redford, Robert, 47, 263
Reformation, 303
Reischauer, Edwin O., 165
relativism, cultural. *See* cultural
  relativism
religion, 54, 87, 127-128, 159, 185n,
  198
religious right, 128.

See also fundamentalism
Renaissance, 46
Reproduction of Mothering, The.
  See Chodorow, Nancy
Republican party, 148
revolution, 12, 18, 24-25, 30, 35,
  36, 51, 72, 96
"Revolution is the festival of the
  oppressed," 35, 95
Rip Van Winkle, 331
robber barons, 158
rock music, 12, 95, 275
Roe vs. Wade, 124, 126, 152, 308
roles, gender, 6, 11, 12, 29, 70-72,
  179, 205-206, 219, 228, 240,
  242, 258, 260, 283-284, 293,
  294, 340.
 See also femininity, masculinity
Rolling Stones, 95
romance novel, 116-119
Roman Empire, 162, 299
Romantics, German, 233
Roosevelt, Eleanor, 6
Roosevelt, Franklin D., 8
Rousseau, Jean-Jacques, 233
Ruether, Rosemary, 55

sadism, 302
sadomasochism, 90-91, 106-108
Samoa, 169, 171-173, 176, 191, 251
Samoans, 179, 182, 251
San. *See* Bushmen
Sappho, 46
Sartre, Jean-Paul, 46
Schlafly, Phyllis, 97-102, 103, 146
Schreiner, Olive, 162
Schwarzenegger, Arnold, 275
science fiction, 48-49, 261
Scott, Anne, 307

Acknowledgments

This book was originally conceived as a joint project with Earl Nelson. To Earl, thanks for continuing support and inspiration.

The ideas expressed were first organized in writing in a paper for William M. Johnston's extraordinary intellectual history course at the University of Massachusetts at Amherst. To Professor Johnston, my thanks for perceiving the serious intent beneath what was then a very tentative content. Thanks to Professor Keith M. Baker, of the University of Chicago, for forbearance and for the example of his relentlessly high standards. These scholars, however, bear no responsibility for any aspect of the content of this book and may disagree in part or in whole with its conclusions.

In specific areas adequately covered by other authors, I have not presumed to duplicate their work, but have contented myself with summarizing and making use of it. This applies in particular to the superb work of Megan Marshall on the psychology of the feminist generation and Sara Bonnett Stein on nonsexist child rearing.

A special case is Steven Goldberg's classic study of the sociostructural effects of male aggression, *The Inevitability of Patriarchy*. I had originally prepared a section on Goldberg's thesis for Part III, on science and gender. But given the distrust in which "male-centered" arguments are currently held, it seemed tactically sounder to make the same case purely from the female point of view (primarily through an interpretation of Carol Gilligan's work). Those wishing to fill the resulting lacuna in *The Failure of Feminism* are directed to Goldberg's own excellent book.

As a number of writers have recently experienced, it is still extremely difficult to find a publisher for a work critical of feminism. My appreciation to all who assisted in that long search and of course to my publisher, Paul Kurtz of Prometheus Books. Thanks to Doris Doyle for her competence and enthusiasm, and to the excellent staff at Prometheus, who are a pleasure to work with.

It is a pleasure to acknowledge my debts to George Gilder, Michael Levin, and Midge Decter.

My brother Charles supplied an especially sharp-eyed reading of the first draft. Very special thanks to my brother Roger for critical stylistic advice and for giving me the shelter of his roof for several months while I finished the book.

The word "xenocentrism" was created as a cooperative venture with Cyril C. Means, Jr., of New York Law School. To Cyril, my appreciation for this and his other kindnesses over the years. Thanks to Enno Hobbing, for commiseration, with admiration. Thanks to Shirley Glubok Tamarin for introducing me to the world of the writer as she once introduced me to the world of art.

I would like to express my appreciation to Jean Pedersen for interpreting several points of feminist doctrine for me with her usual grace and balance. Kate Brooks has provided valuable insights into the trials and joys of the contemporary housewife. Bob and Noëlle Bennett have helped me to understand the problems of following a traditional lifestyle in a unisex age. Thanks to Carol Iannone and to Chilton Williamson, Jr.

Finally, thanks to my parents, and to all the other friends, family members, and intellectual peers who have in various ways contributed to this book.

Nicholas Davidson

New York City
November 1987